# Talisker

# Talisker

## Book One of
## The Last Clansman

MILLER LAU

EARTHLIGHT

SIMON & SCHUSTER

London • New York • Sydney • Tokyo • Singapore • Toronto • Dublin

A VIACOM COMPANY

First published in Great Britain by Earthlight, 2001
An imprint of Simon & Schuster UK Ltd
A Viacom Company



Simon & Schuster UK Ltd
Africa House
64-78 Kingsway
London
WC2B 6AH

Simon & Schuster Australia
Sydney

A CIP catalogue record for this book is available
from the British Library

ISBN 0 7434 0893 4

1 3 5 7 9 10 8 6 4 2



Typeset in 10/12.5pt Melior by
SX Composing DTP, Rayleigh, Essex

Printed and bound in Great Britain by
Omnia Books Ltd, Glasgow

## Acknowledgements

Writing is something we all do in isolation. Without the fellowship of other writers, it would be difficult at times to continue. My heartfelt thanks therefore, go to the 'Js and A's' – Jerry, Jim, John, Jessica, Andrew and Aly – Fen Farmers and writers all, so watch this space!

Thanks also to my test reader, Joy Mance, whose boundless energy and enthusiasm is enough for a thousand books.

Finally, my love and thanks to my husband, Bill: pragmatist, critic and keeper of my dreams.

To Windy and Wiffy – Gotcha!

*Sutra*

The lynx moves silently through the rugged landscape watching the white figure ahead of it, keeping downwind, alert for any change in direction. Occasionally the diminutive grey cat stops and looks back the way it has come, wary of pursuit, its ears twitching, feeling the sounds of the moorlands through every pore. Eventually, satisfied that nothing is hunting the hunter, it moves on, watching the bright outline that walks quickly through the bleak brown and grey of the heather.

As the dying rays of the sun leach the colours from the moor, the white figure reaches its destination. The dark angular shapes of ten standing stones splay outwards, reaching to the sky like the fingers of some buried giant. The lynx stops, crouching in the heather, its posture betraying its fear and uncertainty. The white figure continues on until it stands in the middle of the circle where it also stops, waiting. In the weak red light of the sunset it can be seen that the figure is a young woman, as she pulls back the hood of her white cloak and casts her gaze over the moor. Small clouds of steam escape into the chill air as she fights to get her breath back.

'Deme? Deme? Are you there?' she calls, in a hoarse whisper.

The lynx still crouches anxiously, twitching its tail.

'Deme?' The woman seems nervous now, shifting from foot to foot and glancing up at the sky. With a small noise somewhat like irritation, the lynx stands upright and bounds forward into the circle of stones as though afraid its nerve will desert it.

'Deme! You came, my friend. I knew you would.' The woman laughs. The lynx makes a rough purring sound and rubs against her legs, and the young woman strokes the creature's soft fur affectionately.

'I must tell you, Deme,' she says 'we have serious business to discuss. Can you be sure you weren't followed?'

The lynx sits down and fixes her with its wide yellow gaze. '*I was not followed, Mirranon . . .*' Deme's voice, a soft, slightly sibilant sound, travels directly to Mirranon's mind. The cat blinks owlishly.

'Good. Now, where to begin?' There is a long pause. The wind blows across the moorland like a sigh, whipping Mirranon's robes and hair, sending dark clouds racing across the darkening sky. 'Come, let's take shelter behind the stones, Deme, there is to be a storm.'

The two friends stand in the lee of the largest stone. 'I know you put yourself in danger coming here,' Mirranon continues, 'seeing me when I am outcast, but the favour I am about to ask you will stretch the bonds of even our friendship. I will understand if you do not agree. I need you to get something for me. I cannot go myself.'

'*It does not sound too arduous a task.*'

'Oh, but it is. And it is so important, Deme. Look.' From the folds of her robe Mirranon takes a pouch that was looped around her belt. She tips the contents into her hand and holds them before the lynx's face.

Deme stares at the black shrivelled things and wrinkles her velvet nose in an expression of disgust. '*What are they?*'

'Well, they were flowers, insects, this largest one was a wren. Do you see its shape there?'

'*I don't understand, Mirranon. Surely they have simply been burned in a brush fire.*'

'Look closer, Deme.'

Deme peers at the bird. *There is something odd about it . . . 'Gods.'*

The remains of the creature has the appearance of many black legs, most of which sprout at strange jagged angles from the middle of its back. The whole of its body is disjointed as though the tiny bird had suffered some awful spasm. The insects – although it is less obvious that they have suffered pain – also have the spindly black growths. The flowers appear shrivelled and burned. There is something frightening and unnatural about the death of the tiny creatures. Deme growls.

'It is . . .' Mirranon looks around nervously . . . 'it is Corvus.'

'*Who?*'

Mirranon laughs unexpectedly at this and Deme twitches her tail in annoyance.

'I am sorry, my friend. I simply forgot you were so young and that your kind do not speak of the past in the same simple terms as the Fine.'

Deme stiffens slightly. '*My kind are yours also, Mirranon. At least, some of us consider it so.*'

'And I am honoured by your kind thoughts, Deme,'

her friend replies gravely. 'I can tell you only that a great evil will be soon abroad in the lands of the Fine. For the moment it is contained but the force holding it is weakening, dying, and I need help.'

The lynx looks serious also, narrowing its yellow eyes and wrapping its long tail around its front paws. '*It is sad, and ironic, is it not, that you should be expected to care about us Mirranon, White Eagle, when we have treated you so poorly?*'

Mirranon smiles, recognising that the use of her name by one of the Sidhe is a rare recognition and that her friend would never dare use it among others of her kind. 'I can only say that this danger threatens all, Sidhe or Fine. Our differences are made small in the light of it.' She replaces the remains of the creatures in her pouch. 'I am working now to contain—'

'*Let me go to the Council of Tema,*' Deme protests. 'You know there is strong magic still in the Sidhe. Surely they can help us?'

'No.' Mirranon's tone is firm but saddened. 'It's all politics to them. They will take no action until it is too late. Also, they will not believe I speak in the best interests of the Sidhe. No, listen, Deme. There is only one . . .'

The storm grows stronger, and a freezing drizzle gusts across the moors, heralding the coming darkness. Mirranon's voice carries on the wind, moving among the standing stones, a tiny defiant spirit in the face of the elements, her white robes billowing like a window of purity against the blackness of the giant shapes. The lynx sits perfectly still, so it appears as though the woman is speaking with a small grey statue. The wind draws circles in Deme's fur with cold mischievous fingers. Some minutes later the small cat stands up and shakes itself. For a few seconds, a warm golden glow suffuses the stone behind it like a smaller sunset, the only warmth in the coming dark. When the light fades, two women stand within the circle, Mirranon and Deme – a tall golden being who wears the silver grey of her lynx caste. They embrace briefly as sisters, then Deme walks to the centre of the stones. She looks back once, seeking Mirranon's encouragement. A great flash of lightning rends the sky as the storm breaks suddenly above the circle. When the purple-white after-image fades, Mirranon stands alone.

It seems her task is completed only just in time. From the north, the sky darkens further as a kindness of ravens moves through the storm, black on black, an inky cloud possessed of a sentient purpose. Mirranon begins to run, unsure if they have seen her among the standing stones but knowing that any distance she can put between herself and them is valuable. A dark green light moves about the contours of her form, and as she runs, she changes and grows; the white robes become feathers, her arms extend and become huge wings. Within seconds, the White Eagle takes to the sky. Spiralling, moving swiftly through the cloud, she climbs upwards above the front of the storm. As she feels the clean cold current whip through her wing feathers, she turns in the air, the lightning flashes behind her, and the White Eagle faces the clumsy onslaught of twenty ravens. Flexing her massive talons she utters a harsh cry, which echoes loud across the moor, and joins battle.

**Edinburgh**

**Before this time**

*At the top of the close sits an urchin; almost androgynous in his grimy streaks and tatters, listening idly to the sounds of the early evening. Shadows are gathering at the bottom end of the narrow space and a black cat detaches itself from them. It stalks the distance between the grey ruined walls in seconds but, before disappearing again, it turns and bestows a fathomless gaze on the urchin, who shudders. This place – Mary King's Close – is a place of darkness. The boy fingers a stone he is holding; it is large and reassuringly round. The idea had been to come and stand at the top of the close and throw the stone to show how fearless he was, but now he sits, listening. Can the sound of singing be coming from the close? The sound of children?*

*On impulse he hefts the rock as though to throw it, but instead, he bowls it. The close is so steep it will surely roll into the pool of dark at the end. He watches breathlessly. At first the rock spins smartly down the centre and then, on reaching one of the uneven steps, it begins to bounce. The sound it makes is curiously loud. At the bottom it vanishes but can still be heard, spinning like a penny. Then it stops. And then . . .*

*And then, from the shadow steps a being, surely a Sidhe of legend. It is tall, golden, beautiful, frightening. It says nothing but holds the stone forward as though it would return it. Then, the sweet stench of decay crosses the distance between the two frozen figures. The urchin's hair moves in the tainted breeze and obscures his vision. In those seconds the creature is gone.*

# CHAPTER ONE

The last thing Malcolm McLeod remembers is dying. Actually it hadn't hurt that much, just a brief searing light and then an even briefer moment of peace before nothingness claimed his soul for millennia. Now, the darkness takes form once more, awareness rushes in on cold grasping fingers, awareness of who and what he now is. 'Why have you s s-summoned me?' He has forgotten the sound of his own voice, thin, nasal, quite unpleasant to the ear; he pauses, unsure if he is stuttering because he is nervous or if he has always sounded that way.

Within the darkness and shadow the figure he has spoken to moves, and a greasy orange light flares, washing the walls of the space with reluctant brightness. Malcolm steps forward, his hand dropping automatically to the hilt of his sword, and the figure steps back involuntarily. There is a sickly sweet smell in the chamber – the reek of the grave – and he realises fleetingly that it emanates not from the creature before him but from his own ghostly form. He stops. 'Ah know you.' He shakes his head, looking confused. 'But how's it possible? If Ah'd met onything like you, Ah'd remember.'

The being appears uncomfortable for a moment, as though his recognition is some veiled accusation. It steps back again and sits down on a thin metal-framed seat. 'Sit down, shade.' The voice is female, as are the contours of the form beneath the voluminous grey robes she wears. Her features have a soft golden colour upon which the light of the torch dances and moves, reflecting in eyes darker than the deepest shadows of the room.

Obediently Malcolm folds his legs beneath him and feels little surprise that he can simply hover in the space before her.

She sits back in her chair. 'What do you remember?' she asks.

It seems a strange question. 'Remember? No' much,' Malcolm says briefly. The creature relaxes slightly. 'Ah remember . . . Ah remember who Ah am. Ah remember this place . . .' He nods towards the dark outlines of the vicious steel hooks that hang in long regular rows from the ceiling. 'It used tae be the butcher's shop. We're in the close, aren't we? Mary King's Close?'

She nods.

'Ah – Ah – died here.' Malcolm's voice trembles slightly at the memory and he glances down at his wounds, shaking his head as though he would deny his own statement. 'So why?' he demands again. He stares at the creature, a dark piercing stare, but then he relents, and smiles grimly to encourage some explanation.

'I need your help,' she says quietly.

'Oh, aye?' he replies. 'And whit's in it fer—'

'Malcolm. It concerns your last descendant.'

He starts. 'My last . . .' he echoes. It seems as though the creature has found the power to reach out and slap his ghostly form. The news takes him unexpectedly hard and he frowns. 'Ma last . . . Ah'm one of eight boys, y'know.'

The creature smiles for the first time, her sympathy for his lost lineage apparent in her features. 'I am sorry, Malcolm. I will tell you what I can, and then, if you agree, perhaps I will introduce you to the last of your line.'

Outside.

A bleak dawn wraps the city in its grey blanket. Edinburgh wakens at its own pace; a leviathan, its ancient weary soul reluctant to shrug off the calm of the night. The hills surrounding the city leave it exposed only to the sea, and it is the elements of the sea that characterise its weather. Fingers of damp mist linger in the closes and alleyways of the Old Town, leaving the sandstone buildings slick and wet, waiting for the warming touch of the sunlight, which will not arrive until mid-morning. Gulls' calls break the morning quiet; their harsh cries echo like a scream in the face of the new day. Sounds trickle in like a salt wave encroaching around the buildings, as though they are simply larger pebbles, and the city a natural extension of the shore. Perhaps it is. The city is very old. The light that steals slowly across its craggy face will not illuminate its secrets. As ever, in this time between the darkness and the light, the city has an air of waiting. A silence that hangs above it, above the wave of sound. Silence and waiting.

He was a free man.

As he walked towards the red wooden gates the idea appalled him. If it was what he really wanted, why did the impulse to run back seem so real, so immediate?

What lay beyond the red barrier that had the power to frighten grown men as though they were simple children? He'd always wondered. He'd watched his contemporaries walk this same walk, some laughing, some tearful and some seemingly indifferent, yet when they reached the black shadow of the portal, as he had now, they all did it: they paused. They stopped and stared ahead. Those who were watching would shout encouragement as though otherwise the man would turn back. Talisker had always wondered what they felt, what the look on their faces was at this moment. Some would turn back towards the grey brick walls and wave, others squared their shoulders as though bracing themselves; but they all paused.

And now he knew. The look on their faces was fear, because when those gates opened, a different world lay beyond. A world of changes. Nothing would be the same as when they left, people, places, shops, nothing. The fear was sudden and unexpected, and the realisation that this moment, *only this moment*, was the real execution of their punishment, was overwhelming. It was time that they had lost, the days, hours, minutes and seconds of their lives. Talisker had lost fifteen years.

In fact, the great red gates did not swing open. He was prepared for this but he still felt cheated as the smaller door, inset lower down, was unlocked by a warder. Even these last few moments they stole were not allowed to be remarkable. As the little door opened, a square of light appeared, a square of reality. Talisker knew it was no lighter on the other side of the door than it was in the yard where he stood, yet the light seemed blinding as *new*, unused, unbreathed minutes and seconds spilled across the threshold. He stared at the bright rectangle until the warder coughed sarcastically. 'Ur you goan, then? Or dae I have tae push ye out?'

The creature begins her tale, her low voice echoing in the cold darkness, her sadness like a low, haunting song, each word dropping into a well of sorrows. Malcolm listens in silence, at first.

*'My name is Deme and I have waited a long time. Hundreds of your years. I come from another place which . . . is beautiful. Although these alleyways were grim and stinking then, at least they were still open to the sky . . . the blue sky . . . the only thing, it seems, that this place shares with the land, Sutra, from which I was sent. Even Sutra is exile to my people . . . My waiting has not been entirely uneventful, however. It seems the city did not want me here. It seems I brought with me . . . a plague.'*

Malcolm sits forward then, his jet eyes round with horror, his hand on the hilt of his sword.

'You!' he hisses.

'I – I am sorry.' Deme looks shocked by his reaction and bows her head, touching her forehead with her middle finger in a gesture of abject sorrow. His fierce frown does not leave him, however, and she flinches, then becomes angered by his refusal to accept her apology. Her delicate mouth sets in a thin line.

*'Do not berate me, warrior. I know that you were here then, but think not that I hid myself away. I saw what you saw. Eight hundred men, women and children, sealed in this place to die; soldiers posted at the top and*

*bottom of the close so that none could leave and infect the rest of the city. The stench of death haunts me still . . . I watched them all die. I watched the mothers drown their weakened, feeble children to end their suffering and throw their bodies from the top floor of the close into the waters of the loch. I watched lovers take each other's lives rather than watch the swelling and living decay of one another's bodies. Warriors, fathers, crying like babes as their wives begged for death by their sword . . . I cannot tell it all for it is bitter . . . but I saw you, Malcolm. I saw your stand against those who sealed in the eight hundred. You and a few of the men who were left in the second week. You died bravely. A hero.'*

At this Malcolm gives a short cynical laugh. 'It wiz nothin' personal. Ah mean, you do realise how close we are tae the castle? Tae the King? We all understood the reason they did it, it didnae make it ony easier, though. Oor wee attack on the guards – it wiz mair a defiant gesture, if ye like; we didnae want tae die like dugs.' He shakes his head, looking sad and slightly pensive: he'd sold his life too cheaply. Deme watches him bleakly, her expression one of sorrow; in all her dealings with men, she has never understood them. She is about to continue with her tale when Malcolm forestalls its telling. 'So where were ye, then? If no hiding.'

She laughs at his confusion and, as if in reply, throws back her robe to reveal her golden body, which is sheathed in a black and grey gown. Malcolm, still pale as the grave, blanches visibly as she stands up.

'Do you not know me? Do your legends not speak of my race? Of those we come and take? You call us the Sidhe. We are shape-changers. Watch.'

It is hard for Deme to remember the form she took when she nursed the sick, her desperation to atone for their plight burning as brightly as their fever, but looking at Malcolm helps to remind her of that time. Moving her hand before her face she summons an everyday magic and when it drops away she wears another visage.

'C-C-Constance?' Malcolm is shaken. The transposing of the young girl's face on the Sidhe woman's form appears strange.

In an effort to calm him, Deme makes her human face smile and takes on the voice of Constance. 'Aye, it's me, Malcolm.' Her young clear tones ring around the darkness of the hall, evoking that tragic time more poignantly than she had anticipated.

The effect on the young warrior is astounding: his face contorts and he seems unable to speak although his lips are moving. Finally, the words come rushing out. 'Christ! I loved ye! I mean I . . . ohmigod!' It seems strange indeed that a ghost can pass out, but pass out he does, before Deme's chair.

Constance's bemused voice echoes once more around the chamber: 'Ah. Yes. I'd forgotten about *that*.'

An old woman walked across the red frame of Talisker's vision. She wore a bright blue hat and a tweedy granny's coat. She had a little dog with her – some mixture of terrier and dachshund – and it wore a blue coat, which she had knitted. She was talking to it. '. . . no allowed tae poo there . . .'

The words floated across the space, bizarrely, absurdly poignant. She didn't even glance toward him, stock-still on the prison's threshold, before her life was gone from his reality, but that moment that touched both of their lives was the first he had *owned* for a long time. He crossed the last space, without acknowledging the warder, to step through the door. He was smiling.

As he passed through, something happened. There was a seal around the prison, he knew that now, he felt it. The time in there was stale, dirty, second-hand; and it was held in by this weight, this *force*, which was now trying to push him back. There was nothing to see yet he reached out his hands in front of him as though pushing. Doing time. It wasn't your own time you did, it was everyone else's.

He was through. He stood feeling slightly foolish, knowing as the autumn sunlight claimed him that he had imagined the experience yet still feeling the residual traces play around his body. It was like awakening from a nightmare. He looked back towards the prison and grunted something at the warder, who was closing the gate. No one else would be leaving that day. The seal was complete.

He began to walk down the street reeling with sensation. The traffic noise was so close, so immediate, it reverberated through his body. He was on one side of a wide road, which had railings down the middle so that people could not cross except by using the subway that ran beneath. Without thinking, he changed direction to walk obediently towards the dark mouth of the tunnel. As he did so, a young man of about twenty dashed out into the stream of traffic. Talisker started, was about to shout something but stopped himself. The youth wove between the two lanes of cars then vaulted the barrier; he did this every day. 'Time.' The word had been trembling on Talisker's lips. 'You could die . . .' Then a sound distracted him. It was a tree: its noise in the wind was like rain, its hard leathery leaves seemed to dance a vibrant dance. Talisker sat on the bench beneath it to listen. He realised that he wasn't doing very well, hadn't managed to catch the bus yet or anything, but the tree soothed him: this wasn't wasting time, it whispered, but savouring it.

Once recovered, Malcolm is ashamed by his outburst and equally ashamed that Deme has known him so intimately. The Sidhe tries to make light of his discomfort but he will not meet her eyes again, even though she now wears her own features once more.

'I only tried to give you solace, Malcolm. And I did. All around you people were dying. What happened between you and Constance was sweet and bitter. It gave you heart and you died a slightly happier man, did you not?'

He does not answer but hangs his head, his expression unreadable but somewhere between anger and bewilderment. Deme decides to change the subject and continues with her tale.

*'When all had died, my footsteps echoed hollowly in this place. I would have left instantly to search for my goal yet I was torn by indecision. If I left, I might carry the plague to the rest of the city, and although I had gained little respect for the people of this place, I did not wish to be responsible for more deaths. I had seen enough courage in this dark time to know that mankind was not without a soul. However, the decision was*

*wrenched from my hands for good so that now, when the time is near, I am incapable of leaving. I am a prisoner.*

*'Ten years after the plague, a few families moved back into the higher houses, on the level of the High Street. I kept away, wishing them no harm. But then . . . a man . . . a powerful man, named Elias, became interested in what had happened here. He was the only being I have met in my sojourn in your world who has possessed magic, and he came looking for me. He sensed my presence immediately and one night he sought me out. We spoke at length, and I admired him and would have liked to know more of his magic, but he hated me. You see, his wife and child had been victims of the plague and his heart had turned bitter and hard. He tried to destroy me. We fought here in this room – you can see the scars on the walls – but I was stronger and he fled to the higher levels, mortally wounded. He did not die immediately, no, his hatred was too strong. He returned the following night but instead of daring to face me once more, he placed a capstone, a seal, outside the close so that I might never leave. All of his failing strength and magic he poured into the final spell he fashioned. A spell of binding. It is still there: men call it the Heart. The Heart of Midlothian. He died thinking that he had won some victory and I suppose he had, for in the long years since that time, as the memory of the eight hundred has faded, as my dreams have become peaceful once more, I think I would have ventured out into the world of men. No, I should speak the truth, I know I would have. Elias has rendered this impossible. Should I curse or bless him? I know not.'*

Telling this seems to have tired Deme. She sits back in her chair, feeling for the armrests and looking suddenly weary; she closes her eyes briefly.

Malcolm's voice floats across the space towards her, as disembodied as the rest of his being. 'So. What's a' this got tae dae wi' me and my ancestor? I ken if Ah had a chance I'd kill ye. Aye, I'd kill ye fer the eight hundred. Bloody selfish loathsome creature that y'are . . .'

She opens her hooded eyes and holds his gaze, her slow anger burning into the space between them. 'Take care, little man,' she hisses.

He flinches but does not back down. 'What? Goin' tae kill me?' he mocks.

Deme stares harder. Her gaze is unmoving, penetrating. 'Just believe,' she says coldly, 'that I can hurt you.' There is a frozen, uncomfortable silence and finally she sighs. 'I do need your help, Malcolm, but I will send you back if necessary.'

'Naw,' he says, in a less confrontational tone. 'Let's jist say you've got ma curiosity.'

She laughs once more, and the sound rings loud in this void where two beings who should be dead are speaking. 'It is not your curiosity I require. It is your descendant. Watch now.' Deme conjures a seeing spell and, in the centre of the room, the blackness of the air slowly peels back to illuminate a lazy, grainy image of the world above. It is an easy trick, almost beneath her, but Malcolm is impressed. 'You understand,' she says quietly, 'thanks to Elias, I cannot go to meet him. Even you, as my agent, may be hampered from bringing him here. I know not how the magic will manifest itself . . . But watch! Watch now . . . I have waited long for this.'

*

Talisker was about to leave the solace of the tree and move to the bus stop when suddenly shouting was coming from the subway. A young couple appeared in the daylight, the girl walking at a fast pace, clearly uncomfortable, clutching her handbag against her body defensively. The boy was almost running to catch up with her. 'Wait up, Sus,' he called. He was blinking owlishly in the light and sweating slightly because of his leather jacket, which did not sit well on him and was more reminiscent of upholstery than street cred. He stopped, hawked and spat loudly into the road. The girl carried on towards the bus stop without looking back.

'Fuck,' the youth swore quietly.

There was more shouting, quite close now, and then the culprit, an old tramp, came into view.

'Right doon the side,' he was yelling, 'wide open. Aye, wide open!' This didn't seem to be directed specifically at the girl, though, just the world in general. The old man reeled and looked as though he would fall over. When he regained his balance, which he seemed to achieve in slow motion, his demeanour changed. 'It's arright, hen,' he said towards the girl at the bus stop. 'It's arright.'

Talisker sat forward, something about the man's confused distress pricking at his memory. Before he reached a conclusion, the tirade began again. 'Ye're a whore!' the tramp shouted at the girl he had just sought to reassure. She stood tight-lipped, trying to ignore him.

It struck Talisker that the old man was wearing bright

yellow trainers with his dirty grey clothes, which should have looked sad or even comical, yet . . . he had an innate dignity.

The situation blew. The tramp crashed forward into the boyfriend, screaming, 'Oh, God! Yer leg! Yer leg!'

The boy had had enough. He grabbed the man by his lapels. The tramp didn't seem to be aware of the threat, his unfocused gaze seeing only . . . only—

Shell-shock. Talisker was off his seat before he was aware of it. The old man was one of the few, like his uncle had been, to have shell-shock. They were doomed for ever to see their friends blown apart over and over again; a relentless horror film unlike anything the video generation could envisage. It crashed through into the sufferer's reality and played itself whenever it wanted, gradually unhinging the wretched minds of those who had once been heroes.

'Fuckin' old freak!' the youth snarled.

Talisker was a second too slow and the boy smashed his forehead into the old man's face. There was blood everywhere and the tramp looked dazed and frightened. The boy wasn't finished yet, though. He hauled the man back towards him. 'Fuckin' old freak,' he said again. His fist was an angry tight ball and he aimed a punch at his victim's ribs.

'Put him down.' Talisker's voice was quiet but firm. He was behind the boy now with his hand on his shoulder. He didn't really want to hurt the stupid kid but he would if necessary.

'Put him down, kid.'

The boy didn't look round and seemed undecided. As a final gesture he spat forcefully into the old man's bloodied face. Talisker's grip on his shoulder became vice-like, and he let go.

'He upset my girlfriend,' he whined pathetically. 'She was nearly greetin'.'

There didn't seem much to say to this, so Talisker pushed him hard towards the girl, who was only now crying at the prospect of her man nursing a few broken ribs. 'Get out of here. Now.'

The boy stumbled forward then straightened up, pulling down the front of his jacket self-consciously. He turned back quickly to make some defiant gesture at Talisker but, on seeing his aggressor for the first time, thought better of it. He left the scene to walk to the next bus stop.

The old man was sitting on the pavement cradling his head in his arms.

'Come on, old yin. Let's get you on to this bench, shall we?' Talisker helped him up and sat him down. People who had stopped to stare drifted away. Drama over. Just an old tramp with a bloody nose.

For the moment the man seemed coherent and grunted his thanks when Talisker offered him a handkerchief.

'It's not broken,' Talisker said. He'd seen enough broken noses to know.

'I'm not drunk,' the old man said, as though it was an answer.

'I know. My Uncle Charlie . . .'

'What's yer name, boy?'

'Duncan.'

They shook hands solemnly and the tramp introduced himself. 'Zak.' Then he nodded towards the gates that Talisker had just exited. 'Kid'll end up in there,' he said.

Talisker smiled, suddenly at a loss for something to say. 'They just don't know,' he muttered. 'Kids. They don't know about time.'

Zak nodded sagely. 'I don't suppose you've got a fag on you, son?'

Talisker had only one so they shared it. While Zak had a puff, Talisker's gaze was drawn once more to the yellow trainers. 'I like your trainers, Zak. They're . . . excellent.'

Zak twirled his arthritic ankles to display them better, grinning toothily. 'They're mah fashion statement, boy.'

At first Talisker thought he was serious and tried not to laugh, but when he looked up at Zak's battered hero's face he couldn't help it. 'Fashion statement, eh?'

They both cracked up, their cigarette smoke and laughter mingling with the breeze and drifting cleanly over the walls of the prison.

*'There.'* Deme's voice is choked with emotion. *'The Music he brings will bind for ever the scattered clans of the Sidhe and the Fine. Be proud, warrior, that he is of your blood. He brings the dawn of faith, the end of lamentation. He is Duncan Talisker. And you must bring him to me.'*

## CHAPTER TWO

He'd been home for ten days now and the dreams kept happening.

*Across the battlefield he is running. A warrior. Filthy, mud-streaked, caked with the blood of his enemies. His battle-cry is a berserker roar that rises through the tumult of the fight.*

*'McLeods! Tae me! Tae me!' Then he continues to hack his way through the living wall. The limbs of his foemen fall twitching and bleeding. The noise gets louder and louder . . .*

*Then his face is there. Right up against Talisker's, filling his vision with his anger, his snot- and blood-covered features. His breath is foul, tainted with the bile and fear of the battlefield. Then he smiles, a big yellow-toothed grin, lifts his sword and makes a tapping motion with it, as though he is framed inside a picture – but he can't be because of the smell and the chill wind that blows from somewhere around Talisker's neck and shoulders.*

*'Duncan,' he says, 'Duncan, it's me.'*

Each time Talisker awoke, the anxiety was stronger. In the darkness of his tiny bedsit the warrior's words hung in the still air like an accusation. *'It's me.'* Talisker was a pragmatic man and he'd never had recurring dreams before. Not that they were exactly the same; the vision became ever more insistent, more desperate. It was beginning to worry him.

This time Talisker had reached out his hand towards the face in the dream and when he woke he found himself lying with his arm in the air, fingers stretching towards nothing. He felt instantly self-conscious, still unaccustomed to privacy. He sat up coughing and straightening his T-shirt.

'I don't know you,' he growled quietly, into the black corners of the room. He went to fetch himself a glass of water, reflecting on the way that his skeletal threadbare furniture – courtesy of the DSS – looked better in the dark. When he got back to bed he couldn't sleep, and when the first bus stopped outside the flats at six o'clock that morning he was still awake, his tired eyes red and burning.

He walked all day. It was his first real day out; agoraphobia had seized him after his release and he had spent as little time as possible outside the safe confines of his flat. Today, after the dream of the previous night, he felt he would go insane if he didn't feel some air about him, but once he stood in the street outside, he trembled. The life and colours of the city assailed him in a great – but bitterly familiar – wave. He began to walk, soaking in the people and the sights as though he could possess them for ever, reclaim fifteen years' worth in one day.

Striding through the streets of his city, he was unaware of people instinctively making way for him, unaware that his tall, gaunt frame and haunting eyes could cause discomfort, a prickling tense feeling in those with whom he came into contact. He was too preoccupied. Talisker had hated Edinburgh once, had blamed the city – the whole city, as though it were a sentient entity – for turning against him. Now he knew better. Only people could betray. The old granite and sandstone buildings had seen bigger, more tragic betrayals than his, but the stones of the Old Town kept their own counsel.

He had walked the length of the High Street, from Edinburgh Castle to Holyrood Palace, and then, as though completing his act of reclamation, he had climbed Arthur's Seat and looked out across the city as he had when he was a boy. The tourists who were gathered around the cairn at the summit left quickly as though a storm had blackened their bright communion with that place, which to them meant mainly rain, whisky and tartan.

Talisker stood there for a long time, waiting for some feeling, some sense of reconciliation, but there was none. He stared out to the Firth of Forth, thinking about leaving, and unexpectedly the idea struck him as gloomy and sad; the city had not forgiven him then, but it would not let him go either.

'Mister.'

He looked down the slope and saw a small girl climbing up towards him. Her mother was trailing quite far behind. The child was only about eight and not pretty, her mousy hair looked unwashed, plastered to her head, and she was flushed with the exertion of the climb. She wore a dirty blue summer frock and pink plastic sandals. In one hand she had three or four dandelion seed-heads, and was making her climb more difficult by holding them away from her body.

'D'you want one?' she said boldly, as she reached the summit. Talisker frowned, not immediately understanding. 'Look, I'll show you,' she said, in a pretend grown-up tone. She took a dandelion from the bunch and blew on it. The seeds were borne away by the breeze, and Talisker watched entranced as they seemed to cross the city towards the open water. He had done this when he was a boy, of course, but it had never before seemed so beautiful in its simplicity. More and more ephemeral white dancers whirled into the breeze as the girl continued to blow until there was only one seed-head left. 'D'you want it?' she demanded, as though of one of her peers; she thrust the last one towards him. Talisker shook his head, not trusting himself to speak to her in case she ran away. She looked crestfallen, so he picked her up and stood her on the cairn. Her eyes widened with surprise. 'My mum's coming,' she said.

'Go on, then.' He nodded at the last dandelion, and she smiled.

'Right.'

She blew the last white head. This time she sang out between breaths, 'One o'clock . . . two o'clock . . .'

Talisker watched the tiny clusters rise high in the air, where they seemed to pause before the wind caught them, and whirled to join the others suspended over the hillside. The sunlight made them silver, and Talisker and the child watched in silence.

Talisker started down the other side of the hill as the little girl's mother crested the summit. She did not see him. He turned briefly to glance back at the child, and as he did so, he felt his second-sight descend on him, like an unwelcome old friend. In his vision a young girl no longer stood on the cairn but a beautiful young woman. She wore a white wedding gown and she was smiling as she waved goodbye to him. The traces of poverty, which so often marked the faces of those who lived such a childhood, had passed her by: she would be happy and well. As she raised her hand in farewell the white veil was lifted by the wind and drifted over the crest of the hill to join the silver dancers as they moved across the city skyline.

The vision was broken by the voice of the girl's mother which drifted on the warm air: 'What're you doing up there?'

And shortly after, a quiet, ''Bye, mister.'

He was heading back across the Queen's Park towards Holyrood when he saw it. At first glance he thought it was a small dog, but when he looked again he stopped in his tracks. It was a hare. He'd never seen one before but he was sure that they didn't normally live in the city. There was nothing cute about the creature, which seemed almost impossibly huge. Its brown flanks were sleek and shiny, and it sat back on powerful-looking hind legs. There was something in its bearing that was almost – it seemed ridiculous to think – regal; but it was the eyes that caught and held his attention. They were a bright yellow-gold and they held his gaze without a hint of fear.

It could only have been for seconds that they stared at one another, yet Talisker had an irrational impulse to say something to it. He took a step forward and in that instant the bond was broken: the hare turned and fled towards the crag so fast that he could hardly follow its flight. He blinked. It seemed that the hare had not run into the bushes or bolted down a hole, but vanished. He dismissed the idea – he was looking into the sun. He took a few paces forward, as though to follow its path, and noticed something in the grass where the creature had been sitting.

When he crouched to pick it up, he was still staring at the point where the hare had disappeared so he felt the coldness of the object before he saw it: an emerald about the size of his fist. Talisker let out a low whistle. If it was real it would be worth a fortune. He had only to turn his head to see Holyrood Palace and was instantly sure that that was where the gem had come from. And yet . . .

He stared at the green stone: the sunlight glinted sharply, caught within the facets. Already it was growing warmer to his touch. His distorted image stared back at him from the stone's largest surface: by some trick of the light his face seemed wider, softer, the bitter lines less apparent, his red hair glowing a soft halo of orange. He looked . . . innocent. He gazed at the gem for some minutes before he slipped it into his pocket. Something like a smile flashed across his face and he felt duty-bound to mutter: 'Curiouser and curiouser.' Instantly on the heels of that thought he glanced at his watch. 'Shit, I'm late.'

He was supposed to be meeting Shula in ten minutes.

The gallery tea-room was really a large conservatory stuck on the side of the building. Brilliant sunlight shone through the glass roof like solid bars of yellow, giving the place an air of designed positivity. It was too bright for Talisker. He stood just inside the huge glass and pine entrance, inhaling the mixed odours of polish and cappuccino. He didn't belong here but he couldn't say why. He felt dirty inside, grubby and sweaty. In one of the pools of sunlight, Shula was sitting, absently stirring her coffee. Talisker had been watching her for a few minutes now. She couldn't see him standing in the doorway, but after a while she seemed to sense that he was there and an expectant expression came over her face. He stepped forward.

'Shula?' After all the rehearsal, the word still sounded like a plea for clemency.

She turned her face towards him, stood up and reached out her hands. 'Talisker.' She smiled as though not fully committed to the idea that she was happy. He drew near and she touched his face lightly, feeling the damage that fifteen years had wrought, frowning as though she absorbed his pain. As her fingers traced the lines around his mouth, he smiled tremulously and hot tears welled in his eyes as his emotions conspired to suffocate him. He imagined grabbing hold of her, weeping, holding her so tight, burying his face in her black hair. He checked himself as the first tear escaped and pushed away her hands before it could reach her fingertips. His ploy failed, though: when he bowed his head to kiss her hand the tear landed on its back. It moved almost in slow motion and he watched its journey with a strange mixture of emotions. It caught the blue-white light streaming through the gallery window and glinted like a tiny diamond. Hastily he wiped it away with his thumb and looked up into her face; it had not been unnoticed, and her smile became softer, less forced.

'Shula,' he said again. He could think of nothing else to say and the irony of the situation was lost upon him as she led him, trance-like, to the table and sat him down.

Haltingly, she began to speak. Most of it she had told him in her letters but Talisker didn't care: he watched her rather than listening. These people she was telling him about, their lives had gone on and they didn't care about him – in fact, most would probably cross the street to avoid him. It was different for Shula: she had loved him once.

'Shula,' he interrupted, 'I don't care about them. Why did you stop writing?'

A shadow crossed her face and, although she could not see him, she tried to fix him with her gaze. 'I had a relationship. It's over. I have a daughter – Effie.' She could not help but smile. 'She's so beautiful, Talisker . . .'

He had reached across to hold her hand and his grip tightened. 'I'm glad for you, Shula. About your little girl, I mean. Really.'

And he was. In the pool of bright sunlight Shula was a joy to see, her long black hair, her quick positive movements and her dark eyes, which were still capable of expression and laughter. She wore light, feminine clothes, a long flowery skirt and a lemon cardigan over a muslin blouse. She smelt good. Suddenly it seemed to Talisker that all the colours he had lost, replaced by grey and shadow, were reappearing as he looked at her.

He could imagine a smiling child, a copy of her mother perhaps, could see them laughing together, and he was glad.

'Hold on, I'll get some coffee.' He let go of her hand and she looked saddened somehow. 'When I come back I'll tell you a secret,' he promised.

'Secrets already?' She sounded incredulous. 'You've only been out for ten days!'

They talked for a long time although he couldn't remember afterwards what they had said. She relaxed gradually in his company and, for a short, blissful hour, the past fell away and they were the same couple who had loved each other years before. Eventually, in their determination to ignore the bitterness and anger, they talked of people with whom they had been at school.

'Do you remember Mando?' He laughed.

'Oh, yeah. He was weird. A bit of a nutter.'

'Yeah. You never really knew where he was coming from. He was a bit, you know, on the edge. Like he was ready to flip out.'

'That's good coming from you, Talisker.' He saw shock register on her face as she realised what she had said. They had said Talisker had murdered in a frenzy. His victims were mutilated. 'God, I'm—'

'It's all right, Shula.'

Still, the shock-waves coursed through him even as he spoke. She didn't believe him. That's what she had said. All this time she had assumed his guilt; incredibly she had come past it, and forgiven him. He felt his throat constrict as he choked down his next words: I'm innocent. Who cared any more? His numbness returned. When next he looked up at her she had returned to the shades like all the rest.

There was a long, awkward silence.

'Talisker, I'm really . . .'

'It's all right, Shula.' He couldn't keep the frustration from his voice. 'Really.'

She sucked in her bottom lip, looking close to tears. Finally she said quietly, 'What do we do, Duncan? Where can we go from here?'

He sighed, wishing her colours back, clinging to the smell of her perfume lest he lose her altogether. 'Can we just be friends, Shoo?'

She laughed at his use of her old nickname and reached out for his hand once more. 'I think that's an excellent idea.' She sounded shaky. 'You've forgotten, haven't you? The secret?'

'Ah. Yes.' He reached into his pocket and took out the emerald. As he opened her outstretched hand to place the gem in it, he joked, 'The King of all Hares gave it to me.'

She looked mystified and excited when he told her the story. As she listened, she turned the stone over and over in her palm, frowning slightly. Finally as he finished his tale she said, 'Duncan, are you going to go there?'

'Where?'

'To the place where this comes from.'

By the time he left the gallery he felt slightly better. Shula had invited him to meet her and Effie in Princes Street and go for a burger. Vague disappointment had flashed through his mind that she hadn't invited him to her house, but he understood her desire to take things slowly. Even being friends after all the years would need some work and, above all, time. She had also told him about a drop-in centre for 'ex-cons' – she had said the word haltingly, unsure of his reaction – where she helped out. Talisker wasn't too sure about it but she pressed him into saying he'd give it a try.

On the way up from the Waverley station he stopped to buy a small bunch of flowers from an outdoor stall. He stared down at the mass of red and yellow as soon as the florist put them in his hands, wondering what had possessed him to buy them. He didn't think he had ever bought flowers before. 'Colour,' he muttered. 'Colour.' He thought about the dark, muted tones of his bedsit and smiled grimly.

The smell was the first thing. Although it had never been so strong before, Talisker knew it was decay. He'd once had dental treatment for an abscess, and been appalled by the cloying stench that had risen from his own mouth like an accusation; this was worse. As he pushed open his front door, it wafted out on to the landing, not in teasing wisps but in great big slices. Wrapping his scarf around his face he advanced past the door and gazed around the room, feeling the first touches of fear. Would they know already that he was out? His release had been kept quiet and low-key in case the media got hold of it. People hated him, and he feared their hatred.

When he saw the source of the smell, in the corner by his bed, there was a millisecond of relief, but that was all. A cry of revulsion escaped him, then a spasm of coughing. Closing the door, he leaned back against it and stared.

It was a ghost. Once it had been a warrior, a berserker. Faint echoes hung in the air between them – *'McLeods, tae me! Tae me!'* – but the glory of the battlefield was long ago. The skin on his face was white, bloodless and bloated – it reminded Talisker of a rotten apple. The features were almost obscured within the swollen flesh and further hidden by ropy clumps of red hair. The black glimmer of the eyes could be sensed rather than seen. Under his right arm a sulphurous yellow stain spread from armpit to waist, gluing the shirt to his flesh, and across his chest, bloodstains; stab-wounds. He wasn't bleeding now but the gashes had just dried up, not scabbed over. The ragged puckers were obscene and hard to stop looking at.

He wore a clansman's kilt, not some tourist skirt, more like a blanket that was wrapped round him and held about the waist by a broad leather belt. At the shoulder a pewter brooch gripped the fraying end of his mantle to the roughly spun cloth of his shirt. In his left hand he held a short-sword, his fingers like white puffy roots around it. Dimly Talisker thought he'd never eat parsnips again. There was no feeling of malevolence about the apparition, and Talisker found that somehow unsurprising. They stared at each other in their frozen postures from the darkened edges of the room. A block of yellow sunshine rested across the middle of the space, and Talisker felt that if he walked into it he would become as insubstantial as the figure he faced. His initial feelings of revulsion faded, replaced by empathy and irritation.

''S that you making that smell?' he growled.

'Look, Ah canny help it. See how sweet you smell after a couple o' hundred years.' The Highlander's voice was surprisingly high and reedy. He hadn't sounded like that in the dream.

Talisker was amazed by his own feelings of calm. There was a short pause while he considered his next statement. 'You've come to talk to me, haven't you?'

The Highlander nodded, and Talisker felt sick as a vision of the ghost's head falling off came to mind, the sound it would make . . . 'I – I can't talk to you like this. Can you not do something?'

The shade considered this. 'Aye, mebbe . . . all right, then. But dinny go away, right?'

Talisker adjusted the scarf around his face. He couldn't take much more of this smell. 'I live here,' he joked weakly. 'Where would I go?'

The smile that split the Highlander's face was sickening to see; in life it might not have been much better, but the blackness of the gums and the few rotting teeth were frightening reminders of his lost mortality. 'Aye. That's true. I'd find ye onyways.' With that he vanished.

Talisker dropped the flowers he was still clutching, which spread across the dirty beige carpet like a liquid rainbow. He raced over to the window to fling it open, only to discover it was painted shut. 'Shit-shit-shit . . .' he cursed. He grabbed a dirty knife and stabbed ineffectually at the paint but suddenly, mid-hack, he realised the smell was gone.

Half an hour later, he was sitting at his table with a glass and a half-empty whisky bottle at his outstretched hand. He hadn't drunk it all at this sitting but he was on his third glass. The solid little tumbler he clutched like a life-line was smeared with greasy fingerprints. He didn't know how he felt about being haunted because he never examined his own feelings on anything. That way madness lay . . . but what could this be anyway? He'd always considered himself a pragmatist, felt it had helped him to endure – so why, when a ghostly decaying body appeared in his room, did he not doubt? He was having difficulty getting even slightly drunk.

'Is this better then?' The ghost had reappeared across the table from him. He looked more like the warrior Talisker had seen in his dreams. His face was still pale but his wounds were either gone – not yet inflicted? – or covered up. He was wearing what at first seemed to be the same outfit, but on closer inspection was cleaner. He smelt of cow-shit, and wisps of straw clung to the folds of his dress and his hair, but it was a distinct improvement. 'This is much mair difficult. See, Ah didnae look like this when I died. Aw that pus an' stuff. It wiz relevant, ye might say. Ah hope ye appreciate the effort, ye big jessie.'

Talisker grunted and drained his glass. 'So, come on, what do you want?'

'Weel . . . where tae start? Ye do realise you're ma descendant, don't ye? Ah'm Malcolm McLeod – but you kin ca' me Malky. Ah'm yer great-great-great . . .' he waved his hand vaguely to indicate more greats '. . . grandfaither.'

Talisker stared across the table. Now that it had been mentioned, there was a resemblance around the eyes –

and the red hair, of course. Strange that his however-many-times-great-grandfather should have died at about the same age as Talisker was now. The knowledge was shocking and the memory of how Malky had looked when he died was worse. 'I'm sorry, Malky. You were just a young man when—'

'Aye. Cut down in ma prime.'

'So. Why are you here?'

'Ah canny really tell ye that, Ah'm afraid. I've kinna been sent tae watch over ye and guide ye.'

Talisker gulped his next whisky, ignoring the sharp nipping of his eyes. He could feel the buzz now. He snorted derisively as he put down the glass. 'You mean like a sort of stinking Jiminy Cricket?'

The ghost managed to look offended and mystified at the same time. 'Eh?'

'The voice of my conscience.' Talisker sighed.

'Jings, no. Dinny be daft. From what I've seen, ye've got enough o' that tae be goin' on wi'.

'So. I don't actually need you to watch over me, do I?' Talisker sounded peevish. He knew the whisky was affecting him – he had eaten nothing all day and the coffee he had drunk with Shula was the only thing in his stomach. Now, the reality of conversing with his dead ancestor was too much. He felt everything slide. He glared at Malky, whose indistinct shape was wavering in time with the rest of the room. 'Fuckin' acid burn,' he muttered. 'That's what you are.'

'Look, ye're goin' tae need me, all right? I canny really explain. Jist trust me.'

'Aye. Right.' Talisker belched loudly.

Malky looked pointedly at the empty glass in

Talisker's hand, a prim, sour expression on his face. 'That'll kill ye, y'know.'

Talisker belched again as though in reply to the criticism.

'Aye, very funny.' Malky wasn't laughing. 'Mebbe I should be your sense o' humour instead of your conscience, 'cos you've obviously no' got one. A real hero, you are . . .'

Talisker lost his patience. 'Why?' He slammed his glass on the table. 'Why the hell would I possibly need you? You're a ghost. I could put my hand right through you. It's not exactly practical, is it? Fer Chrissakes, Malky. Get—'

'What?' Malky was frowning.

'Get real.' Talisker's voice had sunk to a whisper. Suddenly he wasn't coping. 'Look, no offence, Malky, I'm for my bed.' He stood up and walked towards it, his gaze continually on Malky until, by the time he reached it, he was looking back over his shoulder at a neck-crunching angle. 'Huh. No offence, Malky. No offence. Get it? That's good coming from me.' He made a strangled noise and flung himself on to the quilt. 'Now that's funny.'

Whether the noise was laughter or sobs was impossible to tell.

# CHAPTER THREE

The raven lands in the blackness of the void. Here, there are no landmarks, no shapes by which to measure the span of the blue-black wings, but the noise and backdraught caused by their beating is sufficient that any soul lingering in that dark space would know that here stood a creature of godlike potency. An immense creature of power and magic. For a moment, the bird pauses, its glittering eyes sweeping the empty reaches for movement. Satisfied that there is none, it transforms into a man.

He is tall, and his blue eyes still hold something of the quickness of the raven. As he is garbed in black robes, his shape is indistinct except for the face and the long, angular fingers. Striding forward purposefully a few paces, he stops suddenly, frowning. He takes another halting pace forward, then another, and stares at the ground as though it is about to open up and swallow him. It might. At his feet lies a chasm as near bottomless as would make no difference should some unfortunate stumble across its rim. Raven-being smiles and, leaning forward, spits into the darkness with apparent contempt. Then he waits.

A long white shaft of light lances from the darkness of the chasm. The being blinks uncomfortably but does not draw back. There is silence but the sensation that he is being watched pervades the space, intensifying with each moment. There is another creature in the void. Lit by the harsh whiteness, something is oozing from the lip of the chasm like a black stain. Its semblance of life is some dark parody. Nothing from that place could create life or form yet the viscous slurry moves towards the raven-being, with an air of malevolent determination. After taking a few cautious steps backwards, the raven-being, who has called it forth, stops. Stooping down, he touches the cold mass and the void is illuminated by a sulphurous green light. Then, a male human form stands before the raven-being, its stance hunched, animalistic. It is naked and its skin has a sickly yellow pallor. The hair and features mirror those of its creator but the eyes are blank, dark and soulless. Also, the hands appear too large, while the waxen fingers shake and tremble. And yet it is adequate for its purpose.

Raven-being grins, a wide, outrageous grin.

'Welcome, demon,' he says. Then his laughter fills the emptiness of the void with wicked delight. The spirit form says nothing, merely waits to be given purpose. 'But you cannot go forth on your journey naked,' its creator chides. 'Here . . .'

Moving forward he places his hands on the creature's chest just beneath the breastbone. Then, he pushes his fingers forward sharply and takes hold of the loose flesh. He pulls slowly and the form of the spirit changes once more so that it appears to be wearing garments the waxen colour of its lifeless skin. The process seems to cause the creature pain: it blinks and its blank expression tightens in something like a grimace, but it says nothing and does not move away from its creator.

Even when the raven-being pulls hard on the malleable flesh of its calves to form the outline of trousers, the spirit does not move.

Finally the job is done, and the artist steps back to admire his handiwork. 'Some colour, I think,' he mutters. He waves his hand almost absent-mindedly and, again, the sulphurous light fills the void. The demon now wears the garb of the place to which he will travel: blue trousers, a short-sleeved black vest and a loose black overcoat. He has no shoes, however: his feet are large and splayed, with no loose skin on which to work.

'Hmm.' The raven-being eyes the effect critically. 'Perhaps a hat will hide those eyes.' He touches the lank hair of the demon and forms a soft grey hat, which he pulls down to shade the blank expression. 'Now, creature, listen to me. I am Corvus, your creator, and you must obey me before I allow you solace of darkness once more. Existence is pain, is it not?'

The demon moves its head in a tiny motion of assent. As it does so, its features begin to melt away as though the pallid skin is wax and something is burning inside. As the features disappear, they reveal a stranger form beneath, another face, closer to the creature's true nature. It is composed of the vibrant greens and reds of flayed, rotting flesh. The shape is that of a human face that has been unnaturally twisted and contorted. The mouth is lipless – merely a few yellow teeth stuck into the core of the jaw – and the eyes blazing black pits of anger and pain.

'No,' Corvus hisses. 'Hold your form. Hold it, damn you, or I will send you screaming into the eye of the sun.'

The face changes again, reverting to the human form, the eyes assuming their blankness. Corvus knows, however, that should he lose control, for seconds even, the demon will attempt to destroy him, and that within this space, the balance of power is tenuous, could change from moment to moment. Cold fingers of sweat prickle on to his brow but he retains his composure. Holding up his hands, he conjures an image of the place to which he will send his unwilling servant: an ancient city in darkness, the streets lit by unnatural light from tall stone or iron sconces, and on the streets large, brightly coloured boxes bearing many people, move as though by magic. The people inside do not meet one another's gaze as though they fear something intangible. Corvus moves the image on, down the streets towards the sea, towards where the shore-dwellers live. Finally he stops before a small iron bridge. It crosses the last of the river that runs through the city to meet the sea. The street there is less brightly lit, and beneath that bridge one might easily conceal a magic that is alien to the people of this time. Beneath that bridge one might plant a seed that will destroy the hopes of the Fine and the Sidhe before they are given voice or form, before the name of their so-called saviour is even spoken aloud.

Corvus looks up at the demon; he can sense the creature's pain, which emanates from the silent hunched form. It is good, a useful weapon to combine with the natural, directionless anger that constantly consumes any spirit from the pit. With a blanking, calming charm, Corvus sends instructions straight into the seething mass of the demon's mind – far safer than speaking to it directly.

'Go now,' he says finally. 'I will watch and guide. Fail me not or I will destroy you. No . . . wait.' He waves his hand, and on the creature's black vest an outline appears of a bird, its beak hooked and vicious, a raven. Corvus grins. 'Just my bit of fun,' he mutters. Once again he waves his hand, almost absently, and the demon disappears.

Corvus sighs, and only then allows himself to wipe the sweat from his brow. Transforming back into a raven, he departs for the relative safety of his prison.

It was raining. The thin grey light of an October morning enveloped the landscape, draining the colours to sepia tones. Beneath the iron bridge the professional atmosphere of a murder investigation was only hampered by a young WPC, who was sobbing quietly into a handkerchief. The dismal scene was lit intermittently by the blue flash of a camera.

Chaplin arrived. He bounced down the steps two at a time, beckoning the sergeant over to him. His figure caught the light that spilled down the sides of the steel bridge and was thrown into an austere relief against the darkness. He was that unusual combination, a tall, heavy man, not fat but big-framed and muscular. He had dark hair tied back in a pony-tail; his hair was thick and strong-looking, and his olive features proclaimed his Mediterranean origins – his father was Sicilian although his mother was a Scot – and he moved with the quick energy of his father's race. Already his gaze was sweeping the scene under the bridge. He was wearing a crumpled dinner-jacket. The neck of his shirt was open and his bow-tie missing. He seemed unperturbed by this inappropriate garb and was munching distractedly on a sandwich.

Arrogant, that was how most people described Alessandro Chaplin. No one said it within earshot, but the thought was often there. However, Chaplin had the respect of his men although few could say they liked him.

'Bit of a mess, sir,' the sergeant remarked. The vision of Chaplin in a dinner-jacket was disconcerting and he found it difficult to keep the questions from appearing on his face – his eyebrows were twitching uncontrollably.

'Got a problem, Sergeant?' Chaplin fidgeted with his lapel. He frowned at the sandwich crust and flung it into the water.

A duck appeared as though from nowhere, quacking possessively. Chaplin frowned at it, for no apparent reason, and then smiled.

'Ducks, eh?'

A cold gust of wind blew downstream causing the duck to move uncontrollably away from its prize. It paddled desperately against the current and then stretched its neck forward as far as possible and grabbed at the crust. Chaplin shuddered in the breeze and pulled his flimsy jacket tighter around himself.

'Bravo, duck,' he said quietly, 'Now Sergeant, let's have a gander . . . haha! Get it?' He turned away and began to walk toward the body. He wasn't smiling. The sergeant followed, bracing himself again.

Underneath the bridge, the murder scene was being photographed and studied. The death of a young girl always hit the team hardest, perhaps because they were men, although none of them would admit to it, of course.

It reminded Chaplin of that clichéd answer people gave when asked what sex they'd like their unborn child to be: 'we don't care as long as it's alright . . .' For some it must be true, but their reluctance to favour one sex over the other, to tempt fate by their admission, hung unuttered over each murder scene he had ever attended. What sex would you like your murder victim? A boy, definitely . . . The sadness and vulnerability of a female corpse was hardest to bear.

He leaned against the cold steel of the arch, staring fixedly at the decapitated head, wondering yet again why people did such things. He could hear the sergeant talking about her identity and contacting the parents. God, he thought, I'd rather be here than on the cold comfort trip. Then he felt a chill within him that spread in a wide band across his stomach and ribs. The sensation puzzled him – he knew it did not arise from squeamishness or fear – until he realised it was recognition. Shadows of the past flared at him from the empty eyes and the shock was like a physical blow.

'Are you okay, sir?' The sergeant's voice had lost its sureness, as he saw the head picked up and deftly put into a black bag, staring like a tragic Medusa.

When the sergeant turned back, Chaplin had composed himself. 'I know who did this,' he said, wearily triumphant.

'But—' the sergeant began, but Chaplin ignored him.

'I'm telling you, I know.' His tone was determined. He would suffer no argument once he had made up his mind.

'It's not possible, sir.'

Chaplin stared hard at the sergeant, his face a bleak mask. A dark, haunted look passed across his eyes. There was pain in it too, as though something shut away safely in the detective's mind had lurched out into the open. 'There,' he said softly. His voice had dropped to a barely audible whisper.

A bus passed over the steel bridge, its diesel engine racing loudly, and the sergeant was unsure of what Chaplin said.

'There,' Chaplin went on. 'The darkness that consumes us. You've never met him, Sergeant. He brings chaos . . . The seed of complicity. Duncan Talisker did this.'

'Er . . . are you all right, sir?'

'Wake up laddie! Wake up!'

Talisker would have groaned but his tongue was stuck to the roof of his mouth. He felt stewed, as though every drop of liquid in his body had mysteriously evaporated overnight. This couldn't be a hangover, though, he decided, because he never got hangovers. Anyway, he remembered everything. He groaned. He had remembered that he was going mad. It was ironic, really, to have kept his sanity all these years only to lose the plot on his release. He kept his eyes shut.

'If that's you, Malky, piss off and haunt somebody else.' There was no answer and Talisker risked opening one gummy eye.

Malky smiled at him from the end of the bed. He was less opaque in the sunlight, and motes of dust sparkled disconcertingly through his body. 'That's no very nice,' he chided. 'It's a guid thing Ah'm no easily offended.'

Talisker groaned again.

'Onyways you've no' got time for a' this denial or whatever they call it. Ye're goin' tae be arrested.'

Talisker sat bolt upright. 'You what?'

'Sorry. That wisnae very subtle o' me. Aye, they're on their way over.'

'Why? What have I done?' Talisker was confused.

'You've no' done anything, ye great lummox. Ye were here wi' me gettin' drunk last night.' He looked serious. 'There was a wee girl murdert last night, Duncan. Just a young thing. Anyway it wiz your . . . MO? That's what they said.'

'Who said?'

'The polis. What does it mean?'

'Never mind. How do you know, Malky?' Talisker was out of bed now, stripping off his sweaty clothes from the night before, oblivious to the chill.

'Well, Ah'm kinna tuned in to you, you see, and anything that affects you is like . . . relevant. Like ripples in a pond. See?' He seemed quite pleased with his explanation. Talisker frowned at him, exasperated. 'They were talkin' about you, so I heard it.' Malky shrugged lamely.

The sudden image of Malky's head falling from his shoulders returned to Talisker and he felt faintly sick. 'Who?' he asked.

'Polis blokes. One's a forriner.'

'Chaplin?'

'Yeah. Where are you goin', Duncan?' Talisker was striding towards the door, pulling on a thick cream jersey.

'I'm running away, Malky,' he said grimly, without looking back.

'Well, that's no answer, is it? It's no' what a real clansman wid dae.'

Talisker stopped by the door, a look of amazement on his face. 'This is the twenty-first century, Malky. I can't hack them to pieces with my claymore. You don't understand.'

'But I do,' he protested. 'I know, Duncan. I know everything. Ye're an innocent man.'

Talisker blinked in disbelief. He had waited so long to hear any voice, other than his own, say those words. He had hoped it would be Shula's. Suddenly, the realisation that the statement had come from what he considered a figment of his imagination hit him, and he felt ashamed. 'I know who you are,' he said. 'You're something to do with my ego. A projection. I just wanted to hear someone say that . . .' His gaze dropped to the floor, and he held on to the door handle as though the small brass lever were the last vestiges of his self-assurance. 'I thought only children had imaginary friends . . .'

Malky was staring at him in horror. 'Christ, laddie, ye're a mess. Look, Ah don't know about the other victims, but Ah ken last night you were here wi' me. I'm sorry Ah don't know . . . an' if Ah did, Ah widnae be allowed tae tell ye. Don't you know? It's no' somethin' ye could forget.'

'I used to know,' Talisker whispered, 'I just got so confused. It's difficult to explain. I think I do know.'

'What?'

Talisker looked back at Malky and tried once again to

smile. 'I'm innocent, Malky. That's what I think I know.' He stepped back into the room and threw his coat back over the chair.

'Well, then,' Malky said firmly, 'say it with conviction.'

There was a knock at the door. Talisker froze. 'Christ, Malky, what am I going to do?'

Malky shrugged. 'There's no' much you can do, Duncan. Just remember what you told me about being innocent. Hold that thought. Ah'll come wi' you tae the station tae see fair play.'

'Thanks, pal,' Talisker muttered. He strode over to the door and swung it open abruptly.

The expression of wild ferocity on Chaplin's face froze as his eyes rested on Talisker. Such naked expression was unusual for Chaplin and was only matched by Talisker's own. They stood almost nose to nose, their gazes locked, the air between them so charged with their enmity that the sergeant, who had accompanied Chaplin, took a step backwards. For a long moment neither man spoke. Fifteen years stretched between them like an invisible wall of complicity and guilt. Fifteen years ago, much had been left unspoken.

Eventually, Talisker backed away. 'Come in.' He motioned the men into the room. His hatred of Chaplin was now subsumed by an air of bleak resignation, which he wore like a grey blanket. It was familiar to both police officers from their dealings with long-term prisoners, but it always angered Chaplin; made him want to lash out.

'What can I do for you?' Talisker asked.

'I'm afraid it will have to be down at the station, Mr Talisker.' Chaplin was gazing around the room. A poster caught his attention and he walked towards it, the sergeant trailing in his wake. 'Cuff Mr Talisker, please, Sergeant,' Chaplin said mildly. 'Ah, Michelangelo, *bellissimo*. You'll have to see the real thing, Talisker, it's sublime.'

'There's really no need,' Talisker muttered, as the sergeant bore down on him eagerly, reaching into his pocket for the handcuffs.

'Eh? Oh, procedure, I'm afraid. The thing is, you really don't get the true colours in these reproductions. In the flesh as it were, the reds and whites especially are quite bright – they give the whole thing more movement.'

Malky was standing on the bed out of the way bouncing up and down slightly, causing tiny indentations to appear in the quilt. 'Kin they really do this, laddie? Don't they need proof first?' he was squeaking.

Talisker wondered vaguely what would happen if someone walked through him. 'No, they don't,' he murmured.

'Pardon?' said the sergeant sharply. 'Wouldn't be getting abusive, would you, Mr Talisker? I wouldn't if I were you, 'cos me and my colleagues have just spent the morning picking up the pieces of a dead girl by the canal, so I'm not in a very good mood.' He had wrapped something around Talisker's wrists that looked like a plastic freezer-bag tie and he jerked it tight to emphasise his point. Talisker frowned down at it.

'I know,' Chaplin said. 'They're just not the same . . . Are we ready, then?' He smiled brightly, and a sharp ray of morning sunlight gleamed on the whiteness of his canine teeth. In Chaplin, the beast was always there, whether or not it was wearing a dinner-jacket.

Talisker had opened his mouth to say something and seemed to think better of it. A muscle worked in his jaw.

'What is it, Talisker?' Chaplin's tone was unreadable.

'It all begins again, doesn't it, Chaplin?'

Chaplin sighed heavily. He surveyed his charge with an unfathomable look then gave a tiny nod. 'Yes,' he said.

They knew Chaplin was bringing him in and the atmosphere at Ladyfield Place was edgy. About fifty pairs of eyes were watching from vacant-looking windows when Chaplin pulled Talisker from the back of the car.

Once inside, nothing was said to either man, as though Chaplin was tainted by the evil of his charge. Policemen went about less glamorous tasks than processing a murder suspect while all the time feeling the presence of that man in the station, like a silent itch. They hustled burglary suspects down the corridors; even smiled at a couple of confused joy-riders on their way to the cells. It was relative, after all.

It was all a blur to Talisker; his body was on autopilot and went wherever it was led. He was glad of the quiet dignity with which Chaplin was treating him, but puzzled by it too. What did Chaplin want?

A young policewoman was coming towards them. He would have to step aside to let her pass. As he did so, she smiled at him, a polite but natural smile. She obviously didn't know who he was. His gaze flickered and his dead eyes tracked her progress down the corridor. As he turned back he saw the barely concealed look of loathing on Chaplin's face and knew exactly what he was thinking, but nothing could touch him.

The police station, for all its grimness, was somehow more substantial, more solid than Talisker's flat. It seemed that its walls held on to the daily traumas that must occur there, stored them up. Here, Malky was just Talisker's shadow. Of course, no one could see him and, in some small way, his presence was a comfort. It was good to have a friend at your back. Malky strode along behind Talisker, grimly silent, his hands fidgeting around the hilt of his short-sword, his eyes darting back and forth, gleaming with a cold feral light from beneath his muddy locks.

Alone in the interview room for a few minutes, Talisker laid his forehead against the cold Formica table-top. It might even be the same room. It smelt the same, of vomit overlaid with wax polish. To him it was the smell of abject defeat, carried in his sensory memory for the last fifteen years, evocative of his shame. His expression was blank.

Malky paced the room for a while then stopped in Talisker's line of vision. 'Ye've got tae snap out of it, Duncan. Ye've got tae do something tae make them ken they've got the wrong man.'

'What can I do, Malky? What do you want me to do?'

'I don't know,' Malky admitted, 'but you're running away already – no' physically mebbe but. . . It jist cracks me up.'

There was a despairing silence while both men stared at the floor. Malky started as he heard footsteps coming down the passage. 'Look, can ye no' jist tell them you were wi' me?'

'Don't be friggin' stupid,' Talisker grated.

Malky returned to pacing the floor.

The door opened and Chaplin came in with an unknown officer, carrying a tray of coffee with a packet of fags – JPS. He'd sent out for them specially. Talisker was staring into the middle of the room.

Chaplin seemed nervous, but whether because of the situation or the other officer it was impossible to gauge. He fidgeted around with the cassette tapes for a moment, then handed round the coffee as though he was hosting an afternoon tea-party. Once he was satisfied that the tape was running, he looked directly into Talisker's eyes. Talisker looked back, unblinking. *It all begins again, doesn't it?*

'Duncan. Mr Talisker. This is Chief Inspector Stirling. He has offered to sit in on our . . . little chat because he feels that I am somehow personally involved in this case.'

'Involved?' Talisker's gaze shifted to the man sitting next to Chaplin. He was small and stocky with glittering dark eyes and a well-trimmed moustache. He looked like Poirot, Agatha Christie's finest. Talisker almost smiled at the man when a tiny shift in Inspector Stirling's expression said, 'Guilty.' He didn't avoid Talisker's appraising look, however, and Talisker admired him for that.

'Involved? Because you nicked me fifteen years ago, Chaplin? Because you milked a confession out of an innocent man? Don't flatter yourself. You were never involved – you just made the frame they put me in.

Anyone could have done it. I was awake for three whole nights. Seventy-six hours by the time I confessed.' He gave a humourless laugh. 'I would have confessed to shooting John F. Kennedy, given half a chance. What is this really? Does your supposed involvement imply that in some sick way you actually *care* what happened to me? Is this some new policy? Well, fuck you, Alessandro. I don't think you give a shit. You never did.'

Chaplin started to fiddle with his pony-tail. Talisker remembered this habit and knew that he'd made Chaplin uncomfortable. 'One day, Chaplin, I'll be cleared,' he went on. 'I'll be cleared.' He was fighting the raw emotion that was creeping into his voice. He swallowed hard.

'And then what, eh? Compensation? Will you buy me a beer, tell me that you're sorry? That you were only doing your job? Isn't that what the Nazis said at Nuremberg?'

Chaplin stood up suddenly, the plastic feet of his chair scraping across the floor. A blue vein ticked ominously at his temple and the lines around his mouth tightened.

Stirling leaned forward. 'I think,' he remarked quietly, 'they said that they were only taking orders.'

Talisker had no opportunity to respond.

'Sorry?' Chaplin hissed. 'Sorry? Yeah. That's right. Tell me, Mr Talisker, do you think you're the only one here who's done fifteen years?' He stood over Talisker, who could smell the policeman's cologne. 'Let me tell you, Mr Talisker,' he said quietly, 'there are other kinds of prison.'

'Bullshit.' Talisker didn't know what Chaplin was talking about, but cursing into that big face felt good.

Chaplin turned round and moved to the other side of the room, lighting a cigarette – he walked straight through Malky, who had been standing behind him.

'Don't mind me,' the Highlander yelped.

'I thought,' Chaplin began, 'that you were innocent, Talisker. I suppose that comes as something of a surprise to you. You thought nobody believed you, didn't you? Yeah, well, I did.' He paused as though to let the implication of this sink in, then he took a deep drag on his cigarette and continued. 'It was hell. Probably not the hell you thought you were going through, I admit, but a kind of hell all the same—'

Stirling interrupted him: 'Is this relevant, Inspector Chaplin? We are here to question a murder suspect, irrespective of the past history you two share.'

'Yes.' Both men spoke at once.

'Yes,' Chaplin repeated, 'it's all relevant. Please let me finish, sir.'

Stirling nodded dourly.

'I lived your case, Talisker. Took it home with me, dreamed it, ate it, slept it. You see, the excitement it created when we nicked you – it's difficult to explain to anyone who wasn't around at the time – it defied the evidence, it defied you to deny it. You, of all people, know it was all circumstantial. Six murders, Talisker. Six young girls . . .'

'I know.' Talisker closed his eyes.

'We were all so convinced we had the right man. So damn fucking convinced . . .'

'Inspector Chaplin.' Stirling threw Chaplin a warning look, which Chaplin chose to ignore.

'Then I interviewed you. Do you remember? And after about thirty seconds I knew, or I thought I knew, that you were innocent. I told everyone who asked me, and quite a few who didn't, but by then it was too late. You seemed near to confessing so the machine rolled inexorably along. The rest is history, as they say. I couldn't look at you in that courtroom.' He stopped pacing the floor and fidgeted with his hair again. Cigarette smoke snaked around his head in acrid curls. 'I suppose this is not so relevant, after all,' he mumbled. 'Anyway, I tried to forget about it. Tried to tell myself that it was an inevitable part of the system that sometimes we get it wrong. But it changed me, made me cynical . . . It's a feeling I carry in the pit of my stomach, like so much bile. I've lived with it for nearly sixteen years. Until this morning . . .'

His demeanour changed with lightning speed. He rushed back to the table, flung aside the plastic chair, and struggled to pull something out of the pocket of his dinner-jacket. Talisker somehow knew what was coming. Don't do it, he thought. Don't show me those . . .

'Goddamn it, man! They were right all along!' Chaplin was shouting now, almost out of control. He slammed a sheaf of photographs on to the table. As they fell from his grasp they fanned out in a tableau, somehow grimly beautiful. In the black and white tones, the photographer had somehow restored the girl's lost dignity.

'You scum! You bastard! They were right, weren't

they? It *was* you! I put myself through a wringer for fifteen years for nothing!'

Talisker wasn't listening. His horrified gaze danced around the edge of the photographs as though they had the power to kill. He buried his face in his hands, all reserve gone. 'Please, Chaplin. Don't do this to me again.'

'You were guilty all the time, you bastard. Look at them! Look at what you did to her!'

Talisker groaned again. 'No,' he said, through his fingers. 'No, no, no.'

# CHAPTER FOUR

*'Malky? What's happening?'*

*'Ye're dreamin', laddie. I think.'*

They were on a mountain. It was snowing – not beautiful snow, but treacherous, indelicate flakes that whirled around them in a cold-sick dance, before disappearing into the chasm below. Talisker was clinging to the sheer cliff face, staring upward at his own outstretched hand. It was gripping a tiny crevice in the silver rock above, his veins standing out like steel cord. He knew that he must continue to climb. He would put all his strength into that hand, all his weight on to that tiny crevice. He knew that if he moved his head and looked down he would see his feet – toes curled within the strange boots he wore – in an equally insignificant crack. Every muscle, every sinew in his body ached. He groaned aloud.

*'I can't do it, Malky. I can't move. Where are you?'*

*'I'm right beside you, Duncan. Ah don't know how Ah got here either. Ghosts dinny gan intae folk's dreams withoot, like, requestin' permission.'*

*'Permission? No . . . never mind. I'm slipping, Malky. I'm slipping. I'm going to fa—'*

Falling. The rocks and snow whizzing past, frighteningly silent. There, at the top of the cliff, a light, first green then silver. Somewhere, carried on the wind, his voice, Malky's. *'Ye're only dreamin', laddie! Wait fer me!'*

He thinks he'll wake up when he lands. He's had dreams of falling before. Relaxes. Watches the rocks. Watches the snow.

Lands. Still dreaming?

There's a woman. Except she's not a woman, not really. It's difficult to tell because she's swathed in green cloth from head to toe. A dark hood covers her features but from within the folds a sharp glimmer of green eyes is just discernible. She has been sitting here for some time in the heavy drifts of snow, and beside her there is a large copper bowl. It had been filled with water but she has tipped it over in her alarm; flower petals are scattered in a violent pink stain across the distance between them. Her movements are jerky, panic-stricken, and she moves towards Talisker, reaching out her hand. *'Wake up, Duncan.'*

Her hand is golden. The skin catches the light, which is arcing over the crest of the mountain. Her fingers are claw-like, but the gesture she makes is of supplication.

*'I can't wake up.'*

'Tal-ees-ker?' Her breath comes softly from beneath the green swathes of cloth. 'I have summoned the One?'

The wind howls around them, a constant mournful backdrop of sound. It whips up the snow that has already fallen and flings it once more into the fray. Talisker remembers the dandelions. For long seconds the two seem frozen in their poses: Talisker still crouching in the snow, she reaching to touch him with her golden hands.

*'Wake up, damn you.'*

Her hand falls back to her side and, even through the cloth, Talisker is sure she is now smiling. Her green covering begins to glow, like a warm emerald. Like *the* emerald. Inside the light, her form is shifting, transforming. He knows he doesn't want to be here when the transformation is complete but he cannot tear away his gaze. Something frightening is happening to the shape, yet it is beautiful to watch. It causes no pain to the figure but is an affirmation, or celebration of its existence. It possesses its own music. Feathers become visible, silver-white as the surrounding snows, and the shape is growing slowly, majestically.

And then the light is fading, and the creature within is revealed. In place of the female being there stands a white eagle. This new form is three times the height of the original; the huge white feathers gleam against the snow and she gazes down at Talisker through the same green eyes, except now an inner eyelid flickers across the surface. There is no doubt it is the same being.

From the slow heartbeat to heartbeat rhythm, the dream changes. The eagle takes a few ponderous steps towards Talisker and beats her vast wings in preparation for taking off. Talisker is backing away on his hands and knees, and realises he is slipping again. The cold and wet is all-pervasive, and as he feels the last of the solid rock disappear beneath him, a despair born of the misery of this place seizes him and he cries out a word of which he has no knowledge: *'Mirr-an-non!'*

The eagle opens her great hooked beak and gives harsh answer. Her wings slice the air for seconds and then she begins to dive. Talons like a steel trap close around Talisker's waist, and then they are rising high towards the pinnacle of the mountain, the air currents taking his cold breath from his lungs.

*'I'm waking up. I'm waking up.'* His lips are mouthing the words. The last thing he is aware of as they crest the mountain is the strange gathering on the plateau. A silver-grey figure stands there surrounded by dark skulking shapes, dogs or wolves. The wind whips at the figure's robes, forming them into the contours of another being. At the sight of the eagle, it lifts its arms in the air and beats against the wind in a gesture of frustration and futility. The great eagle cries again as though in triumph, her grip tightening possessively. Talisker cries out in pain, a weaker echo of its call. And wakes.

The noise from the traffic was immediate and deafening. The doors of a bus just leaving the stop outside the flats had jammed and the persistent hissing, coupled with the irritated cursing of the driver, was the first thing Talisker became aware of. The second was Malky, sitting on the end of the bed and frowning thunderously at him.

'Do you think that because I'm getting used to you, Malky, it's a sign that I'm mad?' Talisker asked sombrely.

The dream was fading, the harsher reality of his day and evening in police custody overwhelmingly bitter. He started to sit up then fell back groaning as a sharp pain gripped him around his ribcage. He rolled off the bed and went to stand in front of the mirror. Gingerly, he pulled back his shirt, which he had kept on from the night before, and gasped at a purple ring of bruising, startling against the prison pallor of his skin. 'They didn't beat me up, did they? I would have remembered that.'

In fact, a beating would have been preferable to the poison of their contempt, which had hung in the air while he had been in their custody. At least it would have been honest. But Chaplin hadn't beaten him up: he'd shown him the photos instead. And as Talisker had stared down at the grim black-and-white tale, it had happened to him again. His second-sight had re-created the poor girl's last moments.

He had seen it all. The girl, sobbing, her face white with fear, her lips blue, as the dark shadow of her murderer hacked and slashed, first at her clothes and then at her. Her tiny fluttering hands moved across his line of vision, like white birds. She had been menstruating, and the sight of the dark cyclic blood mingling with fresh arterial plasma had incited the killer to greater frenzy, which continued long after her pleading screams had stopped. He had held her up against the stones of the bridge in the lurid yellow glow of the lights and watched the two red tides meet in the dark crux of her thighs. Talisker had tried to stop the vision, had scrubbed his eyes and fought to keep his face a blank mask, but he had vomited across the table, blotting out the images and adding another layer to the room's smells. Chaplin had eyed him coolly, no trace of sympathy in his gaze. 'I think I might just join you, Duncan. You make me sick to my stomach.'

Stirling had leaped up from his chair and held a handkerchief over his nose and mouth. 'I think that's enough for now, Mr Talisker,' he said, his voice muffled. 'I'll take you to a cell while we get cleaned up here.' He didn't wait for a response but guided Talisker from the room. As they passed Chaplin, Talisker wanted to say something; he wanted to protest his innocence again, but there didn't seem to be any point.

'Her name was Judith,' Chaplin said.

After three more hours of questioning they let him go. Talisker couldn't quite believe it but he knew, as he'd known when they had picked him up, that they had no evidence against him. They would probably watch his movements for a few days, but he could live with that. He had felt their gaze, their contempt, as he was escorted out of the station, but at no time had this been made physical. Now, as he gazed at the bruising, a kind of cold awe crept over him. It made more sense to believe that he had been drugged and beaten than to admit what he was thinking, that it had been the eagle.

'Do you remember, Duncan?' Malky asked gently.

Talisker remained motionless. He saw the huge silver-white wings, the mountain light arcing from the feathers, felt the heat and heartbeat of the giant bird again. Mirranon. He couldn't give voice to that.

'No,' he lied. He did not meet the Highlander's gaze.

Chaplin sipped his coffee and stared at the snow. He'd taken the tacky paperweight from a young shoplifter three weeks ago and it had become lost in the junk-pile of his desk. As plastic paperweights went, he supposed it was quite a good one: the snowflakes took a long time to fall, and when they did, they almost obliterated the scene. It was supposed to be Edinburgh at night but it could have been anywhere. He picked it up and shook it again. He was thinking about Talisker.

Something had not been right about the man's reaction to the hours of questioning. Chaplin had been forced to admit to Chief Inspector Stirling that a man capable of rape, murder and decapitation was unlikely to vomit when confronted with photographs of his crime, yet something was there. It seemed as though Talisker wasn't sure of the truth any more than he was, and that frightened the man. Chaplin had sensed weakness in his adversary, he'd seen the blankness, the façade, drop and it brought him a predatory joy to see the damaged soul within.

Alessandro Chaplin had been raised to despise weakness: his father had beaten it out of him. His mother had watched with her quiet brown eyes as her son had grown into a man of strength, incapable of self-doubt and unable to forgive what he saw as weakness of character in those around him. Aged twenty-two he had married Diane, beautiful, bright and energetic, able to cope with the dark melancholy that often threatened to engulf him; her smile was like the sun. When she was killed in a car crash eighteen months after their wedding, his grief had left him emotionally untouchable. He missed her still.

His gaze was unfocused as he thought of Diane. The snowflakes seemed larger now, their whiteness filling his vision. For a split second an icy chill touched his face and he heard the echo of a voice. He could not make out the word. 'Diane?' He blinked and reality reclaimed him. Inexplicable anger seized him and he slammed the paperweight down on his desk.

Stirling looked up, raising his eyebrows. 'You still here, Chaplin? Thought I was the only mug staying late to do bloody paperwork.'

'Late?' Chaplin growled. 'Don't you mean early? I'm

going home now, anyway.' He started to rise from his chair when tightness gripped him around the chest. He fell back, but missed the chair and landed heavily on the floor, his arms crossed around his ribcage.

'Christ!' Stirling was by his chair in an instant.

'I'm all right,' Chaplin muttered, but the sweat was forming on his brow.

Stirling ignored him and loosened his clothing. Gently but firmly he moved Chaplin's arms and undid his shirt buttons. He cursed again under his breath. A malevolent ring of dark bruising encircled Chaplin's torso. It looked as though something had tried to crush the man's life from him. 'What happened, Alessandro?'

The light of fear was in the younger man's eyes.

'I don't know,' he whispered.

They sent him home for a few days. Stirling had promised to continue to amass evidence and to get in touch if anything came up. Chaplin knew he was lying: the consensus of opinion in the station was that Chaplin was too close to this case and his collapse had given them an excuse to get him out of the way for a while. He sat on his bed with a large glass of brandy, swirling it around and staring morosely into it.

Sometimes he didn't think about Diane for weeks and then he would hear a song she had liked, or something else would prompt a memory. Such grief never really left you, he thought. It had been so long now since she had gone that if he tried to bring her face to mind, it was faint and indistinct. Sometimes if he was feeling low he would gaze at photos of her and could hardly recognise the smiling young man beside her as himself. It made him feel worse and an ache not unlike heartburn would creep over him – but at least she had caused it. In that small pathetic way he could hold on to her. She could still reach out from somewhere and touch him.

Today, though, each time he closed his eyes – and he wanted to close them, he was tired – her face was there. Not soft and misty-looking but sharp, as though she stood in front of him. Every line, every nuance of her features was tantalisingly clear. But it wasn't the Diane he chose to remember, it was the other Diane. It was the look she had worn when he last saw her. A look of such accusation and scorn that he wondered how anything could have erased it from his memory. He swirled his drink again, watching the brandy adhere to the side of the glass. 'Diane,' he muttered.

No one else would ever know that on the day she was killed, Diane had been leaving him, and it had been Talisker's fault.

In some respects it was the usual policeman's wife story. He worked too hard, didn't come home when he promised and didn't leave his work at the office. With Chaplin, though, it had been one case: Duncan Talisker's. It had dragged on for months and it was all he talked about. She couldn't stand it any more, she said. On that fateful morning, Chaplin had gone to see Talisker sentenced with her screams ringing in his ears. She was an emotional woman just as he was an emotional man, he told himself. Perhaps she would stay away for a few days, but she'd calm down. Her car had collided with a petrol tanker. There was no corpse left for which to hold a funeral. She had gone for good.

There was a mirror opposite the bottom of his bed. In

the early-evening light it reflected his room. It was a sea of colour: clothes and blankets sprawled across the floor and covered the furniture in arcs of unexpected brightness, as though the room's occupant was a creature of chaos. By some serendipity, the mass of brightness fanned outwards, away from the dark outline of the bed, on which lay a large bronzed man, naked, with a circle of inexplicable bruising around his ribcage. He was weeping.

Chaplin slept well. When he woke he felt calm: the cold, all-encompassing calm that lay on the fringes of madness. He remembered that he had wept for Diane for a long time. He had never before shed tears for her, and at the time of her death he had behaved with stoic dignity. This morning he didn't question why she had come to him now with her silent accusation. He knew. It was because of Talisker. Fate had brought back the man who had taken her from him. It did not occur to him that the vision of her face might have been warning him to let it be. When he woke that morning he felt certain that he could avenge Diane's death – for the first time the idea of retribution seemed real – and he wondered if the thought had always lain there, dormant until now. He welcomed it like an old friend. Once it was over, he could continue with his life once more and no one would grieve for Duncan Talisker, especially since now it seemed that he had been guilty all along.

He was parked outside Talisker's flat, unsure what he was going to do but cradling a gun against his still tender ribcage. He couldn't do it here: Leith Walk was always busy and it was Saturday morning. There were no mega-stores, only ordinary shops, a greengrocer, a fishmonger, a small Woolworth's, but people had always shopped here and their mothers before them. Leithers were a breed apart, stubbornness and tenacity part of their makeup. It was nine o'clock and the street was packed, despite the drizzle that had continued almost unabated from the day before. The gun was cold against his chest. At the bus stop a small golden-haired child was talking earnestly to the rest of the queue, while the adults smiled. The child caught his eye and a flicker of uncertainty crossed her face. Chaplin grinned at her briefly and then looked away. He continued to wait.

'What the hell's he doing out there? Why doesn't he just come and arrest me? What's going on?' Talisker dropped the edge of the dusty curtain.

'Look, jist cos Ah'm a ghost disnae mean I have all the answers. If Ah was you, Ah'd go an' ask him.'

Talisker considered this. 'Yeah, I suppose I could. This must be police harassment. Mind you, I've got nothing to hide. If they want to waste their time and resources, let them. I'm going to meet Shula and Effie. D'you want to come?'

'Oh, aye. Ah canny leave ye on yer own. Ah've got my orders.'

'Orders? Who gives you orders, Malky?'

Malky looked evasive. 'It's a long story and Ah'm no'—'

'Let me guess, you're "no' allowed tae tell me"?'

'Em. Naw. Will we be goin' up the High Street at all?'

'Could do after I've seen Shula. Why?'

'Mebbe Ah'll tell you a bit about ma life,' said Malky. 'Or ma death.'

A short while later, the door to the flats opened and Talisker walked out. Chaplin sat forward to watch as he paused next to the bus stop to check his pockets for keys and money. A frown creased his brow and he started towards the newsagent. Chaplin guessed he would come back to the queue, and sat back again. As Talisker passed the first shop-front the policeman did a double-take.

It must have been a trick of the light. Reflected in the window, Chaplin could see someone following Talisker. A Highlander, sword, kilt and everything. His hair looked like matted straw and, although he was short, he walked with a long, ambling gait. He was definitely with Talisker – the impression was that he was walking in the taller man's footsteps. Then he vanished.

Chaplin blinked. His mind was buzzing. He rubbed his face and eyes, kneading the flesh, then kept his eyes closed, attempting to focus back to the feeling of icy calm that had gripped him earlier.

There was a sharp rapping noise on the roof of the car. He opened his eyes reluctantly. Talisker beamed in at him. 'Top o' the morning to you, Inspector Chaplin.' He had affected an appalling Irish accent. 'And what brings you to Leith Walk this bee-ootiful day?'

Chaplin smiled back. 'Fuck off, Talisker,' he said.

Talisker smirked: he had scored a point in their game. 'I may as well tell you I'm going to Princes Street for a McDonald's. Then I'm going to the High Street for a wander round the shops. Now you can take the morning off. I'd get some sleep if I were you. You look like shit.' He rapped on the roof of the car again. 'You have a nice day, y' hear?' Then he turned and crossed the street to the bus stop.

Before Chaplin had time to think about what he was saying, he called after him, 'Who's your friend?'

Either Talisker chose to ignore the question or he didn't hear it over the noise of the traffic.

Chaplin returned to Ladyfield. As soon as he walked into the communal office area he knew that certain officers were missing. They had been called for a briefing; the room reeked of cigarette smoke and Stirling's desk was clear. He had taken all his case notes with him, which meant that the briefing was about Talisker.

Chaplin sat down at his desk and stared blankly at the steam rising from Stirling's abandoned coffee. Something was happening to him; he knew that, but he couldn't stop it. It was as though he was losing control, losing the fight. But until yesterday, he had been unaware of his tenuous hold on reality. He was sweating; voices buzzed in his skull like lazy feeding insects whose limbs were working his mind to a pulp.

*'Have a nice day now, y' hear?'*

*'Her name was Judith . . .'*

He realised he still had the gun. It was warm now. The heat of his bruises had warmed it.

'*. . . collided with a tanker . . . death by misadventure . . . I just can't . . . I just can't stand it . . . any more . . .*'

Chaplin stood up and walked to the briefing room. From inside, Stirling's flat monotone droned on. He stopped at the door and peered through the grimy glass panel.

*I love you, Diane . . .*

On a screen at the far end of the room were the pictures. Seven girls now. Six would have been in their early- to mid-thirties; but the parents of one were still in the first stages of their grief. Some of the younger officers looked pale, their eyes avoiding the grim display. There were two photos of Talisker, his official prison picture and the one taken at the station yesterday. His eyes stared directly at Chaplin. Above Talisker there was a photograph of someone he didn't know, an older man: he was smiling the only smile in the room. Chaplin slammed the door open and walked in.

There was an instant hush. They all knew that someone had decided to hold this briefing when Chaplin was safely out of the way. At the opposite end of the room, Stirling was looking fidgety and worried, while some others, who had known Chaplin for years stared uncomfortably at their shoes. Chaplin reached into the pocket of his jacket, sweat and adrenaline making his movements clumsy. Where his jacket gaped open the gun caught the glare of the fluorescent light and it seemed as though he was about to draw it.

'He's got a gun,' someone hissed.

There was a silence. Chaplin was a policeman: it was unthinkable that he might fire a weapon at a colleague. He could still hear the voices in his head as he took the first few steps towards Stirling.

*Let's go away for a while . . . work here is finished . . . go away . . . away . . . I'm leaving . . .*

Stirling was holding out his hands towards Chaplin

as if he was fending off a large dog. Chaplin could see his lips moving, but could only hear the voices in his head and the buzz of white noise. Someone near the back of the room panicked and hit the alarm bell. Soon help would arrive in the shape of armed officers. Not soon enough. Chaplin's hand moved from his pocket.

'Get down!' Stirling bellowed.

Chaplin withdrew a tattered piece of paper. 'Victim,' he muttered dully.

He walked past Stirling's prostrate form and pinned it to the board: a photograph of Diane. He pulled down the picture of the unknown man and stared at it, trying to focus on why it hung beside the murder victims and their killer.

The policemen began to pick themselves up. Chaplin turned to leave the room.

'Wait!' Stirling cried. 'Alessandro!' He crashed past Chaplin without trying to stop him, yanked open the door and raced into the outer office. 'Safe!' he screamed. 'Safe!'

The first armed officer already had his gun trained on the door. On recognising Stirling, he lowered it immediately, unable to keep the disappointment off his face.

Chaplin lurched out behind Stirling. He was feeling sick now and wanted to go home and sleep, but he had to see Duncan Talisker. He heard Stirling call out to him again.

'Wait, Alessandro. There's been a development. Your man Talisker . . . looks like he may be—'

The door slammed behind Chaplin, cutting off the sound of Stirling's voice.

'. . . innocent,' Stirling said wearily to no one. 'We have a new suspect.'

He sighed heavily and started to light a cigarette. He felt like his bowels had turned to water but refused to join the small queue forming by the toilet. He gave a tired smile to the armed officer who looked about eighteen.

'My mother was right,' he sighed. 'I should have been an accountant.'

It was late afternoon and Talisker was drinking in one of the pubs in the Cowgate. It seemed strange to him that the place could be both trendy and scruffy. In his day, when a pub looked like this it was considered a dive; now it had 'atmosphere'. It was the place to be if you were a student or an academic. People sat around old oak whisky casks instead of tables, their feet and legs contorted into impossible positions because there was no table to tuck them under. A real fire was burning and the lucky few had already claimed the easy chairs beside it for the evening. Out of habit Talisker propped up the bar. He had to admit grudgingly that he liked the place, and although he'd had only a pint he felt more relaxed than he had for a long time. To his left was a kind of low-ceilinged tunnel painted a turgid red, in which stood more casks and a few actual tables.

Very Freudian, he thought. Then he checked himself – he'd watched too many Open University programmes in Saughton.

'Psst, Duncan.' It was Malky, and Talisker gave a tiny nod to show that he had heard.

'It's all right, Duncan. Jist think. Ah kin hear yer thoughts.'

*Really?*

'Oh, aye. It's easy. Ah was jist wonderin' if ye'd like a walk up the High Street in a wee while.'

Talisker frowned. *Well, I wasn't planning to . . . Is there something you want to show me up there? Come to think of it, do you know anything about the emerald?*

'Why would I ken anything about that? Ah'm jist a ghost, that's a'. It disnae make you om . . . om . . . thingy.'

*What about Mirranon? Do you remember my dream?*

Malky had the grace to look uncomfortable. 'Well . . . er . . . Aw, naw. Dinny look round.'

*What?*

'It's Chaplin. Just come in. He looks really mawkit. Like as though he's been in a battle or somethin'. He's no right at a'.'

*Where is he?*

'He's goin' tae sit in that red room. He's no' even gettin' a drink.'

'Soon fix that,' Talisker muttered aloud. He smiled towards the barman. 'I'll have another pint of Guinness. You have malt whiskies in here, don't you?'

'Aye, we've got quite a big selection.' The barman indicated a broad shelf above the optics with pride.

'Have you any from Skye? Oh, I see it. The very thing. Could you send a double over to my friend there? Thanks.'

Talisker watched as the man presented it to Chaplin, who raised his head and looked over. Talisker allowed a quick smile to flicker across his face and nodded briefly, as though they were, in fact, old friends. He was expecting Chaplin to mouth an obscenity in return but the policeman merely reached forward and gripped the glass as though Talisker had thrown him a lifeline.

'He's in a bad way,' Malky observed. 'Ah almost feel sorry for him.'

*Don't waste your time,* Talisker thought back bitterly. *He's not worth it.*

'He hates you,' Malky nodded. 'We ghosts know some things. You can see the black stain around him. He's become bitter about somethin' in his past and he blames you. Mebbe kennin' you were inside was enough tae keep him goin' but now ye're oot . . .' He trailed off.

Talisker restrained himself from laughing. *I could have told you all that. He blames me for the death of his wife. Didn't you know that?*

'Christ! Did you murder his wife an' all?'

The question took Talisker off guard. *'What?'* he hissed aloud.

'Pardon, sir?' The barman looked at him in puzzlement. His customers often spoke to themselves but seldom with such venom.

'Sorry. I was just thinking aloud.

*How could you think that? Do I have to keep protesting my innocence to you as well? I thought you were on my side. Anyway, she was killed in a traffic accident.*

'Eh?'

*Don't ask.* Talisker shrugged. *Just don't ask.*

It was dark by the time they made their way up the High

Street. Talisker felt slightly stewed by the warmth of the pub, and the chill of the night air, which held the promise of winter, was welcome. They'd watched Chaplin drink himself almost to oblivion. He looked so miserable that Talisker nearly felt a twinge of sympathy. Just before they left Talisker visited the toilet and when he returned Chaplin was gone.

'He left,' Malky said. 'D'ye think he'll be a' right?'

*Who cares?* Talisker thought bitterly.

'You're a hard man, Duncan Talisker.' Malky shook his head sadly. 'I dinnae think ye'll ever put this behind you.'

Talisker regarded the ghost of his ancestor calmly.

*So have I got some kind of aura, then? Do I carry a black stain?*

Malky looked surprised, as though he'd never thought about this before.

'Naw. No' black . . .'

*What then?*

'Kinna . . . purply-red. I dunno what it means.'

The night sounds washed over Talisker as he stopped to light a cigarette, acutely aware of the hiss of his petrol lighter and the familiar smell of the fumes. It seemed as though his senses were becoming sharper and he toyed with the idea that he might be shaking off the invisible confinements of fifteen years in prison.

'What's going on, Malky?' he muttered. 'Why d'you want me to come up the High Street?'

'It's kinna difficult to explain.' Talisker looked unimpressed. 'Duncan, please come. Please.'

His tone was so beseeching that Talisker turned

unquestioningly towards the top of the High Street. At the edge of his vision, through the plume of white cigarette smoke, he caught the movement of a shadow on the other side of the crossroads. 'Aye. Why not? Nice night for a walk round the Old Town.'

# CHAPTER FIVE

Unwittingly Chaplin had overtaken Talisker and was slumped in the entrance to Advocate's Close, further up the High Street. He was lost in a haze of alcohol. As a rule Chaplin drank little, too smart to fall into the drinking-to-unwind trap. Until now. He had just vomited in the alleyway, and his eyes burned from the smell of undigested alcohol and unshed tears of shame. Resting his back against the cold stone wall of the alley he slid down to the ground. In the still, quiet air, the noise his coat made against the stone echoed around him. In his mind he heard his father's voice: 'You're a Sicilian. If you can't hold your alcohol, don't drink.' He stared upwards to the cold, vacant stars and down the now hushed expanse of the High Street. It was empty: the people, the noise, the lights, all gone. A slow mist was creeping round the bottom of the street-lights and the statues, and a light drizzle was falling.

'What?' The whisper was swallowed by the mist.

The High Street seemed to be waiting, and Chaplin's eyes searched around him for movement. At first there was none, but then he thought he saw something through the mist, back down the way he had come. He wiped the spittle off his chin with the sleeve of his trench coat, stood up and began to stagger in that direction. A flare of lazy orange light reflected off metal, and Chaplin became dimly aware that he was holding his gun.

'Duncan! Get down!'

A gunshot rang out across the silent street, ricocheting twice off the cobblestones. Talisker dropped to the ground and lay flat, confused by the sudden turn of events. The rain soaked through his thin cotton shirt-front, almost freezing him where he lay. 'Malky! What the—?'

'Never mind that! Move yourself, laddie!'

Talisker began to crawl towards the news-stand, a large wooden table propped against the outside wall of a pizza parlour. Just before he reached the safety it promised, another shot was fired, this time from closer proximity. Instinctively Talisker looked up in time to see his left hand shatter into a mess of blood and bone. He screamed.

'Keep goin', Duncan!' Malky yelled. 'Dinny stop or he'll kill ye!'

Talisker reached the news-stand and tucked himself in behind it. He was breathing in the warm smell of his own blood, and he was sure he was badly injured. He tucked the splintered hand inside his coat, afraid to look at it, knowing he'd pass out if he did. 'Malky,' his voice was quiet, strained. 'Malky.'

'Ah'm here, Duncan.'

'He's hit an artery in my wrist. Do you understand?'

'Em . . . naw. Whit's an artery?'

Talisker didn't have the strength to reply.

'Talisker!' Chaplin's shout came from across the road. It contained a note of bewilderment. 'Where's all the people gone, Talisker?' The tone was petulant now. 'What have you done with the people? Have you killed them?' Cracked laughter followed.

'Fuck off, Chaplin.' With painful effort Talisker pushed himself to sit almost upright. 'I can see people, Chaplin,' he yelled. 'What's wrong with you? You losing it?'

'What?' Malky said. 'Ah canny see . . .'

Talisker winked at his friend. It expended less energy than talking.

'Oh. Aye.' Malky frowned. 'That's no' very nice, Duncan.'

There was silence from the other side of the street. The inside of Talisker's thigh was damp and he realised that he was sitting in a pool of blood. Gritting his teeth, he pulled his hand out from under his coat. His arm felt lifeless and with his right hand he pulled it towards his shoulder. Then he unfastened the right side of his braces and used it as a tourniquet, twisted round his forearm. The flow of blood slowed, and Talisker felt inordinately proud of himself.

'Talisker? You still there? Have I not killed you yet, you bastard?' Chaplin's voice again, but this time it seemed closer, somewhere to the right.

'I'm still here, Alessandro.' The mist was thick now and the sounds were muffled.

'You can't call me that, Talisker. I don't even like you.' The sound came from further to the right this time, and Chaplin was definitely losing it.

'Duncan. Kin ye move?' Malky was getting anxious. He drew his sword and crouched in his habitual position, his free hand reaching out into the mist.

'Get a life, Chaplin,' Talisker croaked.

'I think I'll just take yours.'

Chaplin staggered around the corner of the building, and Talisker cursed: Chaplin had kept him talking on purpose.

The hand that held the gun wavered before Talisker's face. Now that he was there, in front of his intended victim, Chaplin seemed to have lost his determination.

Talisker gazed at him implacably. 'Go on then,' he mumbled, 'do it.'

Chaplin's hand tightened on the trigger then a movement to his right caught his attention. He turned. 'You.' He waved the gun at Malky. 'This has nothing to do with you. Back off.'

There was a heartbeat of stunned silence.

'You can see him?' Talisker asked.

'What kind of question is . . .' Chaplin was staring at Malky as he realised that he could still make out the *Evening News* headlines on the billboard behind the Highlander. He spun back towards Talisker, a question forming on his lips, just as Talisker lurched forward and grabbed at Chaplin's legs with his right hand, pulling him down.

The fight didn't last long. More by luck than anything else, Talisker ended up sitting astride Chaplin's chest using his knees to pin the policeman's arms to his sides. He gathered up a fistful of Chaplin's trench coat and shook him almost rhythmically as he talked. 'Why, Chaplin? Why don't you just leave me alone?'

There was a slight pause, then Chaplin's reply came as a strangled sob. He was blacking out. Just before unconsciousness claimed him, he muttered, 'I know . . . about Mirranon.'

Talisker stared. 'Did you hear that, Malky? Tell me I didn't imagine it.'

'Aye. I heard.'

'How can he know about my dreams?' Talisker's voice had sunk to an appalled whisper.

'Em, he's no' deid, is he? Ye're sure you didnae crack his heid oan the pavement?'

'No.'

Talisker climbed off Chaplin's prostrate form. He fought back the impulse to kick the man hard in the kidneys. 'You know, when he sent me down, I quite respected him. He was the only one who really listened to me. I thought, Okay, the guy's just doing his job . . . but now . . .'

'Let's go, Duncan.' Malky seemed impatient.

'You do know where we're going, don't you, Malky? That's what this is all about?' Talisker waved around the deserted street.

'Aye. I know.'

Progress was slow. Talisker had lost a lot of blood and was light-headed. The first time they stopped he looked back towards Chaplin and cursed. 'His gun. I didn't pick it up. Did you see it, Malky?'

'Naw, he must've lost it during your wee fight. Mebbe it went under the newspaper-stand and he'll no' be able tae find it.'

'"Wee fight".' Talisker laughed unsteadily. 'Not much impresses you, does it?'

'I was at Bannockburn, laddie,' Malky said simply. 'Come on, it's no' much further.'

'Where are we going?'

'There.' Malky pointed.

'That's the City Chambers.'

'Aye.'

When they arrived, the main doors to the offices of the Lord Provost were closed, but a small brown door stood open. Although a flight of steps and painted railings led down to it, it was a door that was normally passed by, unremarked. Except for now: the white mist had originated here. It clung thickly around the railings and the entrance itself was filled with thick ivory vapour. Malky started down the stairs. 'C'mon, Duncan.'

Talisker leaned heavily against the railings, his vision clouding over. Malky's voice seemed to come from a long way off.

'Duncan. Please . . . c'mon. There's someone here who can help you.'

Talisker aimed his feet towards the white cloud. Malky's voice was the last thing he heard before the night gave way to darkness.

The darkness was moving. Indistinct shapes, softening to dark grey outlines, drifted slowly across the blank landscape of unconsciousness. Red flashes streaked across the void, and as clarity returned Talisker flexed his left hand.

'Duncan?'

Before he opened his eyes he moved his hand up to his face to force himself to look at the injury. There was no pain.

'He awakes . . .'

Talisker didn't recognise the voice. He opened his eyes.

His hand was healed. Only the streaks of dried blood

that still covered his forearm testified to the wound's existence. He spread his fingers.

Then he glanced about him. 'Jesus Christ!' he yelped, and sat up on the cold surface on which he had been placed.

'It's all right, Duncan.' Malky's voice came from behind him. 'She's a friend. She's called Deme, and she healed you.'

Before him stood Deme Rintoul. She surveyed him with disbelief and awe. In the semi-darkness of the chamber her skin glistened like burnished gold; the firelight danced across her delicate features, bleaching out their sharp, almost reptilian lines, so that she appeared almost human. There was an air of nobility in her bearing, which was calming. She pushed back the cowl of her robe and a long, heavy coil of shimmering golden hair dropped over her shoulder. She smiled disarmingly.

'Duncan Talisker.' Her voice was sweet and melodious. 'My name is Deme Rintoul, although my friends sometimes call me Blueseeker. I have waited many years for this moment.' She inclined her head in a gracious bow.

Talisker was stunned. When he spoke he fought for control of his voice. 'Th-thanks for healing my hand. Em, can I go now?'

She looked surprised and dismayed as he began to push himself off the shelf on which he lay.

'No! No, please stay. Are you not curious to hear why someone would wait for you for two hundred years?'

He laughed bitterly. 'I know some who can't wait fifteen.'

She frowned, not understanding, and Talisker, who had been thinking of Shula, felt ashamed and disloyal for having voiced his disappointment. 'I'm sorry,' he said. 'I'm confused.' There was a short silence, and suddenly Talisker peered closely at Deme's face. 'Do you know Mirranon?' he asked.

Her eyes widened. 'Mirranon? The Great Eagle? What do you know of her?'

Talisker felt the same reluctance to speak of his dream as he had when Malky had asked him, yet he sensed the excitement the name inspired in Deme. Perhaps she could make sense of it. Haltingly he told her of the night on the mountain, the snow, the great creature into which a delicate being like herself had been transformed. As he spoke, the sensation of falling came back to him, and the exhilaration of the flight. The sound of the huge white wings beating the air seemed to fill the chamber.

Deme had sat back on her ancient chair as he spoke, and seemed moved by his tale. Malky was squatting on the floor beside her, which seemed to Talisker a small statement of his allegiance to her. The torches lighting the chamber flared briefly as though a sudden gust of air had reached them.

'Mirranon was my ancestor, even as Malcolm is yours,' Deme said. 'She was . . . is a sorceress of unsurpassed power. It gives me hope to know that she is still able to visit our land.'

'Why did she want to make contact with me?'

'Because of who you are.'

'And who am I?'

Deme laughed. 'How can I tell you what makes

your soul unique of all souls? Only you can know this.'

Talisker stared at the frayed hem of his bloodied jeans. 'Have you been watching me?' he asked, in a quiet, controlled voice.

'Most of your life, Duncan. All of it has brought you to this moment. But there is much that I cannot understand – why you chose to live only among men for so long, why you never walked in the sun or sought the company of kinder companions.'

Malky laughed derisively. 'He didnae choose tae go, he was in the gaol, Deme, a prisoner.'

'What did you do to deserve it?'

Talisker looked up into her eyes but saw no sign of condemnation. 'You tell me,' he said. 'Don't you know?'

This was too much for Malky. He gave a loud exasperated tut. 'Duncan, how come you really dinny know?'

'Know what?' Deme seemed impatient. 'What could you have done to merit such deprivation?'

Talisker was about to speak but Malky interrupted, with a kind of salacious glee: 'They said oor Duncan here killed six women.'

'What?' Deme was clearly shocked.

'Naw, but wait,' Malky chided, 'he says he disnae remember. He disnae actually ken if he's innocent or no' – that's the bit I dinny follow. I mean, you'd surely ken something like that.'

Talisker was annoyed at Malky's apparent enjoyment of the situation. 'Shut up. Something happened to me in prison. I was beaten up, badly. I almost died. There were five or six of them and they were out to kill me,' his voice grew thicker, 'but not without humiliating me first.'

Malky hung his head.

'I suffered head injuries – was in the hospital wing for six months. Afterwards I couldn't remember much of anything. Some things come back to me, you know, like dreams,' Talisker was visibly shaken, 'but some of the memories . . . I can only hope they're not really mine.'

'Yes.' Deme stood up. ' I remember almost losing you. About ten years ago I searched for your mind, your essence, and it was so weak. I imagine you want to know what I have seen of your life but I fear I can be little help. Over the years my vigil became routine, especially when nothing happened for so long. I looked for you every few weeks but nothing I saw suggested that you had killed.' She walked forward and crouched beside where he sat on the stone slab. She touched his face and held his gaze with her yellow eyes. ' I'm sorry, Duncan,' she murmured. 'Believe me, I know what it is to have death on your conscience. However,' she stood up again and began to pace the chamber, her robes swirling about her frame as she went, 'I must be practical. How can I send you to the Fine if you are a killer? You may worsen everything.' She lapsed into silence. Then she went on, 'But things cannot get much worse. The time is near and we need . . .'

'Send me where?" Talisker's voice cut across her thoughts. He looked at Malky but the Highlander shrugged noncommittally.

Deme gazed at him appraisingly. 'There is no simple way to explain this. I would have you leave this world, Duncan. It should be no loss to you – it seems it has brought you nothing but condemnation and pain. In my world your name is – will be – legend.' She inclined her head towards the black expanse of the wall behind Talisker. 'The gateway is there. All I ask is your consent.'

Talisker turned to look at the blank stone, 'Yeah, right,' he muttered. He stood up. 'Look, thanks for mending my hand, Deme, and now I've got to go. If I stay here much longer I'll go insane.' He began to walk out of the chamber, to find his exit blocked by Malky.

'Get out of my way, Malky.' Talisker's tone was level.

'Duncan,' Malky smiled – endearingly, he imagined. 'Pal . . . Look, Ah ken ye're having jist a bit o' trouble coming tae terms wi' all this, an' that's perfectly understandable, but jist hear Deme oot, will ye no? Her an' her people – Mirranon's people – they're in no end o' trouble.' He tried to slap Talisker on the back but, as usual, his hand passed straight through, giving Talisker a passing sensation of cold.

'Go away, Malky. Leave me alone. It's got nothing to do with me.'

'You just don't want tae believe everything,' Malky snarled, trying to block his path even though Talisker could walk straight through him. 'But ye believe in me, don't ye, and I'm a ghost!'

'Please, Duncan. Please listen,' Deme called. 'I can show you if it will help you to understand.'

'I don't want to understand.'

Suddenly Deme's voice filled the tiny chamber and echoed out along the darkness of subterranean passageways that had once been streets. 'Then you leave me no choice.'

Talisker turned back to face her. 'And what's that supposed to mea—'. The chamber flared into white light so dazzling he put his hands to his eyes. When he took them away and cautiously opened his eyes the chamber was dark again, but he realised he could not move his legs. He looked down and saw tendrils of light wrapped around him like an unearthly vine. As he watched in horror, they grew and entwined further round him until his arms were pinned to his sides and the last tentacle anchored itself threateningly around his neck.

'Deme!' he yelled, and struggled violently against the bonds, which only drew them tighter. A movement across the room caught his eye. 'Deme? Let me out of these and I swear I'll listen.' He heard the edge of panic in his voice.

He stopped struggling and slowed his breathing, listening to its rhythm to stop the panic engulfing him. When he called again, his voice was steadier.

*'Malky? You've not deserted me, have you?'*

'Dinny be daft.' There was a flare of light as Malky appeared at the far side of the chamber. The Highlander seemed to be walking through the air – not unreasonable for a ghost, Talisker decided – and beside him stalked a silver-grey cat. It was larger than a domestic cat, with fine delicate bone structure and large yellow eyes. Malky looked down and grinned. 'Aye, I think he's catching oan. It's her, Duncan. Deme. She's a lynx.'

*'Duncan Talisker . . .'* Deme's imperious voice seemed to bypass his ears and arrive directly in his beleaguered brain. '*. . . I'm sorry it has come to this. I did not foresee your reluctance. But, much as I understand*

*it, I cannot allow it to jeopardise the lives of the Fine. It has been foretold that you will bring redemption to the clans in their darkest hour.'*

'Go oan, Duncan. It'll be great. You'll be a hero,' Malky said encouragingly.

'No! Goddamn it!' Talisker struggled against his bonds again, even though he knew it was futile. 'You don't understand, Deme. For fifteen years I've been told how to live my life day by day, hour by hour. There's no self-determination in a prison cell. I've only been out for a couple of weeks and you're trying to do it again! And do you know what they do to you when you step out of line? This! They truss you up like a frickin' Christmas turkey!' he screamed.

Malky looked down at Deme. 'Mebbe this wiznae such a bright idea, hen,' he said quietly. 'It disnae seem tae have endeared him tae yer cause.'

The lynx sat motionless, watching the thrashing prisoner. Only her twitching tail betrayed her discomfort. *'Look at him,'* she thought to Malky, he loses control so easily. She shuddered. *'How can I send him to Sutra if he is so weak and volatile? It will avail us nothing and perhaps break his sanity.'*

*'Naw, wait a minute, Deme. That's no' my experience of him. He's done well to keep a hold o' himsel' the way he has ower the last while. I say he's no a killer like they say he is. I think you've just . . . hit a nerve by tying him up like that.'*

*'I hope you are right, Malcolm McLeod.'* She surveyed him gravely for a moment then made a decision. Turning her attention back to Talisker, she spoke to both men. *'Duncan? Please listen. If you stop struggling*

*the bonds will loosen. I am truly sorry. I will give you what you crave, some measure of self-determination, a choice. I am going to send you through the gateway—'*

'What?' Talisker hissed.

'That's no' much o' a choice if you ask me,' Malky said.

'But wait. I will send Malcolm with you and give him the means to bring you home if you judge it necessary.'

She turned to Malky and directed her thoughts to him: *'Malcolm, you are either an astute judge of character or a fool. I pray for all our sakes it is the first of these. Look in your pouch.'*

Malky did so. As he opened it radiant light spilled out; in its brown folds nestled a gem that seemed to possess an inner fire. He whistled softly. Then he looked at Deme, whose expression betrayed alarm. 'What's wrong?' he asked.

The lynx glanced around the chamber, her whiskers twitching. *'We have little time, Malcolm. This gem is smaller and less powerful than the one Talisker is carrying . . .'*

'How d'you know about that?' Malky demanded.

*'Never mind. He must return that stone to Mirranon. This one,'* she peered more closely at it, as though she couldn't believe what she was seeing, '*will glow like that when Talisker is in danger of losing his life in Sutra or here.'*

'Here? How kin he be here an' there at the same time? That's no possible, surely?'

*'It is, Malcolm. Talisker's soul will be split between worlds. It is part of his . . .'* she glanced to where Talisker slumped in his bonds *'. . . unique charm.'*

Her sarcasm was lost on Malky. The Highlander frowned, struggling with the idea. ‘So time is still goin’ on here? I mean, stuff’ll be happening to him here an’ all?’

*‘Yes, but the timelines are different.’* Deme was distracted. *‘If he is in danger, either here or there, the gem will glow,’* she twitched her tail, *‘like that. You can return him here by thinking of it, Malcolm, while you hold the gem. Do you understand?’*

‘I’m no stupid, hen, jist cause I dinny talk posh,’ Malky snapped. ‘It disnae seem like much o’ a bargain tae me if he kin only come back when he’s in danger – that’s no’ whit I unnerstand as self-determination.’

Deme sighed. *‘I’m sorry, Malcolm. I am only a friend and servant of Mirranon. It’s all I am able to offer. In fact . . .’* She looked shamefaced.

‘What?’

*‘I’m afraid the power of the gem is limited. You can use it only a few times before it dies – but,’ she rallied, ‘Mirranon will assist you further.’*

‘How many times?’

*‘Three. Possibly four.’*

‘What the hell’s going on here?’ a voice slurred across the chamber.

Chaplin staggered across to where Talisker was restrained. ‘What the f—?’ He peered myopically at the bonds and reached out a shaking hand to touch one of the golden fronds.

*No!* Deme’s voice flashed through Talisker and Malky’s minds. *‘Don’t let him—’*

Too late. There was a flash of bright light and Chaplin, who let out a scream of pain, was thrown backwards across the room.

Malky and Deme rushed across to his prostrate figure.

*'He's all right,'* Deme smelt the alcohol on Chaplin's breath, '*just unconscious. Quickly, we have a little time before he wakes. I must open the gateway now. Look away. I must be in my female form to achieve the spell and the light of transformation is bright.*' Without further instruction Deme began to change from lynx to woman, just as Mirranon had in Talisker's dream, bathed in silver-grey light that pulsed softly before it became brighter, more intense. Talisker and Malky had no choice but to look away as the transformation was completed and Deme stood before them once more. Talisker was struck by how catlike her movements were, even in this female form, and how small and delicate she was.

Already Chaplin was moving.

'Ah bet his wee shock's sobered him up an' all,' Malky remarked.

'Deme. I didn't agree to this . . .' Talisker began.

'I'm sorry. There is no choice. Mirranon will explain. Now, stand back from the wall, Malcolm.'

Malky did as he was told, his eyes fixed on the darkness at the far end of the chamber. Deme walked forward and stopped in the centre of the room. Slowly she began to chant, her words unintelligible to the two listeners, their sound guttural and dark. Lifting her hands palm upwards she brought them together before her chest. A white light appeared between her fingers, which suffused her features with uncompromising starkness.

For a moment Talisker thought he saw a shape: a globe-like object between her fingers, which was wrapped around by a tiny, circular rainbow. A promise, he thought, as he always did on seeing a rainbow. He glanced down at the shadowy outline of Chaplin on the floor and up in time to see Deme fling the globe against the wall. Colour flew from the centre of the impact and a sound shattered the reality of the chamber. It was like many sounds, all sounds, compressed into one joyous note that found release within the dark recesses of Mary King's Close. And when the shock-wave subsided an image remained on the wall.

Within the picture was a loch, its pure clear waters lapping gently against a shoreline verdant with green and russet trees. The water reflected the brilliant blue of the sky with such clarity that when a swift entered the image, skimming the loch's surface, it was as if two birds flew, their paths meeting and diverging like a rapturous song.

Each person in the room was silent as they gazed upon the place Deme had conjured. Deme's joy was bittersweet. She could not pass through the gateway yet – she must wait for Mirranon's summons, as her friend had asked – yet there were the sky and the water, tantalisingly close, just as she remembered. 'This place,' she said softly, 'is called Light of the Sky.' She pulled herself together, remembering her duty. 'You must pass through water to reach Sutra. It is written.'

'Sutra?' Malky seemed puzzled. 'I know that name.'

'It is an ancient name and it was once used in your world.' Deme nodded. 'Are you ready for your journey? It will be short but difficult.'

'Kin ye swim, Duncan?' Malky grinned nervously.

'Not with these damned things on,' Talisker grated. 'Deme. You said I had a choice . . .'

'And I wish I had time to talk more to you so that you would go willingly, but I do not.' Deme stood before him, bowed her head and touched her forehead in a gesture of sorrow. 'Please trust me, Duncan. I will loose your bonds as soon as you are in the water. I hope that Sutra will bring you joy and give you reason to forgive my harsh treatment of you in time.'

Talisker smiled grimly. There could be no turning back, he realised. Deme had said, 'All your life has brought you to this moment,' so perhaps everything would be washed away, all the pain and guilt, when he plunged into the water. He was afraid of what was to come, but the fear was edged with the bright tinge of exhilaration. 'I hope so too, Deme,' he said.

Deme stepped aside into the shadows; Malky walked forward and Talisker felt himself propelled by the bonds, which now gripped him tightly: Deme didn't trust him not to make a break for it. And she was right: as he neared the image it dawned on him that he was to be pushed, fully bound, into a lake.

'Take them off me, Goddamn it!'

Then he and Malky felt a pull as a cold, clean force engulfed them. Its effects were more than physical: Talisker's fevered mind was calm and his struggles ceased as clarity washed over him and forgiveness touched his heart and mind. Before them towered a great wall of water and their entry into Light of the Sky was seconds away . . .

'Talisker!'

The voice seemed far away in time and distance but

its tone was unmistakable. Talisker turned to see Chaplin push Deme roughly aside. The image was hazy now, but he could see that the policeman was still disoriented and still had his gun. Realising at that instant that his bonds were gone and the water was about to engulf him, Talisker stretched out his hand to Deme as if to warn her, but it moved slowly through the water. Then the chill enveloped him.

Chaplin didn't understand the scene in the chamber. His head still hurt from the fight and his hands burned as though they had been scorched, but he couldn't remember why. He knew this couldn't be right: how could a lake be under the High Street? He stumbled towards the image of Light of the Sky, pushing aside a woman who seemed to be aiding Talisker's strange escape. Then, as he felt the pull of the place, he tried to retreat, but it was useless, like swimming in sand. Behind him someone cried out and he raised his gun, almost expecting to see Talisker. Beyond the mist a tall golden being was calling him, her hands outstretched to reach for him. 'Take my hand.' The voice was like the echo of a song. The being took a step towards him and he fired. She fell as the waters took him.

This was what drowning was like. The coldness, burning, as his lungs fought to contain the last precious breaths of air and his limbs thrashed violently. His last thoughts were disjointed.

. . . dying . . .

. . . Diane . . .

The last thing he saw was a tiny silver fish, which

darted across his vision seemingly unperturbed by his movements. His legs jerked spasmodically once more and then he was still.

# CHAPTER SIX

Talisker opened his eyes with a groan to be greeted by a dazzling blue sky.

*Deme.*

The name sprang to his mind but he let it go, drinking in the warmth of the sun, the sounds of water and birdcalls. He fought the tiredness that still clung as he tried to marshal his thoughts.

*Deme.*

He sat up abruptly. The movement provoked a spasm of coughing as the water he had inhaled left his nose and throat. Before him lay the loch, Light of the Sky, its crystal waters glimmering in the early-evening sunshine. He was lying in a clearing on the western bank. Around him, their shadows lengthening, were six huge standing stones. They seemed to possess a quiet awareness, a grey calm. Talisker shuddered, both from the chill of his drying clothes and the growing sense that he was being watched. As he scanned the shore of the loch, he saw the hare.

It sat quite still in the patch of darkness where the shadows of the stones merged, and only the twitching of its whiskers betrayed its presence. Bright sunlight silvered the ends. Talisker stood up shakily, expecting the creature to bolt at his sudden movement, but it remained perfectly still, watching him – almost critically, Talisker imagined. He remembered the hare that had brought the emerald to his attention. 'You again, huh?'

Talisker looked back to the shoreline. Malky's body had washed up on the shingle.

'Christ,' he muttered. When he turned back to the hare, it had gone.

Malky had changed. He was solid flesh and blood. It also appeared that he was dead. His flesh was white and freezing cold, his lips blue. The veins of his eyelids and temples showed starkly in the rays of the dying sun. Strangely, the gashes that had caused his original death in Edinburgh were gone, no traces left of the sword wounds. He must have drowned during the journey through the loch. Then he opened his eyes and grinned up at Talisker, his gums horribly white. 'Didn't know ye cared. Whit's the lang face fer? Ah telt ye Ah could swim.'

Talisker sat down again on the damp grass, his back against one of the standing stones, unable to speak. Malky stared down at his hands and pinched his lifeless flesh. 'Oh,' he said. 'There's good news and then there's bad news . . .' His voice trailed off and Talisker could see he was fighting to hold back tears. He composed himself enough to say, 'Weel, mebbe this means Ah'm indestructible,' and gave a choked laugh.

They were quiet for a while as they listened to the calming sound of the water.

Finally Malky spoke: 'Was Ah imaginin' things or did your pal Chaplin follow us doon there?'

Talisker shrugged. 'Who cares? I'm sure Deme could deal with him. We're well rid. So, what do you think we do now?'

'Are ye dry yet? Ah'm still wringing'.'

'Let's see,' Talisker mused. 'We're wet, we've no dry clothes, no food, no weapons.'

'I have,' corrected Malky.

'And it's about two hours to sunset, I reckon.'

'Ah'll get some wood for a fire, shall Ah?'

'Good man, Malky.' Talisker rummaged in the pockets of his saturated black woollen coat which he laid on the grass to dry. 'At least we've got this.' He brandished his lighter. 'I hope the wick's still dry. Oh, and there's this.' He picked the paper off a sodden bar of nut chocolate.

At the sight of it Malky beamed. 'I've always wanted tae try that stuff. It wiznae around in my day, leastways, no' fer poor folk.'

'Malky, you're breaking my heart.' Talisker split the bar in two then laid it aside. 'Let's get the fire going first. There's plenty of driftwood.'

It wasn't long before the men were huddled around a comforting blaze. After only two attempts Talisker's petrol lighter had sputtered into life.

'I think we should take our clothes off before it gets dark,' Talisker suggested. 'If we hang them over those branches they'll have at least an hour to dry out before the sun goes.'

'Aye, all right,' Malky agreed. 'As long as we kin eat the chocolate soon.'

In the gathering twilight both men's thoughts turned inward and for a long time neither spoke as they stared into the bright heart of the fire.

'How dae ye feel, Duncan?' Malky asked quietly. 'Ah'm sorry how it turned out. I didnae think Deme wiz that desperate – jist tae send you onyways, I mean.'

Talisker smiled distantly. 'It's all right, Malk. Although don't think I'm not mad with you,' he joked. 'Whatever happens here can only be better.'

'My ma used tae say that a man is only the sum of his battles. That they made him stronger, mair of a man. Aw these things that have happened tae you, dae you no' think they mean something, that they had some purpose?'

'No disrespect to your mother, Malky, but that's rubbish. People tend to say these things to get them through hard times. All prison does to a man—'

Out on the loch something broke the surface of the water. Ripples spread out in golden arcs from an object that floated in a green tangle of dark weed and driftwood.

Malky stood up. 'Duncan, is that no' . . .'

'We could just leave him there,' Talisker suggested. 'He's probably dead anyway,' but both men began to walk back into the chill waters of the loch.

'Just as I was getting warm,' Talisker moaned. 'Why didn't he stay at the bottom and decay?'

'Aye, well, something else my mother used tae say.' Malky grinned. 'Shite floats.'

Their laughter rang across the loch to the far eastern shore disturbing a flock of black birds, which took to the evening skies wheeling and calling, their harsh cries a reminder of the impending darkness.

When the first grey streaks of dawn lightened the sky above the loch, Talisker awoke numb with the cold. He and Malky had gathered huge armfuls of bracken and reeds to make beds. It had seemed doubtful then, even when they laid Chaplin as close to the fire as they dared, that he would survive the night. Reluctantly Talisker had helped Malky to strip the sodden clothes from the policeman's limp body then wrapped him in his own black coat, which had been drying by the fire.

Now, Chaplin had regained some colour and his breathing was even. Talisker sat up. Malky had gone, probably into the forest in search of food. The fire was newly made and the morning air was fresh. He looked for his clothes and found them folded neatly on a large boulder in a patch of weak sunshine. While he put them on he wondered why Malky hadn't woken him to help with these chores; it seemed that his friend had decided to become some kind of squire to him, which made Talisker feel uncomfortable. He decided to speak to Malky about it when he returned. In the meantime he would wake Chaplin and explain things to him. He smiled grimly at the thought of the policeman's reaction.

In the dappled green light of the forest, Malky was cursing his ill-fortune. It wasn't all bad – he had managed to climb a tree before the bear saw him, but it had spotted him now and was sitting patiently at the bottom. It yawned occasionally and swatted the gnats that rose from the loch. Its sleek brown coat glistened in the morning sunshine and a musky aroma rose from its flanks. The noise of its breathing was quiet but steady, somehow in tune with the sounds of the forest. As he gazed down upon it from his uncomfortable perch, Malky noticed that the bear was wearing an earring. He squinted down: yes, a silver ring pierced the thick brown pelt of the right ear and attached to it was a single white feather. The movement caused the branch to shake precariously. Malky pulled himself back quickly before he could fall. He had to get rid of the creature before he could get down.

'Hey, bear,' he said, in a loud stage whisper, 'are ye hungry? Ah'm no' very meaty, ye ken.'

He had caught two rabbits for the day's meals – the still warm body of a large buck was tucked into the pocket folds of his plaid. He sighed and pulled it out by its ears. 'Here, bear,' he said, and shook the rabbit.

The bear looked up, its nose quivering, sampling the smell. Malky threw the animal as hard as he dared over to the other side of the clearing. For a moment it seemed his gambit had failed, as the bear's warm brown eyes remained fixed on him. Malky found himself smiling down at it. 'Ye daft galumphin' critter, ye. Look. Over there. Fetch.'

The bear gave a snort and lumbered on to its paws to cross the clearing.

'So that's how it is, Chaplin. It looks like you're here for good. You're more than welcome to piss off and get killed in the forest, of course.'

The policeman was sitting as near to the fire as he dared, still wrapped in Talisker's black woollen coat. Bits of bracken had caught in his long thick hair and he was still pale. He was staring into the fire and he had not looked at Talisker since he awoke. Talisker squatted down on the other side of the fire. 'Chaplin,' he said gently, 'can you hear me, man?'

Chaplin's gaze remained fixed on the flames. He had picked up a twig from the edge of the fire and his hands were squeezing it hard in an absent motion that seemed independent of his thoughts.

'I noticed the bruises when we helped you last night. Where did you get them?' Talisker probed gently.

No answer.

'Look, Alessandro.' Talisker lifted his own shirt, and thought he saw Chaplin's gaze flicker.

'When I . . . when we were fighting, you said you knew about Mirranon. What did you mean? Did you dream it?'

Now Chaplin looked up sharply, the movement jerky and odd, as though his muscles were in spasm. His lips were moving. 'M-M-Mirranon,' he said.

'Yes?' Talisker said encouragingly, but Chaplin was staring at his hands, which had begun to bleed from the pressure he was exerting on the sharp edges of the stick.

Talisker reached forward gently and took the stick from his grasp. 'C'mon, Alessandro . . .' he said. He wished his old adversary was back to normal so that he could dislike him once more. 'It's funny—'

'Mirranon,' Chaplin said again. 'The White Eagle.'

The bear had almost reached the rabbit carcass when it happened. Malky had begun his descent from the tree when the creature bellowed. The sound echoed away towards the loch and he froze, his leg muscles rigid with terror. Then he realised that the bear was not charging at him. What he saw instead chilled him so deeply that even as he began to climb up the tree once more, he could not turn away his gaze.

Across the clearing a black shape loomed towards the bear; in the clear light of the morning its outline was still indistinct and murky. Within it, insect-like limbs, feelers and antennae were moving, and it was making strange clicking noises. The bear had reared in response to the threat and bellowed again. This time Malky fancied that the cry was tinged with fear, although the great beast stood almost ten feet tall. As he watched, the shadow shape changed, its contours becoming sharper. A few seconds later a dark shadow-bear, composed entirely of seething squirming insects, opposed the forest bear. Around the shadow-bear a cloud of flies and cockroaches swarmed. Its existence defiled the forest. With a great roar the forest bear charged the monster but the shadow-bear offered no resistance. Instead it opened its limbs in an obscene embrace and enveloped its opponent. Its shape dissolved over the doomed forest bear, which was screaming in rage and fear – a sound so human that Malky's bowels twisted.

He leaped down from the tree and cursed loudly as his legs crumpled and he collapsed into a clump of nettles, losing any hope of stealth or cover. Now, the forest bear appeared coated in jet shadow and the insects had gone. Slowly the shadow faded and the brown pelt was visible. The bear lay quite still.

Suddenly it screamed again as its body began to thrash about. Black blades lanced out from inside the bear, and its blood arced across the forest floor. Long spindly feelers burst out, jerking and twisting to plunge back into the creature's unresisting flesh. The bear screamed again. It seemed impossible that it was still alive. The blades continued relentlessly.

Malky could stand it no longer. Drawing his claymore he raced across the green space, willing his shaking legs to carry him but shrieking his war-cry. As he reached the dying animal, he lifted his blade double-handed, willing himself not to look at the horror that still slashed the length of the prostrate form. At the last instant he looked into the eyes of the bear and saw its agony. With a cry of despair he severed its head from its body with a single blow.

Talisker scanned the tree-line for movement. He was worried about Malky. It was about two hours after dawn now and he had become increasingly concerned that he had been wrong in thinking that the Highlander had gone for food. Perhaps something or someone had come in the night and taken him. His gaze flickered towards Chaplin, who had said no more since he had uttered Mirranon's name.

His reverie was broken by a distant roar that seemed to come from the forest. Seconds later it came again, and Talisker swore. He could be of no help to Malky: he had no weapon. At least the Highlander would have his sword. He threw the last stick on the fire, his face grey and set.

Malky stared down at the corpse. The attack from inside it had ceased. There was no evidence of the crawling horror that had consumed it, just a mass of blood and fur. Only the head retained some semblance to the majestic noble creature Malky had seen enter the grove. As he looked at the face, the pelt split. He crouched low, ready to cleave the skull with his sword, if need be, but slowly he straightened and gasped.

As the pelt dissolved, the face of a young man appeared. His skin was golden, like Deme's, but faded rapidly to a pale yellow. The skull was still covered in the shaggy brown fur and a large patch remained on the forehead, but at the sides were wisps of blue-black hair. The lifeless blue eyes were open and at peace, belying the violence of his death. Malky sank to his knees, stifling an oath. Killing the creature had been the only way to end its torment but he would have held back had he known it was a man. 'Ah'm sorry,' he grated. 'Ah didnae ken what tae do.'

The morning sunlight touched the young face and the dark hair blew across the eyes. Malky imagined those eyes smiling and knew he'd done the right thing. He removed the silver earring and hooked it through the buckle of his belt. 'Goodbye, bear. God speed ye.'

He rose and walked from the clearing without looking back.

The water was calm, as mirror-like as when Talisker and Malky had first seen it the evening before. Now, in the midday heat, it shimmered almost unnaturally and only the sound of the wavelets washing on to the shingle gave the impression of coolness. Talisker sat on the large flat stone at the water's edge, his feet dangling in the water. He had ceased trying to communicate with Chaplin some time ago. He felt a growing sense of unease about the place as he gazed across the water at the wheeling black birds and tried to remember if they were rooks or crows. 'If you see a rook alone it's a crow, and many crows together are rooks,' he said quietly, to himself, smiling at the memory it prompted of his grandfather.

'They lock ye up fer talkin' tae yersel', you know.'

'Malky! Jesus, where have you been?' Malky grinned and Talisker flinched at the whiteness of his gums and the blue of his lips, which he had last seen in the less stark light of the evening. He also noticed the blood on his blade. 'What happened?'

'Ah'll tell ye as we walk,' Malky replied. 'Ah think we should get movin'.' He nodded towards Chaplin. 'Is he able fer it?'

'I don't know, he's hardly spoken all morning, just stares into the fire.'

'Well, he'll have tae walk,' Malky stated, with uncharacteristic sternness, 'else we'll leave him behind.'

Talisker raised an eyebrow at this comment from the normally easy-going warrior but said nothing. The Highlander would tell him in his own time.

'Got any o' that chocolate left, Duncan?'

'Sure have.'

'Lunch can wait, then. Let's go.'

The landscape was in the early stages of autumn, the forest changing to gold and russet, the leaves carpeting the damp ground like copper rain. Away from the shores of the loch stillness prevailed. Nothing moved, no birds sang, and in the afternoon sunshine, the walkers felt enervated by the humidity. They headed west through the forest so that they would still have the cover of the trees for their next campsite.

'I think Deme was being optimistic about the

reception committee,' Talisker grumbled.

Malky said nothing. He was pleased they were not heading back towards the scene of the bear's murder. He was still unnerved by what he had seen and he was watching the undergrowth for signs of movement. As they walked he told Talisker and Chaplin of what had happened. Chaplin did not react. He had been silent all day and walked as though in a trance. Talisker had seemed less surprised by his story than Malky had expected, but he paused to look at the earring.

'Ah've seen deaths in my time, Duncan, but this . . .' Malky shuddered '. . . and he was just a young laddie. Still, Ah did the right thing.'

He looked at Talisker for approval – anything to make him feel better about the boy's death – but Talisker shrugged.

'I suppose so,' he said.

'What would you have done, then?' Malky snapped.

'Nothing,' Talisker replied coldly.

Malky fumed silently for a while. 'Whit are ye sayin', Duncan? Think you're a hard man, do ye?'

Talisker turned. The expression on his face was apologetic. 'No, Malky. I think I'm a coward.'

Nightfall found them around ten miles from the shores of the loch. They hadn't got far because of their late start, and the pace was slow because of Chaplin. It was colder than the previous night, and although there was no real wind because of the trees, the breeze was iced with the promise of heavy frost. Again they collected bracken but they knew that the sparse covering would provide little comfort. As they were about to climb into their nests for the night Malky made a suggestion.

'Look, Duncan, Ah've no' got a heavy coat like you an' Chaplin tae put ower the top tae hold the heat in. Mebbe we should take it in turns an' one man should stay awake and keep the fire goin' a' night. Then at least when we do sleep it'll be warm.'

Talisker nodded, 'Aye, that's a fair suggestion. We know there's bears at least in the forest.'

'And other things,' Malky muttered darkly.

Both men's gaze turned on Chaplin. They were still unsure of how much he was taking in. To their surprise he looked up briefly. 'I'll watch,' he said.

Talisker had the final watch before dawn. He saw the first pale pink streaks colour the sky and felt a quiet satisfaction alien to him, although he was freezing, scared stiff, and Deme's words echoed through his mind in a continuous loop: *'People are waiting for you there, people who need you . . .'* Why? He imagined they were waiting for a warrior. His gaze travelled to Malky, a real hero, who had fought and died in battle. He and his companions had gone in a blaze of glory, however small and unremarked. Malky cared about things with a passion that had died in Talisker fifteen years ago. He looked back up to the lightening sky, where a lone star remained, a bright star. He told himself that he would look for this star each morning when he awoke in Sutra.

He was considering waking the others when he thought he saw a movement in the trees. He tensed, staring into the gloom of the undergrowth, his eyes working hard to focus in the half-light of the dawn. He fixed on a particular tree, an oak, from which it seemed the motion had come. The trunk was gnarled with age, its outline knotted and mottled with lichen. And yet there was something about it . . . He took a couple of steps across the clearing.

The tree had become a person. No, a figure had formed from the tree trunk. In the gloom it was difficult to discern what had happened, but it appeared that part of the trunk had pulled away from the main body and formed a figure. And that figure was an old man.

He was tall, unbowed and carried a long thin stave – Talisker guessed it to be oak. As he watched, the rugged boles and knots of the tree trunk softened and disappeared in a soft grey haze that became the drape of a ragged ankle-length cloak, whose wearer seemed to be speaking to the tree. The man reached out and tapped it lightly with his stick. Then he turned to walk into the forest. In the dawn light his straggly grey locks and short-cropped beard were silver, his dark, hooded brown eyes sparked with intelligence and pain, and his movements were slow and measured. Without a glance in Talisker's direction he was gone. It was the final impression of yellow – so out of context with the elemental nature of the figure – that tugged at Talisker's memory. 'Zak?'

His whisper was swallowed in the sudden chorus of birdsong that heralded the new dawn.

On waking, Malky ventured into the forest but with more caution than on the previous day. Within an hour he had collected three huge parasol mushrooms, five pigeon eggs and a mixture of rocket and dandelions.

Breakfast would be light but nutritious – he wished he had some oats to bulk it out. Talisker had been quiet and withdrawn when they'd woken, either deep in thought or just tired, and Chaplin was the same. Perhaps today would bring him back to himself once more. It had been a relief when Chaplin had woken during the night for his watch: Malky had seen delayed shock kill warriors – they had gone to their bed after a battle to be found the next morning as stiff and white as the corpses on the battlefield. Suddenly he stopped at the edge of the clearing where the campsite was. Voices.

Creeping forward he peered through the lower branches of an oak. At the edge of the clearing a white mule was cropping the damp grass, and around the fire sat Talisker, Chaplin and an old man in a grey cloak whose back was towards him. He seemed to feel the Highlander's scrutiny because he turned and met his gaze as though the cover of the trees was non-existent. He smiled a wide white smile. 'Ah, Malcolm. Breakfast at last. I have some oats, if you're interested.'

# CHAPTER SEVEN

It was always cold here. Today, though, the sun would reach the peaks of the mountains for a few short hours. Corvus stared through dark, heavy-lidded eyes towards the lintel of the window and sighed. Blue sky as ever. It was all he could see through the high archway from his position in the room. Sometimes the scene was varied by stormclouds and, more often, snow, but the elements had long ceased to hold any charm for their captive audience. The only other place Corvus could escape to was the blackness of the void, and he went there as infrequently as possible. Here, in his tower, he had been watching the skies now for longer than he cared to count and he had cursed the blue and the stars with the blackest oaths he knew. He ached for red.

As if in response to his thoughts, a raven alighted on the sill, its movements clumsy, scraping and grasping for the stones, its wings batting the frame with a frantic violent motion. In its powerful maw, it held a tiny scarlet flower so bright that its colour spilled across the sheen of the bird's glossy chest. It hopped from the sill to the seat beneath with a slow, deliberate air. It was a large bird, even for one of its kind and it filled the wrought-iron framework majestically, as though aware that it had once been a throne. Leaning forward, it dropped the scarlet flower on to the latticework of the arm and cawed loudly; an ugly, harsh sound, not entirely bereft of humour.

Corvus threw back his head and laughed in response, but his laughter was less than humorous. It echoed around the cold empty space, its bitter edge sharpened further by the blue ice of the walls. 'She's coming, Sluagh, she's coming!'

The door to the chamber crashed open dramatically.

She stood tall, dressed in black and silver. Her body was encased in silver mail, beautifully fashioned, and a black undergarment that covered her slender neck accentuated her white, almost stark features. As usual, her wide blue eyes, made colder by the light of the chamber, regarded him with a mixture of sibling admiration and scorn.

'Greetings, brother.' She strode into the room drawing her sword in a bright blur of soundless motion and struck out swiftly at the throne where until the last moment Sluagh had been perched, pecking at the scarlet bloom he had brought for his master. She missed. For all his apparent clumsiness the raven was not stupid and had anticipated her action from bitter experience. In the blink of an eye he had transferred his perch to the sill of the high window, out of reach of Phyrr's sword. He gazed down implacably, then opened his beak as though to caw his disapproval, his pointed pink tongue arching forward, but at a withering glance from Phyrr, he snapped it shut.

'Stupid bird,' she fumed. 'I don't know why you use him, brother. He came from a cuckoo's egg.' She spoke with exaggerated disdain, as though she knew this was a particular insult to ravens, and Sluagh obliged by ruffling his feathers. Corvus laughed again, enjoying his sister's passion. His gaze became darker, a look akin to greed passing over his features; her white skin was so fragile-looking, and when she spoke the sinew and muscles that moved there made her face a moving tapestry, beautiful but deadly, as cold as this place. There was never any softness: her long dark hair was scraped back severely from her face and even her smile gave no quarter. In his weaker moments Corvus would long for her to stay so that for a whole day he could watch her, talking, cursing and laughing. But for Phyrr, a hedonistic creature who lived from moment to turbulent moment, a day was far too great a gift for her brother. She was selfish, just as he was. Sometimes it was like gazing into a glass to find his own emptiness staring back at him.

'Bitch,' he said.

'You do know he's here, don't you?' she demanded. She had not sheathed her sword and waved it in his direction.

Corvus's eyes narrowed dangerously. 'Who?'

She laughed scornfully, until she was cut short by Sluagh, whose expression radiated contempt – *If you laugh at my master once more, I'll have your eyes.* 'I'm surprised you don't know,' she said, less sharply than she had intended.

'I've been . . . asleep,' Corvus said, his tone quietly defensive.

'*No.*' She walked over to the wooden throne on which he sat and touched his hand lightly. The contact unnerved them both and she withdrew her hand as though she had scalded it.

'Touch me again,' he said. His tone was neither pleading nor demanding and his gaze was unreadable. She smiled lightly, although her mouth was dry and her heart pounding in her breast. She replaced her hand although her fingers trembled. 'Don't sleep, brother. Please. Promise me.'

'I am weary, Phyrr. Don't people sleep when they are weary?' His face seemed older, the skin sallow and the blue eyes empty of emotion.

She said nothing for a few moments. Then she smiled encouragingly at her brother. 'Talisker has come,' she said simply. 'You can kill him now.'

Corvus's features flared into life. 'Where is he? Has he been found yet?'

'In the forest east of Light of the Sky. He has two companions, who arrived with him. I will get more information from my birds.'

'Sluagh will go.'

Without another word of command the raven soared into the sky, his black outline filling the window frame.

'So it begins,' Corvus said quietly.

At least the journey through the forest had a purpose now: the four travellers were heading towards a city called Ruannoch Were, the largest in this part of Sutra. They had four days, Zak had informed them, to make the remainder of the journey if they were to be there by Samhain for the Gathering, apparently the biggest and best Gathering of all. He refused to be drawn about what happened there, muttering vaguely to himself, occasionally stopping to admire a tree or bird. He seemed to enjoy walking and set a blistering pace, which the three younger men – and his mule – which he told them he didn't often ride – were hard pressed to match.

When he had first appeared in their midst, Talisker had questioned him relentlessly over breakfast. Was he Zak? Had he and Talisker met before? The old man smiled and shook his head. 'You may call me Zak if you like it. My real name is Morias, but men seem to title me often, fanciful names like Grey Oak or Oakshadow.' He chewed his oats and mushrooms with a deliberate air. 'Never been called Zak before, though. What does it mean?'

'I'm not sure,' Talisker admitted, somewhat thrown. 'Does it matter?'

'It's short for Zachariah,' Chaplin said suddenly. 'It was the name of a prophet.'

At this Morias hooted with laughter.

'What are ye then, Morias?' Malky enquired. 'Where are yer people?'

'I don't have any people, just myself.' Morias smiled, 'I'm a *Seanachaidh*. A storyteller.' There was something about his tone which, though polite and unchallenging, did not invite further query. He mentioned the Gathering and assumed they were going there. Talisker exchanged a glance with Malky and nodded; it seemed as good a plan as any. Perhaps Mirranon would be there. Morias agreed to travel with them for their company.

As they cleared up their campsite, Talisker watched the old man covertly. He seemed benign but his finding them could have been no accident. Now, as Malky and Talisker stamped out the embers of the fire, he was deep in conversation with Chaplin, which was surprising, given Chaplin's withdrawal over the last two days. As Talisker watched, Morias pressed something into Chaplin's hand. As far as he could see it was a small rock or pebble, and Morias seemed to be explaining earnestly about it while Chaplin listened and smiled – his old white wolf's grin. It was the first time he had smiled for many days.

The following morning they chanced upon the main road to Ruannoch Were. It was little more than a dirt track, worn smooth by generations of feet and hoofs as people drove their sheep and cattle to market, and wound like a red ribbon through the forest. They began to see people too. Sutra's inhabitants were Celts – at least, Talisker imagined them to be Celts for red hair and green eyes predominated in most of the family groups they passed. The men wore rough-spun checked trousers and surprisingly colourful cloaks fastened with ornate brooches of silver and bronze. Many had plaited the length of their beards and moustaches. Which appealed to Malky, who rubbed the stubble of his blue-white chin thoughtfully. Almost all of the men carried swords similar to Malky's and most had leather-covered shields slung across their backs; they rode shaggy but sturdy-looking ponies while their women and children walked. The women didn't seem to mind this arrangement, which gave them more freedom to control whatever animals they were herding. Talisker was impressed by their beauty and strength, which he would not have expected to see in such apparently poor people: their long red hair shone in the morning sunshine, and the reds and greens they favoured for their skirts and cloaks seemed alive and intoxicating.

No one challenged the newcomers, and they received simple nods in greeting. Talisker watched the eyes carefully – he had learned to do this in prison – but saw in them only caution, no malice. Their fellow travellers must have wondered at the odd garb of the strangers but perhaps assumed that they came from far away and that their dress was not unusual in their own land. At this thought Talisker gave a wry grin. It was true after all.

It was towards the evening of their second day on the road when they heard screams and cries coming from the forest. Malky drew his sword and plunged into the undergrowth, followed by Talisker while Chaplin and Morias hung back. As they reached the small break in the trees, Talisker and Malky froze as the horror of the scene exploded into their consciousness.

Most of the screams were coming from two children who had scrambled high into the branches of a tree for safety; a young woman stood at the foot of the tree clutching a firebrand. She held it before her, protecting the children but the threat was not directed at her. In the middle of the scene, crashing over the ashes of the fire, an ill-matched battle was ending. If rescue was what Talisker and Malky had had in mind when they arrived, they were too late. A young warrior was fighting what appeared to be his shadow, but the shadow was darkening, moving inexorably closer. The warrior's sword dropped from his grasp as the black hand encircled his wrist, and his eyes bulged as the shape began to engulf him.

'No!' Malky roared. He ran towards the figure, his sword flashing silver, but even as he reached the man's side it was too late. The death from within had claimed him. His glance flickered from Malky and Talisker to the young woman, who stood sobbing at the foot of the tree. 'I love thee, Una,' he gasped.

She sank to her knees, racked with sobbing, as his glance returned to Malky. 'Please . . .'

Even as he spoke a black limb erupted from his breastbone, glittering in the light, and he vomited blood. Malky wasted no time. Taking a step back and widening his stance, he gripped his blade two-handed and beheaded the suffering youth with one blow.

For a moment, there was silence in the clearing. Then Una screamed. 'Darr-agh!' She began to crawl towards the young man's severed head, her red hair catching in the brambles, oblivious to the scratches she was inflicting on herself.

Talisker remained rooted to the spot, unable to take in what had just happened. He knew that the creature must have been of the same type that Malky had seen before and that, again, the Highlander had done the right thing. His attention returned to the woman, who was almost at the spot where the head lay.

He stumbled towards her. 'No,' he said quietly. He knelt beside her and gently took her outstretched hand, the rigid claw-like fingers. Her face was shining with tears, mucus and mud, her hair entangled with bracken and twigs. 'Darragh?' she said.

Talisker took her into his arms and held her, the first woman he had held for many years. He pressed her face to his chest, as though to shut out the horror she had witnessed, and stroked her red hair.

*

They did not bury Darragh. Morias made a small platform on which they laid him out, body and head reunited, the join concealed with Darragh's checked cloak. Chaplin helped the children – a boy and a girl – down from the tree and sat with them on a log at the edge of the clearing. He talked to them soothingly, and Talisker recalled that death and bereavement were part of his job.

Una had said nothing since the killing. When she stopped shaking, Talisker let her go and she sat where she was, gazing into space. When she saw that Morias and Malky were laying out Darragh's body, she got up to wander around the edge of the forest. At first Talisker was concerned that she would wander off but then he realised she was picking flowers, ferns and bright sprigs of berries to lay on Darragh's bier.

When they were ready, the company gathered round to make their farewells to the young man. Una and the little girl, Bris, had covered him in all they had picked, Bris sprinkling him with celandines, her grey eyes solemn and her small hand steady. Morias had found an oak with wide branches where they would lay the platform among the leaves, tinged gold with autumn. Before they lifted it Talisker asked Una a question.

'Una,' he said, 'I wonder if I may have his sword?'

Morias shook his head as though in warning, but there was no outburst from the grieving widow. 'Sir,' she murmured, 'what arms will he carry to his rest if I give you his sword?'

Talisker realised his mistake. 'I'm – I'm sorry, Una . . .'

Malky intervened. 'Dinny fret, lassie. Look, Ah'll

gie him my black knife.' He paused, searching for words. 'Your husband's valour will shine before him onyways . . .'

'Thank you, Malcolm,' Una said. 'Darragh was not my husband but my friend.' Her voice broke. 'We grew up together.' She turned her green gaze on Talisker. 'My father named him my protector on this journey to Ruannoch Were. If you carry his sword you must carry his oath to protect me and these children for at least the next four days. My friendship you have already for your aid.'

Talisker bowed self-consciously. With great dignity, Una lifted Darragh's sword and presented it hilt first to Talisker. He gasped; the basket handle was encrusted with turquoise and jet, the steel interwoven with gold threads; the grip of black leather bore the remains of a filigree pattern, but the blade had seen much use. Talisker reached forward to take it with his left hand, at which Una's brows arched but she said nothing. Suddenly aware of an expectant hush, Talisker looked at Morias.

'You must name the blade if it is to be yours,' the *Seanachaidh* explained.

'Oh. If it binds me to keep Darragh's oath, I'll call it my oath too . . . Talisker's Oath.'

'Very good,' Morias said gravely.

'My thanks, Talisker,' Una said. 'Darragh would have been proud.'

Sleep came hard that night. Una wanted to move the camp but the light was already fading. Bris and her brother, Conall, huddled around the fire, as darkness fell, wrapped in grey blankets, their wide eyes scanning the darkness between the trees. Malky took first watch, and made a show of patrolling the perimeter of the clearing.

Talisker's gaze was drawn constantly to the oak where Darragh's body lay, and an irrational fear that the young warrior would rise up played on his mind. Una's blankets were near to his and sometimes he gazed at her copper hair, which glowed in the firelight. The warmth of his blankets and the memory of her perfume aroused his senses and a feeling of contentment passed through him. Just as his eyelids closed, he saw a huge black bird in the tree beside Darragh's body, and thought it had come to escort the young man's soul to whatever passed for heaven in these parts.

He awoke with a start to the sound of voices. It was still dark and the fire was low. Raising himself on his elbow Talisker looked over to the fire. Chaplin was sitting between the two children, speaking to them in the same low tones he had used earlier, but this time there was something different in his demeanour: there was a clarity about his movements. His young audience were entranced by what he was saying and Malky, whose watch had finished, was lying propped up on his elbow like Talisker to listen too.

Talisker turned to ask Una what was going on, only to realise that her blankets were empty. A breath of wind caused the fire to flare and he saw her, a soft dark outline at the base of the oak. She looked so alone and dejected that he got up to go to her. He picked up her blanket as he passed then wrapped it around her shoulders. She smiled her thanks but said nothing, so he sat beside her listening to Chaplin's voice float across the clearing.

'. . . and so Uisdean claimed his prize, the blackest, most beautiful horse that ever travelled the roads of Sutra. He named it Chrruach, like the wind, and all the other chieftains desired his horse but none could ride it save Uisdean mac Fain . . .'

Talisker wondered briefly how Chaplin could have come by such a tale and how his simple telling made the words so alive. In the darkness it seemed that all who heard the story could see the black shapes of Uisdean and his steed.

'Uisdean,' Una said quietly. 'This tale is no longer told here.'

Talisker thought she would say more but when her next words came they were unrelated to the story. 'He said he loved me. Just before he died.'

'Darragh?'

'Yes.' She gripped her blanket tight around her shoulders. 'I never knew.'

Talisker was at a loss. He had had no dealings with love for many years, and even when he had, it had seemed unreal. Love and grief were out of his league.

'Would it have been different if you had known?' he asked gruffly.

'No. He was my best friend, like a brother – but that diminishes our relationship. I was fostered by my aunt to his clan so that I might learn skills to ease a woman's pains when . . .' She faltered.

'You deliver babies?'

'Yes,' she said. 'It is an invaluable skill. Anyway, I met Darragh on the first day in my aunt's service. He was just a boy then, a skinny, clumsy boy with a runny nose, but he earned his sword young and he looked after me. And now I know he loved me as a man, not as a brother. Our parting was to come at Ruannoch Were, anyway, for I am returning to my family . . . but this . . . it was so cruel.' A shudder passed through her and she rocked gently to and fro. She turned her tearstained face to Talisker. 'I am sorry if I speak too frankly. I know that men find these matters . . . difficult.'

Talisker smiled bleakly. 'Not me, lady. I find them impossible. I think we should get some sleep.' He stood up to walk back to his bed, then turned back to her. 'Una, what was the thing that killed Darragh?'

Her eyes widened in fear, the whites shining alarmingly in the gloom. 'Don't you know?' she whispered.

He shook his head.

'I cannot speak the name,' she said. 'They hear all.' Leaning forward, she cleared a space in the soil and began to write with a twig. Talisker crouched beside her.

The firelight flared again, as though even the writing of the name disturbed some restless spirit, and Talisker read the one word. CORANNYEID.

The following morning they set off at first light in a subdued silence. Una, Bris and Conall clustered briefly around the oak to say farewell to Darragh. Bris seemed brighter after the night's sleep and after she had laid more flowers at the base of the tree she skipped up to Chaplin and slipped her hand into his. 'Darragh's gone to sleep now, *Seanachaidh*, hasn't he?' she said. Chaplin nodded.

Conall was more affected by the death of his kinsman and walked close to Una's side, saying nothing but scowling thunderously.

During the course of the morning Talisker tried to speak with him but was met with a glare. It seemed that Conall held the travellers responsible for Darragh's death, and it dawned on Talisker that, although the adults knew Malky had killed Darragh in mercy, it was not clear to Conall.

That day, as they drew closer to Ruannoch Were, many more travellers were on the forest road and Talisker, Malky and Chaplin saw their first Sidhe. It was towards noon when a group of travellers passed them mounted on tall, graceful-looking horses unlike any they had seen so far. As they drew level Talisker turned to nod in the short greeting people gave one another but the sight of the first rider stopped him in his tracks. It was a female with the shape and bearing of Deme. She was clad in loose scarlet robes, and her golden skin glinted a warm pinkish tone in the glaring sunlight. Her long silver hair had been woven with pearls into hundreds of tiny braids. Another strummed on a small harp-like instrument, the horse led by the rider in front. They had said nothing, merely nodded courteously at the group.

Talisker's reverie was interrupted by a giggle from Bris. 'Have you never seen the Sidhe before, sir?'

'Sidhe?' Talisker's gaze was still fixed on the departing horses.

'Don't your clan have any, Talisker?' asked Una. She was puzzled by their reaction and something akin to suspicion showed in her eyes.

'Have any?' Talisker echoed. 'Aren't they free people?'

Una stiffened. 'Well, yes . . . Let's move on, shall we? We will be the last to arrive at this pace.'

That night, the last before they would reach Ruannoch Were, Chaplin told the children another story. Talisker had been watching him through the course of the day and he had changed, physically and mentally. Like Talisker, he still wore the clothes in which he had arrived and he had grown the beginnings of a beard, but he did not question his presence in Sutra. It wasn't so much that he had accepted the place but that the place had accepted him. He seemed happy to talk with everyone except Talisker and Malky. A few times during the day, Talisker had caught Chaplin staring at him. There was no mistaking the gaze: the policeman's feelings towards him were unchanged.

During the afternoon when Bris complained of tired feet Una and she rode on Morias's white mule, while Chaplin walked alongside chatting with the little girl.

'Why are you and Talisker wearing such funny clothes?' she asked.

'It's what everybody wears in the mountains where we come from,' Chaplin replied.

'Don't you wear nice plaid?'

'Oh, yes,' Chaplin said seriously. 'It's so lovely that we wear it on the inside,' and opened his trench coat to show Bris the green tartan lining.

The detail and complexity of the story Chaplin told that night amazed Talisker. All of the company gathered around the fire to hear it. The policeman sat slightly higher than everyone else on a gnarled log, staring into the flames as he spoke. He had reversed his coat so that the lining showed and wore it draped loosely around his shoulders.

He began simply. 'Here is my tale,' he said. 'It is the tale of Kentigern and Rowan. There once ruled a thane of a great clan named Kentigern. He was a mighty warrior, a skilled swordsman and horseman. He was as handsome as he was powerful and all the women in his kingdom loved him and would have married him if he had asked them. But he never did. One desired Kentigern more than any other and her name was Rowan. She was as fair as he was handsome, and some whispered that she was a changeling. She worked each day in the stables of Kentigern's great hall, caring for the horses, and often Kentigern would see her when he went riding and would speak with her about the horses. Time passed and still Kentigern had no wife. Rowan and all the other women of the land, began to despair . . .

'Kentigern had falcons and he spent many days on the moors flying them. Gradually, this time away increased until he was not seen for a week at a time. Then a rumour reached Rowan that worried her greatly. It was said that Kentigern had been bewitched by a faerie lady and one day would not return at all. The next time Kentigern went hunting, Rowan followed him and, sure enough, it was true. Kentigern climbed the steep side of a mountain and when he reached the top, a great white bird appeared, bigger than he, and transformed into a beautiful faerie. Kentigern went to her as though in a trance. They walked forward into the air off the edge of the mountain and disappeared. Rowan waited by Kentigern's horse for two anxious days and then, on the second night, they reappeared. When the faerie lady transformed into a bird once more, Rowan came out from hiding and loosed an arrow, which shot through the heart of the bird. She vanished in a great silver flash, with a cry of despair that echoed through the mountains.

'In his rage Kentigern, still bewitched by the faerie, turned and struck Rowan. She fell, hitting her head on the sharp rocks. As her lifeblood spilled from her Kentigern realised that he had loved her and called out to the gods. Only one heard, the capricious Rhiannon. She decided that Kentigern did not deserve the constant Rowan and turned her into a tree. The red berries of that tree are the beads of blood that ran through her hair. Kentigern returned home alone and remained alone for ever.'

When Chaplin fell silent Talisker shook himself as though he had been dreaming. 'I don't get this,' he muttered.

'What don't you "get"?' Morias, beside him, asked.

'How does he know these stories? He's a policeman, for Chrissakes!'

Morias's eyes narrowed and his gaze became sharper. A hard-edged intelligence showed itself, which Talisker thought he had last seen on a park bench in Edinburgh.

'I know,' Morias said quietly. 'Your friend is a *Seanachaidh*. It is a gift. The land has chosen him to speak its past. Do not question its wisdom.'

'But why? Why Chaplin? I'm the one with no past. I was the one who was sent here.' He gazed at the ground as he spoke. He knew he sounded jealous and petty.

'Not for ever, Talisker,' Morias replied. 'Sutra is changing you. You are the one with a future too full for stone-dreaming.'

Talisker, Malky and Chaplin would never forget their first sight of Ruannoch Were, and even the others of the company seemed entranced by it.

It was dark as they neared the city and the forest road was thronged with people on horseback and on foot. The progress of the company became slower and slower, and it became obvious that the road ahead was obstructed. Talisker, Malky and Chaplin led the way, with the others bunched in the middle for protection. As they drew nearer to the obstruction hundreds of white lights illuminated the spaces between the trees. At first it was impossible to tell the source of or reason for the lights but then it became stunningly clear.

At one moment there was land, at the next water. A huge lake, bigger than Light of the Sky, glinted and shone with the reflected glow of the torches that moved upon its surface. Each was attached to a post in the middle of a tiny round boat, a coracle that held three people – its oarsman and two passengers. Hundreds were moving back and forth across the lake because Ruannoch Were was built on water.

In the darkness it was difficult to judge the scale of the city but as each torch neared the quay it vanished into a pinprick of light. The city walls seemed impossibly high for the inhabitants to have built them, and their black stone gleamed darkly as the water from the lake condensed on them. The city was a fortress with four huge towers at each corner but its forbidding silhouette did not diminish the mood of celebration that wafted across the water to those who waited for the boats. Some enterprising travellers were singing to entertain those in the disorderly line.

'I will have to go on the ferry with the mule,' Morias said. Talisker looked to where he was pointing and saw the larger boat, strung with lamps, moving towards the shore. A different group clustered around its landing-point, largely composed of Sidhe with their elegant horses, waiting to board.

'Does anyone want to come with me on the big boat?' Morias smiled.

Conall and Malky elected to go with him. Bris was excited by the prospect of a ride in a coracle so Chaplin agreed to take her, leaving Talisker and Una to board another.

As she gazed across the water, Una's green eyes sparkled, reminding Talisker of the gem he carried in his pocket. She was barely able to contain her excitement as their oarsman turned his back on them and rowed out into the lake. 'Isn't it beautiful, Talisker?' she said. Her hair caught the breeze and floated out behind her, catching the glow of the lamp. As the sound of laughter and singing on the shore faded she trailed her hand in the water then touched it to her mouth. Tiny illuminated droplets clung to her pale skin.

'Yes . . .' Talisker couldn't tear his eyes away from her.

She looked at him then. 'But you're not looking at – oh.' There was an awkward pause. 'Look,' she said. 'You do it.' She dipped her hand in the water again then pressed it to her lips. 'It's lucky,' she explained.

'Maybe I should drink the whole damned lake,' he joked.

She laughed then, her self-consciousness gone and splashed him. He flicked some drops back at her and a water-fight ensued, accompanied by squeals and roars of laughter. The oarsman ignored them, and within a few minutes they were drenched and spluttering.

'Ssh,' Una said, but she was still giggling as they came within the darker shadow of the city wall. 'Listen.'

From inside they could hear singing. It was unlike any singing Talisker had ever heard: it was a pure, ethereal sound that carried out across the water transforming the night with its echo. All around them, the people crossing the lake fell silent, and Talisker felt something within him lift upwards and out over the water as though his soul would mingle with the voices.

'The Sidhe are singing,' Una whispered. She turned toward him, still dripping wet, fern-like tendrils of hair plastered to her face. Then, as their boat bumped gently against the jetty, she kissed him.

# CHAPTER EIGHT

Ferghus stood on the western tower and watched the lights on the water. The wind stirred his silver beard and he shuddered. His feelings of foreboding returned with the last notes of the song. He imagined he saw again, as in his dream, the dark shadow of the face that haunted him and heard the hollow mocking laughter echo across the lake. But already the image of the dream was fading, like the music that drifted away into the night, a transient brightness that drove before it all things made of darkness and chaos. The night winds tugged at his robes but now he smiled grimly.

Gripping the edges of the cold stones he stared at the tiny golden lights crossing to the city, like thousands of fire-flies flocking to the great golden fires of Ruannoch Were. 'I am the Thane,' he reassured himself.

'Father?'

He turned to see his daughter framed by the lintel of the oak doorway, the light from the torches playing on her silver-white hair, fine tendrils playing in the breeze. She was so like her mother.

Kyra smiled brightly. 'I thought I heard you speaking, Father. Was someone here?'

'I was rehearsing my speech for the *Seanachaidhs*,' he lied easily. 'I wouldn't wish to offend them.'

'Oh, yes.' She walked towards him and took his hand. 'Let's see, you've only given it twenty or so times before.'

They laughed together.

'Well, I'm glad that someone around here can still laugh.' The voice was broken, croaky, and although Ferghus and Kyra were smiling as they looked back towards the doorway, their mood was broken. Ulla stood there. Now, where brightness was held sway just moments earlier, it seemed that a dark shadow or stain had been left behind. Ferghus's second daughter had been blighted as a child, her strong young frame twisted mercilessly by a cruel disease. Ferghus had tried many times to find love in his heart for her but he knew there was little. His daughter was sullen, given to inexplicable rages. He knew that her limbs pained her and she seldom complained, but even this quality did not endear her to him. Her mother had understood her and loved her well, but she had been dead five years now.

'What ails you, sister?' Kyra asked. 'Come and look at the lights. I will not allow you to be sad tonight.' She said this so kindly that Ulla gave a grudging half-smile and allowed her sister to help her to the side of the turret. Her movements were slow and difficult. She is an old woman already, Ferghus thought sadly, and she has only twenty summers.

When she reached the wall, Ulla gazed out at the boats, her dark features betraying some enjoyment. Her right side, untouched by her illness, was towards her father and, for a moment, he studied her face. She would have been beautiful also, he thought. Perhaps not as lovely as Kyra – she was dark where her sister was fair, her features were not as fine, her brows heavier – but she would have had her own qualities. Tonight, the knowledge seemed especially poignant, for Eion would ask his permission to marry Kyra. He knew this because he was a good thane who knew most things that happened within the walls of the city. Kyra would be happy to accept a suitor of such high standing and the young man seemed genuine in his admiration of her. Ulla would be left behind, like the shadow she was fast becoming.

Kyra interrupted his thoughts, chattering to her sister. 'You can't wear that dress, Ulla. It's horrible. We'll find you one of mine.'

For a moment Ulla looked annoyed, but then she sighed and hobbled back to the doorway, Kyra's arm around her waist. Ferghus smiled: the girls' occasional camaraderie was a great comfort to him.

The smile froze. As they reached the doorway, it seemed to Ferghus that the black depth of shadow which was always with Ulla had begun to spread unnaturally, so that the white of Kyra's skirts and the gold of her hair was swallowed by darkness. When they paused in the doorway Ferghus could see the sisters only as a black shape. A sound like laughter rang out across the lake. 'No,' he gasped. 'No . . .'

Then the shadow was past and Kyra glanced back at him. 'We'll meet you in the Great Hall, Father. I've got something to tell you,' she called.

'I'll be there soon. Ulla?' He seldom addressed his younger daughter directly and she stiffened slightly as though surprised. She turned back with difficulty and Ferghus didn't know what to say to her. 'You know I . . . you know . . . Be happy tonight, won't you?'

She nodded. 'If the Thane commands it,' she said, without a trace of irony.

'No,' he said sadly. 'Your father just wishes it.'

For a moment she met his gaze with honesty and they understood one another.

Kyra coughed. 'Let's go and find you a dress, shall we?'

As the Sidhe began a new song, Ferghus was left alone once more.

Ruannoch Were was a vast maze of streets and alleyways through which laughing, screaming people ran seemingly at random. They waved blazing torches in the air, the bright orange glow leaving streaks across Talisker's vision that he could still see when he blinked. Even the smallest children carried lanterns with a glowing rush-light inside that illuminated their excited faces. Talisker's first impression of the city was that it was full of light and fire. Una's kiss still lingered on his lips, he could still taste it. He was not sure what it had meant – after all, she had just been through a great trauma. Now she took his hand to hurry him up the gangway. The warmth of her touch was almost more than he could bear.

'Una?' he said, unsure of what he wanted to ask her, but she didn't hear him: she was waving to Bris and Conall, who had just stepped out of their boats.

The small band of travellers was reunited by the city gate. The children had caught the excitement of the evening, and Chaplin had Bris on his shoulders where she jigged up and down irrepressibly. Only Morias was quiet, his mood solemn and reflective. He nodded in welcome to Talisker and Una as they arrived. 'It seems we have arrived in time,' he said.

'What for?' Talisker asked.

'The procession, of course, silly,' said Bris, 'and the stories. Morias is going to tell one and Alessandro. Can I have a big torch, Una?'

'No,' Una said firmly, 'You will have a lantern like all the other children.'

'I can't . . .' Chaplin said. 'Morias? I've no story ready for Samhain.'

Morias slapped Chaplin on the back. 'Don't worry, lad. I don't think they'll have time for newcomers this year.'

Malky walked out of the shadow of the gates with five flaming torches in his hands and two rush-light lanterns. He grinned broadly at Talisker and Una. 'Here we are. They were jist gi'in' them away. Said tae tell ye, they're frae the North fire, white're that means.'

Morias pointed upwards. 'There,' he said. Two huge bonfires could be seen on the towers to the front wall of the city. 'There are two more fires on the back towers. Brands are lit and distributed at random and your luck for the year determined by which you are given. North is not the best of luck; at its worst it can mean tragedy, but we have seen that already.' He smiled at Bris and Conall. 'Not you two, of course, you're too young to have grown into your luck. That's why you have rush-lights.'

Conall scowled. 'I'm old enough for battle,' he complained. 'I don't see why I can't have a torch.'

'Come on!' Bris wailed. 'Let's go!'

The crowd thronged the streets of Ruannoch Were in festive mood. A great deal of good-natured shoving was going on but no one took offence. In doorways and alleyways entertainers juggled or ate fire, while a few stalwarts appeared to be singing but their music was lost in the bedlam. Talisker was unsure if they had joined the end of the procession or not. The only indicator seemed to be that everyone was heading the same way, but, as their section of the crowd turned a corner at the top of a slope, Talisker saw the leaders. They carried huge effigies made of straw, the shapes demonic and menacing in the lurid light of myriad torches. Without thinking, Talisker nudged the person next to him. 'They're amazing, aren't they?' he began.

It was Chaplin. Their eyes met and the spark of the enmity was there, but then Bris patted the policeman's head with her lantern. 'Faster, *Seanachaidh*, faster . . .'

Chaplin quickened his pace and disappeared into the crowd.

At last the procession seemed to be reaching its destination. In the heart of the city there was a large flat square and in the middle of that a tor; its sides were steep and inset with four flights of narrow stone steps. Around its base, fires were burning in a bright ring. Talisker could see now that the processions had converged on the square from the four corners of the city, and that the massed crowd was easily two thousand strong.

'Can you see the Thane?' he heard Bris gasp in excitement.

At the flat summit of the tor were three ornate chairs, two placed slightly behind the largest one, which was undoubtedly the throne in which sat Ferghus mac Ferghus, Thane of Ruannoch Were and the Eastern Dominions. Even from the distance at which the group stood, there was no doubt that his stature was immense.

He wore a plaid of dark green and a silver chain-mail shirt beneath; at his left shoulder his gathered plaid was fastened by a large silver brooch and he wore a circlet of silver around his brow. As he moved upon his throne – slightly impatiently, it seemed – the reflected lights flashed and glinted spectacularly. By the sides of the throne, raised up so that all his subjects could see, stood a large ornate war-axe and a leather shield, heavily studded with silver. The hands of the Thane, gripping the arms of his seat, were broad and strong. Talisker had the impression that he was well capable of using the ceremonial weapons, despite the grey of his beard.

'Who are they?' Talisker nudged Una, and indicated the other seats behind the Thane.

'Thane Ferghus's daughters,' Una replied. 'Kyra and Ulla. They are like night and day, are they not?'

Talisker was about to answer when the Thane stood up. The crowd was immediately hushed, and all that could be heard was the sputtering of the torches and the quiet breath of the night breeze. The Thane began to speak. The language – an ancient ceremonial dialect – was unknown to Talisker and Chaplin, but his voice was sombre, resonant, carrying over the heads of the crowd into the darkness beyond.

'He is giving thanks for the harvest,' Una whispered, sensing Talisker's lack of comprehension. 'He calls upon the gods to keep us over the coming wintertide . . . especially now.'

'Why now?'

'Ssh,' an elderly woman chided them. 'Show some respect.'

Talisker lapsed into silence. As the speech

continued, he observed the crowd. It seemed that most of the travellers who had come to the city were like those he had seen on the forest road: peasants and farmers who, in the main, looked prosperous and well fed. Here and there, a few men stood out in the crowd, tall and rugged with hard eyes. They carried weapons and no torch to hinder their sword arm, warriors he supposed, mercenaries with no army to fight in. Perhaps they would have been hired to protect the wealthier travellers or merchants as they brought goods to sell in Ruannoch Were. It struck him that none of the Sidhe were in the crowd.

The singing had ceased when the Thane had risen to give his speech and when he finished the crowd made a ritual response. Then Una grabbed Talisker's arm. She began to jog back down towards the market square. 'Where are we going?' Talisker asked.

'We have to get a good view, Duncan. Morias will be telling his story in the Tannery Square. He's very popular.'

By the time they reached the square, Morias was already seated on a mounting block. He was watching calmly for the movement of people into the space to cease. Others would have gone to hear lesser *Seanachaidhs* in Miller's Barn, the Quay and the Piggery – which was popular as it backed on to a tavern. A large fire had been lit beside the *Seanachaidh*'s set, and the flames danced over the expectant faces of the hushed crowd.

'Where to begin?' Morias stared intently into the fire.

'Not so very long ago, by the reckoning of stories – that is, about three hundred years – the gods still lived on the face of Sutra. Their magic filled the land, flowing like lifeblood through the things that were dear to them, such as plants, trees and all things elemental. As a consequence of this, mortal man prospered also and the land was gold and green, the nights filled with laughter and song . . .

'Of course, this is not to say that the gods were beneficent to man. No! Rather, they found mortals curious and interesting. Occasionally man's great passions surprised those they worshipped and perhaps over time the gods developed some . . . paternal feeling for their mortal charges. Still, the gods lived apart in their great halls, which only their chosen acolytes might approach. All was peaceful, in balance. Those were halcyon days . . .' He sighed.

'Anyway, all things must change. As many years passed, the gulf between the clans of men – the Fine – and their gods grew greater. The location of the halls of the gods became lost in the mist of legend, which is often not as ancient as we would assume, but merely convenient to some. The clans of Sutra governed themselves without recourse to the magic of their ancient mentors, and as the gods lost interest, slowly, imperceptibly, the colours of Old Sutra began to fade for ever . . .'

Morias gazed at the rapt faces of his audience. Before him sat a small boy, his eyes round and shining with delight. Morias smiled kindly at him. 'What is your name, child?'

'Rory, sir,' the boy whispered.

Morias held out his fist palm upwards. 'Blow on it, Rory,' he said.

Rory did as he was told, and Morias made as if to throw something into the air. A bright green light shot upwards like a firework, but it remained fixed in the air and formed a picture of the face of an infant child, with black hair and bright blue eyes.

As the image faded, Morias went on, 'Then, as happens only once in a millennium, a new god was born. Some say his origins were evil, for darkness covered the skies as his mother, the goddess Matrona, lay in childbirth. They say he was created from the stuff of chaos – indeed, his father was unknown even to the other gods. I cannot believe that a babe can be born evil incarnate, but who can say? Soon after came another babe; a weak, mewling thing who was expected to die. They were twins: Corvus the boy and Phyrr the girl. Yet she survived – and some suspect through dark magic, for her soul was surely tainted.

'As the pair reached adulthood it was clear that the ill-omens of their birth would be proved correct. Phyrr was seldom to be seen in the halls of the gods, for she had become interested then obsessed by darkness and death. She was as a beautiful shadow often to be seen in the company of mortal men, usually before she killed them for her pleasure . . . but Corvus was worse. Would that the death of a single soul could amuse him . . . He interfered in the affairs of the Fine, first provoking petty border disputes but, as time passed, he progressed to warfare, and fashioned himself as a great war chieftain such as had never been seen before on the face of Sutra. As he conquered he assimilated. Each clansman was made to foreswear his allegiance to his own lord on pain of death – not his own, of course, Corvus was too clever and wicked for that, but those of his wife and children. It is told that within the first year of his campaign, thirty thousand families died on their own swords. So began the reign of the Raven King.

'What of the gods, you may ask? What indeed? Having lost interest in the Fine, they were slow to see the danger that Corvus presented to the land and, long before that time, the Fine imagined themselves forsaken. As their belief diminished, so the magic retracted from the land, pulling back to the seat of the gods' power; for that power is ever dependent on the faith of men.

'Finally, the days of the last conflict approached. Five clans were left as freemen and they were the mightiest clans of Sutra, their leaders great legendary heroes; Uisdean Finnach, Red Raghnald, Kentigern Murdoch, the youngest of them all, Conner mac Roich and the beautiful Maura McLeish. On the eve of the conflict their spirits were low, and around their campfires the lamentation could be heard of women soon to be widows. As midnight silence fell upon the campsite, a young woman was brought forward to the meeting of the heroes. The sentries had found her just beyond the edges of the site, near the river. Four of the five were agreed to slay her as a spy but something in her bearing made Uisdean bid them stay their hand . . . something about the quiet way she smiled in the gathering dark. She admitted she was a sorceress of great power but said she had come to aid them. If the heroes would give their leave she could summon help for the duration of the battle. This caused much argument as there was naturally a backlash of suspicion in the land with regard to magic, but finally, even before the first light of dawn paled the skies, the leaders agreed. Their situation was such that they could not do otherwise – even then the dark stain of Corvus's hordes could be seen across the river.

'And so the sorceress made a spell. It was simple, she said, but its like has never been repeated. She sent a signal – a huge shining jewel – into the sky. It flew upward over the river so that its bright flare illuminated the massed warriors on each side. It trailed a green light like a dying star, so that to see it was to hope – or to despair, were you the legions of Corvus. Then it vanished.

'For long moments there was silence. All that could be heard was the sweet sound of the river. Then, just as the heroes feared betrayal and as furtive hands reached for daggers, a flash of green lightning blazed across the night sky from end to end. As the after-glare faded only a small glow remained, which appeared to be drawing closer through the heavens. Finally a huge clan of warriors could be seen walking through the skies behind their chieftain, the blades of their axes and swords flaring with eldritch green fire. Their chieftain carried the green gem in one hand and a mighty sword in the other. They descended from the skies and approached the waiting army with grim smiles of greeting.

'The chieftain stopped before Uisdean and handed him the gem. Then he took his wrist in a warrior's grip and smiled. He was a large man, head and shoulders taller than Uisdean. His beard and hair were red gold and his smile was like the sun. "Brothers," he said, in a strong voice that echoed through the valley, "we received your call for aid. We have come." A rousing cheer carried through the ranks of the heroes but, after this introduction, neither he nor his warriors spoke again. Their deeds spoke for them.

'At dawn a mighty battle was joined on the banks of the river. The Fine were greatly outnumbered – although then by his magic Corvus controlled few ranks of the Corrannyeid. The mere sight of these creatures was enough to fill the stoutest heart with fear. Their appearance was unpredictable – they can change shape at will as can their antithesis, the Sidhe, who were not then abroad in the land – for the Corrannyeid have no spirit, no creative power of their own, and mimic the likeness of their foe. Of course, the likeness is primitive, and, in battle their shapes can often be seen only as a black shifting mass of insects and decay as they swarm between one victim and another. Above the battlefield that day could be heard the high-pitched clicking and whirring as of millions of such creatures.

'Many acts of heroism were performed, as the ballads of the time recall. All of the heroes fell beneath the seething mass but for Raghnald and the Nameless Chieftain. They were surrounded atop a grassy hillock by the black swarms of the Corrannyeid and the soldiers of Corvus. All seemed lost. Around them their foes walked across the bodies of the slain, the sky was black with wheeling, carrion-eating birds ready to pick the flesh from their still warm bones. Raghnald and the Nameless Chieftain embraced as brothers when the moment of final conflict approached.

'And then the gods intervened. Their powers were

weakened by the loss of faith of the Fine, yet together they could still be strong. Together in their shame that one of their number could wreak such havoc upon the green fields of Sutra, they united to create one last spell.

'It was a spell of binding so powerful that it could contain a god. Lightning filled the skies once more, and where it touched the earth between Raghnald and the Nameless Chieftain, a bright staff appeared that dazzled those closest to it so that they fell to their knees. The saddened faces of the gods could be glimpsed in the boiling heavens. The staff flared bright arcs of white light outwards, and Corvus, who was watching the battle from behind the lines of his soldiers, was pulled upwards into the sky. Sensing the nature of the spell he thrashed and screamed, black bolts of magic flashing through the air. The final malicious shaft grounded on the broken bodies of the heroes, which some faithful clansman had placed on the hillock near Raghnald. All were instantly turned to grey stone including Raghnald, the luckless survivor. Only the Nameless One remained on the knoll and he fell to his knees and wept for the passing of the gods and all his comrades. The Corrannyeid vanished as the flaring light of the staff touched them and a strange, stunned silence fell on the battlefield.

'As the last bright flares died, the goddess Rhiannon appeared to those few still assembled. Her shape was indistinct. "We have failed you," she said, "so we are leaving. Do not mourn our passing. In truth, perhaps you do not need us . . . If ever your peril should be so great again, seek us in the quiet places of the world, the places of mystery. The spell will hold the darkness from the land for many generations, as long as we can sustain its life. As long as there are souls such as these, whose love of this land exemplifies its spirit, we will not fail."

'She turned to the Nameless Chieftain. "Gather up your dead and I shall return you to your homeland. Know that as long as there are Celts through all of time, your deeds this day will be spoken of." She handed him a banner that unfurled in the breeze. It was scarlet, the colour of the blood of the fallen. "Take this emblem with you. As long as it remains in your halls, no man of your clan will ever fall in battle again."

'And so the clan of the Nameless Chieftain returned whence they came, taking their dead and wounded. As he walked into the mists Rhiannon had conjured, the chieftain turned and saluted, touching the flat of his blade to his brow. "Until the light calls again, Lady Rhiannon." Then they were gone.

'The lands of Sutra recovered soon enough. Perhaps some unknown hand was at work in the healing process and the gods' desertion not as final as they claimed. Men forgot their wartime allegiances within a generation and the reign of the Raven King was spoken of only in whispers. The day after the battle, Sidhe were first sighted riding from the south. People believe the gods sent them for their powers of healing and music. Soon, each clan had their own small band of Sidhe aligned to their halls to remind them of what brightness there could be in the world.

'Yet, a seed of darkness remained. Phyrr, the sister of Corvus, was forgotten, and for many years after, her black shape was to be seen on a battlefield where fair young men died. This might be conjecture, but I wonder . . . It seems to me that the darkest soul was the one who fought hardest to survive. This is the end of the *Seanachaidh*'s tale.'

The last words of the story seared Talisker's heart. Why would the darkest soul fight hardest to survive? What did that say for his embattled soul? Suddenly he was aware that he was clutching Mirranon's gem, which still lay in the pocket of his jeans. Until the light calls again . . . Talisker gasped aloud, and as he did so, Morias caught his gaze and gave a tiny shake of his head.

The audience had erupted into a wave of clapping and cheering. Morias smiled and nodded, in modest acceptance of their praise, but Talisker could see in the light of the fire that the old man was tired. Chaplin was already by Morias's side speaking quietly with him, and Talisker walked towards them. He stopped next to Morias and was about to speak when the *Seanachaidh* held up his hand to silence him. They watched the audience leave, their torches burning low, dark streaks of smoke rising into the midnight sky. Within minutes, only Talisker, Malky, Morias and Chaplin remained in the square. Una had taken the children to their bed in the house of a kinsman. The night was now silent.

'But that cannot be the end, Morias?' Talisker demanded. 'The end of the *Seanachaidh*'s tale?' His voice was hoarse, his tone more demanding than he had intended and Chaplin, thinking he meant the old man harm, stood up and placed himself between them. The glint of a silver blade caught the moonlight, and Malky grabbed at Talisker's jersey to pull him out of reach.

'Oh, very good, Chaplin,' Talisker fumed, 'just the

excuse you've been waiting for. It didn't take you long. I don't suppose you care what's actually happening here, do you?'

'Now, dinny be daft, laddie,' Malky growled at Chaplin.

'Leave him be, Sandro,' Morias said mildly. 'I suppose my tale has somehow raised more questions than it answered.'

Talisker sidestepped Chaplin and pulled the stone from his pocket. 'What about this, Morias?' he demanded.

The gem was shining as it had in Edinburgh. Green fire lanced from its facets, illuminating the scene, bleaching the features of the four men, making their eyes sparkle with reflected brilliance. 'Put it away!' Morias hissed, 'You'll kill us all.'

'Christ,' Chaplin breathed. "Until the light calls again . . ."'

Talisker slipped the gem back into his pocket, and Morias nodded wearily. 'Yes,' he said. 'The light has called again, but this time there is no mighty clan of heroes. This time there is only one, and he is a less than perfect man. I think we should speak about this in the morning. I am very tired. I think this will be my last Samhain.'

'But, please, Morias,' Talisker protested, 'I need to know everything. I don't understand – why me?'

Morias sighed. 'My tale was true, Duncan. You – and Malky – are the last descendants of the clan that was pulled through the ether at Sutra's greatest hour of need. How many people would you say were in the crowd tonight?'

'I'm not sure. About two thousand? Why?'

'Within the last week more than double that number left their homes to travel here for Samhain.'

'What?' Talisker hissed. 'What are you saying?'

'They were killed, like Darragh, in the forests. The Corrannyeid stalk the land once more.' He made a warding-off gesture as he said the name. 'The people have not realised yet the scale of the killings. But this night, believe me, through all the homes and taverns of Ruannoch Were the truth is dawning. The spell of which I spoke is decaying. It was created by great alchemy and its nature is close to what your world would consider a chemical. At a certain point, it can no longer sustain its structure. It will fail, and Corvus knows that. He will be free and two hundred years have done nothing to mellow his spiteful nature. All we have to level against his power is a handful of vague prophecies, the gem and you. It looks bleak indeed, does it not?'

There was a stunned silence.

'I think I will sleep now,' Morias said, as though they had been discussing the weather. He rose to his feet unsteadily and Chaplin took his arm. 'I have taken rooms for us in the hostel,' he pointed with his staff, 'the third street down, the Black Swan.' He moved away, Chaplin and Malky with him.

'I'll be there in a minute,' Talisker muttered.

His star was still there, and Talisker stared at the sky for a long time. The fire around the mounting block was dying back, its embers losing tiny brilliant sparks into the wind. He picked up his jacket and put it on – he had taken it off earlier as he listened to Morias's tale but now the night air was tinged with cold and the promise of mist coming in off the lake with the morning. Two thousand people, Morias had said, murdered in the forest on their way to Samhain, the festival of light, by the same evil that had claimed Darragh.

'Talisker?'

Una stood in the shadow of the tor, the moonlight giving her delicate features an ethereal glow. He smiled at her but tiredness threatened to overwhelm him.

'Many people have died,' she said quietly. 'They are talking about it in the taverns, women and children—' She broke off as a tear slid down her cheek. He went to her and held her close as he had the first time. Neither spoke, their shared warmth and grief enough for now. Her hand stroked his chest and she laid her head against his shoulder. When she next spoke her voice was as quiet as a sigh, but it seemed to Talisker as though she shouted from the rooftops.

'Will you lie with me, Duncan?'

'Una,' he whispered, 'you don't know me. You don't know who I am . . .'

She didn't lift her head but he felt her cheek move as she smiled. 'It's no disgrace to want a man, Duncan. You will not dishonour me, not on Samhain. Besides, I can hear what's in your heart and I want it for my own.' She moved her hand down over his hip until it rested gently against the top of his thigh, the warmth of her touch almost searing through the fabric of his jeans. He felt again the slow heat creeping through his veins as he had when she had slept next to him. But this time the warmth came from Una and it demanded answer.

'Fear,' he said, 'that's what's in my heart.'

She looked up, her face radiant. 'Then let me take your fear, Duncan Talisker, and keep it safe.'

He kissed her then, his anxiety melting like spring snow. In the silence of the night, the festival and music finished, the dark pall of death crept across the sleeping city and the only singing was in Talisker's soul.

As the green light of Mirranon's gem had flared across the empty market-square a watcher looked on from the crenellations of the north tower. Behind her the bonfire that lit the Samhain torches was dying, the burnt timbers collapsing inward. She stayed until she saw Talisker and Una move off in the direction of the tavern, Una leading the tall man as though he was in a trance. Kyra smiled. 'How sweet,' she muttered. 'The hero of the hour . . .' Pulling her wrap tighter around her shoulders she left to rejoin her betrothal party.

Much later, Kyra tried to let sleep claim her. It was hard to still her thoughts. Would he come to her again in her dreams? Would he still want her? He was all she wanted. She moaned quietly as sleep engulfed her like a velvet hand, and she felt the blackness against her cool skin, felt the sensation of falling as though it were a lover's touch. He would catch her. She knew he would.

'Kyra? There you are.'

'Corvus,' she said.

He stood a few feet away from where she had landed on her feet, although all around was darkness still. The sensation of falling had stopped. He was naked but for a black cloak, and his blue eyes danced with a feral light. 'You know me?'

She nodded. 'There was a *Seanachaidh* at Samhain and he told your story.'

'Are you afraid?'

She shook her head defiantly. 'I don't believe you are evil,' she said.

He threw back his head and laughed. 'You are so very young, Kyra. I can assure you I am evil. What do you say to that?'

'No,' she said. She wondered why he had made no move towards her, wondered if he was somehow bound in this dream to where he stood. She walked forward, tears pricking at her eyes, her chin tilted upward. 'How can you be evil if someone loves you?' she demanded. 'Doesn't love redeem all?'

She stood within arm's reach of him and itched to touch the face that had seemed so strong and gentle each night for the last month, but something made her hold back. His grin had turned to a maniacal leer and from the back of his throat a harsh, dry chuckle emerged, which mocked and shamed her. Before she knew what she planned, she acted. She spat in his face.

'Bastard,' she squealed. She turned to run.

*This is a dream. This is a dream.*

The words ran through her mind as her fear mounted. From behind her, a sound, an animalistic roar. There was a rush of shadow, black on black, then sharp lancing pain, as her back was ripped open by huge dark talons. Warm blood covered her buttocks and thighs. As she fell she twisted and saw him. She screamed.

He was a raven. His wings filled the darkness as far as she could see, blotting out all else. His talons were silver, streaked with the fresh red of her blood. But it was Corvus. The same blue eyes filled with malicious delight bored into her soul. He descended on her and as he did so, he changed. By the time he lay pressed against her his features were those of a man, but against her bare breasts, for an instant, she felt the animal warmth of his feathers, the heartbeat of the giant bird. Then it was skin on skin.

He put his wings/his feathers/his cloak around her and drew her to him. He entered her, his hands sliding down in the warm river of her blood, slick and wet. She cried out and he pressed a bloodied finger to her lips. 'Darling.' He laughed.

She struggled, fought and screamed. She was the daughter of the Thane and her resistance was impassioned and strong for a woman of her size, but it was useless. Eventually, she lay weeping in exhaustion and self-disgust, until she felt the dark seed take hold within her. Her eyes widened with the horror of knowing that she was losing her soul, but then she closed her eyes and a tiny malicious smile appeared on her face, which mirrored Corvus's own.

Chaos had claimed her. Kyra was dead.

She opened her eyes. 'I'm yours, my lord,' she whispered.

'I know,' he said.

# CHAPTER NINE

The air was silver. The air was music. Above the mists the eagles flew, and Makhpiyaluta was the greatest eagle of all. His huge wings split the air currents with the sound of steel whispering through steel. Higher and higher his spiralling flight took him, until he looked down on the brown backs of his fellows and his cry echoed through the forests and over the sleeping city. He hovered on the peak of a thermal and watched their ascent as they followed his lead. They would follow him wherever he flew, he thought smugly, even if he flew up and up to where the air became too thin to support his flight, until the sun scorched his feathers.

A movement distracted Makhpiyaluta from his self-satisfaction. It came from beyond the narrow windows that dotted the roofscape, light reflecting off a red-gold surface. It intrigued Makhpiyaluta and, folding his wings, he descended. As he neared the window that framed his prize, he twisted so that his feathers met the resistance of the current and his flight slowed. He saw into the dark cramped space. The red-gold flash had come from the hair of a sleeping woman, illuminated by the first touches of the dawn light. Two people lay on a rough pallet, their limbs wrapped around one another, their features softened in sleep. Somehow the man seemed alert even in repose, his muscled shoulders tense, as though ready to spring into wakefulness should the door open unexpectedly. A bright sword lay on the floor, just within his grasp. Makhpiyaluta called again and this time the echo seemed tinged with sadness.

In the attic room of the tavern Talisker awoke to the cry and glanced up at the window in time to see the flash of brown feathers.

'Christ,' he whispered. Seven or eight huge birds flew past in quick succession, their wings sending a freshening downdraught into the unlatched window. As the last passed by, he met its gaze and it seemed to Talisker as though it smiled. He laughed aloud at his imagining and stared at the sleeping form of Una beside him.

'Una,' he said quietly, 'there's massive birds outside. Eagles, I think.' She stirred in her sleep, pressing her warm body against him. Reaching out he gently moved the hair from across her face and she smiled without opening her eyes. 'Una,' he whispered, unable to keep the passion from his tone, 'are you awake?'

She giggled and squeezed him to signify that she was. He groaned. Without warning she whipped the pillow from beneath his head and leaped up to stand over him. She beat him hard with it, feathers escaping, to dance through the air with her laughter. 'Don't you know, Duncan Talisker, that in these parts a man must fight for his woman?' She hit him again. White feathers caught in her red hair and she blew theatrically at one, which came to rest on her breast.

Talisker thought he'd never seen anything more erotic or beautiful. 'That's not what you said last night . . .' he replied, stood up and gathered her into his arms.

*

Outside, the streets were still relatively deserted but already a feeling of tension filled the city, the revelry forgotten. The air was crisp with the promise of an autumn morning, and Talisker decided to go in search of eagles. The tavern was by the south wall, near the main gate to the city, so he followed the streets towards the gate and climbed a flight of stairs to the watchtower over the lake. There, the eagles flew.

There were nine, deep brown and golden in the morning sun, which arced off the surface of the lake making their colours vibrant against the blue of the sky. They flew high above the waters, passing within a wing-tip of each another then spiralling upwards on a thermal. Their harsh calls filled the morning like a joyous song.

'Beautiful, aren't they?' It was Morias. The old *Seanachaidh* had climbed the tower behind Talisker. He was breathless after the effort and Talisker gestured to a wooden bench by the side of the inner wall.

Morias sank down thankfully. 'I've seen them fly many times,' he said. 'It always moves me.'

'Do they live in the city?' Talisker asked, still watching the display. The eagles were fishing the waters of the lake now, swooping down with breath-taking speed on their hapless prey, whose silver scales flashed in the sunlight.

'Don't you know?' Morias seemed mildly surprised by the question. 'Have you forgotten already who called you here?'

Talisker turned towards the old man with the answer on his lips. 'Mirranon? The White Eagle? They are . . . like that? Like Deme?'

'Sidhe.' Morias nodded. 'Do not speak the name of the White Eagle here. She is outcast from her kind. Watch them now, they are coming in.'

They landed to Talisker's left, each bird on one of the crenellations of the battlements. Then, as though with one thought, they spread their vast wings outward and upwards, and sent a keening call to the heavens. There was a bright silver flash, so intense that Talisker's eyes watered. When he looked back seconds later, nine Sidhe stood on the battlements, their silver hair snapping in the wind, their robes of grey brown and white feathers fluttering. With a lightness of step still suggestive of their recent flight they leaped off the battlements and began what seemed friendly banter in a strange guttural language while they straightened their robes. In the middle of the group stood the tallest, a male of stately bearing, somehow detached from the others although he spoke with them. He seemed to sense Talisker's scrutiny for he turned towards him. Their eyes met, and in that instant Talisker knew him as an enemy, although a smile lingered on the Sidhe's lips and he moved towards Talisker and Morias. He stopped before Morias and inclined his head respectfully. 'Greetings, *Seanachaidh*. It is a fine morning, is it not?' He sounded amused as though he and Morias shared some joke to which Talisker was not party.

Morias inclined his head gravely, with no trace of humour. 'Prince Makhpiyaluta. As usual the flight of the eagles brings me joy.'

Makhpiyaluta nodded in acknowledgement of the compliment, and looked enquiringly at Talisker.

'This is Duncan Talisker,' Morias announced flatly.

There was a second's pause as the Sidhe tried to hide his reaction but he had blanched as Morias said the name.

'Talisker?' he said.

'Yes,' said Morias coolly, 'he came for Samhain.' He was about to continue when Chaplin appeared in the stairway, followed closely by three warriors of the Thane's guard.

'Morias, we've been looking . . .'

'*Seanachaidh.*' The largest of the guards pushed past Chaplin. 'Thane Ferghus bids you attend on him with such healing herbs as you have with you. His daughter is very sick, sir . . .'

'Ulla?' Morias frowned. 'She has her own healing and can deal with her pain.'

'No, sir, it is Kyra.' The warrior was distressed. 'She won't wake up.'

Morias's eyes narrowed and a look of dismay crossed his features. He patted the soldier's huge biceps reassuringly. 'Lead on, Eion. We shall see what we can do for your lady.' He motioned absently to Talisker and Chaplin. 'You will come too, and meet the Thane.'

At the turn of the stair, Talisker looked back at the Sidhe. Most were still talking but Makhpiyaluta had taken the seat Morias had vacated. His scarlet cloak was bunched around him, trapping the morning breeze; his long fingers rested lightly on the fabric of his breeches and his head was tilted to one side in the manner of a huge bird, silver wisps of hair drifting in the breeze. He was as much an eagle now as before, and his blue eyes were fixed on Talisker.

*

Thane Ferghus was striding up and down the antechamber to Kyra's apartment, his anxiety at fever pitch. He had woken to the news that many of his subjects had not survived to celebrate Samhain, and the tales of horror he heard had chilled him to his bones. As if to confirm the ill-omens, Kyra, his golden one, had been pale and cold when her maid went to rouse her that morning. She was still breathing, but her sleep was unnatural. And there was the smell. It filled the bedchamber from corner to corner – although, could he bring himself to admit it, it was centred on the bed.

'Father, don't worry. I'm sure one of the *Seanachaidh* can help.' It was Ulla, who smiled nervously as best she could, which resulted in a poor contortion of her features. Her eyes radiated concern for her sister, but Ferghus could hardly look at her in case she saw his thoughts reflected in his eyes. Why Kyra? he had thought in his despair. Why my precious one? Now his thoughts shamed him and he stared morosely at the hem of Ulla's habitual brown dress.

'Go away, Ulla,' he said, his voice leaden. He did not look for her reaction, merely watched the movement of her skirt as she scuttled into the shadows at the corner of the room.

Shortly after this exchange Morias arrived with a small group of people. Two soldiers hastily crossed long spears across the entrance to Kyra's room and only Morias was admitted. Ferghus greeted him warmly as an old friend. When Ulla came forward from the shadows, Morias took her hands in his and kissed her cheek.

Talisker watched keenly from the doorway, his

questions about the *Seanachaidh*'s identity returning. He was sure now that Morias was the old tramp he'd met in Edinburgh, but that seemed irrelevant now. Here, he was shown such respect that it was obvious he was someone special. He remembered the moment of laughter they had shared on the bench outside the prison. What power must the old man possess that he could simply 'visit' Edinburgh when Deme had been forced to wait two hundred years in her dark prison?

'Checking me out,' Talisker muttered.

'There, did you see that?' Eion pointed towards the horizon. 'That movement.'

It was late afternoon and the westward shores of the loch were bathed in mellow autumn sunlight. In the middle distance, stretching as far and as wide as the eye could see, was the great forest of Or Coille. At first glance, the trees seemed impenetrable, impervious to the sunlight, a huge canopy of deep greens and ochre through which it now seemed incredible that thousands of people had travelled for the festival. Then, as the eye became attuned to the forest, breaks in the landscape were more noticeable: in placcs sharp grey splinters of rock and earthslides of the loamy brown soil created patches and clearings devoid of tree or bracken.

Talisker shielded his gaze and stared into the forest. 'I can't see anything,' he said. 'Just . . . No, wait.'

Across a clearing, slightly to the east of the fortress, something was moving. Talisker stared. It was difficult to judge because of the distance but the creature was about the size of a small horse. Another entered the clearing and another, further south, broke from the cover of the trees. All of the creatures were black and from this vantage-point, with the sun moving west, appeared as if in silhouette against the background. Something about their gait . . .

'*Dogs*?' Talisker's voice was quiet, incredulous.

As he spoke, more shadows appeared in the forest, moving silently with an air of purpose that was alien, as though a common thought controlled and bound their feral nature.

'Fuck.' It was Malky. The Highlander stood behind Talisker, also staring. It was the first time they had seen one another since Talisker had shown Mirranon's jewel the night before.

'Dogs, Malky.' Talisker still sounded disbelieving.

'Aye, black dogs, Duncan.' Malky spat over the battlements. 'Big basturts, aren't they?'

Talisker turned towards him and, as he did so, realised that all along the battlements warriors were staring out at the forest in horrified fascination. They stood in small groups of two or three but no one was speaking. Many of the younger soldiers looked pale with fright, but the elders looked on with grim resignation.

'What does it mean, Malky?' Talisker's voice had fallen to a hoarse whisper. As if in reply Malky nodded out towards the forest once more, where hundreds of dogs could be seen now. The hairs on Talisker's neck bristled as the menacing black wave moved relentlessly through the treeline toward Ruannoch Were.

'Warriors believe that black dogs are an ill omen, Duncan,' Malky said. 'The worst ye kin have, in fact. If ye see a black dog it means death. Each one claims a soul. Each one out there has someone's name oan it.'

Talisker's gaze tracked along the battlements again. The silence was so intense now that the sound of the waves breaking on the rocks below, usually calming, seemed urgent and nauseating.

'But who could've sent them, Malky? You wouldn't see this many by chance, would you?'

Malky tutted under his breath. 'Come ower here, Duncan.' He beckoned Talisker away from the battlements. 'Look, Ah've been asking around last night. Remember the Corrannyeid? The thing that killed the bear and Una's man?'

Talisker nodded.

'Aye, well, there's a whole army o' them oot there. Like in Morias's story. Seems they're growing in power – naebody seems tae know why, but thon Corvus is behind it.'

'But Morias said he had been imprisoned and, anyway, the story happened over two hundred years ago.' Even as he spoke, Talisker realised that two hundred years was but a short time to a god. 'He's powerless,' he ended lamely.

'Aye, but his sister Phyrr's no'. She's like a queen. She's in charge o' the Corrannyeid but Corvus directs it all through her. She sounds well wicked.'

Despite himself, Talisker almost laughed at the Highlander's description, but Malky's face was deadly serious and the atmosphere on the battlements remained one of stark fear.

Suddenly the silence was shattered by a sweet sound that echoed across the waters of the loch.

Makhpiyaluta, prince of the eagles, was perched on the edge of the battlements, his legs dangling over the side, oblivious to the height. He played a gold whistle no larger than his fingers, which moved across its length in an effortless dance. It broke the hypnotic spell cast by the black dogs and, as though under a new trance, many of the men drifted away from the edges of the walls.

'How's the lady Kyra?' Malky asked. 'Folk are saying she's under a kind o' spell.'

Talisker was distracted by the music, and took a moment to reply. 'Between you and me, Malky, she was. Morias managed to wake her, though. He's still with her but he's not happy. She looks like . . .' he glanced around '. . . well, like a zombie.'

'What's that, then?'

'Alive but . . .' As he looked into Malky's deathly white features Talisker was suddenly aware of what he had been about to say. 'Never mind. Anyway, they sent me and Eion to look at this and report back, so I'd better go and tell them. It doesn't look good.'

'Have ye seen yer man Chaplin?'

'Yeah.' Talisker sighed. 'He's with Morias. Do me a favour, Malky. Keep an eye on him. Watch my back.'

'That's why Ah'm here, Duncan.' They began to descend the steep stairs of the tower. Suddenly Malky chortled. 'Aye, I suppose you might be a wee bit preoccupied with a certain red-haired lady.' The Highlander slapped him on the shoulder.

Talisker wasn't used to male camaraderie. He knew that men spoke in jest of women in terms that seemed disloyal to him, and felt his cheeks colour. 'Yeah . . . well . . .'

They reached the bottom of the stairs and Malky looked at him closely. 'Ah'm happy for you, Duncan. She's a wee brammer.'

'She surely is, Malky.'

This time Talisker gained entrance without being challenged to the lady Kyra's bedchamber – perhaps because Eion was with him and the Thane had gone. Kyra was sitting up, looking petulant and frustrated. Talisker instinctively disliked her although he did not know why. Morias was beside her, his bony frame perched on the edge of the bed, talking quietly to her. Talisker caught a snatch of their conversation as they walked in.

'Remember, Kyra. It's important.'

Chaplin, Ulla and Kyra's maidservant hovered ineffectually around the bed.

'Eion.' Kyra held out her hand to her suitor.

His face was a picture of relief and he pushed past Talisker and Malky. As he reached the edge of the bed he knelt down, took her hand and kissed it. As he did so, his back stiffened as though he had been struck. Malky's hand dropped to his sword but Eion rose – unsteadily – to his feet. 'I am gladdened to see you are w-well, m' lady.' His voice was shaking and he looked at Morias as though for reassurance. The *Seanachaidh* frowned a warning at the young soldier.

'I – I must now report to your father. I will speak with you soon.' He turned sharply on his heel and marched from the room, pushing past Talisker and Malky with as much haste as the first time but now distress was written on his features and he looked close to tears.

'Sleep now,' Morias was saying to Kyra. 'It will be a

blessed sleep.' As though hypnotised, she did as she was told, her eyes closing immediately. Morias rose and beckoned the assembled group into the antechamber. The maid remained behind, fussing with Kyra's bedclothes.

'What's going on, Morias? What happened to Eion?'

Morias did not reply immediately but looked to Ulla and reached for her hand. 'I am sorry, Ulla, I fear she may be lost to us. Do you understand?'

Tears sprang to Ulla's eyes. 'I will watch with her, *Seanachaidh*,' she said, and hobbled back into the bedchamber.

'She's dying?' Chaplin asked, 'But, Morias, I watched you wake her – you said to the Thane—'

Morias cut him off impatiently. 'The Thane is a father first, Alessandro, and where there is life there must surely be hope – at least, so I thought, but now I know better.'

'What is it, Morias?' Talisker asked.

Morias stared into his eyes and held his gaze, unblinkingly. 'It is the reason you are here, Duncan. It is Corvus. Look.' From the folds of his grey plaid he produced a black feather. It was as long as the diagonal length of the plaid that had concealed it and the quill at its thickest was as broad as Morias's thumb. There was something else about it: it emanated the blackness of despair.

'A crow?' Malky asked.

'A raven,' Talisker replied.

'I found it in her bed, under the pillows,' Morias said wearily. 'She is dead. Corvus has been with her in her dreamstate and her soul is forfeit. When Eion touched and kissed her he smelt the taint of corruption on her skin.'

'So why has she come back?' asked Chaplin. 'Why did he let her return?'

'I see you have grasped the situation quickly, Alessandro – it is a strong instinct with you, probably because your father's people have much superstition. Yes, he could have kept her soul, made her remain with him between the worlds for his entertainment, but I fear he did not really desire her, beautiful though she . . . was. No, I think he sought to use her, to bring his physical being into this realm. He grows impatient with his sister's efforts on his behalf and longs for sensation once more. It was an experiment. Kyra was too weak a vessel and her mind snapped. I'm not sure why he is allowing her to cling on.'

Talisker glanced into the chamber where Kyra lay like a fairytale princess in a film he had once seen, her silken hair spread across the pillows catching the warmth of the sunlight that streamed in through the window. Her breathing was even, her face softened in sleep. Ulla sat in shadow, only her hand illuminated where she held her sister's. He thought briefly of Una and the warmth they had shared the night before. Perhaps Eion and Kyra had shared such a time together . . . perhaps only once. 'Poor kid,' he muttered.

'Indeed,' said Morias. 'Perhaps we should break the news to her father.'

'We are under attack,' Thane Ferghus announced grimly. 'Or, at least, we will be. An army is amassing on the shores of the loch and our best intelligence suggests they will attack at dawn. I have instructed the Sidhe to gather information about how the army intends to cross the water, but it seems to me that they are confident they can and we must work on that belief. We are assuming . . .' He glared around the room as though daring the assembled men to react. Then he sighed. 'We think it is an army such as has not been seen in Sutra for hundreds of years. We think it is the Corrannyeid.'

There was uproar. Ferghus raised his hands for silence but it was a few minutes before order was restored.

'What about the dogs?' someone called out. 'There's at least as many dogs as we have warriors.'

'Frightened of a dog, eh?' someone else replied.

There was a ripple of nervous laughter and everyone looked expectantly at Ferghus.

'I don't have all the answers,' he replied, 'but it's my guess that some of the Corrannyeid have taken that guise deliberately to . . . to play upon our superstitious beliefs. I have decided to evacuate the women and children from the city through the north passage,' this was met by grim nods by the warriors, 'so I suggest you take the next few hours to say your farewells. Those of you who are conscripts or have no families, report to your captains as soon as possible. That is all.'

'How is the lady Kyra?' a warrior called out. 'We heard . . .'

'The lady Kyra is recovering, thank the gods,' Ferghus answered.

The crowd began to disperse, and Morias walked forward to the front of the hall to speak with the Thane.

*

The maidservant had brought news of the Thane's announcement, without thought of Ulla's reaction. Ulla stared down at her sister, who had not stirred since Morias had commanded her to sleep. 'Did you hear, Kyra?' she whispered. 'They are evacuating the children. I must leave you for a while. Look, I have had Morna bring some herbs and flowers from my room – meadowsweet and lavender. They will ensure you are untroubled until my return.' She laid the rough bouquet across Kyra's chest and regretted it instantly, since it only heightened the impression that her sister was slipping away.

Ulla had never liked Kyra. She considered her spoilt and facile, too concerned with her next gown, and her beauty was superficial, but men adored her. The two sisters were worlds apart, yet Ulla would never have wished this darkness to consume Kyra because such evil was beyond her understanding. She paused in the doorway and glanced back once before hobbling off as fast as she could down the passageway.

It would have been a surprise to Kyra if she could have known where her sister was going. In all their lives she had never considered that any man might love the disfigured Ulla – 'Who could love *you*, Ulla?' she had taunted her. Yet Ulla had found a love that surpassed anything Kyra might have imagined in its quiet passion and strength.

Callum, a dark and serious man, was low in rank in the Thane's guard. When first he saw Ulla she had been half in darkness and he saw only the side of her face that was unscarred. He bowed and asked if she would walk with him in the gardens. Ulla's life was changed. First she spent half an hour cringing in her room, frightened of what the handsome young man would say when he saw her in the cold light of day. Then anger took over when she decided he was making fun of her for a wager. Therefore, she decided, she would give him a run for his money. She wore her best green gown, and when he arrived in the garden, she stood and moved slowly towards him in her lurching gait. He hurried forward and took her arm in a strong supporting grip, his glance never faltering as he looked at her, and they walked and talked all afternoon. Finally, she asked him, 'Callum, did you know that I was scarred? That I am called a drab when they think I cannot hear?'

In answer, he picked a large white rose from a nearby bush and gave it to her. 'What do you see, Lady Ulla?' he asked.

'Why it's beautiful,' she said. 'I believe no one has ever picked a rose for me before.'

'Could you be so unloved?' he said quietly. Taking her hand he turned it over. The rose was blighted with blackspot, its stem covered in greenfly. He turned her hand up again, 'I also see the rose.' He smiled. 'Here, I'll pick you a better one.'

'No,' she said firmly. 'I'll keep this.'

A year later Callum died in a riding accident while hunting boar with the Thane. Ulla mourned him deeply. She was carrying his child and she gave birth to their daughter in the sole company of her trusted maid. Now the child was three, dark and precious as her father, and she had been fostered from birth by an elderly couple who loved her well and lived within the shadow of the castle. Her name was Dom. Ulla visited often, but now she was coming to say goodbye for a long time. She hoped her daughter would not forget her.

She pushed open the door of the tiny casement and the only unequivocal love she had known, apart from Callum, rushed forward like a small bright firework and leapt into her arms. 'Mama! You're here!'

Darkness moved across the inner courtyard where the Sidhe eagles were based, and Makhpiyaluta stared into the flames of the fire he had lit, which flared and guttered in the breeze. He knew on the night before battle that men of the Sidhe and the Fine were the same: reflections on their lives came to them in different guises but all were coloured with melancholy or regret. Makhpiyaluta had elected to sleep outside until his watch in order to be alone with his thoughts. Apart from the distant sounds of drunken Fine, the night was still. The sky, an inky black, was studded with so many stars that the heavens were heavy with silver possibility. It was on nights such as this that Makhpiyaluta felt the weight of bitterness in his soul, when he remembered the laughter of Minosa.

Sometimes, as his eyes closed with the exhaustion engendered by the violence of his days, it seemed he felt her touch: a delicate hand on his shoulder or cheek, or the pressure of her lips against his chest. At times when he ached with spite and bitterness, a rage that remained undimmed by time, she mocked him still. He missed her.

The first time he had laid eyes upon her he knew that

she was the most beautiful woman he would ever see, and then she had been barely more than a girl of thirteen, still unable to give in to her totem and become a great eagle, which was the form of their tribe. That moment was fixed fast in his mind and, for all the blackness of anger that tainted his memory now, remained undiminished, a token she had left behind. She stood within the shadow of a great linden tree, the light and shadow moving across her features as though the strange depths of her duplicitous soul had been there all along for him to see, had he cared to look. Her eyes caught the light of the waters of the river upon whose banks she stood and Makhpiyaluta felt awkward and self-conscious under her stare. He tried to ignore her but wanted desperately to gaze openly at such beauty. Minosa had short-cropped hair, unusual in the women of the Sidhe, which framed her face, pointing wickedly inwards to her mouth. She wore red breeches, a sky-blue tunic and no jewellery.

'Min, come on, don't speak to him. He's weird.' Another girl had appeared, small and fat, already the image of her mother and grandmother. She pulled on Minosa's arm insistently. 'Come on . . .'

For the briefest moment, though, Minosa didn't move. It seemed her eyes bored into his soul. Makhpiyaluta had scowled down at the salmon he was gutting, hoping that the burning he felt in his cheeks was not visible to her. When he looked up, she had gone.

It was true that by choice, none of the others of Makhpiyaluta's age would speak with him. It was not that he was a prince of sorts but that there was something about his nature that set him apart: a kind of permanent melancholy pervaded him. His elders told him that the emptiness he felt was but a space for great wisdom and that when he was older he would lead his people among the Fine with courage. But Makhpiyaluta often wished for the easy laughter of his peers. He knew that Minosa would avoid him when she heard the tales they told of him.

But he was wrong. Minosa was intrigued by the silent youth and showed it in no uncertain manner. The following night she appeared in the darkness of Makhpiyaluta's room. He slept in the largest lodge but access was easy through the large windows, over which only a pelt was draped. The first he knew of her arrival was the sound of her soft breathing and before he could get up she was beside him, her perfume catching in his throat. There was no time to object even if he had wanted to: the feral quality of her smile was immediately arousing and frightening. She pressed her body against his and went to sleep. Makhpiyaluta lay for hours, tense with fear and excitement but eventually the even sounds of her sleeping lulled him into sleep also and the last thing he remembered was stroking her hair.

Minosa was no fool. In the morning, they were discovered before Makhpiyaluta was awake and their parents had them betrothed by midday. He was thrilled, exhilarated that she should have taken such a calculated risk; but Minosa saw what she wanted and made sure she got it. He remembered her radiant smile as the other girls of the village clustered around her when she told them of her betrothal. She smiled at him and the dark shadows of his spirit were lifted.

He loved her well for three glorious years, but killed her by his own hand when he found her in the arms of another. She died unrepentant, cursing him as the breath, which was also her spirit, left her body and showed its true colour. She reached out her hand towards the body of her lover whom Makhpiyaluta had also slain, and the last look she gave him was of defiance. In truth, remorse would not have saved her but perhaps it would have saved the other luckless women Makhpiyaluta had slain since.

He shifted his gaze from the fire to the stars. Deception, duplicity – no quarter was given for such things among the Sidhe. He had not been punished for killing Minosa and her lover, and the flame of righteous anger she had ignited within him replaced the warmth she had brought him with a cold, dark fire. Such women were not to be tolerated, did not deserve to share the earth and skies with the great and the good. She had never flown, cut down before achieving her eagle totem – *Rowwhapneer* – at the age of twenty, and Makhpiyaluta dealt mercilessly with other faithless wives, and wore their feathers in his hair. Consequently he was venerated by some and feared by many. He knew that he would never be loved again, but it mattered little now that he had seen Talisker, the man predicted to bring Braznnair back to the Sidhe. The fate of the Sidhe might be in his hands.

Talisker felt lost and useless. The day had passed in a blur of noise and fear, and the real battle was yet to come. After the Thane's announcement he had sought out Una, who was helping her aunt and cousins prepare for flight but Talisker was dismayed to learn that she herself was not going.

'You must go,' he insisted. 'It could be a bloodbath.'

'No,' she said. 'My skills with herbs will be needed here.' She shot Talisker a steely look as though daring him to argue.

'You're a brave woman, Una,' he said.

'No braver than any other warrior . . .' Her voice trailed off. 'Probably less so, Duncan, because I've seen what's coming.'

He moved towards her but she held up her hands to fend him off. 'Have you no work to do?' she asked sharply.

'Una?'

Her expression softened. 'Just go, Duncan,' she said. 'I will see you after . . .'

He took her hand and kissed it. 'You will,' he agreed.

Now, in the fading light of the evening on the battlements, Talisker was not so sure. He was a coward, he knew that. In prison he had earned a measure of respect from his fellow inmates and the warders and he had done what was necessary to survive – he fingered the thin white scar that ran from his left ear to his cheekbone – but he had never sought violence. It had always come to him. He still shuddered at the memory of Darragh's death, when his head flew from his neck beneath Malky's sword. At one second he had been alive – breathing, thinking, speaking – at the next a bloody corpse.

The night breeze was stiffening. The emblem of Ferghus snapped whip-like on the flagpole behind him. Across the waters, just visible in the gloom, were the dark outlines of the black dogs. Behind them, in the trees, who knew what was massing there?

'Talisker.'

He turned. Chaplin was standing at the top of the stairs holding two steaming flagons. 'Malky told me to bring you this,' he said gruffly. 'It's hot mead, I think. The Thane has sent it to every warrior.'

Talisker took one. Chaplin seemed awkward, at a loss for something to say. He hovered uncertainly by the stairwell then turned to go.

'Chaplin?' There was a long pause. 'Thanks.'

''S okay.'

'Look, we might die tomorrow. Can't we just put all this Chaplin-gets-his-man shit behind us?' Talisker asked mildly. 'After all, you're out of your jurisdiction here.'

'Is that what you think this is about? Me getting a collar? I did what I had to do, Talisker. I put you away. Now all I know is that you were out for a week and people were dead.'

'But that was in Edinburgh,' Talisker protested.

'Here, there, it makes no difference to what you are,' Chaplin sneered.

'A murderer. That's all you see, isn't it?'

'That's all there is to see.' Chaplin took a gulp of his mead.

'Look around you, Chaplin, for Chrissakes!' Talisker spat. 'This time tomorrow we'll all be murderers or we'll be dead.'

'Those . . . things don't count. People count. Watch your back.'

The wind was buffeting the flames of the torches,

which spluttered loudly, so Talisker almost didn't believe he had heard Chaplin's last words.

'What? What did you say? Come back, you bas—'

Chaplin had begun to descend the stairs but it seemed he had a change of heart because he turned, walked right up to Talisker and spoke straight into his face, his warm, honeyed breath blasting his cheeks. 'I'll tell you something, shall I? Something for you to ponder on your last night alive. I can't look at you without thinking of Diane. Pathetic, eh? That's why I hate you. The rest is just dressing. I didn't really care about the rest of them – I didn't know them. Doesn't say much for my integrity, eh?' He stepped back, overwhelmed by his confession and slightly unsteady on his feet. 'Diane,' he continued, 'she was mine . . .' He tried to swig from his flagon but it was empty.

'Chaplin,' Talisker said quietly. 'I didn't kill Diane. She died in an accident.'

Chaplin's face contorted into the scowl he always wore when confronting Talisker. 'Yes, you did – maybe not with your bare hands like you did the others, but you killed her.' He backed away towards the stairs. 'I can't look at you sometimes . . . and I don't care what Malky says, you killed those girls.'

'No, I didn't. Let it go, Chaplin.'

Chaplin seemed to consider this for a moment. 'I can't,' he said.

Talisker stared into his drink. 'Last time you were pissed, you tried to kill me,' he said softly. 'Are you going to try it again?'

'Hadn't thought about it.'

'And are you going to wear that raincoat inside-out

for ever? You still look like a copper.'

It started to rain, a fine grey sheet of mist that made the torches hiss but lacked enough force to put them out. When Talisker looked up from his drink again Chaplin had gone. As he stared out across the water he finished his mead, which was cooling fast. Chaplin's hatred shouldn't get to him the way it did, but it typified everything that had been wrong and hurtful about his previous existence. And Chaplin had brought it here to Sutra, where supposedly Talisker was special, a hero. If Chaplin came after him, under cover of the battle, he decided, he'd get more than he bargained for. With a curse, he threw the empty flagon out into the lake.

'Kyra? Can you hear me, my love?'

In the silence between sleep and wakefulness, life and death, Kyra was waiting for the sound of his voice. Around her the blackness of the void echoed with the voices of disembodied souls. A grief-stricken wail reverberated across the distance, followed by the laughter of a young child.

'Kyra?' The voice was closer this time, its sardonic, musical quality washing through the darkness.

Her blue lips moved to form the sound. 'Corvus? Is that you? I want you here. Please . . .'

There was silence once more. Unbearable. She wanted to move but could not. 'Please. Help me.'

'I want to help you, Kyra. I do. But I can't.'

'Why?'

'You have to let me in. I need to be near you – physically.'

'Do you mean . . . in the light?'

'Yes.'

'You won't hurt me any more?'

'I would never hurt you, Kyra. I was simply testing you. Look.'

Kyra opened her eyes and saw that she was whole once more. Her blood and rags were gone and a warm breeze played through the reaches of the void. Standing up, she twirled round as though dancing, the white cotton of her nightgown billowing, causing ripples of darkness to wash outwards. The warmth touched the bare flesh of her legs like quiet fingers that made their way up towards her taut belly. Remembering the seed that lay there she caressed it with both hands and her laughter rang out into the well of blackness. 'Corvus. You know I am carrying—'

'Yes.' The tone was short, impatient, and Kyra flinched as though she had been slapped. 'I mean, I am impatient to be near you – both. It will be a boy.'

She laughed again, an easy sound. 'What must I do, my lord?'

'Let me in, Kyra. Let me into the light . . .'

Ulla returned to Kyra's bedside. The *Seanachaidh* had warned her to be extra vigilant after dark when the powers of chaos were at their strongest and Corvus would have spent the day planning what to do with his young victim. Kyra lay as Ulla had left her: her face deathly white and bloated, her hands folded across her chest. The flowers and herbs were scattered on the floor as though her sister had sat up suddenly and thrown them from her. The meadowsweet glowed in the light of the torches, its fragrance filling the death-tainted room like a warming shadow. Ulla failed to notice the earth on her sister's feet.

The attack began before dawn.

# CHAPTER TEN

All night the warriors had speculated on the ability of the black dogs to swim – perhaps with demonic warriors on their backs. Or were their masters, the Corrannyeid, building rafts to float them across? At the first light of dawn, the dogs stood up silently and began to walk across the waters of the loch.

Malky woke Talisker by shaking his shoulder as cries of disbelief and curses filled the air. 'Come and look at this,' he said grimly.

They walked to the battlements, and saw that the first of the dogs had reached the jetty already and bounded effortlessly from the water, shaking its thick coat. The cool dawn light played on the black sheen of its massive flanks. More dogs followed, their huge muscular limbs scrabbling for purchase on the jetty, the spread of their paws a wide as a man's chest.

With a cry somewhere between a scream and a curse, one of the watchers hurled a large rock at the leading beast. It glanced off its head, and the great hound looked up to the battlements, curling back its jowls in a vicious snarl.

'Ye gods, it's marked my card.' The young warrior blanched. Talisker was surprised to recognise Conall.

A barrage of rocks followed the first but the dogs stood their ground. They seemed to be waiting for something and stared straight ahead at the walls of the city. The warriors subsided, mystified.

'Steady, lads . . .' Eion cautioned.

A movement from the far shore caught Talisker's eye. A woman was coming forward from among the trees. She wore light silver armour over a white shift and, as she stood next to the last black dog, Talisker saw that she was unusually tall. A few of the watching men spat and cursed as she appeared.

'Is that . . .?'

'Yes,' Eion said. 'She is the lady Phyrr, the Morrigan. We are looking at a legendary evil.'

A sudden chill blew across the water and it seemed to Talisker that his vision shifted and he saw her more closely. In the gale her black hair whipped around the sharp white lines of her face and her contemptuous blue eyes were fixed on him. She lifted the corners of her mouth in a tiny smile and nodded as though in salute.

Talisker blinked, and the vision regained its proper distance. There was a bright flash of silver as Phyrr appeared to draw her weapon, but then she threw her hands forward and the shape of a great black raven could be seen in the sky. At this signal, a cacophony erupted from within the forest as the Corrannyeid let out a chilling battle-cry and appeared from the tree-line. At that instant, the dogs sprang into action. Those in front of the great wooden gates of the city leaped forward, their sheer brute strength and weight of numbers crashing open the old damp wood and breaching the city's defences. The Corrannyeid crossed the loch also, two or three at a time, their dark shadowy forms leaving an oily taint on the water.

Talisker and Malky were grabbing their weapons when the first of the dogs gained a foothold on the battlements and the bloodshed began.

Ulla awoke to the distant sound of a battlehorn, shouts and cries. She stretched in her chair and began to rub her weaker leg, which was often stiff on waking. Her first thought was of Dom – how hard the farewell had been, when the little girl had clung to her and begged her to come too. She had been sorely tempted but knew that, as the daughter of the Thane, her leaving would be seen as an ill-omen by the warriors. She must do her duty and stay. Rising with a sigh, she opened the shutter of Kyra's chamber window. Below, a huge black dog was running across the Thane's gardens. With a shocked cry she slammed the shutter and turned to her sister's bed. 'Kyra!'

The bed was empty.

Talisker had never seen killing like this before. Nothing could prepare a man to become a warrior: the songs of glory, the rituals of weaponry came down to this madness. The sights, sounds, colours and smells of battle were vibrant and cruel, rushing in on his senses, threatening to overwhelm him. His legs trembled, and his grip on the sword he had named Talisker's Oath felt insubstantial. The first of the dogs had landed among his group and swept up a man in its jaws. It shook the screaming youth like a rag until his spine snapped. In his death throes the young man waved his sword chaotically, and unwittingly hacked off a kinsman's arm as the dog crashed among the group of warriors, using his victim as a weapon. As more of the beasts crowded into the confined space of the battlements, men were trampled and crushed beneath their paws.

Dropping his first prey, the lead dog leaped forward and grabbed for another warrior with its bloody maw. The man shrieked, jumped backwards and was impaled through the ribcage on the sword of the man behind. His scream was cut dramatically short as the dog's jaws enclosed his upper chest and throat. Now level with the beast's shoulder, Talisker was jostled forward by the fight behind him. With a yell, he thrust his sword deep into the dog. Even above the bedlam of battle, he heard the sound of flesh slicing. Gasping for air he tried frantically to withdraw his weapon but it was embedded in the muscle and his grip slid from the hilt. The dog turned its head towards him; it was bleeding from many superficial wounds and its right ear was hanging by a thread of cartilage. Baring its fangs with a deep growl, it snapped at Talisker.

'Get back! Get back, you eejits!' Malky's voice came from the stairwell just as Talisker was knocked off his feet by the dog behind him, which backed towards its comrade. Its paw landed heavily on Talisker's arm, which snapped like matchwood. Talisker screamed.

As though in answer, a great eagle gave a harsh call and plunged into a steep dive towards the dog, silver-tipped talons unsheathed. The arc of the dive was perfect, and as the black dog looked upwards towards it, the golden bird wrenched its eyes from their sockets as it snatched minnows from the loch. Someone grabbed Talisker by his good arm and hauled him clear as the beast howled and thrashed about blindly.

Talisker stumbled forward to where Malky stood. The Highlander had collected an armful of long spears or lances and was handing them out to the warriors. 'You all right, Duncan?' he yelled.

Talisker nodded. Surprisingly, his arm was numb, but he knew the pain would come later. His gaze swept along the battlements: he could see about ten dogs, seven of which had been blinded by the Sidhe eagles. It made little difference: the Corrannyeid were swarming over the battlements behind them, their dark outlines assuming man-like shapes. Below, all defence of the quay had been abandoned and a pitched battle was taking place within the market-square. The air was rent by the inhuman screams of the Corrannyeid's victims and the battle intensified as the warriors turned their swords in mercy against their kinsmen.

Suddenly the movement of a Corrannyeid as it stood on the battlements caught Talisker's gaze. Its outline was shifting in shapes unlike the others. For a moment, he was puzzled but then he realised what it was. 'No!' he shrieked in horror. Above the Corrannyeid figure an eagle had begun to dive, unaware that it could not touch the figure of its enemy. It was a fatal error.

'Pull up! Pull up!' Talisker yelled. But it was already too late. As the two creatures made contact, the darkness of the Corrannyeid engulfed the feathers of the noble bird. As its prey vanished it seemed confused and it rose from its dive to circle for another. It had not gone far when its wings buckled and sinuous black tentacles erupted from its chest. It gave a shriek of distress, and Talisker moaned aloud, furious at his impotence. But Malky had seen the death-throes of the mighty eagle and, with one swift motion, he drew a long silver blade from his sock and threw it with deadly accuracy. The eagle was dead as it hit the water.

Talisker was filled with rage. He snatched a lance from Malky and ran back towards the dog in whose shoulder his sword was embedded. His ears filled with a buzzing sound and the thump of his heartbeat was like a war drum. There would be no room to throw the lance, since the creature was surrounded by men trying to keep it at bay. A few had grabbed long lances and were jabbing at it.

'Get out of the way!' Talisker bellowed. He ran the last few steps and used the momentum to thrust the lance forward. It rammed home above the dog's ribcage, piercing it to the heart. The creature fell heavily to the ground and died, trapping a warrior beneath its bulk. Talisker rushed forward, gripped his sword two-handed and pulled it free. As he did so the shadow of a Corrannyeid moved to his left, and with one clean motion, he spun and clove the creature in two. A ragged cheer went up from those who saw this, but Talisker did not hear. A red rain filled his vision as the anger and hatred that fuelled the creatures of the Corrannyeid seeped into him; his empathic soul helpless to resist his deluge. His ferocity grew with each kill as he hacked, tore and shredded. Soon he was coated in their blood and mire, a red slavering berserker. Above the sound of the battle, he could hear himself screaming.

Ulla had searched everywhere that Kyra could be expected to be, and now she wandered despondently through the deserted kitchens in the vain hope that her sister had simply woken up hungry. Most of the servants had left the castle the night before but a fire still burned in the huge open grate, and Ulla rested beside it for a time: her leg was bad this morning and she wished she could go back to bed. Then she heard a noise from the end of the corridor – quick light footsteps, and what sounded like someone humming under their breath.

'Kyra?'

She went to the doorway and looked out. The passageway was in darkness but for a single torch at the far end. This was the route that had been used by the evacuees, and a few scattered possessions lay where their owners had dropped them in the crush the night before: clothes, a couple of shoes, a mirror which lay smashed on the ground. It made a sad, eerie sight. The hairs at the nape of Ulla's neck bristled. She told herself it was because of the cold but she knew it had more to do with the desolation around her. The entrance to the west tunnel was not far away and suddenly she became convinced that that was where her sister was heading.

'Kyra?' she called. 'Are you there?' The question resonated in the empty space. Ulla picked her way through the debris. Half-way along she stopped as the dull gleam of metal caught her eye. It was a roughly made dagger, of the kind men used when feasting. She fingered the blade almost absently and put it carefully into her pocket.

A hundred yards further down, the corridor sloped quite steeply and narrowed. Ulla slowed as her limp became even more of an impediment, and she held out her hand to the right wall to steady herself. As her descent became steeper it slipped against the damp surface of the stones and she realised she was already beneath the level of the loch. The air was colder and she could hear water trickling. A brown rat skittered past her feet but Ulla did not flinch as her sister would. She rather liked the businesslike behaviour of the quick, intelligent creatures.

'What's going on then, Ratty?' she said. Her voice was uneven as she was breathing heavily, so she rested against the wall. Dom would have passed this way the night before, and Ulla peered into the darkness, hoping that the little girl had not been too afraid. Perhaps when the passageways were full of people they would not have seemed so awful, and all Dom's friends would have been going too. Then she heard a soft sound from up ahead. It came again. Kyra! She was singing. Ulla could just recognise the tune – they had sung it together as girls for their father. '. . . *and give me joy, you sweet brown bird, and I will give you flight . . .*' Gathering the folds of her skirts she moved on.

Outside, in the streets and market-place of Ruannoch Were the battle raged on. The disorganised hordes of Corrannyeid slew all in their path, four main groups fighting around the west side of the city, while skirmishes happened as dogs and Corrannyeid broke away in pursuit of some unfortunate prey. Among the chaos Phyrr walked silently as a dark shadow, her calm agile gait somehow distancing her from the frenzy. She killed three times with an air of detachment. The third man encountered her in a narrow alleyway. He was a handsome youth, his features contorted by the rage of battle. He rushed forward, his bloodied claymore raised to strike her down. Phyrr stood very still, her face betraying nothing, and held the gaze of her attacker. His momentum carried him forward, and as he reached her, he thrust forward his tarn to ensure that his chest was protected. In the same instant he slashed with his sword, but the lady Phyrr was gone: she had side-stepped him and her dagger was already through his ribcage and in his heart. As he fell to the cobbles, his face showed disbelief.

Phyrr bent over her victim, and noticed that he was deliciously handsome. 'War makes men so very clumsy,' she muttered. As she withdrew her weapon she dipped a forefinger in the flow of dark arterial blood and touched it to her tongue.

A harsh cry came from the eaves of the building next to her. She looked up. 'Quiet, Sluagh,' she fumed. She looked back at the lifeless body. 'Maybe later, dear heart,' she grinned. 'I've got someone to find.'

She moved on through the streets, clinging to the shadows until she came to the market-square. There she found him.

Deep within his soul Talisker knew he was doomed. The tiny rational voice inside him told him he was failing, that soon he would be a victim of the Corrannyeid. But still he roared and screamed and hacked. He blinked as a stream of blood from his temple stung his eyes but had no time to wipe it away. Above the noise of men dying, he could hear the eagles cry, he could hear the water, his senses stretched out around him, hearing everything in those last seconds . . .

'Tae me, Duncan! Tae me!'

The cry came from behind him. Malky was at his back once more, cursing his roundest curses. 'D'ye like that, ye wee basturt? Here's some mair! Talisker? Kin ye hear me? Kin ye hear me, man? Ah'm here at yer back. Walk backwards. Slowly. We kin reach – Jesus Christ!'

Talisker saw Phyrr enter the square at the same time as Malky did. She had three Corrannyeid with her, their misshapen bulk shifting uneasily in the strong light of the new morning. They were the biggest and ugliest he had seen yet, their dark brown legs and splayed feet the only part of them that held to their form. The mass of their bodies moved and writhed, tendrils of tube-like gristle dancing from the pitted surface of their skin; their heads, small against the great size but moving like the rest of them, formed horns, teeth, skulls and tongues that lapped obscenely against their foam-flecked mouths.

Moving forward, Talisker dispatched a Corrannyeid to his right, slashing the legs from beneath it with a wide-arcing swing then stabbing to the head with a short-sword he had acquired from a dead soldier. It was dangerous to move in so close, and with its dying movement the Corrannyeid snaked out a tendril-like limb and grabbed for Talisker's leg. Cursing, he hacked downwards, narrowly missing his own calf. When he raised his head again Phyrr stood a short distance away. He took a step towards her, his footsteps suddenly leaden, his sword and dagger slick against the wetness of his palms.

'Talisker! No!' Malky was screaming. 'Run man! Ye canny—'

*

Ulla was almost at the end of the passageway. Ahead, the torch her sister carried flickered. 'Kyra?' she whispered hoarsely. 'Kyra, are you—' She stopped. She had heard something that chilled her more surely than the darkness: the sound of a wooden bar being drawn back. She knew what it was: the chamber ahead of her contained the mouth of the tunnel beneath the loch, the escape route through which Dom and all the other children had passed, which had been sealed behind them.

'Kyra. No . . .' She groaned, as her stomach clenched. A scream echoed through the corridor and Ulla drew back against the wall. She was mostly hidden by a wooden support as the first of the Corrannyeid came into view, their dark shapes racing through the shadows like a vicious poison. The fastest runners were to the fore, carrying long spears from which dark red-stained fabric hung. At first, Ulla could not distinguish what was atop the weapons but then an absurd familiarity of movement – a vivacious bounce made bright with red ribbons – brought home to her what the trophies were. She let out a scream that came from the darkest corners of her soul and with it all brightness left her life for ever.

'Dom . . .oh, Dom . . .'

She was pushed aside by the first of the runners, who simply locked his arm outwards and shoved her against the wall. She flew backwards, hitting her head and mercifully was fighting unconsciousness when the banner that held the head of her child went swiftly past her. A drop of blood escaped it and landed on her cheek like an unspoken farewell kiss. The army swarmed forward into the very heart of the city.

Phyrr was annoyed with herself. She had watched contemptuously as Talisker started towards her, aware that he was exhausted. He carried a short-sword and a dagger but his stance, even now, was low and well balanced. His eyes were fixed on her face but her gaze flickered behind him to assess the danger to her from his companion who was dispatching one of her brother's minions.

Then, as Talisker reached her, something changed, something indefinable in his bearing and the way he carried his sword. From somewhere, while she had stood arrogantly and watched his approach, the man had found one final reserve of energy. The cord-like veins that knotted across his forearms twitched as a new wave of adrenaline washed through him. Phyrr's eyes widened and Talisker grinned. With no warning he aimed a blow with his sword, a clumsy hacking arc that Phyrr parried with little effort. As he lumbered forward with his dagger she was already behind him. Before she could strike he whirled round, knocked down her sword, then kicked out with his right leg and brought her feet from under her. She fell hard, which knocked the breath from her, and looked up to see the bright arc of his sword.

'Duncan! Look out!'

Talisker turned swiftly at Malky's shout as a Corrannyeid moved in for the kill. Phyrr scrambled to her feet but did not engage Talisker; even she would be prey to the Corrannyeid if she accidentally touched one. She crouched low, waiting her moment and wondering at her opponent. She had sensed no hesitation in him even though he faced a woman. Something warm flared in her belly. She would enjoy the kill this time.

The Corrannyeid were engaging scattered groups of warriors around the palace. Ferghus and a small band of his bodyguard were faring well, the older, more seasoned fighters learning with each engagement the strengths and weaknesses of their foe. It was the younger men in whom recklessness proved fatal. Ferghus watched more Corrannyeid come through the main doorway out into the street. 'The tunnel has been breached,' he yelled. 'Eion, Angus, you there, follow me.'

Chaplin was in the small group that clustered around the Thane, swords turned outwards to protect his mighty frame. He had avoided much of the fighting so far, although not deliberately – Chaplin was no coward – but had stopped frequently to help the wounded. He had made several trips to the north tower where a makeshift hospital had been thrown together. He had seen Talisker's lady Una there, her apron drenched in the blood of the dying but her smile a bright beacon of reassurance. Few had made it to the hospital; those who had, had been either caught by the dogs or injured in the crush of battle.

Now, Chaplin cursed as he raced along behind the Thane, who was cursing enough for the whole army. Ferghus appeared to take each death personally and moved through his own chambers bright with rage. He bellowed and hacked at any Corrannyeid he saw – engaging the enemy when he could have passed by –

joining small skirmishes with vicious glee, calling out to his men, never forgetting who they were even in the heat of battle. When one young man went down to a Corrannyeid Ferghus decapitated the creature with his axe, yelling, 'This for Liam's father!' Tears of rage streamed down his cheeks to mingle with the blood of the fallen. He inspired all who saw him fight, and Chaplin was swept along by the sheer force of his fury. On the way to the tunnel Ferghus, Chaplin, Eion and three others reached the kitchens, racing forward for the door to the passageway. From the corner of his eye Chaplin noticed a raven, sitting on the lintel above the vast hearth. He registered it as the man in front of him stopped running and they all came to a halt in the middle of the room. Some instinct made Chaplin turn around just in time to see the great oak doors to the kitchen slam shut behind them. From the four corners of the room stepped the Corrannyeid, and instinctively, Chaplin, Eion, and the others turned their swords outwards to form a circle around the Thane, who growled at the advancing shadow-forms, 'I'll not die like a dog in my own kitchens, damn it.'

'There's no way out of this, sir,' Eion panted, crouching low, readying his sword. 'I'll see you in paradise.'

The moment seemed to stretch out endlessly. It seemed the Corrannyeid were in no hurry, for they came forward in a slow lurching motion, stopping just outside the reach of the warriors' swords. Chaplin had the uneasy feeling that they were savouring the moment, relishing the terror of their opponents.

'What are they waiting for?' Eion hissed, his voice dropping to a hoarse whisper.

As if in answer, Chaplin's eyes were drawn to the raven. 'The bird.' He spoke as quietly as he dared. 'Get the bird.'

For a second, no one moved, then a flash of silver flew across the room. Ferghus had thrown a dagger. The raven took off the instant the dagger left the Thane's fingers but, as the weapon thudded into the wall, a black feather from the tip of its wing was pinned there. The bird screamed a harsh call as it flew towards the doors, which crashed open before it, and the Corrannyeid surrounding the group disappeared.

'Get it!' Ferghus bellowed. 'Get that cursed thing!'

Two men bolted after the raven as Ferghus turned his attention back to the passageway. Chaplin and Eion walked slowly towards the fireplace, and Eion removed the dagger and the feather.

'It's a real bird,' Chaplin mused. 'The feather's the proper size, not like the one Morias found under—' he stopped.

'It's all right,' Eion said briefly, 'the *Seanachaidh* has told me about the lady Kyra. I am mourning her although it seems she still lives. I shall remember her as she was.' He glanced towards Ferghus, who was sifting through some of the refugees' bits and pieces. 'It is beyond tolerance,' he said quietly. He looked so pained and spoke with such dignity that Chaplin simply nodded, thinking of Diane.

'Are you two coming, then?' Ferghus demanded.

It was tempting to run while he still had some energy left. Talisker had given ground to Phyrr and stood with his back against the wall of the stable block. If she had wanted to she could have killed him by now but twice she had given quarter when he would have died. She had just laughed, a short sound like a vixen's bark. She was enjoying herself. Her blue gaze was as draining as the sharp efficient blows she dealt with her sword. She carried a dagger also and Talisker was aware that she used this for the kill.

'Come away, you wee beauty.' Suddenly Malky appeared beside Phyrr, blocking the blow she had aimed for Talisker's arm.

She turned on Malky, eyes bright with rage. 'You will die for your insolence,' she said, without inflection.

With no further warning she pressed her attack and he was driven back. 'Canny kill me, hen,' he grinned horribly showing his white gums. 'Ah'm deid already. Ow!'

'You still bleed, though, sir.'

Talisker dropped his sword and dagger. Clutching the top of his arm he staggered into the stable groaning quietly. He felt as though he was going to die. Blood streamed from cuts and wounds he had hardly noticed before; now they ached and throbbed. He had a large gash at the top of his thigh, which was bleeding profusely, his right eye had puffed up and turned purple, his sword arm was a tapestry of fine cuts from Phyrr's sword and his left arm was broken; he was certain he had also cracked a rib. Pitching forward on to the sweet-smelling straw, he lay with his eyes open, his mind empty.

Ulla had been unconscious for some time and when she woke it was to a sharp wave of anger. There was no blessed moment of forgetfulness, the image was right there: her daughter's head on a pike.

'Kyra. You did this.' Her lips moved before she knew what she was saying, before her crumpled body had time to shift from its position on the floor. She raised herself up, holding on to the beam. 'Sister!' she yelled. 'Kyra!'

She ran as best she could the rest of the way to the tunnel entrance, the dagger in her hand glinting in the light of the torches. As she entered the chamber she saw her sister immediately. Kyra was trapped behind the heavy oak door, which had been sealed the night before. She had been pushed aside in the same way as Ulla had been, and the door had crushed her against the wall, breaking most of the bones in her body and her spine; she was pinned at a seemingly impossible angle, her body skewed to one side. She was still alive, though. She turned her head as Ulla came through the door, and there was a faint glimmer of reaction in her eyes.

'Corvus? When are you coming, my love?' Her voice was thin, pathetic, and a thread of blood trickled from her mouth.

'Kyra,' Ulla hissed through her teeth. She pulled back the door and Kyra's broken frame crashed to the ground, like a puppet whose strings had been cut. Ulla felt no pity for her sister: she herself had attracted too much and knew it to be cheap emotion. She kicked her sister on to her back, ignoring the faint incoherent cry of pain, raised her dagger and plunged it into Kyra's chest, killing her instantly. She stabbed her again and again in a frenzy of grief and rage.

*

*She stops. She is on her knees now. On the floor next to her lies her sister, Kyra; Kyra the golden one. She is not golden now. She is red.*

*'Red,' Ulla says, her tone sullen, emotionless.*

*Kyra's famous gold hair is a crimson sunset as it soaks up the blood. In death – real death – her face is quite, quite beautiful. Ulla starts to sing: ' "And give me joy, you bright brown bird, and I will give you flight." Come, sister, why don't you sing with me?'*

*Hearing a noise behind her she turns. It is the Thane. 'Father.' Her eyes fill with tears. 'There's so much blood, Father. She won't sing.'*

*'Ulla? Oh, gods, take my eyes. What have you done?' His gaze flickers towards the mouth of the tunnel. 'You have betrayed us all.'*

*'No, Father. It was Kyra. She—'*

*The Thane will hear no more. Drawing his sword he rushes forward screaming his war-cry as though he faces an army rather than one frightened young woman. Realising his intent, Eion and Chaplin yell and try to tackle Ferghus to the ground. They fail.*

She was in the stable now. He could hear her breathe. Pushing himself backwards into the straw, Talisker wondered what had happened to Malky. He held his breath – there was no fight left in him.

'Talisker?' Her voice was tinged with mocking laughter. 'I know you're here. Come now, let's finish this, shall we?' She turned to the entrance of the empty stall in which Talisker lay prostrate against a heap of straw. The tiniest part of his soul that was not preoccupied with dying had to admire Phyrr. Only the faintest flush of colour in her cheeks belied that they had been in combat for the best part of an hour. Her black hair had fallen across her face and her gaze was like sapphire in obsidian. There was no pause, simply a feral grin of triumph and the instant kiss of her sword. Then blackness.

The grief in the tunnel was all-pervasive. No one spoke. Thane Ferghus knelt by the bodies of his daughters and wept. After some time he reached forward and pushed aside Ulla's lifeless form, reaching for Kyra.

Chaplin frowned: it seemed obvious to him that Ulla had only just killed her sister when they arrived in the chamber and had not been the one to open the gateway.

Eion, who knew more of the relationship between the Thane and his daughters, also felt uneasy. Ulla had been a gentle soul all her days and it was difficult to see what could have driven her to this. She hadn't deserved such treatment.

Without exchanging a word, the two men stepped forward to arrange Ulla's body. As they did so, Chaplin felt quietly for a pulse and stifled a gasp of surprise. His eyes widened and he nodded silently to Eion in case Ulla's father decided to finish the job. Eion looked back to where the Thane was crouched over Kyra then moved over beside him, signalling to Chaplin behind his back. 'Sir – Ferghus, she is at peace now. Look at her face.'

It was true. Kyra's features had returned to their normal beautiful state. It was the face Eion had loved dearly, the face of the girl he had danced with on Samhain. He would remember that smile always. As the two men gazed wordlessly at the bloodied form, Chaplin scooped up Ulla's body and walked quietly to the door, waiting for an explosion of rage from her father. Nothing happened. Ferghus didn't glance away from his favourite daughter. Chaplin could not know that Ulla had lived with his indifference all her life: to him it seemed worse somehow than the Thane's anger.

Watching through the eyes of Sluagh, Corvus was exultant when Phyrr killed Talisker. In the cold reaches of the tower, Corvus's body lay unmoving on the narrow space of his bed, as still as the death he had bestowed that day on so many. His eyes were closed but he saw the sharp visions of the raven. 'Did you find it, Phyrr? Does he have it?'

'No.' Phyrr turned towards the raven, her face wearing the stark expression of the battle-weary. 'It's gone. He must have hidden it somewhere. What does it matter? Without him the prophecy is broken. You will be free.'

Corvus frowned at his sister's apparent lack of enthusiasm. Perhaps some recreation would cheer her. 'You may do what you will with the body,' he ventured. He was aware of Phyrr's strange predilection and found it mildly amusing.

'No.' Her voice was strained. 'Leave him. He died a good death although the end was a touch inglorious. Just get me away from here. I've had enough.'

'Very well, sister.'

The battle for Ruannoch Were ended. Without warning, the Corrannyeid vanished, leaving only their dead and a sickening smell behind them. The city was burning and fewer than two hundred of the three thousand warriors remained alive while only four of the nine great Sidhe eagles survived. In the stable block lay the body of a man who was known to few in the city, an innocent man, who had never killed until that day. In the twilight, a dark pall of smoke drifted across the loch, and the sparking of the flames was the only sound to be heard.

# CHAPTER ELEVEN

*'One o'clock . . . Two o'clock . . . Three o'clock . . .' a child-like voice sang. In the dark, white motes danced across the void. 'My mum's coming . . .'*

*'Did ye see him? Did ye see him fight? He's no goin' tae wake up, is he?'*

*'Duncan. I know you can hear me . . .'*

The voices, both heard and remembered, clamoured in the darkness, but Talisker was powerless to respond. A spark of his unconscious mind could feel the dying of his nerves and cells like a thousand tiny supernovas exploding into oblivion. He watched the death of his body as if from a great distance but he knew that his vantage-point was merely a trick of his brain. The last starburst would come and then the silence would be absolute.

Singing. It was a strange song. The voice was old and shaky, the words meaningless, and yet it was a sound unlike any Talisker had heard. It was the sound of another soul making contact. The song reached into this dark space and touched him.

*'That's why I hate you . . . bottom line . . .'*

*'Mirranon?'*

*'Please wake up, Duncan. Can you feel me touching your hand? It's so cold.'*

He wanted to wake up. He felt that now. A small

certainty that danced like the dandelion seeds. He wanted to . . .

Morias shook his head wearily at the small group of people who clustered around Talisker's bed. 'I don't think it's possible.' He sighed. 'His physical wounds are so severe that his mind is simply giving up.'

'No,' Malky said, adamantly. 'Duncan widnae dae that. He widnae jist gie in.'

'Yes, he would,' Chaplin replied. 'You haven't known him long, Malky. He was in prison for fifteen years. His mind won't see it as giving up exactly, just accepting, waiting. Biding his time.'

'That'd suit you though, eh?' Malky snarled. 'You hated him.' The Highlander looked more than ever like a walking corpse. The tiredness of battle and a kind of numb disbelief wrapped him in an invisible shroud. The impending death of Talisker, his only contact with the world of the living, frightened and saddened him: something deep within Malky's warrior soul knew that he would follow his friend into the darkness. He already felt detached from what was happening around him and, although he told himself he was simply weary to his bones, his unease persisted.

'You're right, Malky.' Chaplin's voice carried to him as though from a great distance. 'I don't like him. But I think there has been enough dying, don't you?'

'Enough dying . . . Aye . . .' Malky repeated.

'Malcolm, I think you should rest.' The voice was that of the Sidhe Prince Makhpiyaluta.

'No,' Malky protested.

'Please.' Makhpiyaluta's voice was quiet and

persuasive. 'We' – he indicated Morias and himself – 'think we understand how you must feel. Your spirit is reaching out, like Morias's song, into the void. But you need your strength, Malcolm. You cannot lend what you do not possess.'

What Makhpiyaluta had said made sense to Malky. 'You will wake me, though, if there's any change?'

'Of course.' While he spoke Makhpiyaluta had walked Malky to another bed in the makeshift ward, where he lay down and slept.

Those around Talisker's bed remained silent. Only Morias and Makhpiyaluta knew that the Prince had spoken the truth to Malky. It was possible that the Highlander's strength could help his friend but neither knew how. It was merely a shared intuition. Una, Chaplin and the Thane also kept vigil by the dying man, deep in thought and sorrow.

Finally, Morias broke the silence. 'This cannot be allowed to happen or the prophecy will be broken. Don't pretend you do not know what I'm talking about, Makhpiyaluta. I must ask you to put aside your personal feelings for the time being. Allowing Corvus his freedom cannot be in the interests of the Sidhe or the Fine.'

'What you call my "personal feelings", Morias, are the shared beliefs of my generations of people. Were I a less reasonable being, such as my grandfather Narragansett, I would have slain Talisker ere he had a chance in battle. But beware, as civilised we Sidhe may be now, the voices of our ancestors are strong. You know what I am, I speak for the Council of Tema. You know what that means.'

'What *does* it mean? Murder? Can the Sidhe collective soul benefit from the evil of Corvus as the honeysuckle does from the tree which it strangles as it grows? Would you see the Fine crushed, Makhpiyaluta?'

'Enough!' The Prince seemed confused. 'I do not know.'

'Know this. Your fears are well founded. Talisker carries the gem of Mirranon, the White Eagle. What do you say?'

Makhpiyaluta looked astonished and appalled. 'Braznnair is here? Where is it?'

Morias gave a self-mocking laugh. 'In truth, Makhpiyaluta, I do not know where he has put it. But I know he had it two nights ago.'

'What's going on?' Una looked suspicious. 'Why do you want Talisker's gem?'

'Do you know where it is, lady?' Makhpiyaluta's tone was solicitous, heightening Una's feelings of distrust.

'I might,' she said simply. 'But perhaps you should tell me first why you want it. I would like to know if it can help Duncan in any way.'

'This is outrageous!' Makhpiyaluta spluttered. 'Who are you to make demands of the Sidhe? Just give it to me – us.'

There was a low rumble as Thane Ferghus stood up, his hand dropping to the hilt of his sword. 'She is a woman of my clan, Makhpiyaluta, of which precious few survive. I will not allow you to address her so. Bloody birds!' The Thane seemed confused but his anger was real enough.

'Please, I meant no offence.' Makhpiyaluta bowed.

Morias stepped between the Prince and the Thane. 'Lady Una, it is true that perhaps the Sidhe would not have Talisker's best interests at heart. His coming was foretold long ago but the interpretation of prophecy means different things for the Fine and the Sidhe. However, I give you my word and Makhpiyaluta will give you his – won't you, Makhpiyaluta? – that no harm shall come to Talisker if you give us the gem.'

'What do you think, Alessandro?' she asked.

Chaplin shrugged. 'I don't understand much of this,' he said, 'but you can trust Morias.' He eyed Makhpiyaluta as he said this, his meaning clear to all, then reached into his pocket and withdrew the gem.

The Sidhe Prince gasped as the rough facets of the stone caught the daylight. 'How do we know it is the real thing?' he said. 'Can I hold it?'

'No, you can't. And in answer to your first question, we know as much as you do. Talisker found it in . . .?' Chaplin looked towards Morias questioningly.

The *Seanachaidh* inclined his head. 'He found it in a park, in our world, the day after he dreamed of Mirranon.'

'*Your* world?'

'Makhpiyaluta, Talisker and Chaplin come from the same world as the Nameless Clan of legend. They were summoned by the White Eagle.'

Una was stunned by this news. 'He is not from this world, then?' she whispered, gazing down at Talisker's battered form.

'What of Malcolm? Where does he come from?' the Thane enquired. 'He fights like a warrior of our world. Ha, he curses like one too!'

Everyone smiled at this, but Morias sighed and shook his head. 'It's difficult to explain. I'm not sure why he was sent to us but he comes from an earlier time than Talisker and Chaplin.'

Makhpiyaluta frowned. 'But the prophecy says only one . . .'

'Prophecy is often uncertain, I find,' Morias mused, 'but let us see if we can give this one a helping hand.' He took the gem from Chaplin. 'Makhpiyaluta and I will need to be undisturbed for this,' he said. 'Perhaps you should all get some rest and food. There is much to consider.'

'Aye, a city to rebuild and mourning to be done,' the Thane agreed. With that Chaplin, Una and he left the hall.

Makhpiyaluta watched them go. 'I hear Ferghus lost both his daughters in the fighting,' he remarked. 'They say he killed the lady Ulla himself. What happened, *Seanachaidh*?'

'They say?' Morias raised his shaggy brows. 'How unlike a Sidhe to speculate on the affairs of the Fine, Makhpiyaluta.'

'Are you mocking me?'

'It was merely a comment on changing times. We will have need of our allies, Prince. Soon, the Sidhe must decide for whom they are – themselves only or the Fine too. Come, we have work to do.' Morias held out his gnarled hand, which contained the stone. Makhpiyaluta hesitated. 'Would you watch him die, then realise you had made the wrong decision?' Morias said quietly, but with a note of warning.

Makhpiyaluta laughed nervously. 'Have I your

permission to kill him later if I'm wrong?'

'I think not.' Morias smiled. 'Come now, we are friends, let us enjoy working a little elemental magic together, eh?'

'For now, *Seanachaidh*, but only because I like you.'

Morias inclined his head graciously and Makhpiyaluta reached out and placed his hand over the stone.

Talisker is weeping. At least, his mind is weeping, still feeling the dying of his flesh. Lost to warmth and hope. In the void the voices have stopped, the singing has ceased. He wishes it would start again.

*Help me.*

The voice of his conscious mind is younger than the age of his fading life. It is the voice of a young man on his first day in prison, unable to believe that this could happen to him; a nineteen-year-old who has been beaten to within an inch of his life by prisoners who were capable of the things they said he had done. It is the voice of a young man who has been kicked and punched, spat up on and raped. He is not new to the wasteland of the void but aware that this time there is no going back. Weeping silently in his cell, curled into a tight ball, rocking back and forward.

*Help me.*

One o'clock . . . Two o'clock . . . Three o'clock . . .

The dandelion motes of light move across the darkness. The young Duncan stops crying and holds out his hand to catch them.

*Game's up the pole . . .*

He knows his mind is playing tricks on him, knows he can't really see the silver seeds, the bed which he, the young Duncan, is curled upon. He's still there watching it happen. The final stages of the dying of the light.

A large brown hare appears, just by the end of the bed. Young Duncan gets up to walk towards it. It sits there looking at him with big golden eyes and then, as he draws near, it moves suddenly and swiftly away into the dark. He runs behind it. He can see his bare feet and the legs of his stripy pyjamas.

'Duncan, hey, Duncan! It's me!'

'Malky?' His voice sounds younger. It echoes through the endless space. 'I – I can't see you.'

'Over here . . .'

Duncan walks towards the point where the hare vanished. Malky is there. He looks real, alive, younger. He wears a green plaid that makes his red hair glow like spun copper. Duncan laughs. 'Look at you, Malky. You're real here!'

'There's different kinds of real, laddie. Look at yersel'.'

'I suppose this is really me, Malky. This is what I was then – full of possibilities.'

'Aye, it's sad, all right, but listen, ye canny give intae it. Ye've got tae come back, Duncan. I mean, ye canny die. They need ye.'

'They?'

'You know, Sutra. You're important.'

'Nah. You go, Malk. You know about fighting and killing. No offence like.'

The hare appears again and Duncan walks past his friend to follow it once more into the darkness.

'Don't go, Duncan.' Malky's voice seems far behind

him already, although he has only walked a few paces. 'Wait for me. We'll miss ye. I'll miss ye . . .'

'It's no good, *Seanachaidh*. We must rest for a while.' Makhpiyaluta was concerned for the old man, who looked strained, his features ashen.

'I feel we almost reached him then,' Morias replied, 'and I know I'm tired, but Makhpiyaluta, if we stop we will lose ground.'

The Sidhe Prince nodded unhappily. 'Very well, but my conscience will not allow me to continue much longer.'

'But mine will not allow me to stop.'

'Who are you?'

A woman stands in the darkness where the hare had been moments before. She is beautiful – her ivory features soft in whatever pale light illuminated her – but she wears a brown dress and a grey woollen cloak that seem unlikely on one of her bearing. 'Do you not know me? I am the lady Ulla,' she responds.

The young Duncan stares wonderingly at her face. 'But how can you be in my death also?' he demands. 'Is this a dream? Will I wake up?'

Ulla looks sad. 'I do not know if you will awake, nor I myself, but my heart hopes that you will. You seem so young.'

'Ah, well, I'm not actually so young. This is . . . er, really me. If you see what I mean.'

She nods. 'I understand. But I think this is not a dream, it is the time-between-times. We are waiting.'

'I've done a lot of that.'

Ulla studies the young face closely, 'It seems to me,' she says, 'that we can travel through this place together. I am awaiting another soul here but I will be happy if you can return.'

The young Duncan smiles.

'Here,' she says, 'take my hand.'

They walk for some distance, an easy silence between them. Ulla's hand is warm in his, and the young Duncan feels a strange contentment creep through him. He knows he should be asking questions, he doesn't understand about this place, but he walks in silence, feeling the care of the lady Ulla's touch.

'Duncan, wait for me . . .' The sound echoes from far away. Ulla stops. 'Is he your friend?' She smiles. 'If so, we must wait. We need our friends in this darkness.'

Young Duncan nods obediently. The call comes again and Duncan shouts back. Immediately, he is engulfed by a chill that drains all energy from his limbs. His rational mind knows that this is the dying of his body, which he has been expecting, but the suddenness shocks him. He finds himself on the floor, the lady Ulla looking down at him. 'Duncan,' she says, 'if you falter here there is no going back. Do you understand?' He tries to respond but cannot make the mute cold flesh of his face move. This is all a dream anyway, his mind is telling him. How can I die in my dream?

Malky finds them. 'I fear it is too late,' Ulla says to him. 'I think he has gone before us.'

'No,' Malky replies grimly. 'No' yet. Duncan widnae go without me.' He touches his friend's face, and the flesh is indeed cold and white.

'I must go,' Ulla whispers. 'I am sorry for your loss,

sir, but I must say a farewell of my own.'

Malky looks up and takes her hand, his eyes bright with tears. 'And promise me that then ye'll go back.'

She considers this. 'I will think about it, warrior, but my heart is empty. All those I have loved await me here. Goodbye.'

Ulla walks away and is swallowed by the darkness. 'God speed ye,' Malky whispers.

He stares down at the young Duncan, his features wearing the peculiar blankness of grief.

'Duncan, ye canny die – like we said, folk need ye here. An' if ye die here, ye die in Edinburgh an' all. That's what—' He stops. 'Aw, shite,' he groans. 'Ah canny believe I forgot.' Reaching into his pouch he pulls out the gem Deme gave him. As the gatekeeper had promised, it is glowing with white fire and Malky's features are illuminated by its light. 'I hope I'm no' too late,' he mutters. 'Duncan. Duncan, kin ye hear me?'

'Kin ye hear me?'

'Huh?' Talisker mumbled. He turned over in his sleep, pulling the cover around his shoulders against the chill. 'Go away, Malky . . . Malk?'

Consciousness.

Talisker opened his eyes sleepily. It was still dark, but not the darkness of . . . that place. He was in a small room that smelt of . . . flowers. Sleep still pulled at the edges of his awareness but he didn't want to wake; didn't want to think about battles, Phyrr . . . anything. He wondered dimly why he wasn't in more pain; he felt bruised all over, the sharpest sensation in his left hand and arm, but he knew it should be worse. He opened his eyes again and scanned the darkness. Something was niggling at his exhausted mind. It was the smell, he decided. It had an edge to it, which, although not unpleasant . . . The thought slipped away as his mind tried to make sense of what he was – or wasn't – seeing. His eyes were adjusting now and his gaze rested on the coverlet over his chest. There were dark blotches on it, which appeared in a haphazard pattern. Roses. He picked up the cover and held it closer to his face, unable to fathom why this should bother him. His heart was thumping wildly and he was sweating.

Straining his eyes to see into the further reaches of the room he picked out the dark looming shapes of furniture, and there, near the end of the bed, a lower item with a square box-like object on it. As understanding dawned, he groaned. The smell had a chemical edge because it was air-freshener, and the box was a television.

He was back.

'Duncan? What's wrong?'

He froze. That voice. There was a rustle beside him and a light – a bedside lamp – illuminated the scene with a night-time yellow glow. He was in bed in a beautiful, feminine room. And beside him, her face radiating concern, was Shoo. Shula Morgan.

'Good morning, sir. Would you like some coffee?' Chaplin opened his eyes and stared groggily at the person before him, a young woman dressed in utilitarian clothes. She wore no jewellery or cosmetics and her dark hair was ruffled by the morning air. In her hand she held a steaming polystyrene cup. A familiar rumble came from behind the girl, who blotted out most of his range of vision. Traffic. Chaplin had grown up in the city, the noise was in his blood. He peered past the girl, squinting against the bleak winter light just as a number-two bus moved along the road behind them. He knew instantly where he was, orienting himself almost automatically by the position of Edinburgh Castle, whose looming form squatted on its slick basalt platform to the top right of Chaplin's vision. Still, it didn't seem quite right . . . Reaching forward a trembling hand he took the cup. The faint bitter smell of the coffee assailed his senses. He hadn't had coffee for a long time – had he?

The girl was watching him closely, concern on her face.

'If you don't mind me saying so, you're a bit young to be . . . well, you know, here. Younger than our usual crowd.' She waved her hand behind her as she spoke.

'I am back in Edinburgh, aren't I?' Chaplin asked.

'Back? Well, yeah,' the girl laughed. 'I was referring to the fact that you're in the Grassmarket, sleeping in a doorway. You missed the curfew at the hostel last night, didn't you?'

Chaplin groaned. 'No, you've got it wrong. Look.' He rummaged in the pocket of his coat, hoping he'd find what he was looking for. 'Here,' he held up his ID, 'I'm a policeman. I was on . . . surveillance last night. Must have nodded off.'

'Oh.' The girl looked aggrieved.

'I suppose you want your coffee back,' Chaplin joked.

'Nah, it's okay.' She smiled back. 'It's a bit late for it now – I mean, you could've done with it last night.' She stood up to go and a blast of cold air entered the doorway. She saw that Chaplin was looking at her blankly. 'So's you didn't fall asleep, like,' she explained.

'Oh, yeah . . .'

'Well, I hope you get yer man as they say.' The girl made to go, turning up her collar against the chill.

'Excuse me,' Chaplin called after her, 'I know this will seem like an odd question, but what day is it?'

She turned back. 'You're jokin', right? It's Friday – you know, the day after Thursday.' She peered back at Chaplin's face. 'Are you sure you're not from the hostel?'

'No, sorry, I've just come back from Australia and, you know, you lose a day . . .' Chaplin trailed off, wondering why he was bothering to lie. He had just come back, he knew, but he couldn't remember where from. It was odd. 'Thanks for the coffee. I'll go home and have a shower, I guess.'

'Bye then.'

He watched her go then searched his pockets frantically. He still had his keys and some money. Also, in the deepest corner of his pocket he found a smooth round stone. He stared at it and was about to throw it away, but something stopped him. He put it back into his pocket for later consideration. Now all he had to do was remember where he lived.

It was one o'clock in the afternoon when Chaplin walked into Ladyfield police station. He wore a smart blue suit, a white shirt and a red tie; his hair was scraped back into his habitual pony-tail, he was close-shaven and smelt as expensive as the Chief Constable, having spilt half a bottle of Chanel L'Égoiste down his front. In short, he was ready to come back to work and would brook no argument on the subject. His appearance was a façade, however. Chaplin was wound up so tightly that he was ready to explode. Stalking down the corridor, his eyes darted left and right, flinching at shadows.

Having trusted to instinct and jumped on a number-six bus, he'd found his apartment in the Dean Village with little trouble, his memory sparking as he moved along, recognising buildings, hedges and gardens. As he put the key into the door of his apartment, he realised that this was a lonely place and no one would be waiting for him, asking where he'd been. Where *had* he been? It was just as he'd left it, he knew – clothes everywhere, a bright chaotic kaleidoscope that centred on the bed. A complete mess, the sign of his degenerating mind. Something had changed, but he was unable to guess what it was. Without taking his coat off, he flung himself on to the bed and stared around him. He remembered being here, weeping for Diane . . . Snorting at his own actions he reached for the bottle of Jack Daniel's at the side of the bed and poured some into the smeared glass on the bedside table, then knocked it back. He felt the warm flare of the drink spread through him, and rested his head against the wall. He shut his eyes, reached into his pocket, curled his fingers around the stone for comfort; it brought none.

It wasn't like remembering something. Not really. You don't get the sounds and sensations when you remember. Chaplin knew that he was still in his room, propped up on his bed, an empty glass in one hand and the stone in the other, yet what he was seeing and feeling was so violent, so bright, that he was sure he cried out.

He saw himself running up the High Street then into darkness. Heard someone cry out as he looked behind him and fired his gun. Then confusion, water, the drowning sensation again, gagging for air. Another scene: a battle. Men dying all around him, screaming, confusion, sobbing. There was a woman, too, her hair copper red, and scarlet where it had trailed in the blood of the fallen. Behind him, the noise and screaming were louder and he turned to follow it . . . 'No,' his lips were moving, sweat forming above them, 'no, don't go there. Don't . . .' But the vision continued.

He was climbing stairs now to a turret from which he could look down on to battlements. There he saw the whole scene: monsters, moving shapes of clicking, sliding insect-like swarms, gripping men, assimilating them, and then – oh, God – and there in the middle of it all, covered in blood, screaming, cursing, hacking, was—

His eyes snapped open. Talisker.

Now, back at Ladyfield, Chaplin strode along to the incident room, his anger burning like a brand across his features. He'd rationalised the situation as best he could and didn't like the conclusions he had drawn. As usual, Duncan Talisker was the instigator and the key. Last night he'd followed his old adversary to the pub in the Cowgate, and Talisker had bought him a drink. It had been drugged, Chaplin had decided. It was the sort of perverse, stupid thing Talisker would do, designed to keep Chaplin from following him while Talisker completed his grisly evening's entertainment in the Old Town. While Chaplin had hallucinated then slept in a freezing doorway, Talisker had killed again. At first, Chaplin had simply jumped to this conclusion but his suspicion had proved correct when, having showered and dressed, he switched on the television. *Reporting Scotland*, the local news programme, was in a furore over the latest murder. There was a difference this time, though; the victim was a youth of eighteen.

Chaplin crashed through the doors of the incident room with such force that all the officers inside looked up. There was a momentary silence before Stirling walked forward. 'Sandro, how are you today?' He was rubbing his hands together as though he was washing them, which he did when discomforted.

Chaplin frowned. 'I'm absolutely fine, Bob. Really.'

'Sandro, I don't think you should—'

'I have evidence,' Chaplin interrupted. 'I can place Talisker in the High Street last night. He was drinking in the Cowgate until midnight.' Pushing past Stirling he walked over to the table where black-and-white photos of the victim were spread out. 'Pete, do we have a time of death for the victim yet?' He addressed one of the younger officers, but didn't wait more than a second for his response. 'C'mon, let me have the information, dammit! We haven't got time to dither around.'

The officer snapped to attention. 'Approximately one-fifteen, sir.'

'Good.' Chaplin grinned. 'Now, which interview room is Talisker in? I want a word with the bastard.'

There was a loaded silence, broken only by the sound of ringing telephones. Stirling spoke quietly but his tone was firm. 'Sandro, I need to talk to you urgently. In my office now.' He turned to the assembled men. 'Brian, we need Inspector Chaplin up to speed. Can you make sure a full dossier is on his desk as soon as possible, please. As you were.'

In his office, Stirling closed the blinds and turned on Chaplin. 'Sandro, what the hell d'you think you're doing? Correct me if I'm wrong, but didn't we send you home yesterday unfit for duty?'

'Yessir, and it won't happen again.' Chaplin hardly flinched. 'Look, I'm fine. Do I look ill to you?'

Stirling was an astute man, not about to be bulldozed by Chaplin. He'd seen stronger officers burn out and, for all Chaplin's protests, there was something about him that Stirling didn't like the look of. 'It might have been a stroke, Sandro,' he said gravely. 'It's only because we care. You know that.'

'It wasn't a stroke.' Chaplin swallowed, unwilling to appear vulnerable. 'It was an anxiety attack.'

Stirling didn't look convinced.

Chaplin felt he was losing ground. 'Look, I admit I've been a bit . . . edgy since Talisker was released, but surely that's understandable? Especially since the murders have started again. Just don't shove me off the case, Bob. I'll do anything – light duties, whatever. You can't afford not to have my experience on this one.'

It was his trump card, Stirling had to concede that. None of the original officers from the Talisker case were still in service. 'All right, Sandro. But I'm in charge of this case.' Stirling sat down and rocked back in his chair. 'If I decide to pull you out at any point, I don't want any argument from you.'

Chaplin grinned. 'That's fine. So where is he, then? You'll need me to sit in on the interview. I know the way his mind works.'

'If you mean Duncan Talisker, we haven't brought him in yet,' Stirling said mildly. He watched closely for Chaplin's reaction, trying to gauge whether the man really had lost his objectivity.

'What? Why not, sir? Isn't he the prime suspect?'

'Well, yes. And we probably will pull him in later today. But there's something else we want to look at first. We've found hair samples that are definitely not Talisker's.' Chaplin frowned. 'They're jet black,' Stirling explained, 'not the infamous red, and the victim was blond. We're checking it out with Forensics now. Look, take the rest of the afternoon to get up to speed on the new case but come and see me around four. There's someone I want you to meet.'

Shula's house was what most of Talisker's peers would term 'dead posh'. She had inherited from her parents a Georgian four-storey building in one of the crescents near the west end of Princes Street. The bedroom in which Talisker had woken was so crammed with antique furniture, mostly Arts and Crafts or Georgian, that it was disconcertingly like waking up in a display at an antiques fair. At the far side of the room facing the bed, the weak morning light filtered through the heavy curtains that hung at the huge bay windows.

'Duncan? Are you all right? Speak to me,' Shula demanded.

Talisker stared at her. Her arm was still outstretched to the bedside lamp and with the other hand she held the rose print quilt up to her chest. Her fine black hair was ruffled at the back where it had rubbed on her pillow. Talisker noted that she was wearing a loose white nightdress and also that, although she was under all of the bedclothes, he was covered only by the quilt. He felt a tinge of disappointment as he realised that whatever it was he couldn't remember, it did not involve Shula and himself being lovers. That had happened only once, well in the past now.

'Yeah, I'm – I'm okay,' he said hoarsely. 'I'm just a bit disoriented. Shoo . . . I can't . . . We need to talk.'

'I know, Duncan. I'll go and make some coffee first, though. You stay there and I'll bring it back to bed. This house never heats up until midday.'

He watched her walk across the room, spellbound by the way the light picked out her delicate form beneath the nightdress. She moved confidently, not feeling her way around the furniture as one supposed blind people often did, but straight across the middle, reaching for the door at the right moment. Talisker realised she knew the layout of the room exactly, despite its cluttered appearance. When she had gone he sat back against the pillows. He was more tired than he'd ever felt in his life. He closed his eyes and almost drifted back to sleep, but suddenly visions of the battle for Ruannoch Were assailed him. He saw himself in the midst of the fighting, covered with blood, hacking like some demon. He shuddered: there had been no control, he had lost it completely – even if it had been to save his life. As he watched the vision of the fight against the

Corrannyeid that some might term 'heroic,' he felt disgusted – not only because the monsters were so vile but because, in his desperate flailing defence, he had become as low as they, as unfocused, as mindless.

He opened his eyes again and rubbed them, as though attempting to scrub away the image. 'Those things don't count,' Chaplin had said, when Talisker had pointed out that they would all commit murder during the battle or die. But they did count. In a moment of clarity, Talisker knew that the essence of what made the Corrannyeid monsters was that they reduced their foes to their own level before they killed them. Those moments of mindless desperation were dehumanising. Now he was back in Edinburgh, where people believed *he* was such a monster – and he was armed with the knowledge that after all, he was capable of what they'd always said. Was he being rational? It was possible that he was in shock, he supposed. He cast his eyes around the room, and absorbed the warm tones as though they were a salve for his weariness. He couldn't understand why he was here, in Shula's bed, but he was glad that he was not alone.

'Here we go, Duncan, coffee and biccies.' She was walking across the room carrying a large silver tray.

'Can you man—?' Talisker began to get up.

'I'm fine,' she said. 'Is the bedside table still here or has it flown away in the middle of the night? Ah, yes . . .' She put down the tray, got back into bed, and deposited a plate of biscuits between them. Hobnobs, if he wasn't mistaken. He grabbed one and crammed it into his mouth. It tasted strange, artificial, of saturated fats, emulsifiers, refined sugar. 'Ah, civilisation,' he joked, through a mouthful of soggy oats, quietly pleased that only he would understand the irony. His satisfaction was cut short, however.

'Duncan. We really do need to talk.' Shula sipped her coffee. 'Where were you last night? What happened to your hand? I couldn't get a sensible word out of you. It took a while to stop the bleeding.'

Talisker looked at his hand, and registered that it was neatly bandaged. He flexed his fingers, and felt pain in the centre of his palm. It was not an injury from the battle of Ruannoch Were: all he had brought physically from there was tiredness. 'It was Chaplin,' he said uncertainly. 'He shot me.'

This morning the view from the window was bleak. The autumn clouds leached into grey drizzle, which hung over whatever view Corvus was not allowed to see. His mood of grim impatience was heightened by the distant rumble of mountain thunder. He glanced down at the clear halo of light that circled his ankles, shackles of a mystic energy strong enough to contain a young god. The light was fading, though, as his power grew; with the prophecy broken, the source of that energy would be lost for ever. Then, what revenge he would wreak on the puny gods of Sutra! And the Fine would be his means of achieving it. In the process, Sutra would be laid waste but such was the price of his anger. Also, after Kyra he had decided he enjoyed mortal women; their pliant weakness made them easy prey, which both aroused and amused him.

He walked over to his bed. On the side table was a bowl of water in which floated a large black feather.

Corvus sat down and stirred the bowl with his index finger. It grieved him to resort to such a lowly method of scrying but he was conserving his energy. Besides, Sluagh was injured and unable to be his eyes. The great raven had returned from the battle with a large gash in the thin layer of flesh and cartilage at the tip of his wing. He was perched on the bed head and cawed quietly as his master stirred the bowl.

'Hush, Sluagh,' Corvus chided. He stroked the glossy black feathers absently. The wound hampered the bird's flight and Corvus had confined him to quarters to speed his recovery.

Corvus stared into the water looking mainly for his sister, who had not returned since the battle. This did not worry him, she was probably off whoring somewhere . . . An image had formed in the bowl; a tall slim youth, perhaps in his twentieth summer. He wore unfamiliar garb, a shirt and breeches coloured alarmingly with red stripes. There was something about the flame-red hair that Corvus recognised . . . The boy seemed lost, searching, surrounded by darkness, but then – as Corvus watched in horror – the image shifted and changed. The boy became a man, freshly battle-scarred and weary, the eyes harder, more cynical, the bearing stronger, the shoulders broader. He carried a sword in his left hand, which flared in the darkness; his right arm was broken.

'No!' Corvus screamed. 'No! Phyrr! I'll kill you for this!'

The copper bowl accompanied his howl of anguish and went where Corvus was unable to follow. Through the window, out into the rain.

*

Four o'clock. Chaplin slapped the file down on the desk and left his office to see Stirling. After an hour or so, he'd realised that he wasn't taking in the information he was reading. He'd drunk three cups of coffee and smoked four fags, which he'd had to scrounge from one of the younger officers but nothing had worked. Looking round almost furtively he wondered if anyone had noticed his discomfort, but the rhythm and pulse of the station provided a comfortingly familiar backdrop of noise. Phones rang, people rushed in and out clutching bits of paper and photos but no one noticed that Inspector Chaplin was 'trippin' out'. That's what it was, he'd decided, flashbacks to the hallucinations he'd suffered when Talisker had drugged him last night. He knew some drugs – LSD, for example, had such an effect, although he'd always assumed these flashbacks occurred years later, not the following day. Moving about the office as little as possible allowed him to escape attention and he buried his nose in the file as though deeply engrossed.

He'd almost forgotten about Stirling when Pete Caithness tapped him on the shoulder and reminded him. 'Are you due in to see Stirling, sir? Only, I've got to see him at four-thirty . . . Are you all right? You look terrible.'

'I'm fine,' Chaplin snapped.

Stirling had company: a man was sitting beside him and at first Chaplin assumed he was a suspect or a witness. He looked uncomfortable and out of place in one of Stirling's big leather chairs. He wore casual clothes, jeans and a baggy sweatshirt with DM boots. Although he appeared in his early- to mid-thirties, his lip was pierced and his peroxide-blond hair was carefully ruffled. The retro-punk look was negated by the narrow black-rimmed glasses that gave his face an owlishness despite his apparel.

'Sandro.' Stirling smiled as Chaplin walked in. 'This is Findlay Willis – Finn. Finn, this is Inspector Chaplin.'

The man's reaction surprised Chaplin. He seemed to shake himself, then said, 'Alessandro Chaplin?' almost disbelievingly. He didn't get up to shake hands and Chaplin scowled.

''S right. Do I know you?'

'No no,' Stirling assured him. 'Finn here is a journalist. Orders from on high, public consultation and the like, probably so they can make a documentary about it in a couple of years' time . . .'

'We're going to be working together for the next few weeks,' Finn explained. 'Don't worry, I won't get in your way, just shadow you and observe.' As he spoke, his gaze never left Chaplin's face, which annoyed the policeman. Also, his voice was quite thin and reedy. It reminded Chaplin of someone. Malky – but posher. But he didn't know anyone called Malky, did he? A picture arrived in his mind. A clansman? He tried to dismiss it.

'Yeah, right,' he muttered. 'I've heard that before.'

'Sandro!' Stirling looked surprised. Finn held up his hand, imperiously Chaplin thought. 'Nah, it's okay, he's right. Some of us do get over-zealous when we're on these assignments, but that's not my style.'

'I've warned him to expect long irregular hours and

issued him with a mobile and pager,' Stirling said. 'For the next while at least, he goes where you go.'

Chaplin was appalled. 'Do you think that's a good idea, sir? I mean, now?'

'Are you questioning my decision, Sandro? Because it doesn't come just from me.' Stirling was irritated. 'This is a murder enquiry. There's no "good" time.'

'Well, no.' Chaplin knew when to shut up. He looked at Finn, who was radiating an air of smugness. He sighed, gritted his teeth and smiled insincerely. 'Well, welcome to the Murder Squad, Finn,' he said.

# CHAPTER TWELVE

Talisker spent the morning with Shula in the big old house. They sat in the drawing room – crammed with so much furniture that it seemed like a homely antiques shop – in big overstuffed orange chairs, talked and drank coffee. Effie, Shula's daughter, was staying with her aunt for the half-term holiday so they were alone in the house. Outside, an early frost had painted the shrubs and trees of the communal crescent gardens with sharp white contours and the area was quiet. For just a few hours, Talisker felt something akin to peace. He sipped his coffee and told Shula everything he could remember about last night in the High Street, editing as he went. Without Malky and Deme, it acquired a much simpler aspect.

Alessandro Chaplin had followed him to the pub in Cowgate, watched while he sat drinking then trailed him up to the top half of the High Street where Talisker had been planning to catch a bus. Chaplin had shot him through the hand then passed out from too much drink. She listened avidly to what he said and didn't seem to doubt him.

'Shoo, can I ask you something?'

'Of course.'

'When we met in the gallery, you said something that made me think you didn't really believe in my innocence. If you think I killed those women, how can you stand to be here with me? How could you offer me the comfort of your bed? I don't understand.'

It was some moments before Shula replied. A car passed by outside, its lights dimmed against the uniquely Scottish grey of the morning sky. Then she asked quietly, 'Do you believe that people have souls, Duncan?'

'Yes, I know they do.'

She looked faintly surprised by his answer. 'I am a Christian – you know that, don't you? But not in the normal sense. I mean, I don't know if you remember, but Mum and Dad were evangelists. They travelled the world in their Mission from God.' She smirked. 'They did everything, Duncan, exorcisms, speaking in tongues, healing, much of it in this house. It left me with a unique perspective and a personal relationship with God. Anyway, I carry a few fundamental beliefs with me from those years, and one of those is that no soul is ever truly lost to God.'

He stared at her. 'I'm sorry, Shoo, but that can't be true. I didn't kill those women, at least I don't think I did, but whoever murdered them is evil. Their soul is worthless. And, God forbid, if one day I get my memory of that time back and it turns out it was me, I'll still think the same.'

She reached out and took his hand. 'You must never believe that, Duncan. If forgiveness was easy, it wouldn't be a virtue, would it? I will keep praying for you.'

'Thanks,' he mumbled.

At around lunchtime Talisker remembered. 'What day is this?'

'Friday the twenty-second. Why?'

'I think I've got an appointment with my probation officer this afternoon at three.'

'What's he like?'

'About sixty, bald, can't stand the sight of me.' Talisker shrugged. 'I guess I'd better head back to the flat and tidy myself up. Not sure how I'm going to explain the hand, though.'

Shula nodded. 'I'd wait and see what Chaplin has to say for himself first.'

Talisker stood up to go.

'Wait. Can you hold on five minutes?' Shula said. 'I've got something for you. I'll be right back.' Without waiting for his answer she headed for the door. Talisker sank back into the easy chair.

'Psst.'

'Wha—'

'It's me, ya plum.'

'Malky? Where are you?'

'Ah'm no manifestin' mahsel'. I reckon that lassie o' yours is a wee bit sensitive.'

'Well, you could be right.' Talisker addressed the chair facing him as that seemed to be where Malky's voice was coming from. 'But I feel stupid talking to myself. Can you not just appear till she gets back?'

'Aye, all right then,' Malky replied grudgingly. He was suddenly sitting in the chair, as Talisker had imagined. He was still wrapped in the plaid he had worn at Ruannoch Were; it was stained with so much blood and grime it was hard to see what the original colours had been. 'Look, we've got tae talk. Ye've got big trouble.'

'D'you know what *déjà vu* is, Malky?'

'Eh? Naw. Look, we've no' got time tae mess around, there's been another murder. Hey, Ah jist remembered sayin' that tae you afore!'

Talisker groaned. 'But it's only been one night, Malk—'

'Well, that's no' the worst o' it. Chaplin's back an' all.'

'From what I can gather, he never left physically and neither did I. It was more like a split in our consciousness or something.'

'Well, aye. But like you never left but are back, so's he and he's no' a happy man.'

'So what else is new?'

'Is that no' enough?'

'What? Eh, it's just a figure of speech Malk, a rhetorical question. Do you think he'll come after me again? Does he remember Sutra?'

'He'll come after ye sure as anything. The murder was in the High Street where you two were last night. Ah think he remembers Sutra but it's hard tae tell. He's got the look o' a man who kens he's recently been in battle, hauntit like.' The Highlander stood up and began to pace the floor. 'Tae be honest with ye, Duncan, Ah'm no sure what I should be doin'. Ah mean, Ah'll keep an eye out fer ye but it's down tae you now. I canny take ye back unless yer life's in danger onyways. Maybe we should go' and speak tae Deme again, but the High Street's no goin' tae be the safest place for you now.'

Talisker cursed roundly. 'I can't believe it, Malky. It's just never-ending with Chaplin . . . Well, I've had enough of waiting for justice to win out. That's it. I'm leaving. You can always find me anyway, can't you?'

'Oh, aye, nae bother . . . Ssh, yer lassie's comin'! I'd

better go.' With that Malky vanished, leaving Talisker staring at the wall.

'Did I hear you talking to someone, Duncan?' Shula came in carrying a small blue box.

'Bad habit from prison.'

'Here, I'd like you to have this.'

Talisker took the box and opened it. Inside was a gold St Christopher. 'It's – it's lovely, Shoo,' he stuttered, embarrassed.

'Put it on.' He did so and she reached out to touch where it nestled against his chest. 'It's to keep you safe on your journeys and to remind you of what we've said. Your soul will never be worthless, Duncan. Not to God, and not to me.'

'Shula . . .' He felt almost overcome, took her by the shoulders and looked into her eyes, wishing she could see him because his sincerity was surely evident in his face. 'You might hear something soon, which will cause you to doubt me. But I promise you, I swear, the murders since I came out of prison had nothing to do with me. Please keep believing that.'

She pulled him into a warm hug, standing on tiptoe to reach his height. 'I'll keep the faith if you will.'

At three o'clock he was standing by the sea wondering whether to walk into it and end it all. Keeping the faith must be easy, he mused, if you only had to do it in an abstract way. After leaving Shula, he'd caught the bus home to Leith, packed a few odds and ends in a rucksack and left. Almost as an afterthought, he put a gun at the bottom of the bag. An acquaintance from prison had insisted he have one 'for protection' and delivered it to him on his release; Talisker had never imagined he might use it. As he turned the corner at the bottom of the street, a police car arrived at the other end, missing the fugitive by moments.

He had planned to catch a train to London. He wasn't sure what he'd do when he got there, but being away from Scotland seemed like a wise idea in view of last night's murder. He sat down on a boulder and gazed out at the cold grey water. In the face of Shula's trust and fragility he had let down his guard, if only for a few hours, and it had drained him. It had also made him realise he missed Una. He had no idea if she was alive after Ruannoch Were. She should have been safe tending the wounded but the Corrannyeid had been swarming all over the damned city; anything could have happened to her. He'd never know now that he was back here.

Of course, he hadn't made it to London; there had been police on the train – well, he'd seen one. As the 125 had snaked its way down the east coast he'd watched the bleak winter scenery for a while then decided to pretend to be asleep. Just as he shifted his position, trying to tuck his legs beneath the seat, a woman had leaned towards him across the narrow grey table. 'Do I know you, son?' she demanded.

'I don't think so,' he replied, his tone neutral and uninviting. She stared at him almost defiantly, an elderly woman, seventy or eighty perhaps, but the faded blue eyes were still sharp. 'Funny. I never forget a face usually. Must be getting old, eh?' Talisker smiled, still trying to avoid being drawn into conversation. 'Never mind. Would you like a toffee?' She shoved a bag of Woolies' finest pick 'n' mix towards him, 'Go on, dinny be shy.'

He took one but he knew he couldn't talk to her for long – his gut instinct told him she would remember him. Glancing down the central aisle he could see the uniformed policeman making his way along the train about three carriages down: he was stopping to ask the passengers something, possibly showing them a picture. 'It's my stop next,' he muttered to the woman, as he stood up. 'Thanks for the toffee.'

She looked a little disappointed. 'Aye, right, son. 'Bye, then.'

So he'd ended up here – Dunbar. Or, more precisely, John Muir Country Park. He'd walked here from the station after dismissing the idea of going into the town for fish and chips. If the police were looking for him, the coastal park was the ideal place to lie low for a couple of days. Perhaps he would chance the train after that. For the first couple of hours he'd felt almost smug at his escape from the city: the swathe of estuary salt flats and forest that ran between Dunbar and Tyninghame was quiet as well as beautiful. Generally, people came here only at weekends and he was sure he could easily evade the occasional solitary birdwatcher. It began to rain hard, forcing him back up the beach to take shelter in the tree-line. Sitting beneath a large conifer, the thought struck him for the first time: he was on the run.

'Do I know you?' Chaplin frowned across his desk to where Finn was writing in his notebook. As Chaplin finished his background reading on the new murder, he felt the younger man's gaze on him. When he glanced up, however, Finn was apparently engrossed in his notes.

'No.' Finn shook his head. 'I know you, though. Your infamy precedes you.' He chuckled, a dry, grating sound. 'I was a trainee journalist at the time of the first murders. Fascinating stuff. Rather convenient conviction you guys got there, don't you think?'

Chaplin spoke quietly. 'I wouldn't go voicing that opinion around here too loudly,' he warned.

Finn smirked. 'Freedom of the press, Sandro. I can draw my own conclusions.'

Chaplin felt an almost overwhelming desire to grab the little upstart by his sweatshirt and punch him in the face. You couldn't do that here, though, he reminded himself, it wasn't like Sutra . . . Whoa! Where had that come from? He blinked hard, trying to focus on Finn. 'Draw your own conclusions? You couldn't draw the fucking curtains,' he mocked, 'and it's Inspector Chaplin to you.'

The phone rang before Finn had a chance to respond, but he looked angry at Chaplin's rebuttal. His thunderous frown changed his whole demeanour, and Chaplin almost flinched. 'Let's walk and talk, shall we?' he said as he put the phone down. 'We've got something interesting at Forensics.'

The labs, on the same basement level as the temporary mortuary, always smelt of some chemical, which Chaplin thought was formaldehyde. It was quiet and cold down here; the Forensics crowd were a reserved, studious bunch of people and the atmosphere akin to a library or museum. Bodies were occasionally stored in the mortuary overnight if the main buildings in St Mary's Street were full but autopsies were generally performed either at St Mary's Street or Fettes. Finn seemed curious about the place and was about to walk through the double doors when Chaplin grabbed the back of his jacket.

'No, we're in here,' he said. 'Better not look in there today if you want to sleep tonight. They're still tagging and bagging Talisker's latest handiwork. We've got a much nicer treat in store.' He paused before he pushed open the door to one of the side rooms. 'This lady's a friend of mine.'

Finn arched his brows. 'So?'

'Nothing,' Chaplin muttered.

'Ah, you mean best behaviour,' Finn mocked. 'I can do that, you know. You just need to ask me nicely.'

'Sandro! How lovely to see you!' A tall blonde woman raced across the room and grabbed Chaplin in an unyielding embrace. 'How the devil are you?' she demanded. 'You look like shit.'

'I'm fine,' Chaplin protested. 'Beatrice, this is Finn. He's a journalist. Don't ask. Another bright idea from on high. Today's his first day so we're not showing him body parts.'

'Right,' she smiled, 'but I've got something much more interesting for you.' She put her arm around Chaplin's shoulder – one of the few women who could reach his height – and led him further into the room. Finn followed, his eyes scanning the equipment benches. As they neared Beatrice's section of the lab, the room degenerated into a disaster area: drink cans, food wrappers and half-eaten biscuits cluttered the surfaces. However, there was also a warmth that seemed out of context with the rest of the labs, and music was playing.

'C'mon, Bea, it might be your idea of exciting but it's just hair samples, right? That's what Stirling said, anyway.' Chaplin watched almost indulgently as Beatrice pushed aside a stack of brown folders, clearing a space into which she hefted a microscope.

'Well, not really,' she replied. 'Finn, be a love and get us a coffee, will you? The machine's at the end of the hall; mine's an eighteen and Sandro's is a two-three-eight.' Finn hesitated, seemed about to object, then turned on his heel and stomped off.

'Bea, you're a marvel,' Chaplin said wonderingly. 'I need to speak to you alone. How did you know?'

She winked. 'Woman's intuition – you're bustin' with something, Sandro, and your shadow'll be gone for at least ten minutes – the machine's broken so he'll have to get the lift and use the one upstairs. Spill the beans, fella.'

'Bea, you know about the effects drugs can have, right?'

'You haven't . . .'

'No, nothing like that,' he assured her. 'It's just that I think someone might have drugged me yesterday. I've been having flashbacks or waking dreams . . .'

She stared into his face and pulled down the skin under one of his eyes. 'You're certainly anaemic and dehydrated, Sandro . . .'

He took her hand. 'The things I'm seeing, they're horrible, Bea, but they make some sort of sense, like a big story, and they're impossible.'

'Such as?'

'I – I can't tell you. It sounds ridiculous.'

'C'mon, Sandro.'

'Well, it's like a battle scene mostly. But the fighting . . .' He licked his lips. 'I really need that coffee . . .'

'Here.' She picked up a cup. 'It's one I made earlier. Better get rid of it before your journalist gets back.'

He took a large gulp. 'The fighting is between people and creatures, monsters who can change into the form of the people once they get hold of them and destroy them from within. It's disgusting to watch, they die in agony.' He was sweating and pulled out a handkerchief to dab his brow.

'Very Freudian,' Beatrice murmured.

'That's not all,' Chaplin added. 'Talisker's there, in the fighting. He's completely lost it, foaming at the mouth, covered in blood.'

'It doesn't surprise me that he's there,' Bea said. 'I know he figures largely in your consciousness. But perhaps you should consider that this may be your brain's way of warning you about loss of control.' He frowned at this and she added, 'Just a suggestion. Are there any other symptoms?'

'Well, just that my brain and my body are somehow suggesting to me . . .'

'Yes?'

'. . . that I've been away to this place . . .'

'Where this battle happened?'

'Yes. For weeks.'

'Hmm. Can you remember anything else that might have happened when you were there?'

'Not really. Look, I know what you're thinking. It's

ridiculous, right?' He stood up. 'Forget it, Bea. Show me the hair samples.'

Bea pressed him back into the chair. 'Sandro, don't tell me what I'm thinking. You know it makes me cross. Of course it sounds ridiculous, hallucinations always do. What you're describing is quite possibly the result of some grotty little street drug, but I don't think I've ever known people to imagine time passing quite so vividly. It doesn't necessarily mean you're losing your marbles.'

'It might, though.' He grimaced.

'Of course, there's an easy way to find out. Speak to Duncan. How is he, by the way?'

Chaplin shrugged wearily. Beatrice had known himself and Talisker for years. They had all been at school together although she was in the year above them. She'd always had a soft spot for Talisker and, Chaplin suddenly realised, all through his trial and imprisonment she had never ventured an opinion, simply done her job assiduously and well. A few years later, Chaplin and she had dated for a brief period but nothing had come of it. Chaplin had found her too challenging and individualistic, too like Diane for comfort. And it was too late now: Bea was engaged and would marry in the spring. 'I'm sure he's fine,' he grated. 'I'm going to bring him in again later today.'

Neither of them spoke for a few moments and then Bea muttered, 'Does it never end, Sandro?' He said nothing, so she went on, 'I think the best thing for your hallucinations would be a couple of days in bed. Ride it out. The drug, whatever it is, should clear your system in a couple of days. But if you get any blinding headaches and vomiting, call the doctor.'

'Thanks, Bea.' He reached out and squeezed her shoulder. 'And now show me the damned bits of hair.'

'I'd better, before they're all gone,' Bea observed.

'What d'you mean?'

'Look.' Bea picked up a specimen bag, which contained a tiny patch of black fibres. 'Exhibit A, presumed to be hair, right?'

He watched as she took a hair from the packet, placed it on a slide and beneath a microscope. She peered down the eyepiece. 'Quick, take a look.'

'What the hell?'

The hair seemed to be dissolving beneath the lens. Shimmering motes of greenish light danced around for a few seconds then burned out like tiny suns. After only ten seconds or so, there was no hair left. Chaplin let out a low whistle. 'But the hair's all right until you take it out of the packet?'

'Yes, until you look at it directly like that. If you hold one in your hand and stare at it, it does the same thing although it takes a bit longer. I'd show you, but I'm going to run out of samples.'

'I got the coffees.' Finn was surveying them dourly from across the room.

'Oh, cheers, Finn.' Bea smiled innocently. 'Wasn't the machine working again?'

'I had to go upstairs.'

'Bea, have you shown these samples to Stirling yet?' Chaplin asked.

'Well, no. What would I say? Scientifically, it's a mystery.'

'What's so special about the samples?' Finn sniffed.

'I'm afraid they're probably animal hair of some kind,' Bea explained gravely. 'Perhaps the killer had a dog.'

Chaplin felt a strong impulse to laugh and gulped his coffee. He coughed. 'So, we can eliminate them from our enquiries, Miss Walker?'

'Yes indeed.'

'Okay. Well, I guess Finn and I had better go and pull in the one and only suspect.' Chaplin grinned at her broadly. 'Thanks, Bea.'

They turned to leave the lab. 'Take it easy, Sandro,' she called.

As they walked back down the corridor, Finn said, 'It doesn't seem like much to drag us down here for, dog hair.'

'You know how it is, Finn,' Chaplin replied. 'Some people just don't have much excitement in their lives. Looks like this is your chance to meet the man of the hour. Want to watch me make an arrest?'

A haunting chorus of birdsong echoed across the saltflats. It was dusk and the thousands of wading birds that used the estuary to feed and roost were gathering for the night. From the tree-line Talisker watched them massing, trying to identify them as a way of keeping his mind occupied. He couldn't face thinking about Ruannoch Were and Una: she and Sutra were lost to him now, as far as he could tell. He fiddled with his St Christopher, thinking dimly about the loss of Shula too; she must have heard about the latest murder by now. For all she had said about his soul, he couldn't believe she would keep faith with him now.

His mood was sombre as he stared down at the dull cold metal of the gun he held and wondered if he had the courage to kill himself. But as darkness fell and the pounding surf retreated, Talisker felt sick with despair. It was as though he was no longer capable of the emotional detachment he had wrapped around himself during his time in prison. Sutra and Una – perhaps even Phyrr – had done this to him, had forced him to feel, and with feeling came pain. He felt as though he might cry. But he couldn't. He raised the gun to his face and stared down the barrel. Then, with a sound between a strangled sob and a sigh of exasperation, he dropped it and buried his face in his hands. He heard a sound then, a weak grating sound, which was swallowed up by the rustling of the trees, and realised he was crying after all.

Where was Malky when you needed him?

At five-thirty the following morning, Ladyfield police station was quietly gearing up for the day. Cleaners busied themselves around the cluttered desks, dusting where stacks of paper allowed and Hoovering among the forest of legs and cables. Finn arrived punctually, as instructed by Chaplin the night before, to find the policeman asleep at his desk, face down with his right arm outstretched towards the phone as though sleep had claimed him mid-ring.

'Inspector Chaplin?' He shook Chaplin's shoulder, gingerly at first but then firmly when he got no response. 'Have you been here all night?'

'Christ, what time is it?' Chaplin yawned. 'No, don't tell me. Just feed me coffee, quick.'

Finn wandered off to the machine and Chaplin

grinned sheepishly at one of the cleaners, who wore a disapproving expression.

He knew she could smell the booze on him and cursed himself for not going home. The cleaners were the worst conduit for gossip in the station. He started to tidy his desk as she wound up her Hoover lead and left.

'Sandro, it's me.'

He froze. The voice came from behind him but, for some reason, he didn't want to turn round and look. All the hairs on the back of his neck and his forearms prickled. He knew that voice – didn't he?

'Who's me?' he asked, knowing somehow he wasn't going to like the answer.

'Malky.'

'I don't know anyone called—'

'Look, dinny start playin' silly beggars wi' me, Sandro. Duncan's in trouble.'

Chaplin started to write something on his notepad, pretending he was absorbed in what he was doing. 'Go away,' he muttered.

'Ah don't think so.'

'Who are you talking to?' Finn appeared in the doorway with two cups of coffee.

'The cleaner.' Chaplin waved distractedly without looking up. 'Oh, has she gone?'

'Ah'm still here,' Malky growled.

'Are you okay, Inspector?'

'Fine, fine . . .' Without warning, Malky appeared in front of Finn. Chaplin choked on his coffee.

Malky grinned, almost viciously. 'See, Ah knew I could make you see me!'

Chaplin was caught in a paroxysm of coughing, his

eyes welling with tears. Finn rushed straight through Malky to bang him on the back. The Highlander seemed to take this as an insult and glared at him, his hand dropping to his sword. 'Hey, watch yersel'!'

''S all right, Finn,' Chaplin gasped. 'It was just a bit hot.' He grabbed a tissue from the box on his desk and tried to mop the coffee off his tie. 'I'll just go to the loos and tidy up.' He sprinted off down the corridor leaving Finn shaking his head in bewilderment. Alessandro Chaplin wasn't quite what he'd expected.

Once in the toilets, Chaplin checked to make sure no one was in the cubicles. Satisfied that he was on his own, he stood by the wash-basins with his arms folded. For a few moments he listened to the quiet gurgling of the pipes before he spoke. 'All right, if I'm going mad, let's hear it.'

There was no answer and Chaplin shifted uncomfortably. He decided to take a different tack. Turning to the mirrors he began to wipe his tie with a dampened towel. 'Huh, Talisker can go hang himself for all I care.'

'What? That's no' very nice, Sandro.' Malky appeared behind him. 'I ken you've got yer differences, but he fought beside you at Ruannoch Were. Does that no' mean anything tae you?'

Chaplin turned and looked at the ghost. 'I know what you are. A side effect from the drugs that bastard gave me.'

'Awk, no' again!' Malky groaned. 'Ah had all this wi' Duncan. Ah've no' really got time tae convince ye Ah'm real – well, a real ghost onyways – but Ah can tell ye, Talisker didnae do the murder the night afore last. After ye shot him . . .' Malky paused when he saw Chaplin blanch at this. 'Oh, aye, forgot that bit, did ye? Dinny worry, he's no dead – yet – ye jist got his hand. After that he went to Shula Morgan's house. She'll tell ye.'

'We spoke to her last night when we were trying to find Talisker. She says he turned up at her place between two and three o'clock. That still gives him time to have done the murder before he went there . . . Why the hell am I discussing it with you anyway?'

'Don't pretend you don't know me,' Malky growled. 'I fought beside ye an' all, *Seanachaidh*. Ah'd begun tae revise mah opinion of ye. But now Ah'm no sae sure . . .'

Chaplin didn't react overtly to the title but Malky could see the muscle in his jaw ticking as he clenched his teeth and blinked rapidly.

'So, what is it that you want from me?' Chaplin snapped. 'Just supposing I'm interested.'

'Ah want ye to go and speak tae Duncan. He's suicidal. Nearly killed hissel' last night when I wiznae there. I've no' spoken to him yet today. Ah'm only assumin' he's all right 'cos I'm still here. We're kinna connectit like . . . as if ye dinny know already.'

'Are you saying you know where he is?'

'Well, aye . . . but Ah'm no' going tae tell ye jist so's ye kin go an' arrest him like.'

'Why did you come, then?'

Malky groaned. 'Look, he's no' got anybody, right? Naebody cares about him 'cept me an' Shula, and he widnae want her involved in this.'

Chaplin was struggling to come to terms with the conversation he was having with a ghost who, he could not deny it, seemed familiar to him. If Malky was a projection of his subconscious, he reasoned, he –

Chaplin – must already know where Talisker was. This vision could not tell him anything he didn't already know. 'If I arrest him, at least he'll be alive,' he said reasonably. 'He'll still be able to fight to prove his case.'

'Aye, ye mean like he did the last time,' Malky scoffed.

'It's all right, you don't have to tell me. I know where he'll be.' Chaplin turned to the mirror again and fussed around with his tie.

'How?'

'I know because you're not real,' Chaplin said, 'so the answer is in here.' He tapped his brow.

'Aye, right.'

'He's at Dunbar. John Muir, isn't he?'

'*What?*' Malky was horrified. 'Wh-why wid he be there, like?'

Chaplin spun round triumphantly. 'I'm right, aren't I? There's no point denying it. We camped there a couple of times with the school and I know Duncan used to go walking there. He knows the area well.' Malky's expression confirmed Chaplin's suspicions. 'Well, off you go. Tell him I'm coming to talk to him.' Chaplin grinned nastily and walked through Malky to the door. ''Bye then.' He didn't look back as he left.

'Let's go, Finn.' Chaplin strode back into the office, a man possessed of all the self-confidence in the world. 'I've figured out where he is and I'm going to bring him in.' Unlocking the top drawer of his desk, he took out his revolver, which he had cleaned and replaced the previous day.

'Inspector Chaplin, you'll need back-up.' Caithness was putting on his jacket.

'That won't be necessary. I'll have a better chance of persuading him to come in on my own. Duncan and I go back a long way.' He finished strapping the leather holster around his chest.

Caithness did not look convinced and glanced at Stirling's office: it was empty. 'Where exactly did you say you were going?' he asked nervously.

'John Muir,' Chaplin replied. 'The radio will be out of range, but Finn here's got his mobile. Give Pete the number, Finn.'

They walked out to the car, Chaplin exuding an air of vindication that intrigued Finn. 'Did you get a tip-off, Inspector?'

'You could say that.' Chaplin smiled. 'By the way, Finn, do you know what a *Seanachaidh* is?'

'A clan story-teller, like a Celtic bard. Why?'

'*Times* cryptic,' Chaplin replied. 'Crossword puzzle. It's a bit of a bugger.'

The demon was getting harder to control. In the void, Corvus waited impatiently for the creature to respond to his summons. It had no choice but to come: it was bound to its master by dark magic. And yet Corvus knew that such magic had a price. His power was finite, after all, or he would not be bound by the chains with which the gods had cursed him. Each time he worked with the demon to harry Talisker, his powers in Sutra had been compromised: his hold over the Corrannyeid, his continual railing against his bonds, his freedom, all within his grasp, were threatened by his inattention. But he had no choice . . .

Finally, the creature appeared. Incapable of speech, it

slumped forward, its gangly gnarled arms hanging loosely before it. Corvus was shocked by the creature's degradation: its waxy skin had been broken or gouged in some places to reveal a pulsing red ichor. The clothes Corvus had created to conceal its true shape were tattered, and patches of hair were missing from its scalp. The face – which admittedly he had fashioned somewhat crudely – was askew, the jaw hanging slackly.

'Existence is pain,' he murmured to himself. 'Listen, creature, soon I will release you to nothingness, but first we must resolve matters with Talisker.' He sent an image of Talisker into the simple maelstrom of the demon's mind. The creature shifted but did not react. 'Go and find him,' Corvus instructed. 'He must die. I cannot release you until he is finished.' He stepped back and gestured at the being, which vanished.

Sighing, Corvus transformed himself into his raven form to quit the void. He flew lazily for some distance, enjoying the illusion of freedom. As he flew, he brooded; the hunt for Talisker brought him no pleasure when he had never even sighted the man. It wasn't his preferred method of hunting. Where was the chase, the thrill, the glory? He checked himself. This was no game. It had been foretold by the cursed half-breed sorceress, Mirranon, that Talisker would destroy Corvus. But, still, he would like to see for himself what was so different about this man whose soul could encompass two worlds.

'Talisker! Talisker!' The call echoed through the woodland towards where Talisker sat huddled beneath a larch tree. He leaped up. It was Chaplin!

'Duncan!' Malky appeared beside him just as he began to stuff his sleeping-bag into his rucksack.

'Where have you been?' Talisker asked.

'Ye've got tae run, Duncan! He's guessed where ye are. Ah didnae tell him, honest. Ah mean, Ah went to see him, like, but—'

Talisker stopped. 'You went to see Chaplin?'

'Look, jist believe me. Ah never telt him—'

'Are you saying he just guessed? How could he just guess, Malky? '

'It disnae matter,' Malky squeaked, as Talisker tried to push past him. 'He's comin'.'

'Talisker!' The voice came again, closer now, through the trees.

'Aw, no.' Malky groaned. 'This is no' about the polis stuff really, is it? Ah think he's got a gun, Duncan.'

''S all right, so have I,' Talisker replied quietly, clicking the safety catch off his pistol. 'And I've had enough, Malk.'

'Aw, shite.'

Talisker made his way back along the beach towards Dunbar, keeping the tree-line to his right and the estuarine river to his left. He reasoned that if he could get back to the town and the railway station, he could avoid detection for a while and Chaplin would be forced to quit the search and go home. His route took him past the car park where Chaplin's Ford Cosworth was the only vehicle, looking forlorn and abandoned beside the deserted children's play area and the toilet blocks. It had begun to snow and large white flakes whirled noiselessly around Talisker disorienting him.

The peculiar stillness that accompanies heavy snow filled his ears with crisp white noise, muffling the sounds of the sea.

He considered taking Chaplin's car, but although he'd spent fifteen years among hardened criminals, he had no idea how to hotwire it and it was unlikely that the keys were in the ignition. Then he spotted someone beside the car, a man who was shuffling from foot to foot to combat the cold. He seemed to be watching the tree-line for movement, and Talisker crouched lower beneath the level of the ragged dunes hoping the watcher hadn't seen him.

'That's Finn,' came a whisper from beside his shoulder.

'Jeez, Malk, I wish you wouldn't creep up on me like that.'

'Sorry. He's a journalist – what's that mean, by the way?' Malky asked amicably.

'He writes for the newspapers,' Talisker replied distractedly. 'C'mon.' He moved forward in a low crouch, keeping the line of the building between himself and Finn, hoping the snow would obscure his movement.

'Where the hell are ye goin'?'

'To try to get the car,' Talisker whispered. 'Now shut up . . .'

Hardly daring to breathe, he crept up behind Finn, first ducking behind the building, where he dumped his rucksack, then running to the car in the same low crouch. Finn was standing with his back to him, leaning against the passenger door.

'Don't move,' Talisker said, in his best low,

threatening voice. Finn didn't react. Talisker was about to repeat himself when he spotted the cable running from Finn's pocket to his ear: he was wearing earphones for a Walkman.

'Shit.' Keeping his eyes firmly on Finn's back as though this would transfix him, Talisker reached down and picked up a small stone, which he flung quite hard at the man.

'Hey!' Finn spun around. When he saw Talisker holding the gun over the bonnet of the car, his expression changed to a mixture of fear and awe. He put his hands in the air.

'I need the keys,' Talisker said.

'I haven't got them. Honest.' Finn's voice was remarkably calm. 'Chaplin took them. He didn't want me messing around with it.' He nodded towards the car, 'It's collectable apparently. You're Duncan Talisker, aren't you?'

Talisker cursed his luck. He didn't want to shoot anyone. 'Turn round,' he commanded. 'Keep your hands in the air where I can see them.'

'You're not going to shoot, are you?' Finn's nerves surfaced, his voice catching, but he did as he was told. 'Please don't shoot. I'm a journalist, I can tell your story for you.'

Talisker backed away keeping the gun trained on Finn's back. Once he had gone about twenty paces he would run, leaving Finn standing, hopefully too frightened to turn round for a few valuable minutes. Trouble was, he didn't seem very frightened.

'Are you still there?' he was calling. 'Think about it, Talisker, your chance to tell your story. To redress the balance. I know you protested your innocence all the time you were inside.'

Talisker was almost back at the level of the toilet buildings, but Finn's voice carried through the snow with remarkable clarity. Rubbing the snowflakes from his eyes, he tried to keep watching Finn's back for movement. The idea was compelling.

'My story,' he said quietly. 'You'd never believe it.' He moved forward again, keeping the gun trained on his target.

'What d'you think ye're doin'?' Malky appeared between Talisker and the car. 'Get out o' here, man. It's a trick, Duncan. He's just appealin' tae yer vanity, can't you see that?'

'No, he thinks I should tell my story, Malk. Maybe I can—'

'What? Explain? "I didnae do it" is no' goin' tae take much tellin', is it?' To Talisker's amazement Malky drew his sword. 'Get back, Duncan,' he growled.

'Is – is someone else with you?' Finn was getting anxious.

'What do you think you're going to do with that?' Talisker mocked. 'Put it away, Malky, you're not real here.'

'Naw, neither is this,' Malky replied. 'If he does tell your story, he'll make it all wrong.'

'No, it's just me,' Talisker called. 'Look, turn round slowly. Put your hands on the bonnet of the car.'

Finn did as instructed.

'I dinny believe you sometimes.' Malky threw down his sword in disgust.

Talisker surveyed Finn more closely: he seemed

young to be covering murder cases, late twenties perhaps. 'How old are you?'

'Thirty-five,' Finn replied.

'Huh, older than me.' Talisker blinked away the snow. He had to act more quickly, his outstretched arm hurt, the muscles cramping with the cold.

'I haven't got time to tell you my story. Where's Chaplin?'

Finn jerked his head back towards the woods. 'He went that way, but you're right, you haven't got time. He's probably able to track you quite easily in the snow. Look, I can give you my card and you can ring me. I promise you I won't have the call traced or anything.' He moved his hand towards his jacket and Talisker jabbed the gun at him. Finn withdrew his hand. 'Easy, I was just getting a card.'

'Okay, but do it slowly.'

Finn took out a wallet and produced a business card. 'Here we are.' Talisker reached forward to take it and their fingers touched. His mind flared as the sight claimed him. Not now, he thought desperately, not now . . .

*There is a boy in a darkened room. He is sitting on the floor, sobbing his heart out. Not a contained cry, a wild, frightened noise. His eyes are scrunched shut, long silver strands of drool escape from the corner of his mouth. He is rocking back and forth hunched over something in his lap, a dog or cat, perhaps: black fur is just visible across the knees of the boy's jeans. He is sitting in a dark, expanding pool of liquid. The vision shifts so that Talisker can see clearly. The room is in chaos, furniture thrown around as though some gargantuan hero has tossed it across the room; surely not this frightened weeping boy . . . It's a head, he can see now, the boy is sitting in a pool of warm blood, and he's cradling . . . a head.*

Talisker took the card.

'Are you all right?' Finn asked mildly. 'Perhaps you should give yourself up. They say it's going to snow heavily and you look pale, cold.'

'Going now,' Talisker muttered. 'I'll – I'll call you, maybe.' He backed away with the gun as before. 'Turn round,' he called, almost as an afterthought, and Finn did so. This time Talisker followed his original plan and ran back down to the estuary. He was aware that Malky was running alongside him through the snow, his plaid and long hair streaming behind him, and he appreciated this: Malky could appear and disappear anywhere Talisker was and he didn't need to travel in this way.

'Whit did you see, Duncan?'

'Tell you later, Malk. Save your breath.'

The snow was beginning to lie now, and the going was difficult. Twice Talisker slipped and fell on rocks concealed by grass and snow. Running was hard and he felt as though his blood was freezing in his veins while the aches and bruises acquired across two worlds conspired to haunt him. He was about to stop when he heard Chaplin's voice just behind him to his left. 'Talisker!'

In one smooth motion he pulled the gun from his pocket as he turned and found his target straight away. Chaplin was standing just twenty feet away, his revolver pointing at Talisker's chest. Neither man fired;

both were breathless, their lungs burning from the frozen air. No one spoke.

'Inspector Chaplin!' Finn came running up the beach and Talisker's gaze flicked briefly to him.

'He's not armed, Talisker,' Chaplin said evenly. 'Finn, stay back.'

Finn stopped in his tracks almost midway between the two men.

'Come back here behind me,' Chaplin ordered calmly.

'Chaplin.' Talisker had regained some measure of control now, his breath easing. 'Listen to me, Chaplin, you know it wasn't me. You know where I was last night and for the last week or so.'

'Aye, listen to him.' Malky was standing beside Talisker again.

Chaplin scowled. 'You stay out of this, Malky.'

'What? Who are you . . .?' Finn was thrown.

Talisker laughed hoarsely. 'He'll think you're crazy if you keep talking to Malcolm.'

'So where – were you?' Chaplin asked haltingly.

'Sutra. So were you, *Seanachaidh*.'

'You're lying,' Chaplin had rallied. 'Put the gun down, Talisker, I'm taking you in.'

'*Seanachaidh*?' Finn muttered. 'Wasn't that in the crossword?'

'I'm not coming. You're going to have to shoot me.'

'Put the gun down,' Chaplin ordered.

There were a few seconds of silence. Slowly, inexorably, Talisker felt his finger tighten on the trigger. He was trapped within this scenario and the only release would be the end for him and Chaplin.

'Stop this now!' Malky ran into the line of fire.

Although he was almost transparent, certain areas of his body and clothing were more opaque than others and he disrupted the view of both men.

'Get out of the way, Malk!' Talisker yelled.

'No, Ah canny let you boys do this.' Malky faced Chaplin. 'Sandro, please, you've got tae remember, the battle, Ruannoch Were, Una, Morias, Bris, Conall. You've got tae remember the stories! Morias made you *Seanachaidh*. You were so proud, you fought beside Ferghus—'

'No! No!' Chaplin was shaking his head, his whole body entering a state of denial. 'You're lying – it's the drugs. You're lying!'

'You do remember, though, don't ye?' Malky accused him. 'What about Mirranon?'

'Mirranon? No . . .' He dropped his gun back to his side, his eyes focused on Malky. To Finn he seemed to be falling apart, and the young man was appalled. 'What the hell's going on here? Inspector?' He took Chaplin by the shoulder, obscuring the officer's line of vision, and Malky signalled to Talisker to run.

Chaplin looked at Finn, unsure for a moment who the journalist was. Malky knew it was dangerous to relax his assault on Chaplin's beleaguered senses. 'You know it's true, Sandro,' he went on. 'Jist think about it. Ye can see me, can't you? That's no' normal either but it's true.'

'F-Finn, I don't think I'm . . .'

'You an' Duncan wiz both there,' Malky continued, labouring the point.

Chaplin's gaze darted back to where Talisker stood.

But Talisker was gone.

# CHAPTER THIRTEEN

Running through the snow-covered woodlands again, Talisker thought about his confrontation with Chaplin. The strength of his anger at Chaplin's denial of Sutra had surprised him, but he knew that what the policeman really rejected was their shared experience. He would rather believe that Talisker was a sadistic murderer than acknowledge the truth. The next time they met, there would be a reckoning. As he ran, Talisker fingered the gun and considered how much simpler it might be in the real world without Chaplin, how easy it would be to—

His foot caught on the roots of a tree and he fell headlong, his momentum carrying him on until he landed, face down on the rough frosted earth. For a moment he simply lay there, realising distantly that he was about to pass out.

*It's not real unconsciousness, though. He's in the void, he knows. But how is it possible? Surely he's not dying? It was just a fall. And, anyway, Malky hasn't brought him here. He looks around. It's difficult to pinpoint, surely all blackness is the same, but he doesn't think he's been here before, in this part of the void. It feels different, threatening and oppressively warm. Also, he knows that someone, or something, is watching him.*

*'Hello?' He walks forward.*

*There's a loud rasping sound, and two steps ahead of him, a huge chasm opens in the fabric of the void. A fault line of radiant white light splits the ground before him. Its rays shine upwards into infinity, like bars of liquid silver, and he cannot see what lies beyond their brilliance. He hears a voice, which seems to come from the other side of the chasm.*

*'Talisker. At last. I knew I could attract your attention.' The obsequious tones echo across the space, and he strains to see into the light.*

*'Am I in the void?' he calls. 'What do you want?' He can see a figure now. It's in silhouette but its outline is clear, leaning almost casually against some other unidentifiable black shape.*

*'You know why you can come here to the void, don't you?'*

*'Well, I—'*

*'Your soul is divided, Talisker, across the worlds. And, unfortunately for me, that makes you difficult to kill.'*

*'Who are you?'*

*The being gives a derisive chuckle. 'Really!' he scoffs. 'I wanted to give you something to think about. The murders.'*

*'What about them?' Talisker takes a cautious step forward. 'Do you know who's doing them?'*

*The same dry chuckle. 'Oh, yes. And they won't stop, Talisker, until you do something about it.'*

*'Like what? I'm not responsible.'*

*'Well, yes and no.' The voice is loaded with amusement. 'You see, I want to keep you there, in your home city . . . Have you heard of personal demons? Well, in*

*your case they're very personal – custom made, you might say.'*

*The air between them is hotter, the light brighter. Soon it will be unbearable to stand in that space. As Talisker watches, the silhouette shifts and changes. It becomes larger but there is no light connected with this change, as there is for the Sidhe. Where the silver of the lights catches the edges, the impression is of feathers.*

*'I don't understand,' he begins.*

*The shape, now identifiable as a huge bird, moves its wings, preparing to fly from the chasm. The voice echoes around him. 'Every night, Talisker. It will kill every night. Until it kills you.'*

*He can feel the back-draught as the bird flies, causing the bars of light to flicker. Its wings fan the scorching air towards him and Talisker puts his arms before his face to protect himself. 'But that's not fair,' he shouts.*

*'Fair?' the voice replies, and dissolves into malicious laughter . . . which changes into the discordant cry of a bird . . . a raven . . .*

Talisker sat up. He was sprawled in the undergrowth, his nose bloodied and his back and legs covered with snow. His journey into the void had taken only a few minutes for the blood on his upper lip was not yet dry. The snow was soaking through his clothes now, making him cold and wet. His teeth were chattering and he stood up shakily, knowing he had to keep going before the cold overwhelmed him. There was no way of knowing if Chaplin was pursuing him now, or if he had gone back to Ladyfield to recuperate and get reinforcements.

His thoughts, drifting and unfocused, returned to the

void. He realised, somewhat belatedly, that the power which had drawn him there was not Mirranon's or that of the Sidhe, and although it was chained, it could still send fingers of wicked influence to his world. For long moments he stood shivering in the snow-soft quiet of the forest, crippled by fear and rage. In Sutra, the death of warriors in battle could be counted in thousands but they weren't his deaths; here in Edinburgh they could be ascribed directly to him. Young women, killed by the beast that stalked him, as a warning and punishment to him. It made sense now.

'Corvus,' he muttered.

Stumbling, as the circulation returned to his legs, he continued through the trees.

At first he thought it was a man. He had caught sight of a movement through the green and white shapes of the woodland and instinctively drew back behind the nearest tree. It wasn't until the figure passed within a few hundred feet of where he stood that he realised that it was unnaturally tall, the top of its head brushing the overhanging branches without heeding the shower of snowflakes this released on to it. Also, its gait was strange: although it was moving quite fast, it stumbled along as though it was constantly about to fall on to its face in the snow. When Talisker glimpsed its skin, he knew it was not a man: the skin was waxen, greasy, like candles made of cheap tallow, while its hands were huge, its feet bare.

This must be as Corvus had said, his own personal demon. Hardly daring to breathe, he drew back behind the thick tree trunk and listened for sounds to indicate the creature's direction. It seemed to be moving towards the edges of the estuary where it dipped inland at high tide.

Then he heard a noise close behind him. Whipping round, he saw the creature and it saw him – or so he thought. It appeared to be looking straight at him but did not react. Talisker prepared to bolt as soon as it got too close or broke its stride to charge. It was ten feet away . . . five feet, and now he had left it too late to run. Still the creature did not react. When it was so close that Talisker could have touched its ragged clothes, it turned on its heels and began to walk towards the water, crashing through the trees and bushes as heedlessly as before.

'Duncan.' Malky spoke softly, sensing that Talisker was on the edge of endurance. 'Ye've got to run now, haven't you, or the beast will catch up?'

'Let it,' Talisker replied. 'I don't care. Corvus wants me dead. That's why those women died.'

'But if ye kill it, Duncan, that's goin' tae be tellin' him, isn't it?' Malky reasoned. 'He's feared o' you. That's why he's done this.'

'It's a fucking demon, Malk. Corvus says you can't kill it.'

'Well, he would say that, wouldn't he? He wants you tae give up. Ah hope you're no' goin' tae give him the satisfaction. Look, this is what I think. The beastie is trackin' you, right? But no' like a dug would. He's following you through time an' all. D'you see?'

Talisker frowned. 'How do you know, Malk?'

'I kin see your tracks,' he shrugged, 'so I bet he can. We'd better plan our attack – it'll catch up soon. I dinny think it stops where you stopped, leastways, I keep hearin' it an' it's been goin' fer hours already. And the gap is goin' tae keep gettin' smaller each time you stop.'

Talisker sighed. 'God, I wish I had a sword instead of this bloody gun. All right, Malk, you've got a point.'

'So, let's keep movin',' Malky grinned triumphantly, 'till we can make a plan.'

'I don't reckon we can kill it just by walking up to it. We've got to do the same thing it's doing. Let's backtrack. I say we take the fight to it. Now.'

'There's just one thing, Duncan. I canny help you here, remember? Ah'm a ghost. You're on your own.'

Something happened as they walked back through the woodland retracing Talisker's steps: a connection flared along the pathway of their footsteps, between Talisker, Malky and the demon. A glowing pathway became visible in the trees, criss-crossing like the web of an indecisive spider. It seemed as though their journey trapped Talisker and Malky within the timeline that they and the demon followed, unravelling the day. The afternoon, which had been gradually darkening, lightened and turned back into morning. Talisker noticed the strange motion of the waves: they too were moving backwards, the tide slowly creeping out. He returned his attention to the trail. 'At least Theseus had the sense to get out of the maze,' he observed.

Malky said nothing; their retrograde journey was unnerving him. Apart from the sound of the sea, the only other noise was the demon. The way the snow was disappearing upwards into the heavens was . . . creepy. The Highlander drew his sword and was satisfied by the quiet hiss of the steel.

'Malky.' Talisker had stopped and was observing his

friend closely. 'I know you can take me back to Sutra.'

'Only if ye're dyin', Duncan.'

'When we catch up with this thing, don't interfere, Malk. If it kills me . . . let me go.'

'But—'

'No, I mean it. It'll be over then. A conclusion. Do you understand?'

'Aye.'

'Promise me, Malcolm.'

'I promise.'

Twice, the creature passed within feet of them but ignored them. Its unseeing gaze swept the forest trail. Malky whistled quietly when he saw it closely for the first time. 'Jings, it's a big beastie,' he whispered.

Talisker had lost all perspective but he was sure they had been walking for about an hour when the trail they were following became brighter and moved spasmodically. 'It's close,' he muttered. He pulled out the gun and picked up a thick branch from the forest floor. 'For back-up.'

There was complete silence, and Talisker cast around wildly, his breathing becoming faster, panicked, wondering how such a creature could make no noise. Then, from the forest dead ahead, there came a loud, screeching call and the demon was charging towards them. Talisker fired, once, twice, but it didn't break its stride.

'Ohmigod . . .' He fired again. There was a click. The chamber was empty. Talisker threw aside the gun and raised the branch above his head. 'C'mon, then!' he bellowed, as the first wave of adrenaline coursed through him. 'Come on!'

As the creature came into range, their pathways from past to present and present to past, met in an instant of conflagration. The forest, the snow, the sea, all physical landscape vanished, to be replaced by a lurid red nothingness. Talisker and the beast were in the moment and the moment was out of time. Slick cold fingers of sweat moved down his back and legs; he felt simultaneously freezing and sticky hot. For what seemed like an age, he was powerless to move, could only watch the darkened figure that filled his horizon, his eyes wide in terror, as it continued its slow-motion charge. It was an absurd parody of a man. Its clothes, hair and large areas of yellow flesh hung loosely from its frame and moved in an insanely slow dance. Only when the moment was upon him did Talisker shake off the pall of dread that held him spellbound and find the strength to move. He drew back his makeshift club in preparation to strike . . .

'Go oaaan!'

Contact.

He landed a blow across the demon's neck and head, and heard a sickening dull thud. The demon was knocked sideways and Talisker allowed himself to think it would topple over. Seizing his advantage, he struck again with the branch hoping to catch it off balance, but the demon was surprisingly fast and had recovered. Reaching out a huge malformed hand, it grasped the branch, snatched it from Talisker and flung it aside. Then, the repulsive yellow hand was around his neck, the huge fingers easily wrapping around and meeting at the back. Talisker felt himself lifted from the ground. He kicked and squirmed, hearing the choking, rasping sounds he was making and the hissing breath of the demon. Red shapes crowded his vision, flares, after-images of nothing he had seen. Kicking out wildly, he made contact hard enough to give his tormentor pause and, just as unconsciousness threatened, the creature released its hold on his neck. There was no time to escape, however, as it transferred its grip to his hair. Talisker heard himself scream in anger and frustration as he flailed wildly for a grip on anything. A sick certainty was forming in his mind that the creature would grab him somewhere around the middle then simply pull him apart. The punch to his head, therefore, took him by surprise. Blood gushed down his face and neck and he choked and spluttered as he swallowed it.

'Duncan! Do something!' he heard Malky yell.

Another punch. And another, to his ribcage this time. There was a horrible sound of breaking bone. For a second the beast let go of his hair, and Talisker felt his legs as far removed and disconnected as they could be while still attached to his body. His eyes were clouded by blood and sweat. He began to slump to the ground but the creature would not let him fall. It grabbed him by the waist and neck. This time it was going to tear him apart. He felt himself lifted high in the air . . . Dear God, he was going to die now. Twisting, twisting, a sick crunching sound. Himself, screaming, pain, pain, pain . . . Then nothing.

Long moments of blackness. But he was aware.

'You've done it, Malk.' The voice drifted disjointedly through the ether. 'What did I tell you?'

'Ah'm sorry, Duncan. Ah couldnae stand it.'

'Duncan? Duncan?'

He opened his eyes, felt the warmth of someone holding his hand. His head felt too heavy to turn but he knew it was Una. Malky's stark white features came into view. 'Ah couldnae watch it kill ye,' he said again. 'Ah couldnae jist stand by . . .'

''S all right, Malk, I'm not angry.' He tried to smile but his lips and skin were cracked and sore. 'Was I really there?' he whispered.

In response, Malky took Talisker's free hand and moved it to his throat. Something hung there, something that had come with him: a prayer from another world. He felt the round shape of Shula's St Christopher, and a tear trickled down his cheek, through the blood and grime. 'I'm not worthless, then.'

He wanted to sleep. With his last vestige of energy he turned his head and looked at Una: she had been crying and her face was puffy. She said nothing, but smiled and shed more tears.

As he drifted into sleep, Talisker smiled contentedly. There was something else in the smile, though, which Una could not fathom but which Malky understood. It was malice.

'Is Chaplin here?' he muttered. 'I want to see him.'

When he awoke, it was morning, possibly the second day after the battle for Ruannoch Were, but it was impossible to tell: he might have been gone from Sutra for days. Talisker made a mental note to check with Malky – he was the only one who knew everything, except Chaplin, of course. Anger flared in his belly at the thought of the policeman but he didn't want to think about him now. Chaplin could wait, assuming he'd come back with them from Edinburgh this time. Right now, Talisker was enjoying the cosy weakness of the invalid. He felt shaky and infirm as an old man but, also, warm and secure: it reminded him of being allowed to stay off school when his mother would bring him cups of sweet tea and let him read his comics in bed. Weak winter light was streaming in through a small window opposite his bed, and half closing his eyes again he wondered if anyone would bring him some food. A smell wafted in through the window, an autumnal smell, a bonfire. He opened his eyes. There was something worrying about it.

'Talisker?'

It was Chaplin. He was leaning against the door, observing him coldly.

'Chaplin,' Talisker hissed. 'You came back, then?' The policeman shifted uncomfortably and Talisker thought he was building up to an apology. 'Just don't bother apologising, 'cos I don't want to hear it,' he snapped.

'Apologise?' Chaplin appeared genuinely surprised. 'Lose a few brain cells between here and there, did you? Coming back wasn't a matter of choice. But, like I said before, it makes no difference to what you are, you murdering scum. You must only have been back hours before you killed that girl. A hundred Corrannyeid not enough for you? Or did they put up too much of a fight to be any sport? We both know it's how you get your kicks, Talisker – Oh great fucking hero.' He turned to go.

Talisker was furious. 'But you denied everything!' he yelled. 'Are you still denying it? What do you think this is? A game?'

Chaplin turned back, his face pinched and angry. 'Okay, Talisker. I'm only gonna say this once. It's real. But it changes nothing.'

'But you know I was here. You know I couldn't have . . . but . . .' Talisker was beside himself.

'You're a murderer, Duncan,' Chaplin said quietly. 'Nothing changes that. I'll bring you in if we ever get back to Edinburgh. Here, just watch your back.'

'Are you threatening me?' Talisker got out of his bed without thought of any lingering weakness. He stood there in the tattered nightrobe someone had dressed him in while he was unconscious. 'Come on, then!' he yelled. 'Come on, Chaplin, just you and me!'

He was walking towards Chaplin, who did not move from his position in the doorway. Too late, he realised his legs would fail him and he fell to his knees, clutching at the empty bed beside him.

He gasped in pain as a sword cut in his side split apart.

'You're pathetic,' Chaplin said. He turned and walked away, his footsteps echoing down the corridor.

'Stay away from me, Chaplin,' he screamed, incoherent with rage. 'You bastard! Stay away from me or I'll kill you. D'you hear me? I'll kill you!'

He dragged himself back to the edge of his bed and perched on the side. Chaplin was consistent if nothing else. All he'd done was reiterated where they stood, so nothing had changed. But it had. Talisker realised that he'd wanted to hear Chaplin – his oldest friend and enemy – say sorry. In fact, he *needed* to hear it. But he had made things worse. As he pulled himself back into bed, two things dawned on him: first, the bonfires were probably burning the bodies from the battle to stop the spread of disease, and second, maybe he should have mentioned something about Finn to Chaplin, but he couldn't remember what it was and he was too tired to care.

The lady Ulla was waking up. She could tell that she was because the pain had broken through her daze to assault her. She thought first of Dom, but that pain was less now: Ulla had spoken with her daughter in the void and made the final farewell that had been denied her in life. Something else came to her as she woke, not a coherent thought, more a sensation, of being picked up and carried. A voice had spoken to her also, a gentle voice, reassuring and kind. She hadn't felt cared for like that since Callum's death. She let the sensation enfold her, remembering the bittersweet smell of the stranger's body, and drifted back to sleep.

When she woke again daylight was streaming through the rafters of the roof in bright golden bars, dust motes dancing in the light. From the inner reaches of the wooden beams, the call of wood-pigeons drifted down to her.

'Lady Ulla? At last.' It was Morias, the *Seanachaidh*. The old man stood at the foot of her bed, bathed in a pool of the yellow light, leaning heavily on a wooden staff. 'We feared the worst, lady. How do you feel?'

She remembered the horror and pain that had brought her to this tiny golden chamber and shrank back into the comfort of her feather covers. 'As well as can be expected, *Seanachaidh*,' she whispered. Her throat was dry and Morias came forward to offer a drink. She sipped feebly from the cup as he supported her head. 'Does my father know I'm here?' she asked when she had finished. The *Seanachaidh* looked uncomfortable and avoided her gaze.

'Please, Morias, tell me,' she urged quietly. 'Did I really kill my Kyra?'

Morias sighed. 'You did, although you must remember what we discussed when she was taken by Corvus. She was already gone from this world.'

'And my father? Can he forgive me? I know he struck out in confusion.'

There was a pause. Morias sighed again. 'Lady, he thinks you dead. It has been three weeks and he has not asked where you lie.'

'Three weeks!' Ulla was dismayed. 'Tell me something, Morias . . . When I was struck down by my father . . . who carried me away? Who brought me here?'

'I believe it was my successor, the new *Seanachaidh*, Alessandro Chaplin.'

'Alessandro.' She smiled. 'Could you send him to me, Morias, so I may thank him.'

'I cannot, lady. He is gone. He left with Makhpiyaluta three days ago.'

# CHAPTER FOURTEEN

The sound of horses' hooves carried across the otherwise silent landscape, muffled by thick snow. The scene was so starkly white that black specks danced before Talisker's gaze and he lowered his head to look only as far ahead as the red-brown rump of Malky's horse. He was warm enough in the heavy new plaid and cloak he wore, which Una had given to him, but he was ill at ease on the back of a stallion. He'd never ridden a horse before he had set out on this journey and when he had confessed this shamefacedly to Una, she had agreed to give him a couple of lessons. They had risen before dawn and gone to the stables, where Una had chosen a small skewbald gelding; the beast had plodded obediently in circles but Talisker had decided he didn't like horses. He understood their place in the culture and lives of the Fine, but he felt no affinity with them.

He had told Una everything. The night before he left, they had sat together outside the north gate looking out at the water. Talisker felt completely relaxed with her and she listened intently as he talked about Shula, how she had spoken of his soul. 'In our world,' he explained, 'most people believe in only one God, not many different ones. Shula is very devout.'

'And very wise, it seems.' Una nodded. 'Did you love her, Duncan?'

The simple question caught him off guard. 'Well . . . I

don't think . . . I'm not sure. She's special to me because she's the only one who cares. I suppose I love her in a way.'

'Duncan, I'm not jealous. We are worlds apart, are we not?'

He went on to tell her about Corvus, what he had said about the murders during Talisker's enforced visit to the void.

'He really wants to keep you away from Sutra, doesn't he? He must be frightened of you,' she observed.

'That's what Malky said,' he agreed, 'but it doesn't change the facts. Women are dying there because of me or because of my failure to stop it.'

'But here, Duncan, you are just as important. You will take the gem to Mirranon and she will make magic such as has not been seen here for hundreds of years. She will destroy the Corrannyeid, and you will destroy Corvus. The Fine and the Sidhe will be saved from another dark time of tyranny. You will save thousands of lives.' Her eyes sparkled.

The people who remained at Ruannoch Were spoke of little else as they restored their scarred city. It lifted their spirits and they treated Talisker, Malky and Chaplin with quiet respect. It made Talisker nervous.

'Do you think so?' he asked. He allowed himself a moment of selfish vanity as he looked into her face. She was beautiful, and she was looking at him with such belief it humbled him. 'It doesn't change the facts, though, Una. Maybe if I wasn't here, the Fine and the Sidhe would manage to contrive another way out of this mess. I've brought the gem – Braznnair – so surely someone else could do the rest. In Edinburgh, no one can change those girls' fate except me. And one will die each night. No one else can kill that thing. It's directly my responsibility. Do you see?'

'But the demon almost killed you already,' she pointed out.

'Well, Corvus never said it would be easy. But I've got to go back and try again, Una. Somehow, I've got to finish it.'

She squeezed his hand. 'Then you can come back to Sutra for ever, Duncan.'

'I'd like that.'

The next day, when it was time to leave with Malcolm, to his dismay – and Una's quiet amusement – Thane Ferghus presented him with a grey stallion; it was almost the tallest horse Talisker had ever seen. He mounted apprehensively but the animal was well behaved. Chaplin, too, was leaving that morning with Prince Makhpiyaluta; they were travelling on foot back into the forest, Or Coille. Apparently the standing stones by Light of the Sky were magic. Both Talisker and Chaplin had instructions from Ferghus and Morias but neither wanted to discuss anything with the other; they had hardly spoken since their argument at Talisker's sickbed.

Just as Talisker and Malky were about to ride off, Makhpiyaluta came over to them.

'May good fortune attend your journey.' He nodded stiffly and held out his hand.

Talisker shook it firmly. 'And you,' he muttered. He cast around for something to say. 'I will pass the good wishes of the Sidhe to Mirranon when I see her.' Too late, he remembered her outcast status. 'I mean . . .'

But Makhpiyaluta inclined his head in agreement. 'As you wish, Talisker. We need our allies.'

Talisker glanced over at Chaplin, who was sorting out his pack and studiously ignoring his existence. '*Ciao*, Sandro,' he called.

Chaplin glared at him but said nothing.

They left on the ferry and Talisker stared back at the city. The devastation of the battle had left Ruannoch Were burned, jagged and broken, but his heart lifted at the sight of Una, who waved then stood and watched the slow progress of the ferry as it drifted away.

Three days later, the two riders crested the ridge, their mounts steaming and blowing white gouts of air into the chill. Not far behind a huge brown bear loped effortlessly on all fours, its pace unhampered by the snowdrifts that reached up to the height of its shoulders. It moved easily and fast but the riders were in difficulty, their horses slipping and balking at the slick rock face beneath their hoofs. Malky risked a glance behind him. 'We're goin' tae have tae stop, Duncan,' he panted. 'We canny outrun the bear. He's no even tired an' we're gonny injure the horses if we keep on.'

Talisker looked back at it. Malky was right. It had been following them for about half an hour and it didn't even seem winded. Reaching behind his saddle he withdrew his sword. They would have to kill it, because once the horses were lame or worse, he and Malky would be stranded in the wilderness.

'C'mon, Malk,' he grated, 'turn on three. One . . . two . . . three . . .'

Both men turned their mounts to face the bear as it started up the lower slopes of the ridge. It stood up on its back legs, rearing to a height of about eight feet. Talisker cursed.

'At least we've got the high ground,' Malky pointed out. He had drawn his sword and didn't seem worried about engaging the creature. Silence fell as the horses reluctantly picked their way back down the slope. Then the bear made a curious baying noise, moving its head from side to side, watching them come.

Suddenly a warm rose-coloured light suffused its outline, spreading outwards like a stain across the snow. Talisker and Malky stopped to watch.

'We should have known,' Talisker said.

'Well, I wiznae goin' tae stop and ask it,' Malky grunted.

Eventually, the light faded and before them stood a young man. He wore black robes and a heavy leather gauntlet on one hand. His delicate features were human in comparison with those of the Sidhe and his blond hair was cropped short. He said nothing but surveyed them through narrowed eyes, then held out his gloved hand and gave a high, piercing whistle. A bird of prey landed there. It was bigger than a kestrel but smaller than a buzzard; its breast was blue-grey and its yellow beak and talons seemed particularly sharp and vicious-looking. It was looking at Talisker and Malky with the same distrustful expression as its owner, who seemed uncomfortable.

'What do you want, laddie?' Malky called down the slope. The boy seemed only about fifteen.

'N-nothing, sir. Just to speak with you.'

Malky and Talisker exchanged glances. The bear clan Sidhe was a girl.

Talisker sighed. The snow was falling again, and the sounds on the high moors became muffled, closing in on them. 'What's your name . . . young lady?' He added this as an afterthought – she might be royal, like Makhpiyaluta.

'Tayna, sir,' she said, 'and this is Breeze.'

'Well, Tayna, let's make camp before we talk. The storm is closing in. Will you help?'

She began to climb the ridge towards them.

'There.' Malky pointed to a patch of darkness among the rocks. 'C'mon.' The three travellers made for the gap, which was low to the ground, more of a hole than a cave.

'We'll no' be able to get the horses tae step doon,' he pointed out.

'There is a little shelter in the lee of the slope,' Tayna suggested. 'If you let the horses go they will find the best place.'

'But they'll no' come back tae us, lassie.'

Tayna pressed her face against the soft muzzle of Talisker's grey. 'I will fetch them for you, sir,' she said. 'Trust me. I am good with beasts.'

Talisker shrugged and nodded. There didn't seem much option: if they stayed above ground with the horses they would freeze. Tayna held the reins while Malky unsaddled and unpacked the provisions, then she walked off down the slope talking gently to the animals, her black robes blowing in the wind.

Once inside the cave, the noise of the wind stopped abruptly. Talisker busied himself lighting a torch, which Malky had made the previous evening. Malky stared back towards the entrance, seemingly preoccupied. 'You know, she could just be a clever horse thief,' he muttered.

'Hey, I'm the pessimist in these parts, Malk.' Talisker handed the Highlander a torch and they looked around the cave. It was much bigger than they had dared to hope, and the flickering light failed to illuminate the furthest end. The rock walls were a soft grey, covered with lichen and moss, wet and slimy but for one dry area where the sun must have reached in during the afternoon. The two men set out their packs there. Tayna returned and stared into the back of the cave. 'Would you like me to check for bears?' She smiled.

Talisker grinned – she had a quiet sense of humour.

'I'm just joking. It's the wolves you have to worry about in these parts,' she added and strode silently into the darkness to return a few minutes later. 'All quiet,' she reported. 'I was serious about the wolves, though. You are crossing wolf clan land now. They are the most radical of all the Sidhe. They would kill you as soon as look at you. That's why I was trying to warn you.' Having made this pronouncement she sat down cross-legged before the fire and closed her eyes.

'Excuse me, Tayna,' Talisker said.

The girl opened her eyes again.

'Why would the wolf clan want to kill us?'

'You are the One, are you not? Tal-ees-ker? You are bringing the gem Braznnair to Mirranon, the White Eagle?'

'Yes,' said Talisker warily. 'How do you know?'

Tayna laughed lightly. 'All the Sidhe know this. We

have the speed of the beasts whose forms we command and messages travel faster between us than they can with a mere rider.'

'If the Sidhe are so good, how come one o' you lot canny take the bloody thing tae Mirranon?' Malky growled. 'How come me an' Duncan are freezing oor bollocks off?'

Tayna looked serious again. 'None will touch it, sir. No Sidhe would take that responsibility. Already the arguments rage among the southern tribes . . . Whoever gained possession of the gem, well, it might provoke a war between the Sidhe.'

'Yeah, we heard that from Makhpiyaluta.'

'You have met the Prince!' Tayna's eyes widened in childish wonder. 'What is he like? Is he handsome?'

Talisker and Malky laughed, the sound echoing through the cave, and the young Sidhe looked crestfallen.

'I'm sorry, Tayna,' Talisker said, 'but as we are human and male, it would be difficult for us to judge. He seems a . . . good man, though. A man of integrity. He has gone with a friend of ours on a—'

'I know,' she interrupted, 'with the *Seanachaidh* to awaken the heroes.' She looked solemn. 'He has gone to delay the decision of the Sidhe further. The others of the Council of Tema cannot act without him.'

'How d'ye know this, Tayna? Ye're jist a young girl,' Malky said.

Her pale golden features turned a warm pink. 'I . . . follow news of the Prince,' she admitted. 'He is . . . special to me, I cannot explain, although my mother has warned me that he is . . . unclean.'

Malky raised his brows. 'Ye mean he disnae wash?'

Tayna giggled. 'No, sir. It's what we say when one of us prefers their beast form and stays with it as often as possible. Makhpiyaluta is more often an eagle than a Sidhe, and some think this means he thinks less of his subjects and more of the skies.'

Malky thought of the Prince's anguish on the night he had helped to heal Talisker. 'What do you think, Tayna?' he asked.

'I think he is a great prince, sir. I think the eagle is his true soul but he will never abandon us.'

'Ye're right,' Malky nodded.

'Tayna, what do the Sidhe believe Braznnair could do?' Talisker asked.

Just as she seemed about to answer, Breeze flew into the mouth of the cave carrying a large white hare, which it deposited beside its mistress. It began to peck off the flesh until Tayna shooed it away. 'Dinner, I think,' she declared. Taking out a small sharp knife, she pared off some meat and threw it to Breeze, who hopped across the floor of the cave to retrieve it. Malky took the hare to draw its innards.

'How d'ye make her come back to ye, Tayna?' Malky indicated the bird. 'I thought ye had to be there and bribe it with some meat or something.'

'Perhaps a human master would, but I can commune with Breeze when I am Ashka, my bear form. I did not name her. She told me her name. We are friends.'

'So, Tayna, what about the gem?' Talisker prodded gently.

'I'm not sure I can say, sir. If Prince Makhpiyaluta has not told you he must have had a reason.'

It seemed to Talisker that Tayna was wise beyond her years. Makhpiyaluta had refused to discuss with him the prophecies of the Sidhe. It was obvious he did not trust Talisker.

'Tayna's right,' said Malky, from the far side of the cave, 'Makhpiyaluta wiznae saying much. Mebbe he jist wanted time tae make the decision – whatever that is – himsel'.'

Tayna bit her lip. 'You are not angry with me, sir, are you?' she asked anxiously. 'Many Sidhe hearts are with you. A great number of my tribe have been cruelly killed by the Corrannyeid and some feel there is naught to be gained by looking to the past—' She caught herself suddenly as though she had said too much and flushed once more.

'I saw a bear,' said Malky distantly, 'when we first arrived. Remember, Duncan? I had to kill him because the Corrannyeid were doing their stinkin' thing to him.' He spat on the cave floor. 'Funny thing, that. When he died, he took a human form. A young lad he was, the most beautiful face I had ever seen.' After all the deaths he had encountered since, Malky was still moved by the memory.

'Yes,' replied Tayna quietly. 'The Fine call we bears "the least changed". They think us the most human-looking. Should you see Ashka with no hair on her face, she would look quite human.'

'Here.' Malky reached into his purse and passed something to Tayna. It glowed a warm gold in the firelight.

'Where did you find this?' she asked, her voice trembling.

'The bear wore it in the top part of his ear,' Malky explained.

'It means he was a *Raknnawr*, a messenger,' Tayna said. 'They are greatly revered among our people and all the tribes of the Sidhe. He was probably going to warn of the attack on the city. Our own halls are to the north-east of Light of the Sky, but still on the fringes of Or Coille, the great forest. It is likely that the Thane sent him to warn us that the Corrannyeid were abroad in the forest. My older brother is such a Sidhe . . .' She handed the earring back to Malky, tears welling in her eyes. In the silence that followed Malky busied himself with placing skewered chunks of meat over the flames of the fire.

'Tayna, I'm sorry if we have upset you,' Talisker said gently. 'Why are you so far from your halls anyway? There is a war coming in the north. Surely you should be at home with your family.'

Tayna sniffed, with a defiant air. 'I left,' she said shortly. 'I thought I'd travel a bit.'

'You've run away, ye wee minx.' Malky grinned. 'Maybe you should stick with us for a while. You'd like to meet the Great Eagle, wouldn't you?'

It was Tayna's turn to laugh. 'I'd get there quicker on my own. You have travelled two days too far south. And I must meet someone in the Lowlands.'

Talisker groaned. 'Great. I told them they'd be better sending someone else. For Chrissakes, I've spent fifteen years sitting in the same room. What did they expect?'

'You've been in prison?' Tayna asked, with interest.

Malky changed the subject. 'It's a boy, isn't it? You're going to meet a boy?'

'Maybe . . .' she agreed guardedly. 'Can we eat now? I'm starving.'

A couple of hours later the trio settled down for the night. Tayna had agreed to travel north with them for a day until the landmarks she had described would be easy to follow. She couldn't afford more time than that, she confided, because the person she was meeting would be unable to wait longer than two days. When pressed for information about him, she stared fixedly into the embers of the fire. 'He's not a Sidhe,' she admitted. 'His name is Owen and he's a clansman from south of Linfar where Huw's clan are settled. There are no great cities further south than there, and the landscape is different. Owen says it is green for most of the year and flat. You can see the sky for miles and miles, he says. We will live there on the plains and I will never be Ashka again.'

'But, Tayna, you will be outcast like Mirranon. How can you do this?'

'I love him,' she said simply. 'He makes me smile. When I am with him, all the colours of Sutra seem alive. I can see him standing beneath the big blue sky, a plainsman . . . Have you never loved like that, sir? It is such a simple thing.'

Talisker said nothing. On the surface, it seemed a simple thing indeed, but in his experience . . .

'Aye,' Malky spoke quietly, 'it wiz like that when me an' Morag were first together. Great days . . . But then we found another love, Tayna. The love for our daughter Ilsa. That's no tae say we didnae still care fer each other – we did – but it all changes then, when you have a child.'

'I didn't know you had a family, Malk,' Talisker said. 'What happened to them?'

'They died, doon there in Mary King's Close. Morag died quite quickly but the bairn . . . I had tae smother her in her sl—' He broke off. Talisker patted his friend's shoulder in a useless gesture of comfort and no one spoke for a while.

'You should go back tae yer parents, Tayna,' Malky said eventually. 'They must be frantic. Ye're jist a wee lassie after aw.'

'I am sorry for your loss, sir,' she replied, 'but this is different—'

Her words were interrupted by the sound of wolves baying quite close at hand.

'Quick. Extinguish the torches!' she whispered. Malky grabbed all three, moved silently to the back of the cave and dipped them in a pool of water. The travellers sat motionless in their blankets for a long time staring at the entrance hole. Outside, the driving snow seemed bright against the dark winter sky, and once a lithe black shadow crossed the opening but did not look into the refuge.

For most of the following day Tayna travelled with them, running tirelessly beside the horses in her bear form. When they stopped to eat she transformed back into her Sidhe shape and chatted with Malky, who related to her in a fatherly way that Talisker found both touching and awkward. It was early evening when she stopped running as Ashka and, transforming to Tayna, told them she must leave. 'Over there,' she said, pointing north-west, 'in the Blue Mountains there is a pass in the high slopes, which is remarkable for a rock shaped like an eagle in flight. Cross the pass keeping the river to your left. Follow the river through the rocks, and when you come through the other side you will see the valley where Mirranon is to be found. I expect she will send someone to guide you if she does not come herself.'

'Thank you, Tayna,' Talisker said. 'Are you heading south now?'

'Yes. I must leave you if I am to catch Owen. Be careful. I think it will get colder. Beware the wolves.'

Malky clasped the girl to him in a warm embrace. To her credit she did not flinch at the touch of the undead Highlander, but returned his hug. 'I still think ye should go home mind,' he said, 'but jist you make sure this Owen is worth it, eh?'

'I will,' she promised. 'Goodbye. Goodbye, Talisker. The gods travel with you.'

Without more ado she changed once more to Ashka and loped off into the snow, stopping only once to look back. Both men waved and turned their horses north towards the mountains.

'Whit a lovely lass,' Malky remarked. 'It disnae happen often ye know, that folk feel so easy with each other. I mean I felt as if . . . I knew her already. Mebbes if my wee Ilsa had—'

'C'mon, Malk, we can get another couple of hours in before nightfall,' and with that Talisker spurred his horse forward.

That night they camped in a copse of birch trees. The delicate branches did not afford much shelter but they were the only cover for miles. Talisker was sure they were being followed by wolves and thought he had seen silent grey shapes a few times, but it was always from the corner of his eye and he couldn't get a decent view of the creatures. He said nothing about it to Malky but as they lit a fire the Highlander remarked, 'We'd better keep this goin' all night if we can. I dinny want tae alarum ye, Duncan, bit I think I may have seen a couple o' wolves.'

They decided that one or other of them would keep watch all night. Talisker had the final watch before dawn. The cold was biting and he hugged his blanket around himself and stared into the fire.

The next thing he knew, Malky was shaking him awake. 'Duncan. Wake up. The horses are gone.'

Chaplin regarded the eagle coldly. What liking he had had for Makhpiyaluta when they started out had faded over the past five days as they travelled through Or Coille. He understood the Prince's actions but that didn't make it any easier, and he hadn't wanted to make this trip in the first place. Separating himself from Talisker and the gem – which as far as he knew was his only ticket back to Edinburgh – was the last thing he planned, but Morias had pleaded with him to go: 'It's my guess that Mirranon will be unable to do anything without you. Three came through the gateway and three must return. It is simple common sense,' the *Seanachaidh* lied easily. 'Chaplin, I don't think you understand. The land has chosen you. You are the new *Seanachaidh*, the only one who can raise the *Fir Chrieg*, the heroes. I would go myself but I am an old man.'

'So why didn't you tell me this before?' Chaplin

stormed. 'You found Talisker and me at the standing stones. Why didn't we do it then?'

'I did not think it possible. It was Makhpiyaluta's idea.'

Makhpiyaluta . . .

After the first attack by a band of Corrannyeid on the second day, Chaplin had changed his mind about the journey. If he was quick, he reasoned, he could loop back round the city and catch up with Talisker and Malky. As soon as he turned though, the eagle had landed on the path in front of him.

*Where are you going?* The thought arrived in his mind like a slap. The huge bird eyed him unblinkingly.

'I've had it,' Chaplin snarled. 'We'll be killed out here. The place is crawling with Corrannyeid and I'm not even on horseback.'

*'A horse would be of little use to you in the forest. You know that. Are you frightened?'*

'No,' Chaplin lied. 'I just don't want to throw my life away on a wild goose chase.'

*Craven coward.* The bird blinked.

'What?'

*'You heard me. I should have come myself. No, I should have descended on your precious Talisker with a flight of eagles and taken the gem for the Sidhe. But I let the Thane and that old fool Seanachaidh guide me. And now I am wet-nursing you through the forest. You will go on, Alessandro Chaplin, because I have given my word.'*

'You can't make me—' Chaplin began.

*'Oh, but I can,'* Makhpiyaluta snapped. To demonstrate his point he beat his wings and rose into the air.

Picking up a gnarled log in his talons he snapped it in two without further comment.

Chaplin was furious at the implied threat and drew his sword. 'I am not a coward, Makhpiyaluta,' he fumed, but the eagle sent no more thought messages. It rose above the tree-line scanning once more for Corrannyeid. The downbeat of the massive wings caused the breeze in the small clearing to buffet the trees and bushes, catching Chaplin's long dark hair and whipping the edges of his new plaid.

'I am not a coward,' he shouted again, shaking the sword towards the Prince. 'I am a Sicilian!'

But his eagle companion had flown ahead and chose to ignore him. After a while there seemed little else to do but sheath the blade and continue.

Now, on the evening of the fifth day, Chaplin neared the clearing where Makhpiyaluta had stopped for the night. He watched the eagle closely, wondering if the Prince ever slept. The two travellers had spoken little since their argument and normally this would not bother Chaplin – he was capable of holding a grudge for a lifetime, especially when he had been called a coward – but this evening he needed to speak to the Prince.

'Makhpiyaluta, we're being followed.'

The Sidhe looked sharply towards him then shape-shifted into human form. 'That's not possible,' he said. 'I've been circling behind you as you travel. There's nothing there.'

'I'm telling you,' Chaplin insisted. 'Three times now I've heard something.'

'An animal? Corrannyeid?'

'It's just a feeling . . . but I think it's a person.'

'I will go and look,' said Makhpiyaluta coldly, annoyed that his talents had been called into question. 'Perhaps you would be so good as to set the fire.'

Chaplin nodded curtly as the Prince returned to his eagle form and set out into the twilight forest.

Two hours later he had not returned. It was dark and Chaplin sat close to the fire, listening for animals or worse in the undergrowth. He was sure that Makhpiyaluta was staying away to spite him and was watching from some vantage-point, enjoying his discomfort, so he kept his movements relaxed around the small campsite. For some reason, he had been thinking about his father today, how he would have loved all this, the battle, the mission to raise the *Fir Chrieg*. He would have been a dark passionate warrior about whom stories could legitimately be told. All his days he had raged against something, had carried a profound anger in his soul that flickered beneath the surface of his life . . .

A scream echoed through the trees. Chaplin leaped up and grabbed a brand from the fire, his heart racing. A shadow loomed over the clearing and just as Chaplin recognised the eagle's shape, Makhpiyaluta dropped a grey bundle from his talons, which landed hard in the bushes emitting a low groan.

*'Here it is,'* the Prince announced to Chaplin. *'It pains me to admit that you were right but we were being quite inexpertly followed.'*

Chaplin ran towards the grey shape, his sword in one hand, the brand in the other.

'All right. Drop your weapons,' he commanded. The figure staggered out of the bushes, its grey robes snagging on the brambles. Makhpiyaluta had landed behind Chaplin, transformed swiftly and ran forward, drawing his sword.

'Please. It is I . . .' The voice was female and familiar. The men looked questioningly at each other. She pushed back the hood of her robe. 'It is I. The lady Ulla.'

Makhpiyaluta was mortified. He ran forward and helped Ulla towards the fire, uttering a stream of apologies. Chaplin tried to control his mirth at the arrogant Prince's discomfort but his first sight of Ulla's face in the firelight sobered him. She was haggard, her eyes were unfocused, and the disfigured side of her features was raw and sore. Surprisingly she walked smoothly to the fire with Makhpiyaluta's support, then sat down gratefully on Chaplin's blankets.

'My lady, are you well?'

'I am as well as can be expected, *Seanachaidh.*' She touched her face. 'I miss my salve, though, and I underestimated the ravages of the journey. Pain I am used to . . . but this irritation—' She broke off, obviously in distress.

'My lady, allow me to make amends for my dreadful behaviour,' Makhpiyaluta grovelled. 'I saw some suitable herbs earlier, and it will be a small task but my honour to make you a salve. We Sidhe are adept at such things.' He bowed stiffly.

Perhaps Makhpiyaluta could not see from where he stood but it was clear to Chaplin that the lady Ulla was crying. Her features remained calm and only the warm flicker of the fire highlighted the stream of tears, which must have burned and stung her. He felt at a loss and was searching for something to say when unexpectedly

Ulla gave a strained laugh. 'Makhpiyaluta, we are not in the palace now,' she said. 'There is really no need to bow, especially since we have become so . . . intimately acquainted. Please address me simply as Ulla . . . and, yes, thank you, I would be most grateful if you could concoct a salve.'

The Prince bowed again automatically, then coloured and beat a hasty retreat in search of herbs, leaving Ulla and Chaplin alone.

There was an awkward silence, then both spoke at once.

'Ulla, why—'

'*Seanachaidh*, I—'

'Sorry,' Chaplin smiled, 'you go first.'

'I expect you're wondering why I'm here, but no one will miss me. Only Morias knows I'm still alive and that I've followed you.'

'Eion knows.'

'Yes, but he'll not speak out.'

'Shouldn't your father be told?'

'I have no father now,' she snapped. 'He killed me, don't you remember? He should have done it years ago when I was young enough not to see his petty spite.' Her tone was bitter.

'Ulla,' Chaplin said quietly, 'fathers mark us for ever, whether by the sword or otherwise. We go on, sometimes in spite of them and, if we're lucky, eventually we can forgive.' He surprised himself with this and even more by the ease with which he had imparted it to Ulla, whom he barely knew.

She drew breath sharply and grabbed at her leg.

Chaplin started forward.

'My leg is cramping, that's all . . . you're very wise, *Seanachaidh*, but I suspect your father never ran you through with a claymore.'

'No. But there were extenuating circumstances when your father attacked you.'

'Kyra?' Ulla said, through gritted teeth. 'Traitorous bitch. She opened the gate. You know that, don't you? I had a daughter – Dom. She was one of the refugees . . .' At that point Ulla gave in to the pain and curled up on Chaplin's blankets, sobbing. He moved round the fire, sat next to her and took her hand. There was nothing to say so he held the withered limb and stroked her forearm, feeling a deep sadness. He had seen so much pain in his years as a policeman, which cast his own bereavement into sharp relief. At least he and Diane had known happiness and passion. 'But why have you come?' he asked. 'And how did you catch up with us?'

Ulla sniffed and wiped her face with the corner of her robe. 'I don't really know, *Seanachaidh*, what made me follow you . . . both of you. I . . . used a drug called mirgol, which makes your body move faster and you don't need to sleep. I've been walking continuously since I left the city.'

Chaplin laughed bitterly. 'I never imagined such a thing could happen here. Don't you know there is a price to pay for all drugs? A physical price? How long have your limbs been cramping?'

A dull flash of anger crossed Ulla's face. 'Do not lecture me, *Seanachaidh*. I would not survive without the salves and potions I take.'

Chaplin released her hand and smiled. He had enjoyed the spark in her tone: she was regaining her control. 'My name is Alessandro, lady.' He lowered his voice and added conspiratorially, 'But my best friends call me Sandro.'

Slowly Phyrr climbed the stairs of the tower, her anxiety mounting with each hollow footfall. Her brother had called her suddenly into his presence, and the force of his telepathic command had dealt her an almost crippling physical blow. It would never have occurred to her not to attend when Corvus summoned her. Their bond was such that life and breath seemed a shared experience. Only one existence but two beings, two gods, shared it. It had always been so, and even though she sensed his anger, Phyrr knew that Corvus would never harm or betray her. Still, some prescience of their encounter seized her as she reached for the door. Forcing a bright, winning smile she flung it ajar in her habitually dramatic manner.

Her light-hearted remark died unspoken in the dark recesses of the room. Only one candle guttered in the draught, leaving the main part of the chamber in darkness. In a pool of shadow, Phyrr could see the ice-blue light of the eldritch chains that bound her brother, snaking across the room from corner to corner like sparkling fire. It had always seemed to Phyrr that they were beautiful – somehow desirable – but she could never share that idea with Corvus, who was their victim. In an instant this thought was gone. Corvus was waiting for her on his throne. The blue fire wound sinuous tendrils around his legs and wrists – contained him – she reminded herself. His head was slumped forward as though he was dozing, his eyes shut. An atmosphere of malevolence pervaded the room. Phyrr walked forward, her footsteps uncertain, her hand dropping automatically to the hilt of her sword.

Suddenly, Corvus's blue eyes snapped open.

'Brother,' she said, annoyed that her tone was not calmer, 'what ails you?'

He said nothing, watching, his gaze travelling to her hand, still poised above her sword. When he spoke his tone was quiet and even. 'Phyrr. So kind of you to come.'

'You knew I would,' she responded. 'What . . .'

A deeper shadow moved in the corner of the room as Sluagh ruffled his feathers and Phyrr thought there was an element of anticipation in the movement. Her brother's next action was as unpredictable as it was cruel.

Corvus flung his hand forward, fingers spread wide as though he would grip her face if she were nearer. The bonds that held him prisoner strained, pulling, their blue light pulsing, sparks flying from them.

Phyrr screamed as she was flung backwards by an invisible force, her head hitting the edge of the door. Something was gripping her face, mirroring the movements of Corvus's hand, focusing on her left eye-socket, pulling, pulling. She screamed his name as lightning arced across her vision and the pain stabbed deep inside her skull.

'What's that, sister?' His words crashed in on a sea of pain. 'You want to keep your eye? I thought you were half blind already.'

There was a further sensation of pressure and this time Corvus twisted, his laughter a ringing backdrop to her agony. 'He's still alive, you stupid bitch. Talisker is still alive!'

There was no answer from the crumpled form on the floor. Corvus released the pressure but as Phyrr moved slightly he made a clawing movement and sharp gashes appeared around her eye, blood pouring down her neck in a vibrant stream. Sobbing quietly she clutched the pommel of her sword. Corvus seemed to grow bored of her torment and sat down again. 'All right, Phyrr. I did promise Sluagh he could have the eyeball, but he'll just have to wait. Never let it be said I'm not merciful. Mind you,' he teased, 'I doubt it will be any use to you now. Perhaps—'

'No, Corvus!' she squealed. 'No! It's not true! I killed him myself.'

'Tsk. It's just an eyeball, for goodness' sake. No, you didn't kill him. He escaped through the void.'

Phyrr fought for control. She had misjudged her brother's capacity for cruelty but she was enough of a huntress to know that to show further weakness now might prove fatal. Corvus was stronger: something had changed in him. Opening her right eye she focused with difficulty on the blurred figure in the chair. 'But what about Mirranon?' she asked, gritting her teeth against the pain. She put her fingers to her eye to find it swollen and bloody. 'You still want me to deal with her. You want me to kill her.'

Corvus grinned in a way that had nothing to do with humour. 'Yes, I used to think it was what you did best, Phyrr, but I was wrong. Rutting with corpses is your thing. The White Eagle is being dealt with.' He tapped his fingers impatiently on the arm of his chair and the movement drew Phyrr's eye. White feathers lay on the chair and on the dais, just visible in the glowing light. They sparkled, out of context in this place of shadow.

'Now why don't you run along while you have the chance? Hmm?' In the rafters, Sluagh ruffled his feathers again and cocked his head to one side. Corvus was dismissing her.

'No,' she said. The pain in her eye could not compete with the pain of her brother's contempt. 'You need me.' She wasn't sure if she was crying or not: there was so much blood on her face. 'No one else comes here, Corvus. There's only me to – to care about you. No one else. You'll see . . .'

Corvus's hooded eyes studied her. She knew what he would say before he spoke.

'There's only one thing you can do for me, sister, and you refuse to do it.'

Phyrr walked towards her brother but stopped out of his reach. Normally she would approach him without suspicion, but now she knew her unquestioning loyalty for what it was: weakness. Corvus was a viper among the gods and the thought she had denied to herself even through his last reign of terror now voiced itself in her mind: they had been right to chain him. Still, even as she studied his contemptuous expression, she was between loathing and the dark love she had felt all her life for her brother, the Raven King.

'I will not take your place, Corvus,' she said. 'You would never return and I would be here for ever. You would not do it for me.'

He did not attempt a denial. Phyrr could feel the onset of shock coursing through her body. In an effort to stem the pull of unconsciousness, she dug her fingernails into her palm until it bled. 'I will kill Talisker for you,' she promised. 'This time I will bring you his head, so there can be no mistake and no healing by the Fine.'

'There's really no need,' Corvus replied, dismissively. 'It's all being dealt with. I will send *Bultari*.'

'Then I will kill them also,' she snapped. 'I will kill them all, to bring you my prize.' She turned sharply on her heel and walked out.

Corvus said nothing but watched her go, noting her pause to grip the door-frame and steady herself. He liked her stubbornness, saw himself reflected in it. She had been right about one thing: as the last black fold of her cloak vanished, he was missing her already.

# CHAPTER FIFTEEN

It was so beautiful. And it was killing them. Talisker and Malky stared at the snow, their eyes reflecting the stark white like an echo of the desolation in their souls. In the end, they had simply arrived at a place where they had to stop and both knew that to stop was to die a frozen death. They did not huddle together for warmth because Malky had no body heat. He was not dying for the same reasons as Talisker, but because his existence was inextricably linked to his friend's. He hummed a meaningless tune. It was not the snow but the icy cold from which there was no protection – if there had been more snow they could perhaps have used it to make a shelter. Instead, there was only a small indentation in the rocky surface of the foothills of the Blue Mountains and, initially, they had fooled themselves into thinking it might provide shelter. They had known this time was coming: earlier in the afternoon, just after the weather had turned bitter, Malky had accidentally dropped the blankets into the river they were crossing. There was no way to dry them out, and the men had simply exchanged a glance that said everything.

Talisker was staring at his star. The snow had made him think about the dream he used to have when he was in prison – of the rooftops and the cold quiet. He had always wondered if the figure who haunted the dream was himself or some other creature, looking up at the heavens at the exact moment as he . . . A warm sensation flared in his stomach and he shut his eyes.

'Malky,' he muttered, through blue lips, 'you're a good friend. I mean . . . the best . . . you know.' There was no answer, and Talisker opened his eyes again. Already there was something lifeless about the way the cruel white flakes clung to the contours and folds of Malky's plaid, as though the warrior had turned to stone. His red beard was laced with silver and his deathly white skin seemed part of the landscape, as though he would be absorbed by it. His eyes were shut.

'Malk?' Talisker's mind was too numb to process the idea that the Highlander might be dead. His gaze moved back towards the moorland and there he saw a dark outline moving fast across the snow. For a moment he imagined himself leaping up, summoning help, but his body would not move. The shape was too distant, anyway, to hear a shout. He watched it listlessly – it was a large animal, the size of a horse but there was no rider. Maybe it was a bear.

'Tayna?' he muttered. It was his last coherent thought before the darkness gripped his soul.

*He knows this place. But how is it possible to know a featureless black expanse? He is still for long moments, feeling his limbs burn as blood courses back into them. As he waits for sensation to return, he looks around and knows he is in that place again. But he's afraid this time. His death cannot be like this, can it? Quiet, stealthy, life ebbing away, unopposed and unremarked. This can't be right. There must be other people here . . .*

*'Malk?' he calls. There is no echo. The sound is*

*swallowed by the distance. Looking down at his own body, he sees he is no longer wearing his plaid and cloak but jeans, a jumper and his dark blue jacket. Is he nearer to his own world in death then, he wonders. All down his back and legs he can still feel the cold of the rocks. Perhaps his body is still there, being covered by the snow.*

*'Malky. Help me.' He's afraid of this death. Afraid of dying alone.*

Sounds, lights, smells, sensations suddenly blink into existence. Reality, like an electric shock. Talisker gasped at the immediacy of the colours and blinked as his eyes adjusted to the light.

'Are you ready to order?' A girl was standing beside him, smiling efficiently. He stared at her as he realised where he was. She stared back, her fixed polite expression faltering. Her glasses had thick lenses and she blinked rapidly behind them as she waited for his response.

'Em . . . I'm not quite ready yet. I'm waiting for someone. Can I have a beer just now?'

'Certainly, sir.' She seemed reassured by this and clicked back seamlessly into efficiency mode. 'Bottled or draught?'

'Eh? Oh. A bottle of Budweiser, please.'

'Okay.'

She left and Talisker stared round the pizza restaurant. They were all the same: you could walk into any one of the chain and sit at the same tables, eat from the same plates, with the same salt, pepper and stupid little herb thing that no one used. However, he was sure of which one he was in: he had been outside it when he and Chaplin had had their fight. It was built on one of the steep corners where the High Street intersected the bridges. If you listened carefully, you could hear the rumbling of the trains, pulling in and out of Waverley station, beneath the roar of the traffic outside. He turned to look out of the window, across to the Tron church, and pressed his head against the glass to focus beyond the reflections. It was dark out there. How many days since he had been in Dunbar? One or two, maybe. In this world, this timeline, he must have escaped the demon. By running away, most likely. The creature would still be out there. Why had he come back to the city, he wondered. Surely it would have made more sense to keep going south. A movement across the street caught his eye, a fleeting impression of the way some-one walked – furtively. He frowned as the man was lost from view in the crowds.

'Your beer, sir.' The waitress had come back. She put down a coaster then the bottle and a glass. Again, the efficient smile. 'Would you like to order now or are you still waiting?'

Talisker frowned, not understanding the question.

'For your friend,' she said.

'Oh. No, I'll order now,' he replied. 'He can sort himself out. I'll have a deep-pan, four cheese, please, and a small side salad.'

'Okay.' She left, and returned quickly with a small bowl. 'That's for your salad,' she explained patiently, as though he was five years old. 'You can fill it up at the salad bar.'

'Thanks.' Talisker turned back to scan the street for the furtive man but he had gone. The shops were closed now and there weren't many children around; he guessed it must be around ten.

'Dunky, could you possibly have sat anywhere more public? Like in the middle o' the pissin' street, mebbe?'

He jumped at the sound of the sarcastic voice, but he knew before he saw the speaker who it was – Charlie Henratty, or just Ratty to those with whom he'd shared a cell.

When his transition happened Chaplin had been asleep. He, Ulla and Makhpiyaluta had set up camp deep in Or Coille. The weather was bleak and freezing but the snow was lighter than that which Talisker and Malky had encountered, as it was filtered by the trees. Chaplin climbed into his sheepskin bedroll, gratefully anticipating the warmth; Makhpiyaluta was taking first watch. He muttered, 'Goodnight,' to Ulla, then drifted into a deep sleep.

He woke to the clash of cymbals. The orchestra was at fever pitch. Chaplin's heart raced and his vision blurred in and out of focus. He stared fixedly at his feet for a few moments, breathing deeply. He recognised the music instantly: *Carmen*, probably his least favourite opera. Once he'd taken Diane to see it and she had loved it. He looked up at the stage, still reeling from the shock of transition: the colours were intense, primary blues and reds, the chorus dressed in unlikely bright clean clothes, high-fashion street urchins and factory girls. His eyeballs ached and he groaned quietly.

Someone put a hand on his knee. 'Sandro, he'll be here soon. They're running straight through. It's so exciting, isn't it?'

It was Beatrice. She looked beautiful, in a silk evening gown, her hair piled on top of her head like some classical Greek statue. He'd never noticed before what a long graceful neck she had, and she was wearing a black velvet choker with tiny pearls sewn on to it. Were they on a date? Surely not. And who was she talking about?

The music changed key with one of Bizet's more frenzied flourishes. He recognised the 'March of the Toreadors' and, sensing movement from the audience behind him, turned to look up the aisle. In a flurry of glitter and sequins the toreadors were promenading down towards the stage.

'There he is!' Beatrice squeaked, in uncharacteristic excitement. 'There's Miles! He's playing Escamillo!'

The leading toreador, a small stocky man whose sequins seemed almost to overpower him, was throwing flowers into the audience while he sang and marched, but when he reached the row where Beatrice and Chaplin were sitting, he kissed one and handed it to her before moving on.

Beatrice giggled like a schoolgirl. 'Isn't he lovely, Sandro?' she whispered. 'You are going to come for drinks afterwards, aren't you?'

'Yeah. Wouldn't miss it.'

'Didja miss me?' Ratty grinned as he sat down. 'Hey, miss, two more beers over here, eh?' he yelled, without waiting for Talisker's answer. 'What's up, Dunky? You look rough. I heard you got big trouble from the Sicilian. 'S that right? So whaddya want from Uncle Ratty, huh?' He was chewing gum, opening his jaws wide and making a clicking noise. Talisker said nothing. There was no point in responding to Ratty until he'd asked at least seven questions. You learned a lot about a man's speech patterns when you spent twenty-four hours a day in the same room for three years.

'So, I gotcha worried right? I gotcha worried?' He repeated himself too: it was a cue for Talisker to speak.

'Yeah. You got me worried, Ratty. Good to see you.' They tried not to look shifty as the waitress brought the beers over. In a perverse way, it *was* good to see him. In their time sharing a cell together, Talisker had come to admit to himself – somewhat guardedly – that Ratty, low-life petty criminal though he was, was probably among the least offensive men in Saughton, although you wouldn't want to mess with the little guy.

The pizza arrived and the waitress asked Ratty if he'd like to order. 'Nah, 's all right, hen, I'll just scrounge a bit of his. Just bring an extra plate eh?' She left again, unable to disguise a disapproving look.

'Hey, cheer up, Dunky. No one who knows you believes what they're sayin' aboutcha on the news 'n' stuff. It's that Inspector Chaplin's fault. They should be out lookin' fer the real criminal, yeah?'

'Just keep your voice down, Rats.'

'No worries. I was just kiddin' before. I got your message and I've brought the stuff for you.'

'Stuff?' Talisker was blank. It seemed that while he had been away in Sutra, his other self, the one left behind, was equally capable of self-determination. He couldn't imagine why he'd wanted to contact Ratty, he wasn't even sure if he'd been aware Ratty was out.

Ratty leaned forward. 'The passport, Dunky. If I was

you, I'd go from East Midlands airport. Don't risk Edinburgh, it's too local.'

A passport. So that was it. His other self – maybe he didn't know or remember Corvus, Deme or the demon – was planning to run. Ratty was watching him closely, trying to read his expression. The humour had left his face and the spark of complicity was in his eyes. 'It's the right thing, Talisker,' he said, soberly. 'There's no justice for you here. You don't want to end up inside again. It'll kill you next time.'

A sick feeling was growing in the pit of Talisker's stomach. Welcome back to Auld Reekie, he thought wryly. 'How much do I—'

'This one's on me,' Ratty cut in. 'If anyone needs a break, pal, it's you. Anyway, I owe you one for not shoppin' me to the screws that time I beat up Keithy Jackson.' Ratty took a big slice of pizza as the waitress deposited a plate in front of Talisker.

'Thanks, Ratty.' Talisker remembered the trouble there had been when Ratty had broken three of Jackson's ribs. 'But it was nothing and—'

'No, really, big man,' Ratty insisted. He took a bite of the pizza – without disposing of his gum, as far as Talisker could tell. 'Now, I'll just finish this bit o' pizza and I'm out o' here. Better not hang around if you know what I mean, eh? I'll leave the envelope with the bits in on my chair for ya.' He munched contentedly and took a swig of beer. 'You need to slip one o' those passport pictures you can get from a booth in Woolies or the station under the plastic coating. Then you just warm it up, like, with an iron or something. It makes a bond, see? If ye're really desperate and you canny find an iron, some of those hand-dryers in toilets work, but you have to find a really hot one, yeah?'

'Okay. Thanks.'

Ratty looked as though he was going to get up, then stopped. 'By the way, Talisker,' he said, 'I can take the Sicilian out o' the picture for you, if you prefer. But that'll cost you five-K. You know where to find me eh?' He winked.

Chaplin's pager went off in the middle of a romantic aria, giving rise to a disapproving ripple of 'Sssh' from around where he and Beatrice were sitting. He switched it off and read the message: PHONE FINN ON MOBILE – URGENT!

'Bea, I'm sorry, I've got to go,' he lied. 'I'm needed at the station.'

Beatrice was used to the vagaries of dating policemen. 'Okay, Sandro. Another time eh?' She kissed his cheek lightly then turned her attention back to the stage, where Miles/Escamillo was inviting everyone to the bullfight.

Blinking in the yellow tungsten lights of the theatre foyer, Chaplin rang Finn. 'It's Inspector Chaplin. What's happening?'

'Everything,' Finn replied excitedly. 'The shit's really hit the fan . . .'

'Where are you?' Chaplin frowned: there seemed to be a lot of traffic noise in the background.

'I've tailed Talisker, Inspector. I'm in Deacon Brodie's. D'you know it? In the High Street.'

'Of course I know it. Talisker's there?' Chaplin handed his cloakroom ticket to the attendant.

'No, he's outside, across the street. I think he's lost it. Seems to be talking to himself.' Finn suddenly remembered their last meeting at Dunbar. 'Sorry – I mean—'

'Never mind,' Chaplin snapped, grabbing his coat. 'I'll be there in five minutes. I'm at the Usher Hall.'

'But, Inspector,' Finn continued, 'that's not all. There's been another murder.'

Chaplin was on the steps outside the theatre, buttoning his greatcoat against the bitter air. Taxis were lined up outside, waiting to take the opera patrons on to various functions or just home. Most of the drivers had stopped their engines and were smoking or drinking cups of steaming coffee, the air filled with diesel fumes and engine noise. Behind him, Chaplin could still hear the strains of the orchestra, and as Finn's excited voice issued from the mobile he couldn't believe what he was hearing.

'What? Say that again.'

Finn repeated himself, and Chaplin froze where he stood at the top of the stairs. 'Oh, no,' he murmured. 'Oh, Christ.' He took the phone away from his ear and stared at it. He was suddenly aware that he was shaking with cold and shock.

'Inspector? Are you still there?'

Chaplin made an effort to pull himself together. For some reason, the fact that Finn had given him this news annoyed him intensely. Why hadn't Stirling called him? He put the phone back to his ear. 'I'll be there in five minutes. Don't move.'

*As he steps into a cab, it begins to snow, and he stares out at the darkened city as the taxi climbs up the castle hill, his mind numbed by what Finn has just told him.*

*Huge white flakes drift past the cab windows in a hypnotic dance and Chaplin feels almost as though he is floating over the city rooftops. He shrinks back into the seat and inhales the stale, but comforting smell of hundreds of cigarettes. He doesn't want to get out. He doesn't want to see Talisker. He doesn't want any of this any more.*

It was difficult to argue with Malky in the street when people were walking past – Talisker kept forgetting that he could pick up his thoughts telepathically in this world. That the Highlander argued so passionately made the urge to shout at him quite strong.

'Ye canny go, Duncan. Ye canny leave Scotland.' Malky stood in front of Talisker emphatically barring his way, his hand on his sword.

'Look, it makes sense . . .' Talisker stopped as a young woman at the nearby bus stop flinched and moved as far as possible from the crazy man who was talking to himself. It does make sense, Malk, he thought. I should have done it before. It seems that in my own absence my other half has done some rational thinking.

'But what about Sutra? Are ye just going tae leave everythin' up in the air?' Malky played his trump card. 'What about Una?'

Talisker sighed. *I know. I'll miss her but . . . He trailed off. Malky, look! Over there.*

Down the street, in the shadows near St Giles Cathedral, a dark shape was moving, clinging to the darker reaches of the building. To the few who had seen it before, it was unmistakable, even at this distance.

'D'ye think it's trackin' ye again?' Malky whispered.

'D'you think it's kinna sensitive tae yer movements like me?'

'Maybe.' Talisker frowned. 'But it's not like before. I haven't been where he's standing. I came up the other side of the street. Last time it followed my tracks exactly, as though it had no choice.'

'Well, what else could he be . . . Aw naw.'

'What?'

'The City Chambers.' Malky jerked his head in the direction of the buildings opposite the cathedral. 'Mary King's Close . . .'

'Deme . . .'

In unspoken agreement, both men moved towards the crossroads, intending to cross over and down towards the entrance to the close but before they could get far, the demon also crossed the road. Moving swiftly as it came within the orange circle of the street-lights it disappeared from view into the courtyard of the City Chambers buildings.

'C'mon, Malk. We've got to warn her.'

'Wait. Duncan, look.'

Nearing the City Chambers buildings was a small group of people, in front of whom walked a tall man dressed in white, his face white with makeup, carrying an oil lantern, which he swung theatrically to and fro. Behind him were six or eight normal-looking people and another actor – Talisker assumed that was what he might be – dressed in ragged-looking medieval clothes, bringing up the rear with another lantern. From this distance, it was impossible to hear what the leading man was saying but his voice was raised so that all the members of the group could hear him.

'What are they doin', Duncan?' Malky frowned.

'I think it's what they call a Ghost Walk.' Talisker tried not to smile at the irony. 'He's like a *Seanachaidh*, tells them stories about things that happened in the High Street hundreds of years ago. They don't usually go down the close as far as I know.' But, as though to prove him wrong, the group turned into the City Chambers. Talisker could hear giggling and then a shriek. He broke into a run, reaching for his sword. He cursed as instead he pulled the pistol from his pocket, remembering what little use it had been against the creature last time. As they approached the corner though, his pace slowed. People were still laughing.

'But there's nothing to fear from the ghost of old Burke here,' a man's voice rang out. 'He'd only be interested if you were dead, madam.'

More giggles. Talisker peered round the corner, still in shadow, unwilling to let the group see him, aware that, in all probability, his face had been shown on the local news. He was wearing a simple disguise, a black beanie hat that hid his hair and a scarf wrapped around the lower part of his face.

The group were gathered near the middle of the square and another actor, hitherto concealed, had jumped out on one of the younger women. He said nothing, but staggered about, pulling at something round his neck. The guide carried on in tones designed to titillate and chill. 'Burke here was hanged in the Grassmarket and, in an act of poetic justice, the sheriff commanded his skeleton be put on display in the University's School of Anatomy.'

The 'ghost' of Burke lunged at a young woman who

squealed obligingly. Malky, who had stopped behind Talisker, observed the tour disapprovingly. 'It's no' right, Duncan. Thon Burke, he's no' a ghost at aw. That big guy, he's just connin' them.'

'It's all right, Malk. They know it's not real. It's just a bit of fun.' Malky looked mystified but said nothing. 'The demon's real, though, and I think he's gone down there.' Talisker indicated the entrance to the close: the door was ajar. 'Let's go.'

The tour group were all listening to the grim tale of Burke and Hare, and Talisker and Malky slipped past unnoticed.

Something was coming, something bad. Deme stared at the dark gap of the corridor, which led from the main alleyways of the close. It wasn't a sound; she couldn't yet hear the movements of the demon, it was an impression, a wave of intangible horror and suffering that swept before the beast like a scream. Without sight or sound of it, she knew within her Sidhe soul exactly what it was and who had sent it to destroy her. Rushing into the back of her quarters she fumbled among her meagre belongings and brought out a gemstone. Smaller than the one she had given Malky, it was a ruby and glowed a violent red. 'Oh, gods,' she whispered. 'Mirranon, don't desert me now.' Her legs were shaking and she knelt on the freezing floor of the old room. She could hear it now. By the light of the gem she sensed a shadow move across the antechamber. She could hear its rasping breath. She looked up.

It was hard to find the way down to Deme's chambers.

Talisker had been almost unconscious the last time he'd been here and it felt like a hundred years ago. Malky walked ahead muttering to himself: 'Aye . . . doon here and turn left . . . Naw, right an' then . . .'

In the darkness, all the entrances looked the same and there was nothing to differentiate where Deme might live. Of course, she had wanted it that way for the last two hundred years or so but it was no help to them now. They moved slowly through the cobbled corridors that had once been open streets. Although the furthest parts were inaccessible to the public, the streets stretched on for at least a mile, sloping downwards to the level of Waverley station and Princes Street gardens. When last these spaces had known the light of day, the Nor' Loch had washed against the backs of the lowest buildings; a dirty odorous backwater that carried the stench of marsh gases back up the streets.

Twice they heard noises ahead of them; a definite movement that could only have been made by something large and shambling. The third time, it was less distinct but came from behind them, back the way they had come.

'Duncan, it's the tourists,' Malky whispered. 'They've come into the close. I thought you said they didnae usually come doon here.'

He was right, Talisker knew, and they were walking right into the path of the demon. They could only be half a mile from it. 'What are we going to do, Malk?' he whispered. Behind them the sounds of the tour party were coming closer. The tour guide's voice carried along the empty passageway: 'Mary King's Close is reputed to be one of the most haunted places in

Scotland . . . when it was gradually reopened, people were understandably reluctant to move back in . . .'

'Right, Duncan, you go an' find Deme.'

'What are you going to do?'

Malky grinned. 'Watch this.' For a moment he seemed almost to disappear; his figure became fainter and blurred, as though Talisker was looking at it through a heat-haze. When the Highlander returned to his normal state of brightness, Talisker recoiled: Malky looked just as he had that day they had met for the first time in Talisker's flat, wounds, pus, smell and all. Not only that, but he glowed with some internal light that flickered like a candle flame. 'See?'

Talisker shuddered. 'Brings back memories.'

'Well, Ah'm away tae manifest mahsel'. I'll catch up with you as soon as I can.' Without further ado, Malky headed back up the corridor.

The tour guide knew he was in danger of losing his group – not literally of course, he should be so lucky, but their attention and enthusiasm. He sighed. It was always a danger when half of the tour party were under the influence of alcohol: they were like big kids. The scout group he'd brought the week before had asked far more pertinent questions and none of them had been sick in the courtyard of the City Chambers. Late bookers were always a liability: all they wanted was to get tanked up and scream a bit.

'This tiny antechamber is the spot where most people with any latent psychic perception claim to hear a ghost.' He held his lantern high to illuminate the space, which he was sure had probably been a medieval linen cupboard; he was tired and knew it was evident in his voice. Actually, the group had rallied a bit: they clustered a little closer and were listening intently, their eyes fixed on the space behind him. 'The sound of a young girl crying,' he continued.

'It's very good,' one of the more drunken girls chimed in, 'but it doesnae look like a young girl to me.'

'It's very clever, though,' her friend added. 'Must be a projector, eh? I like the way you can see right through him.'

'What?' The guide turned. And was eyeball to eyeball with Malky, who grinned, showing his white gums and rotten stumps of teeth.

'Erm . . . Ah'm no' really sure whit tae say now,' he began.

The guide had turned even whiter beneath his makeup. His throat was dry, and when he tried to speak, only a high-pitched whine escaped him.

'You all right?' Malky asked. Then, remembering the purpose of his visitation, he drew his sword and started forward. The tour guide, who had been transfixed, turned to flee. 'Run!' he yelled. 'It's real!'

As one, the group fled. Only one had the presence of mind to turn back and take a photo.

Once they were gone, the silence of the close reasserted itself and Malky transformed to his better appearance. Then he heard the crying. It was real, and he knew immediately who it was. 'Ilsa? Ilsa, hen, it's me, yer daddy.' His voice was hoarse. 'Where are ye?'

Nothing appeared. Malky sat down on the floor with his back to the wall. The crying stopped and the atmosphere assumed a listening, expectant quality.

'Look, Ilsa, Ah know.' Malky bowed his head. 'Ah know ye were too young tae understand – how could ye understand? Yer own father . . .' he was almost unable to speak the words '. . . yer own father killed ye. Ah don't know if that means – wherever ye are now – ye'll always be a child,' he sniffed, 'so mebbe Ah can never make you understand. It was the kindest thing, Ilsa. I couldnae stand fer ye to be in such pain, like yer mother was. Ah loved ye too much – Ah loved both of ye. And she made me promise.' He wiped his face on the back of his sleeve. 'I suppose that's how you canny rest, 'cos ye think yer daddy murdert ye. But it wiznae like that, it wiznae like that at aw . . .' His voice trailed off and he buried his face in his hands. There was such darkness in this place, the echoes of despair all around. How could they come here and gawp and giggle?

'Daddy?'

He looked up. There she was: she had always been a tiny girl, with brown hair that hung like a gossamer mantle to her waist. She had been crying – of course she had, he realised bitterly, she had been crying for over two hundred years. She stood a little way off, her fingers in her mouth, her eyes wide with surprise.

'Ilsa?' he whispered. 'My little darlin'. Come here tae me.'

She padded forward on her little bare feet and sat on his knee, wrapping her arms around his neck. Malky was overcome with joy and grief. How could she trust and love him still?

'Sing me a song, Daddy.'

He blinked away his tears so he could see her clearly, although he could feel the spasms of a sob deep within him. 'A song? Well, only if ye promise me not tae cry any more. Will ye promise?'

She nodded earnestly.

'What song would ye like, then?'

She didn't hesitate. ' "Ali Bali Bee",' she demanded.

Talisker was further down the close, minutes ahead of Malky, when the light erupted. A blinding red flash, accompanied by a scream, blazed out of the depths of Deme's chambers, turning Mary King's Close as bright as when it had last seen the light of day, two hundred years earlier. Talisker put his hands to his face, unable to stand the brightness or to bear his failure to reach Deme before this catastrophe overcame her. Then there was a sound like a sonic boom and it was moments before his ears began to recover enough to hear the screams of the fleeing tourists. He gave a wry grin into the darkness before breaking into a run.

The song was ended and he knew he'd have to let her go. Malky hugged his daughter tight to him. 'You know that Daddy loves ye, wee one, eh?' he whispered. 'God speed ye.' When he opened his eyes, another figure was standing there. 'She knows now, Malcolm.' His wife smiled. 'Thank you.'

'Here's yer mammy come tae take ye home, look,' he said to Ilsa. Her head was nestled into his chest but she looked up.

'Mam!' She climbed off his knee without a backward glance and rushed over to her mother, who gathered her up in her arms.

Morag gazed at her husband for long moments before

she spoke. 'Are you coming?' She held out her hand to Malky just as an unearthly howl echoed from the lower reaches of the close and Talisker's voice could be heard yelling for him.

Malky shook his head sadly. 'Ah canny, love. Ah'm needed still . . .'

There was no pleading or recrimination from Morag. She smiled and they vanished.

It was crazy. Talisker was holding the demon at bay using two of the sconces with which Deme had lit her chamber. Each time the beast lunged forward, Talisker lashed out with a sconce and the flames would flare in the darkness as the demon thrashed in pain. Talisker knew he couldn't keep it cornered like this for long and was waiting for Malky to clear the close and come to help. The screams of the tourists had faded but Malky hadn't appeared. Now the faint strains of a song sung in his inimitable reedy tones were wafting down the corridor.

Chaplin and Finn arrived at the City Chambers just after the tour party had come screaming out of the entrance to the close and run into the snow on the High Street. Only two young women and the guides stopped by the statue in the middle of the square. One woman was crying and shaking, her friend comforting her. She rounded on the guides. 'We could sue you for that, you stupid bastards. Are you tryin' to give someone a heart-attack? I'm goin' to complain to the council and you'll lose your licence. C'mon, hen, let's get a drink before the pubs shut.' She led her friend away, their high heels slipping and sliding in the snow. The guides didn't move or even try to protest; they just looked dazed.

Chaplin walked over to them and showed his ID. 'Can I ask you a couple of questions, boys?'

The guide looked surprised, 'Aye, sure, but what's it about?'

'Did you see someone down the close?'

'Well, aye, but . . .'

'About my height, ginger hair, slim build?'

'Eh? No.'

'No? Sorry, but I thought someone had threatened your group.'

'It was a ghost, pal,' the guide said blankly. 'A *bona fide* ghost.' He laughed weakly. 'Talk about value for money eh?'

Chaplin was unfazed. 'A ghost? Was it a Highlander with red hair, small and pale? Pure white, in fact?'

The tour guide groaned in response. 'Is it just me or has the whole world gone mad tonight? Aye, that's what he looked like.' He began to wipe his face paint off with a large handkerchief. 'Hey, Jim, this is goin' to enhance our reputation and no mistake,' he joked to his friend, who was sitting pale and silent beside him. 'Can we go now, officer? Our customers aren't the only ones in need of a stiff drink.'

Chaplin nodded and the two departed, cutting a slightly less jaunty picture than when they had entered.

'What was that about?' Finn was mystified. Chaplin thought he seemed nervous and edgy: something about him had changed while Chaplin had been in Sutra, but it was difficult to pinpoint what it was. Perhaps he was finding police work too stressful: he blinked constantly and his movements were a little jerky. It seemed that he had taken his role seriously: Chaplin was sure that no one would have instructed him to find or follow Talisker, who would be considered dangerous, so he'd just gone ahead and done it himself. This either showed great spark and self-motivation or it was something else, obsessive behaviour perhaps.

'What do you mean?'

'This Highlander bloke?'

'Just trust me, Finn.' Chaplin paused, trying to think of a way to explain that would sound rational. 'If they've seen the Highlander, Talisker's down there. Let's go. You're not armed, are you?'

'No.'

Chaplin pulled out his pistol. 'Stay behind me, then.'

'Shouldn't we call for back-up?'

'No time. Let's go,' Chaplin said. 'But if you do see anything . . . unusual down there, ignore it. It can't hurt you. Not in this world.'

'So, what do we do now?'

'What are you asking *me* for? I canny dae anything.'

'It was a rhetorical question, Malk. Your moral support's better than nothing.' Talisker jabbed forward with the flaming brand again. This time the demon pulled back more slowly.

'D'ye think it's tiring?' Malky asked hopefully.

'No. I think it's learning the pain. Where were you, anyway?'

'Ah'll tell ye later, Duncan.'

'Talisker!' A voice echoed down the corridor.

'I should've known he was back. Malk, pass me that

other sconce. I think this one's going out.'

Malky shifted nervously. 'Ah canny, Duncan.' He demonstrated by passing his hand through the flames.

'Shit.' Talisker's voice held the first note of panic. 'Do you think you can distract it?'

'Ah'll try,' Malky said amenably, and moved forward, pulling out his sword. 'Ho, beastie! Hey, over here! That's it, ye great lummox! C'mon!'

The demon turned towards its new tormentor and growled. It was a chilling sound, and Malky gasped. 'Hurry up, Duncan!' he yelled. 'It'll soon realise Ah canny hurt it.' He screamed loudly and rushed forward as though attacking the creature, which moved back a couple of paces.

Talisker grabbed the last two sconces from the wall and held them together at arm's length in one fiercely burning shield. 'Right, Malk, I'm gonna try and force it back there.' He moved forward again to engage it, with Malky beside him. Little by little the demon was forced back into Deme's chamber until Talisker stood in the doorway, blocking its exit with fire.

'Great, Duncan,' Malky enthused.

'Yeah, great,' Talisker moaned, 'until these run out.'

There was a click behind them as Chaplin took the safety catch off his gun. 'Don't move, Talisker,' he commanded.

Talisker laughed humourlessly. His arms were shaking and the heat of the flames was burning his face. 'Y' know, Chaplin, that's almost funny.'

# CHAPTER SIXTEEN

'There's something in there.' Finn nodded towards the little antechamber.

Chaplin glanced towards him and saw him pull a weapon from his coat. 'Stay back, Finn. You said you weren't armed.' Chaplin frowned.

'Not officially, no.' A strange smirk crossed Finn's features, exaggerated by the flickering of the open flames.

'Stay back!' Talisker yelled. 'Keep him back, Sandro. This isn't some game.'

Finn moved forward. 'Is that your accomplice in there? The Highlander? C'mon, drop the weapon or I'll shoot.'

'Weapon?'

'He means the fire, Duncan,' Malky explained. 'He canny see me. Ah think he thinks—'

'It doesn't matter what he thinks. Chaplin, call him off. Now!'

'Finn, move back,' Chaplin instructed calmly. He still had his pistol trained on Talisker but Finn's behaviour was making him uneasy and he twitched his sights between the two. Also, he could see the shadowy movement of the demon inside and knew that it wasn't Malky.

'Why did you do it, Talisker?' Finn stayed where he was, effectively blocking Chaplin's line of fire. 'Why now?'

'What the f—?' Talisker began. Suddenly Finn lunged forward as though to rugby-tackle him. Talisker had no choice but to move out of the doorway and Finn plunged forward into the antechamber. He was face to face with the demon, whose remnants of clothes had caught fire and were burning with a greasy yellow flare. Realising that the danger of the flames had gone the beast moved out into the main chamber and picked up Finn by his neck. Finn screamed in terror, incoherent noises mingled with words.

'Arrgh – evil – evil—' He kicked out ineffectually, and Talisker knew from experience that the beast could snap his neck and spine at will. There was a metallic clatter as Finn's weapon hit the floor.

'Do something!' Chaplin screamed. As the beast moved and Finn thrashed about in its grasp he was unable to take aim.

Gritting his teeth and fighting every impulse to run from the creature that had almost killed him once already, Talisker moved forward with the flames and thrust them at the demon's feet and legs. With a roar, it threw Finn aside. His limp body smashed against the solid stone wall of the chamber with a dull thud, and Talisker was forced back against Chaplin. He could feel the butt of the pistol against his back. Yelling at the demon he thrust the flames forward again but this time it simply snatched them from his hands.

There was a surreal moment of silence as the demon held the flames to its face regarding them with a dull stare. Then, inexplicably, it began to dissolve: the distorted face peeled back, revealing something red and pulsing beneath. All three men flinched. Its hands and feet vanished, and before their horrified gaze stood something so grotesque, it could only have been the true nature of a demon.

'Aw, yuk,' Malky groaned.

The smell of sulphur filled the chamber and in the next instant the heaving bulk of the demon vanished in a green flare. No one spoke and all that could be heard was the guttering of the torches and people's breathing slowing. Just as Talisker was about to speak, he was shoved hard in the back and sprawled forward on to the floor almost landing on the flames.

'Okay, Duncan, now we've got that little distraction over, let's go.' Chaplin aimed his weapon unerringly at Talisker's head. This time he wasn't taking any chances.

'You don't get it, do you?' Talisker fumed. 'You just don't get it, Chaplin. That thing – that's your murderer.'

'He's right, Sandro,' Malky chimed in. 'Corvus sent it here.'

In the corner Finn groaned, but Chaplin's gaze remained fixed on his prey. 'I don't believe you. I know Sutra's true this time – I can hardly deny it again – but not this. Corvus could never have known . . .'

Something in Chaplin's expression warned Talisker and his stomach cramped as he asked the next question. He thought afterwards that at some deeply subconscious level he must have known what Chaplin was going to say, but nothing could have prepared him for it. His hands shook and as he reached behind him his fingers closed around Finn's revolver. 'Known what, Alessandro?' His throat closed. 'Tell me.'

Chaplin didn't seem to register his fright. His features

had acquired an expression with which Talisker was only too familiar: grim, unreasoning hatred. He licked his lips. 'Duncan Talisker, I am arresting you for the murder of Shula Morgan. You do not have to say anything . . .'

The rest of his words were lost to Talisker, who could only hear himself gasping for breath. 'No,' he whispered. 'No.' His voice became louder as his denial overwhelmed him. 'You're lying, Sandro. You're lying – you're lying.' He repeated the phrase as though it was a charm that would make it true. 'You're lying, you're lying—' His voice broke in a strangled sob. 'Not Shula.' Now Chaplin was walking towards him, a pair of traditional silver handcuffs in his hand. 'Not Shula.' He thrust Finn's discarded weapon into Chaplin's face. 'Stay back!' His hands were slick with sweat and he was dimly aware that he was trembling violently. 'How could you, Sandro?' he snarled. 'How could you lie to me like that? Even you couldn't sink so low . . .'

Chaplin's face was a picture of confusion. 'It's true, Talisker,' he replied. 'She's dead. Shula's—'

'No!' Talisker snapped. 'Don't you say that.'

'You don't remember, do you?' Chaplin continued, in a quiet, even tone. 'You don't even remember killing her. She's dead, Duncan.'

'No!'

'Shula Morgan—'

'Chaplin, stop it, man, you're pushin' him too far.'

'He must remember, Malky. Shula—'

'Shut up, Sandro!'

'Shula Morgan is d—'

Chaplin's world exploded into pain and fire. Talisker

shot him with Finn's revolver and ran from the singing echo of the chamber without looking back. Chaplin was briefly aware of Malky looking down at him, a curious mixture of pity and scorn on his face. Then the world went black.

*It's like a dream. Or a nightmare. His dreams from all those years of waiting in prison, of silent, frightened screams echoing across the crisp cold snowscape of the city. Talisker runs through the muffled silence of the streets and only he can hear the anguish of the screamer. Unreality dances around him in the snowflakes. His running seems less real, less tangible than any demon or any magic of Sutra. He doesn't slip or fall in the treacherous beautiful drifts, he just runs as fast as his long, light strides will carry him. Down behind the dark bulk of the castle and east down Lothian Road, towards the freezing elegance of the Georgian buildings of the West End. Running, running. His face and hands blue-cold as the snow blasts against them as though it is holding him away from the truth he must look upon. His lips are moving. He is saying her name as he runs. 'Shula, Shula, Shula . . .'*

*Then he's there. He sees the blue flashing lights of the police cars and the ambulance. And he knows. But still he won't let it be true. Lights are on around the crescent and people are huddled in little groups, watching the bitter tableau. Some are in their dressing-gowns and slippers, a few women are crying quietly. All are shocked and white, like the snow. Talisker pushes through, getting nearer and nearer, his ragged breath and his heartbeat the loudest sound he can hear except for the occasional static click and voice over the radio of the ambulance. People are looking at him as he gets nearer to the green doorway of Shula's home. People whisper: 'It's him, it's him.' He ignores them, his eyes fixed inside the doorway. He's still carrying the gun. By now it's cold, indistinguishable from his hand.*

*'Stay back,' someone says. But not to him. He walks through the doorway and up the stairs unopposed. 'Stay back. Leave him,' the voice repeats.*

*Then he's in the room. The warm, yellow room with all the lovely furniture, through which Shula can walk without feeling her way because it's part of her life. She's still in the room. On the floor in a pool of congealed black liquid. Her body is crumpled in an absurd heap, her back arched like a cat's. Some distance away, her head sits neatly on the ground, the dark spread of blood covered by her hair. Talisker sinks to his knees, his body spasming with sobs that remain trapped in his chest, clutching at his St Christopher. He reaches for the head, he wants to talk to her. 'There's no pain now,' he wants to say. Bright flashes flare in the subdued light of the room. It's a camera. He thinks of Una. And Darragh. He understands now. Someone grabs his wrist and he looks up at Stirling, aware that his face is wet with tears and spittle.*

*'Duncan Talisker, I am arresting you for the murder of Shula Morgan. You do not have . . .' The voice continues with the caution but he doesn't hear the words, can't make sense of them. His blue eyes are wide open as he watches Stirling's mouth move effortlessly over the phrases he has spoken many hundreds of times. Finally, he finishes and stares at Talisker closely. 'Do*

*you understand?' he asks, not unkindly. Talisker nods briefly. He has shifted position on the floor while listening to Stirling and his hand has strayed in the wetness of her blood. He doesn't want to look at it on his fingers.*

*'Shula's dead,' he says. Shifting forward he curls into a ball. Burying his head in his knees he cries as though he will never stop.*

'Give him a minute,' Stirling says.

In the quietness of the cells Talisker sat on his bed and stared at the floor. The duty doctor had declared him unfit for interview due to shock and mild hypothermia. He'd given Talisker an injection, a sedative, as though he feared Talisker was about to leap off his bed and attack him too. 'This will calm you down and help you to sleep,' he muttered. Talisker didn't look up at him. Other than the doctor, only Stirling had spoken to him; he seemed anxious to treat Talisker correctly and although Talisker knew of old that this was for purely pragmatic reasons – so that the case could not fail on a procedural technicality – he appreciated the man's dispassionate calm.

'Duncan, we're not going to interview you yet.' Talisker had looked up blearily and said nothing. 'But there's something I need to know. Have you seen Inspector Chaplin and Findlay? They're missing.'

'No,' he had muttered. There didn't seem any point in confusing the issue by admitting to shooting Chaplin. They'd find out soon enough, one way or another. If Chaplin was dead, it was just another thing to damn Talisker with. He didn't have the energy to care.

Wrapping his blanket tightly around himself, he regarded Stirling through heavy eyes, feeling the rather pleasant tug of the sedative upon his senses.

'Well, I'll be back to see you in the morning.' Stirling got up to leave the cell and knocked on the door to be let out. Just before he left he turned back and looked at Talisker. He seemed to want to say something, but changed his mind. There was nothing to say.

After Stirling left they put out the lights and the cell was illuminated by the orange of a street-light outside the tiny frosted-glass window. Talisker sat with his eyes wide open: every time he closed them he saw the image of the cadaver that had been Shula. She had been killed by an evil she had never believed in, torn apart. Talisker's stomach gripped again. He'd seen death many times since Darragh's, he'd killed plenty at Ruannoch Were, but nothing compared to this. He felt an inexplicable anger towards Shula for being so . . . innocent? How ironic, now, her claim that no soul was worthless. He wrenched the St Christopher from his neck and stared at the image of the saint carrying the infant Christ through a blur of fresh tears, conjured in this private grief when he thought none could possibly remain.

A sound at the door attracted his attention. Someone was outside, their footsteps furtive and muffled. He frowned. Usually, the police and the prison staff wanted you to know that they were constantly around. The viewing panel within the door slid open. Talisker did not move or betray that he was watching but his eyes were fixed on the space. It was most likely to be one of Chaplin's colleagues come to gloat: in his experience, institutions harboured many such petty-minded individuals. For a moment, nothing happened and Talisker's view of the door was obscured by the white steam of his breathing in the cold darkness. Then there was a tiny sound as something light was dropped through the viewing panel. Talisker briefly saw the fingers of the watcher, white, almost corpse-like in the gloom. Still, he did not move until he heard the panel snap shut again. Even then he eyed the object suspiciously for long silent moments. Eventually he went over and picked it up.

It was a note, scrawled in black marker on a hastily ripped page of a notebook. The message was unsurprising: 'Scum. Do us all a favour, why don't you?' Talisker gasped when he realised the author of the note was deadly serious: wrapped within the bottom half of the page a razor blade glinted silver in the glow of the street-light. He picked it out carefully and held it up to the light as though it were a diamond. It was new, its silver edge unsullied by skin or hair.

Talisker found himself strangely ambivalent about this request for his suicide. He had just suffered a massive shock, yet it wasn't simply that he didn't care about living any more; he knew that death could not be the end for him, not while Malky and Sutra remained to whisk his reluctant, tired soul into further conflict. He perched on the end of his bed, and laid the razor blade to one side.

But Malky wasn't here, was he? Talisker peered around the cell. Where was he? Didn't he care about . . .

Unconsciousness was pulling at him now, and he didn't fight it, looking forward to the quietening of his fevered thoughts. But then, as warmth and blackness enveloped him, the realisation came that he was not even to be allowed this small blessing. He was being pulled towards that part of the void to which Corvus could summon him with the help of his own body's weakness. Knowing he didn't possess the strength to face Corvus now, he began to fight the drug, opening his eyes wide, staring fixedly at the shadow shape of the doorway opposite his bed. It was to no avail; his body was beyond exhaustion and the blackness called to him like a deadly siren. Imperceptibly, Talisker's hands moved slowly across the bed and closed on two objects: in his right, the still warm talisman of Shula's gift, his St Christopher, and in the left, the sharp cold kiss of the razor blade. A numb awareness of falling overcame him and then he knew he was standing in the void. He walked forward into the dark, his arms held up and out from his sides. 'Corvus,' he called, 'I know you're here.'

*The fissure opens just before his feet with a hissing, cracking sound. As before, bars of light spill outwards, dazzling his eyes and stopping him in his tracks. Behind the lights a shape is standing. This time, the god Corvus has chosen at whim to appear as the raven.*

*'Ah, there you are.' Corvus's voice booms out across the space. He sounds self-satisfied. 'And you are just where you belong, Talisker. In a cage. As far away from me as possible. Couldn't have worked out better, really . . .'*

*'I suppose you think of this as some kind of victory?' Talisker says quietly.*

*Corvus allows himself a wry chuckle. 'Merely a return*

*to the status quo. You can't get out of this mess – my demon has made sure of that. I imagine they will lock you up for ever. Not that for ever's very long for you mortals . . . we're not so different, you know, you here in your prison and I in mine. Imagine, Duncan, for ever to a god means just what it says . . . eternity.'*

*'Why did you kill Shula?' Talisker walks forward a step as though planning to walk into the chasm, unheeding of the heat that is building from the energy of the lights.*

*Corvus sighs impatiently, as though dealing with a witless child. 'She was a mere detail, Talisker. I had to make you realise . . . Enough. I'm returning to Sutra and this time I will not be denied. I daresay we will not see one another again.' The raven ruffles its massive feathers, the sound rasping, echoing through the space between them. It seems as though the bird will fly once more, back to Corvus's own prison.*

*'Don't count on it,' Talisker replies. 'I'm coming for you, Corvus.'*

*'And how do you propose to do that, fool?' The voice is like a whiplash, and the eyes of the raven flare with anger. 'You can't get back now. You are contained, just as I am.'*

*'I can get back to Sutra any time I want, if my life is in danger.'*

*'But how can—'*

*'Like this,' Talisker hisses. Lifting his arms again he extends his left hand palm upwards. In the middle, in its own bloody little trough, the blade reflects the light. Warm blood trickles down Talisker's arm.*

*'No. But you wouldn't . . .' The raven blinks rapidly*

*and its beak opens, revealing the pointed tongue.*

*'Just watch me.'*

*'But you may fail, Talisker.' The voice has a desperate edge now; Corvus is used to winning such games. 'I understand you may only pass through the void with the guidance of one of Mirranon's gems, which your companion carries. He's not here, is he? Your death might be absolute.' Corvus's speech is quickening as realisation sets in. 'Is it worth dying to reach me?'*

*'You made it worth while, Corvus, when you killed Shula. I'm coming to get you. Ironic, really, I didn't care much before, but now . . .' Talisker grins nastily '. . . now it's personal.'*

*Without waiting for Corvus to reply, he plunges the razor blade into his arm in a swift dragging motion that severs the artery. Hissing through clenched teeth he collapses and rolls on to one side bringing his knees up to his chest, nursing the pain.*

*'No!' Corvus fumes. But he is helpless to do anything.*

*Talisker rocks back and forth, cursing repetitively. 'Fuckfuckfuckfuck . . .' He is aware of his dual presence in the void and in his cell. For a moment, he sees the tiled walls and harsh light of the cell. Blood is everywhere, pooling on the floor, soaking the blankets, congealing almost instantly in the cold of the room.*

*'He's not coming, Talisker. Your little friend's not coming.' Corvus's voice is everywhere and nowhere. Talisker is in the void and in the cell, and the pain is with him in both places.*

*Talisker opens his eyes; his face is red where the artery has sprayed him and blood continues to pump through it. The blood has settled into all the lines of his face and outlined his intense blue eyes, giving him a crazed expression. 'Malky,' he calls, in a hoarse whisper. 'C'mon, man . . . Malk . . .'*

*Corvus's voice is triumphant, regaining its self-assurance. 'You've a lot of guts for a mortal, Talisker, and a lot of blood, of course . . .'*

*'Whit the hell's goin' on here?' At last Malky appears at the end of Talisker's bed, beside his crumpled form. 'What've you done, Duncan? Ohmigod . . .'*

*Talisker is losing consciousness fast. 'Do it, Malk . . .'*

*'No!' Corvus howls in fury.*

*Talisker and Malky are back in the bloodied cell, and for a moment, so are the great raven and the lights. The bird vanishes but the lights remain, whirling around the walls of the cell, turning into a tornado that centres around the two men, whipping their clothes. The sound of the wind and light is deafening, and it seems that Corvus's voice is in the wind, screaming his fury. Talisker rallies briefly and opens his eyes; his expression is triumphant as he blinks away the red stream and he grins into the centre of the storm.*

*'I'm coming, Corvus,' he whispers. 'And I'm going to make you pay.'*

As unconsciousness claimed him once more and the more familiar darkness of the void took him, Talisker's initial feelings of righteous revenge gave way to cold fear. There could be few souls who had crossed this wasteland as many times as he without their soul being forfeit, travelling into the astral clutches of whatever god they had believed in. Possibly no one else had used this place as some bizarre transit station. But what if Malky had been too late? What if he had been too close to death in Edinburgh or Sutra? Already, the physical presence that represented his body while in the void was caught between his two deaths: his arms and chest were hot and sticky with what he knew to be his life's blood, but his back and legs were freezing as though he still lay on the unforgiving snow of the foothills of the Blue Mountains. Now it struck him that he was lying down, curled into a ball; whether to preserve his warmth or cradle his pain, he could not tell.

He heard Malky calling him but there was no sign this time of his friend in the void. The voice seemed far in the distance but gave him the distinct impression that the Highlander, as usual, was haranguing him, exhorting him to action. Talisker tried to raise his head to look around but his neck was cold and stiff.

Then there was a different sound: the soft, gentle braying of an animal. Talisker looked up into the deep brown eyes of a bear, which was breathing warm moist air on his face.

'Tayna?' he whispered.

The bear licked his face then wrapped its massive arms around him in a life-giving embrace. Talisker felt himself drawn into the pungent warmth of its pelt and nestled there with no fear or hesitation. He sighed, and slept.

Talisker dreamed the dreams of the great bear. They were like a song that followed the rhythm of her heartbeat. *Running through the green. Ashka the brown, the loudest, the tallest. Singer of songs. Mother of many cubs. Soon taken. Soon gone. Talisker ran also, watch-*

*ing his feet move soundlessly across the grassland, hearing the panting breath of Ashka. Laughing like a child, his own heartbeat pounding, racing, making an answer to the call of the bear. Running through the water. Ashka, scourge of moonlit fishes. Dancing. Ashka dance. Tayna dancing. Touching me. Looking out. Sheer delight. The silver splashing, like fireworks in the darkness of the woodland. The water was aflame, vibrant. Ashka danced and spun in the water, and Talisker danced too, shrieking aloud in nameless joy.*

*Tayna running silently through silver woods. Ashka faster. Boy is there. Owen. Ashka still here. Sadness inside. Already, he sensed the anguish of the giant creature. To be left behind. To fade into the darkness of impossibility. Hear me roar. Hear my echo for ever. See my ghost dance across the snow. Dancing in the wilderness. It is cold now. Tayna loving. Tayna sleep. Ashka sleep.*

Her last words seared his heart and Talisker called out to her, pulling into the warmth of the musky brown fur. The warm heartbeat of the dreaming bear faded into the blankness of sleep.

Hear me roar. Hear my echo for ever.

'No! Oh, no.'

Talisker woke to the sound of anguish. For a few moments he felt disoriented, could still see the ghost bear dancing across the snow, its great form strangely graceful. Then he turned without thinking and everything became instantly clear – as clear as the morning.

Malky was on his knees a few feet away before a crumpled body, sobbing like a child. Talisker struggled to rise but his limbs were still heavy, so he hauled himself over to the spot although he already knew what he would see.

It was Tayna. She had come back for them, worried by the change in the weather. She had run for a day in the form of Ashka and found them last night as their lifeblood froze in their veins. Giving them the body heat of the great bear she had died, unable to control the loss of warmth from her Sidhe being. Saving their lives had cost her everything. When she had found Talisker again in the void, she had saved his soul as well as his body. She had saved him twice.

Talisker stared at the girl's delicate body, remembering the spirit voice of Ashka. *It is cold now. Tayna loving. Tayna sleep. Ashka sleep.* She looked as though she was sleeping. His throat constricted and he sighed to ease the tightness of his chest. He felt ashamed, unworthy of the act of self-sacrifice. 'You were right about her, Malk,' he said, his voice shaking. 'She was very special.'

They could not bury her. The earth was frozen solid so instead they built a raised cairn on which they laid her body and covered it with her cloak.

'Wait,' Malky said. He took the earring of the *Raknnawr* and placed it on her finger. 'Perhaps it was her brother's. At least she will have something of her people with her.'

'I'd like to give her something too, Malk.' He opened his right hand; Shula's St Christopher glinted gold in the weak morning light. He wrapped the chain around Tayna's cold fingers. 'It seems right that she should have it,' he said forlornly. 'She and Shula . . . were both special people.'

Together they continued to pile up the cairn. Malky found some flat rocks to lay across the top supported by the smaller stones. Neither man could bear to crush her body. At last they were done. They stood in silence for a few minutes, feeling the warming touch of the sun. A chill wind still blew across the moor. 'We should go,' Talisker said quietly.

Malky looked at him almost accusingly. 'She believed in us, Malk. We owe it to her to reach Mirranon. She believed that what we are doing is important.'

The Highlander turned his reddened eyes to the mountains. 'Let's go,' he said.

It took another day and a half to reach the end of the valley Tayna had described as the place to find Mirranon. When they turned away from the Blue Mountains, the landscape changed, the bleak ruggedness of the rocks softening, turning from sharp scree to gently sloping hill. Here, in the shelter of the mountain range, there were no harsh extremes of climate, and even so late in the year myriad tiny flowers dotted the grass of the plains. The travellers rested for a while on the grassy foothills.

'What do we do now?' Malky wondered aloud. 'It doesnae look as though anyone's coming to meet us, like Tayna thought.'

Talisker said nothing. He was enjoying the relative warmth of the valley, drinking in the green as though it were a salve for his weary soul.

'Look! O'er there.' Malky pointed. A dark pall of smoke was rising to meet the lowest clouds a few miles away.

Talisker was unable to make out its source, which

was concealed by a grove of trees. 'I guess we head that way, Malk.' He stood up, anxiety gripping him. 'Come on. If that's where Mirranon is, it looks as though we've been beaten to it.'

When they arrived at the site of the fire no one was around. Distance had deceived them into thinking the grove was fairly small but it was a woodland that had surrounded a group of buildings until the ravages of the fire. The trees nearest the buildings had been destroyed and the sweet smell of charcoal and smoke drifted on the breeze. Malky gave a low whistle when they saw the site of the buildings. 'This wisnae what I was expecting, Duncan.'

'Nor me.'

Where the few walls remained standing, white and silver filigree could be seen around the windows, and the walls curved and buckled in a way that suggested the shapes had grown from the ground. The largest, possibly Mirranon's home, had double doors of beaten copper, engraved with the image of an eagle in flight. Something about the engraving was so emotive, so suggestive of freedom, that Talisker reached out and touched it.

'Duncan. Over here.' Malky was pointing to something partially covered by a collapsed wall. 'Corrannyeid, d'ye think?'

It certainly smelt like Corrannyeid but the creature was bigger than any they had seen previously. Malky prodded it with his sword. 'Ah hope it's deid 'cos if this thing decides tae get up, Duncan, we're in big trouble.'

They shifted as much of the wall away as possible to get a better view of the creature but by unspoken consent left a large beam across its middle, pinning it down. At first sight it appeared to be a vast bat; it had folded its black wings around itself to protect its body from the falling rubble. Its face, also a leathery black, was quite human, the features delicate and somehow feminine looking, although it was bald. One eye had been dashed out when the creature had died but the other stared out, a bright baleful yellow, malicious even now. Gingerly Malky pulled back a wing with the edge of his sword: the body was repulsively thin and sexless.

'There's another over here, Malk.'

There were four altogether and the last was the most disquieting. Bright splashes of blood had congealed on the wings although there was no sign of a wound, and its left talon clutched a clump of white feathers. Nearby, another flurry of white feathers was scattered across the ground. Malky kicked the dust and cursed. 'We're too late, Duncan. They must've killed her.'

Talisker was suddenly bone weary and sat down. The implications of Mirranon being dead were clear to him: there was no going home to Edinburgh, no way out of Sutra once Deme's charm was exhausted, as it almost certainly was already. Having just suffered another near-death experience to get back to Sutra, he was sure he didn't want to do it again. So, as far as he could tell, this was it. As the thought passed through his mind, he realised that he didn't care very much. Chaplin would care, for he had a life worth returning to – or thought he did – but Talisker had nothing. It seemed that Shula had loved him once, but now she and that love were gone. A picture of Una formed in his mind, her flame hair and green eyes shining like a vibrant beacon . . .

'Look, Duncan.'

In front of the copper doorway a hare was staring fixedly at the two men. It was large, about the size of a small dog, and something about it was reassuringly familiar. Talisker stood up and walked towards it. The hare didn't move, simply cocked its head to one side as though curious.

'Be careful, Duncan.' Malky stood up, his hand dropping to his sword. 'It's probably bewitched. It could be a sending.'

Talisker gestured behind his back for Malky to stay where he was. When he reached the doorway, he crouched until his eyes were level with the bright gaze.

'Take me to Mirranon,' he breathed.

The hare blinked, and for a moment Talisker thought he was mistaken. Then the creature bolted past him but stopped at the edge of the clearing as though waiting.

'Yes!' Talisker grinned. 'C'mon, Malk.'

Mirranon lay in a cave less than a mile from the clearing. She still held to her eagle form and she was dying; her right wing had been ripped away and a great crimson gash coloured the feathers of her breast. She moved feebly when she saw the two men but seemed too weak to communicate. Talisker was bereft, remembering his dream in which he flew with the White Eagle at a time in his life when the freedom of flight was unimaginable. He realised that now two Sidhe beings had shared their souls with him and died because of it. Pushing the folds of his plaid into her side to staunch the bleeding, he sat beside her and buried his head in the soft white feathers.

Malky sat outside the cave entrance in a patch of bright sunshine as though he felt he would be intruding. He sharpened his sword against a rock, not trusting himself to speak.

A short distance away, the hare watched its mistress and Talisker.

'No,' Talisker whispered. In truth, he could not understand his feelings for the great bird. 'Don't die, Mirranon. I don't understand all this.' He paused for composure. 'Why me?' He stroked her side as he spoke. 'There must have been someone better . . . Don't die . . . don't die . . .'

'Duncan.' Malky spoke from outside the cave. 'Didn't you come to give her something?'

Talisker laughed bitterly. He took *Braznnair* from his pocket and stared down at it. His hands were bright with Mirranon's blood. He could hardly speak. 'Until the light shines again, Mirranon,' he whispered. He sat forward and held the stone on his palm towards the eagle. Sunlight streamed into the cave and flared through the emerald, bathing the wounded bird in a warm green glow. Mirranon closed her eyes and Talisker feared she was already lost to them. Then, gradually, the shape of the White Eagle disappeared, and lying in its place was the weak and bloodied body of a woman. Although she was recognisably Sidhe, her features were softer, a merging of her human father and Sidhe mother. She was wrapped in her grey cloak but it was easy to see that her right arm was gone, as her wing had been. As he stared into her face, Mirranon opened her eyes and smiled a tiny bitter smile at him. 'You came then . . .'

'Don't try to speak, Lady Mirranon.' Talisker's voice was gruff with strangled emotion. 'You have been badly injured by those . . . those . . .'

Her eyelids fluttered weakly and her voice was breathless with pain. 'Aye . . . they are *Bultari.* I shall fly no more. It's what Corvus wanted. I was a fool to imagine he was contained at this stage. A damned fool.' She stopped speaking with an alarming intake of breath.

Talisker assumed the worst and bowed his head in silence. For long minutes nothing moved in the woodland: it was as though grief had laid a thin grey shroud on every living thing. Talisker was dimly aware of Malky coming into the cave and reaching out to Mirranon's body.

'Snap out of it, man,' the Highlander chided gently, 'We'll have to build a fire and keep the lady warm.'

Talisker raised his head. 'You mean . . .?'

'Aye, Duncan, she's still alive. Just.'

All through the night he watched her. With the first touches of dawn in the sky, Mirranon lay sleeping, her breathing shallow and weak. Talisker could hardly describe his feelings towards her: Mirranon was the key to an unimaginable change in his life. As he sat watching over her, many things had crystallised in his thoughts; a feeling of fierce joy was connected with Sutra, a realisation that he was needed for the first time in his life. For all the death he had seen since his arrival in Sutra, and all the violence, what burned brightest in his thoughts was its colour and passion. The warriors who had died in the battle for Ruannoch Were had not sold their lives cheaply or devalued it by their death. Rather, they had died as they had lived, their last breaths savoured as their wives and children. If he thought of Edinburgh now, it was as a grey place filled with people who lived their lives by half-measures. Deep down, he knew this was unfair; he had been happy there once, if only as a small boy. He remembered his schooldays when he and Alessandro had been friends. When they first met he had pulled Sandro's pony-tail and called him a big jessie, but after beating one another to a standstill the two boys had laughed themselves sick over it. He smiled at the memory, feeling strange and empty, but he knew that, deep within him, he had formed the decision not to go back even if a way could be found.

'I will be unable to send you back, Talisker. I am sorry.' Mirranon had woken and spoke as though in answer to his thoughts.

'Can you read my mind?' he asked, surprised.

She smiled gently through her pain. 'I would never do such a thing without your bidding. The gem must reach Soulis Mor before Corvus claims the land for ever. He will be free.' She closed her eyes. 'You know his true wickedness now, do you not?'

'Yes,' he muttered.

'I cannot fly there now. I must lie here and preserve my strength.' she continued. 'I sense I have but one task left me and it may not even be in this realm.'

'But Malky and I can take it, Mirranon.'

'It has been a fruitless journey to find me, has it not? No, Talisker.' She swallowed. 'No. I'm . . . I'm not sure my defences will be enough to help the Fine make their stand. We need further help, just as we did before. And I need you and Malcolm to fetch it. In truth, they will not speak with me as I am neither Sidhe nor Fine.'

'Don't say that. Whoever these people are, they know nothing. If it weren't for you . . .'

She laughed then, even though it pained her. 'They are not people, Talisker. I am speaking of the gods of Sutra. If they thought and behaved as people do, our task would be an easy one.'

There was a long silence as this information sank in. For all of Talisker's acceptance of the magic abroad in Sutra, the idea of real gods worried him. When he had had his battle with Phyrr, the idea that she was a goddess had seemed unthinkable; she was alive, just as he was. Even Corvus . . .

'What troubles you, Duncan?' Mirranon asked.

'He doesnae believe in gods.' Malky had joined them by the fire where he held his hands to the dying flames. He grinned his ghostly grin at Talisker.

'How do you know what I believe?' Talisker said, mildly irritated by the Highlander's presumption.

'Ah widnae either if Ah wiz you . . .'

'It matters not whether you believe, Duncan,' Mirranon said quietly. 'I know you have already met the lady Phyrr. Do not let her physical presence distract you. She might have killed you by magic but chose to make sport of you and save her energy. It was most unwise and I'm sure she will pay for her mistake. As for Corvus, you have seen only a shadow of his malevolence. The first of the gods you must contact is their cousin, Rhiannon. It is over two hundred years since she last had dealings with the affairs of man but then she interceded and helped secure the defeat of Corvus – so there is no love lost between them. There has been no word from Rhiannon since that time but I think I know where she may be found. If she will help again is another matter.'

'But if we do this, Mirranon, how can the gem go north to the city? You're in no state to travel, never mind fight off more Corrannyeid.'

'Aye, we shouldnae put aw our eggs in one basket,' Malky agreed. 'If onything happened tae us and we had the gem, well, the game's up the pole.'

'Help is on the way.' Mirranon's voice dropped to a whisper. 'I'm so tired.'

'Perhaps you should sleep, m' lady,' Malky said graciously. 'Me 'n' Duncan here'll go 'n' get some bunny fer breakfast.'

'I do not eat the flesh of animals, Malcolm, but thank you for your consideration.'

The hare popped its head out from behind the figure of its mistress.

'Er, sorry. Nae offence like.'

Mirranon was already asleep again, so the two men ventured into the woods to hunt.

Just behind the ruins of the encampment, only a hundred yards from where Mirranon lay, was a pool. In the first light of the early morning, a shadow moved across it, black ripples spreading outward from the centre. A stag that had come to it to drink changed its mind and skittered off into the cover of the trees. The shadow rose silently from the dark water forming a shape as it came: the black outline of a huge horse, which carried something on its back. It appeared already in motion, as though it had galloped through time and space heedless of anything but the bidding of its rider. As it made contact with the earth, the darkness that enveloped it was pulled back into the water and the true nature of beast and rider were revealed.

It was Phyrr. She rode bareback, her slim frame seeming tiny and delicate on her mount. The horse remained as black as the shadows, its stature massive, yet it wore an expression of fear. Its nostrils flared, its eyes rolled in panic and its ears lay back.

Leaping off while the stallion was still in motion, Phyrr moved swiftly into the creature's path and waved her arms. 'Whoa! Whoa!' The horse checked its stride and stopped within inches of its tormentor. Phyrr smiled sweetly. 'You want to go home now, don't you? Back to the field full of mares, hm?' She clapped its flank in a show of affection. 'Well, I might need you myself shortly but you'll come if I call, won't you?' The horse snorted, and Phyrr kissed its soft nose. Then, a tiny blue glow suffused her fingertips and she delicately touched the creature's forehead, binding the animal to her service. She let it go then, content that it would be there when she needed it, and walked slowly into the woods towards the encampment. She wanted to see what Corvus had done there. She touched the patch over her left eye, which was now sightless and, worse still, ugly. The pupil had turned white, like an opal. Like Corvus, Phyrr possessed no healing power: chaos lent nothing creative to those who wielded its power. This time there was no forgiveness: her brother had gone too far. The desire for revenge burned in the pit of her stomach.

*

On returning from the forest, Talisker and Malky discovered that a new creature had joined Mirranon by the fire. A small silver-grey lynx watched them with wide yellow eyes. Mirranon was more exhausted than when the two men had left her, barely able to speak. Malky, immediately suspicious, drew his claymore and stalked towards the animal, which refused to move and regarded him with an expression akin to amused curiosity.

'Malcolm,' Mirranon murmured, 'is that any way to greet an old friend?' As the enchantress spoke a warm glow shimmered around the lynx and in a few short moments, a tall golden figure stood before them, smiling as though she had come a long way to see them. Which, indeed, she had.

'Deme! Ah canny believe it's you!' Malky chuckled. 'We thought ye'd been killed by the demon in the close.'

Deme embraced them both. 'I managed to escape, Malcolm. Mirranon had given me a gem similar to the one I passed to you. I returned to my people, who were surprised to see me. It seems that time is different here and I am returned only a few months after I left. But now Mirranon requires swift, silent feet for a journey through the forest,' she said. 'There are none better.'

One bright blue eye observed them from the cover of the trees, missing nothing. Its gaze rested on Talisker for some time, and a slow smile spread across Phyrr's face.

At noon of the same day they left Mirranon and Deme. The lynx had decided to stay with her old friend until the next day, when she would set off for Soulis Mor. She spoke to Malky when Talisker was sitting with Mirranon. 'The end is near for the White Eagle, Malcolm. Don't tell Duncan yet. I fear he will lose heart.'

'But she seems better,' Malky protested.

'No.' Deme touched her heart. 'In here, her soul is dying. Her body will fail by tomorrow, I think.'

'Are you sure? Ah mean nae disrespect, Deme, but you don't seem very . . . well, sad.'

'Death is not truly the end, Malcolm. You should know that. We believe that the spirits of Sidhe return to Lysmair, our home, to be welcomed by our people. She will fly again.' Deme glanced back at her friend. 'She is the embodiment of the unity of the Sidhe and the Fine, and her spirit is great indeed.'

'Aye, mebbe, but Ah don't think Duncan will see it like that. He's lost someone very dear to him already.' He told her briefly about Shula, how she had been the only person in Edinburgh to believe in Talisker.

'Perhaps, sad though it is, Malcolm, this may work in favour of the Sidhe and the Fine. It seems Corvus has lit the flame of vengeance within Talisker's heart.'

## CHAPTER SEVENTEEN

On the morning of the next day, Chaplin woke unaware for a few seconds of his transition. However, even before he opened his eyes, the feel and warm smell of his sheepskin bedroll told him he was back. As he tried to rise he felt a crushing pain across his ribcage and fell back groaning.

'Sandro? Are you all right?' Ulla came over from where she had been feeding the campfire. 'What's wrong? Makhpiyaluta, come quickly. Sandro is sick.'

'Stop fussing, Ulla. I'll be fine.' He gasped as a wave of pain gripped him.

Makhpiyaluta appeared beside him and surveyed him dispassionately. 'Remove your shirt, Alessandro,' he ordered coolly, 'so that we can have a look.'

Chaplin did as he was told, which instantly set his teeth chattering.

'I've never seen a wound like that,' Ulla said.

It was obvious to Chaplin that it was a bullet wound, inflicted a world away: the entry-point was just between his shoulder and breastbone but there was no exit wound. The hole had healed over remarkably quickly and Chaplin guessed that the bullet wasn't in there, that his counterpart in Edinburgh was fighting the real battle with it. He hoped that he was right and that he was only bruised.

'But how could such a thing happen while you slept?'

Ulla marvelled. 'And who could have done it?'

Chaplin gritted his teeth as he pulled on his shirt. 'I can't explain, Ulla. I haven't just been sleeping, I've . . . been away. And this wound was caused by Talisker.'

'He tried to kill you?' Makhpiyaluta frowned. 'But he is our ally, is he not? Is there something you should have told me before we allowed him to go for Mirranon? Can he not be trusted? Because he has *Braznnair*! I must go and—'

'No, wait.' Chaplin held up his hand to quiet the Prince. 'I told you it was difficult to explain, Makhpiyaluta, but in this world, at least, I think he may be trusted.'

Ulla frowned. 'But in your own world, Sandro? What is he there?'

Chaplin rubbed his hands across his eyes. 'Actually, Ulla, I just don't know any more.'

That evening, Chaplin, Ulla and Makhpiyaluta stood on the shores of Light of the Sky. An unseasonably warm wind blew across the water, stirring Chaplin's robes as he stared out across the mirror-like expanse. Just out there, somewhere in the depths of the lake, there was a portal to another world and that world was still his. Here, he had been called *Seanachaidh*, and Morias had said he was his successor. Now it seemed like a cruel joke.

The evening before Chaplin and Makhpiyaluta had set out on this journey, Chaplin had sought out Morias. The old man had been sitting in the remnants of the Thane's rose garden, frowning thunderously at a yellow rose even though it was dark and the flower was lit only by the dim sconces of the castle. 'Do you see this, Alessandro?' he asked.

Chaplin, who had approached quietly, had not expected the old *Seanachaidh* to have heard him and he stopped short, a little way down the path.

'It is being choked,' Morias continued, without waiting for acknowledgement, 'choked by the common bindweed. Look.'

Chaplin was mystified by Morias's insistence. All around, the rose garden lay in ruins; hedges that had taken a generation to establish had been burned and hacked in the battle that had decimated the city. The garden was the least of the problems to be faced before the ravages of the winter. However, the flower seemed to be causing the *Seanachaidh* concern so Chaplin peered down at it dutifully. The rose had survived against tremendous odds. Half of the bush had been destroyed in the fighting – trampled by Corrannyeid whose feet would not sense its thorns – and what was left was frail. A tangle of bright green weed was knotted around the stem, robbing the bloom of nourishment. Above this, in fragile triumph, a single yellow rose flared like a beacon in the night, its heady scent claiming back the garden from the realms of chaos.

'It's very beautiful,' Chaplin volunteered. 'Em . . . late in the year too.'

'Yes, yes . . .' Morias nodded absently. 'You've come to ask me about the *Fir Chrieg*, haven't you?'

'Well, yes. I . . .'

The old *Seanachaidh* was scrabbling in the dirt and then he stood up – as triumphant as the rose, it seemed. He had soil on his face and, in the flickering light of the torches, there was a worrying hint of instability in the blue-grey eyes. He grinned and presented Chaplin with the bloom. 'It was dying anyway,' he said. 'Look. You'll just know, Alessandro. You'll know what to do. Trust me.'

And because he had little choice, Chaplin had held his peace. It seemed strange to him now that he had come unprepared to a place where he didn't know what was expected of him just because something about Morias demanded faith.

'Alessandro. We have built the fire.' Ulla's voice was quiet as though she was loath to disturb his reverie but Chaplin knew it was more than that. Ulla was frightened lest she allowed a hint of anger or accusation to enter her voice. He watched her walk back to the fire, her gait still slow and sore as it had been when the drug had worn off the previous day. During the few days they had known each other, Chaplin had come to feel more at ease with her than he had with any woman since Diane. Although her character was unlike his wife's – Ulla was as placid as Light of the Sky – there was an honesty about her that made her easy and pleasant company. Surprisingly, in such a thoughtful, serious woman, she had a sharp wit, and the speed of her perception of others was amazing, if a trifle cynical. During their journey together Chaplin had come to admire her. Her slow smile seemed a warm reward in the stillness of the winter forest, yet when she had slipped silently into his blankets as the first light of dawn touched the forest on the day before he was spirited to Edinburgh he had been astounded. 'Ulla? What are you doing?'

She didn't reply, just wrapped her arms around his neck. Her eyes were still heavy with sleep and he was unsure if she had lost her way in the darkness. Then she moved against him and left him in no doubt.

'No!' Chaplin sat up suddenly, realising that his voice had sounded harsh. 'Ulla . . .' He looked down at the pale outline of her face and realised that in those few seconds she had misunderstood his reaction. She thought she repelled him because she was crippled. She stumbled out of the blankets as though she had been scalded, and her near panic made Chaplin think she would run into the forest to hide her shame. He reached out and grabbed her arm.

'Ulla, listen to me,' he begged.

'Let me go,' she replied, in the most regal tone she could muster. 'Unhand me, or I'll summon Makhpiyaluta to run you through. I got into the wrong blankets, *Seanachaidh*. Let me go.' For an instant, Chaplin believed her but then the sense memory of her touch played on him again and he tightened his grip. 'If I let go, will you listen to me?'

'If you insist,' she replied. Chaplin released her arm slowly, as though he was freeing a captured bird. The pale light of the morning illuminated Ulla's outline as she sat on the grass, her long dark hair streaked with silver, her hands and feet the colour of marble. She had twisted away from Chaplin before she sat down and the unblemished side of her face was toward him, its strong, intelligent lines softened by the dawn.

Chaplin felt like a fool as he realised now how often she adjusted her position like this when she was in his company, and also that without her scars Ulla would have been a hauntingly beautiful woman. ' "Ill met by moonlight . . ."' he mused. 'It's not what you think, Ulla—'

'It's quite all right,' she interrupted archly. 'I do know about men who . . . don't like women. You don't have to explain anything to me.'

'Is that what you think?'

'Then what else, *Seanachaidh*?'

Chaplin felt he was losing ground. 'Look, it's just that I'm . . . I'm celibate.' He was glad of the half-light now, feeling his cheeks colour. 'It was a choice I made when my wife died. It's – it's like my tribute to her memory, you understand? She was killed and . . .' He looked up again and Ulla was gone, leaving him uncertain as to whether she had heard his explanation at all.

Now they had reached their goal of the *Fir Chrieg* – the False Men – on the shores of Light of the Sky. The day had passed quietly and Chaplin had walked slowly, nursing the pain of his ghostly wounds. Each of the travellers seemed lost in their own thoughts. Makhpiyaluta knew that something had passed between Chaplin and Ulla but did not mention it. Although Chaplin had considered speaking again to Ulla about the incident, he had thought less about it as the day wore on and his pain made progress a trial.

He walked back to the fire, heavy-hearted. Makhpiyaluta, sensing something of his despair, smiled almost encouragingly then ruined the gesture with his usual sarcasm. 'Have you worked out yet why the *Seanachaidh* should have such faith in you? I knew the old man was going senile but . . .'

Chaplin was too tired to argue with the Prince. 'If you've any suggestions, let's hear them.'

Makhpiyaluta let the remark pass almost with good humour. 'No,' he admitted. 'I can only suggest we get a decent night's sleep. I'll take first watch and wake you later.'

It was much later when Makhpiyaluta woke Chaplin. The Prince, in his eagle form, needed only a few hours' sleep each night. Now Chaplin stood alone by the largest of the grey stones, listening to the quiet sounds of the water. He wished that the answer would come to him but not even a glimmer of a suggestion presented itself. The image of Morias handing him the rose, in the harsh orange glow of the castle sconces, kept recurring to him but he was well aware that, with a venerable fool like Morias, any gesture might later be construed as wise and meaningful. Chaplin viewed such a search for meaning with a degree of cynicism. But the memory of the rose would not go away and he was forced to admit that his thinking was inadequate, that perhaps an idea was surfacing.

'Sandro?' Ulla's voice carried hesitantly around the rough grey pillar. 'That is what your friends call you, isn't it?'

Despite himself, Chaplin smiled into the darkness. 'Where are you, Ulla?'

She stepped into the light of the torch he carried, her face strained with worry. 'I'm so sorry, Sandro. I've made a fool of myself, haven't I?'

Chaplin wasn't sure what to say so he held his counsel.

'I'm sorry about your wife too. You must have loved

her very much and I have lived with such bereavement. My own sweet Dom . . . At least I could say farewell to her as her soul passed into its rest. I came here to ask if we are still friends, and it seems I will sadden you further.' With a small smile, which said more of courage than humour, she slipped her hand into his and squeezed.

It was such an endearing gesture that Chaplin was momentarily lost for words. He lifted her hand, still entwined in his, and kissed it. 'I hope we will always be friends, Lady Ulla,' he said solemnly, 'perhaps even when my name is synonymous with the word fool.'

'You've made no progress, then, with your thoughts?'

'None,' he admitted. 'I spoke to Morias before I left but he would say nothing useful, just gave me a rose.'

'A rose?' Ulla frowned. 'What colour?'

'What difference does it make? It was yellow. He just said I would know what to do. Well, he was wrong. Maybe we should just head straight for—'

Ulla was laughing, a rusty sound that carried across the silent water and was swallowed by the forest beyond. 'It's me, Sandro. I am the yellow rose. It is my token, although I thought none knew of it except myself. I used to tend a certain bush in the rose garden, which was special to me . . .'

'Was the bush at the edge of the second large bed?' he asked.

'Yes. It survived the fires, then?'

Chaplin nodded, confused. 'Yes. What do you think it means?'

'That I can help in some way, or that I know something that may be of importance to you. May I sit down?'

'Of course. I'm sorry, Ulla. I'll go and get some blankets to sit on.'

They stared up at the night sky. Great cascades of stars swept across the heavens as though they had been painted on some immense dark canvas.

'They are so beautiful.' Ulla leaned back against the stone and patted it. 'Sorry, Raghnald, but I'm tired.'

'You know each one?' Chaplin asked, surprised at her familiarity with the stones.

'Oh, yes. We learn them by rote when we are children – Kentigern, Uisdean, Raghnald, Conniech, Owein and Maura, the heroine of every little girl . . . What's that star there? Why is it shining so brightly?'

Chaplin looked up. It was bright, much brighter than all the others. He glanced at Ulla again – she was fighting sleep to be with him. He told her the story of the star: 'There was a princess once, so beautiful that all men desired her, yet her heart was colder than the deepest vale of the badlands in the north . . .' His voice carried across the water with such clarity and purpose that it seemed almost reasonable that he might touch the star of which he spoke.

'. . . and so he placed the soul of Mafeynwys there in the heavens so that all could marvel at her arrogance. But even the gods could not be unmoved by her beauty so they sent her maids to tend her through all eternity that she might remain untarnished and gladden the sight of man for ever.'

For a few moments, only the lapping of the water at the edge of the lake could be heard. Chaplin sighed and, thinking Ulla asleep, pulled the band from his hair so that he could settle down too. Perhaps inspiration would come with the dawn.

'That was very beautiful, *Seanachaidh*.' Ulla's sleepy voice was muffled by her blankets. 'Morias has named you well. How do you know the stories?'

'I just know them,' Chaplin responded, without thinking. 'I just . . .' He sat up suddenly, his mind grasping for the connection. Ulla pushed herself up on her elbow frowning, as though concentrating on his behalf. 'Morias said that the land has somehow chosen me to tell its stories, to carry them forward so nothing of the land is diminished or lost – that's what a *Seanachaidh* is – but I'm not from this place, Ulla. There must be gaps, things that I can't understand.' He gestured towards the stones. 'I know all their stories,' he said, 'they were heroes, but I don't know . . .'

'You don't know?' Ulla repeated, trying to be helpful.

'I don't know,' Chaplin groaned in frustration, 'and I don't bloody well know what it is I don't know! Agh! It's driving me crazy!' He had sat forward and knotted his hands in his hair as he often did when he was thinking.

'Maybe you should get some sleep, Sandro,' Ulla said kindly. 'Things might look better in the morning.' She pointed to the east where the sky was lightening. 'It's not that far off now.'

Ulla watched him settle down. Her eyes were tired but she wanted to be with him, and she knew he probably wouldn't sleep. In the pre-dawn light, the blue-black sheen of his hair caught the glow of the torches. Although it seemed Alessandro Chaplin did not want a lover, Ulla felt content that such a man would be her friend and companion.

'Ulla! Ulla, wake up!'

It was only an hour or so later and still not quite daylight. The morning was suffused with the pink stain of a glorious sunrise. Chaplin was crouched beside her blankets, his face pale with tiredness but looking excited.

'Sandro?' she said wearily. 'What is it?'

'I've worked it out – where the gaps are.'

'Slow down, Sandro. Start from the beginning.'

'Okay. You said to me last night that as children you learned the names of the heroes by rote, and I said I knew all of their names but there was a lot I didn't know. Anyway, you are the key, Ulla – that's what Morias was telling me. You have the knowledge to put the heroes' stories into context for me. Do you understand?'

'Yes,' she said quietly.

'Well, I'm a *Seanachaidh*, right? Only I didn't choose that, I was chosen. The words that come to me have their own existence. I only channel them.' He was holding her by the shoulders now, his face alight. 'But I need you to tell me what to say.'

Makhpiyaluta had woken and come over to the spot by the stones. Neither Chaplin nor Ulla had noticed him for his tread was silent. He had listened to their conversation, his eyes grave with concern, the morning breeze stirring his silver hair. 'Lady Ulla,' he said quietly, 'I believe the *Seanachaidh* may be speaking of "Ur Siol", the Lineage of the Fine.'

Chaplin frowned. 'A history lesson? What use is that, Makhpiyaluta?'

'Sandro, it is much more than that. Makhpiyaluta is right. I believe it may be what you need. It has never been written down but all children of royal birth are taught it very young. It is a long fable or poem, whose telling takes over two hours. It charts the bloodline of the Fine from their creation to the present day – in fact, the other way round for it must be told backwards through time, ending with the creation of the five thanes by the elder gods. It is seldom told by *Seanachaidhs* or bards because one error is punishable by death. To tell "Ur Siol" is a feat of great courage if you are not of royal lineage.'

'But there's only yourself and Makhpiyaluta here. I am sure you would not put me to the sword for one little mistake,' Chaplin joked.

'No,' Makhpiyaluta agreed. 'We would not. It would be unnecessary.'

Chaplin blanched at his expression. 'Are we talking lightning bolts here?'

'Perhaps,' Makhpiyaluta nodded gravely, 'but I have never seen it told wrongly.'

'It's probably just a super—'

'I have,' Ulla said. 'I would not wish to see such a thing again.'

There was silence.

'Well,' Chaplin said at last, 'we're wasting time here, Ulla. Let's do it. I'm sure I could not have a better teacher.'

She sighed. 'Well, we have all day, Sandro. "Ur Siol" must be told to end on the stroke of midnight.'

'Don't tell me – if I finish early, I'm dead also?'

She smiled gently at his anguished expression but the concern in her eyes remained. 'Yes,' she said.

*

A gale of near hurricane strength had begun to blow, centred over Light of the Sky. The standing stones of the *Fir Chrieg* appeared as jagged silhouettes against the darkness of the night. In the middle of the stones Chaplin stood, marshalling his strength for the telling of 'Ur Siol'. Between each of the stones Ulla and Makhpiyaluta had placed huge beacons, which Makhpiyaluta had worked all day to produce. Even in the gale, they stayed alight, the lurid flicker from the flames lighting the night sky with a troubled orange glow.

Ulla had spent the whole day rehearsing with Chaplin. Now, she sat between the stones of Conniech and Maura, sheltering from the gale and ready to signal to Chaplin when he should begin his task. Makhpiyaluta had transformed into his eagle shape, which he described as more windproof, and sat hunched between the stones of Kentigern and Maura, with his feathers ruffled up, the light of the fires catching his eyes.

Chaplin's thoughts were in turmoil, and as he looked at Ulla, he realised he could not remember one line of one verse of the poem. Fighting to control his panic he began to walk towards Ulla.

'Stay there,' she shouted, over the noise of the wind. 'It's almost time.'

'Someone doesn't want us to do this,' he called back. 'Perhaps it's a warning.'

'Stay there, *Seanachaidh*,' she repeated.

Suddenly the wind seemed to enter the circle of stones as a concerted force. Invisible hands pushed

Chaplin backwards towards the middle, pulling at his plaid and hair. He tripped and fell on to the grass, the wind pushing him down, holding him there.

'No!' he yelled. 'I will be heard.' Words tumbled through his mind, not the words of the 'Ur Siol' but other, words just as old and powerful. They were an ancient language known only to generations of *Seanachaidhs* and bards, which he did not understand. Instinctively he said them aloud, his lips forming the shapes and sounds of incantation, which fled from his throat as though they were alive.

The pressure of the wind dropped as the gale retreated outside the stones, and Chaplin sprang to his feet, drawing his sword. Now, cruel curls of a biting white mist drifted into the circle and Chaplin's sword became so cold that he dropped it with a yelp.

'Gods . . .' he heard Ulla whisper. 'It's so . . .'

'Ulla?' He could no longer see her for she was obscured by the mist.

'Ulla?'

'Sandro. It's time.' Her voice floated through the mist and Chaplin strained his eyes to see her. The voice came again more urgently. 'It's time, Sandro! Can you hear me? Speak it.'

Unexpected strength, from the earth itself, flowed into Chaplin as though he was indeed a focus for the will of Sutra. He threw back his head in exaltation, and Inspector Alessandro Chaplin, chosen *Seanachaidh* of the land, began to recite the 'Ur Siol'.

And it seemed to him that time stood still. His perceptions shifted, moving aside into that space where gods and spirits drifted, that space where none could walk and hope to return. Still, he felt his lips moving, reciting the 'Ur Siol', forming the words Ulla had taught him, feeling each sound so that each word he spoke became real – had power and sentience – carrying into the sky like an echo of time. Unable to move, instinctively knowing he must not, he stared around at the altered landscape. Only the stones and the torches remained. Outside, there was nothing but a bitter dark. Turning his head slowly he stared at the stones and saw the warrior souls within. He could feel his eyes burning in their sockets as his lips moved. Suddenly, he imagined himself flaring like the lights around him, growing larger and larger, striding the land, calling the generations to him, gathering the strength of the dead. Somewhere inside him, a tiny flame of fear burned but he knew there could be no going back. Already he had said too much. As the warmth of power flooded through Chaplin he didn't want to stop. The souls of warriors called to him and, reaching his hands to the heavens, he made his answer. As he neared the last verse, he felt the first pull of resistance, and looking out on the brightening wasteland he saw beyond the stones a huge shape in silhouette against the sky. Within it, the stars shone and outside was only darkness. It was the outline of the torso of a man, the lower half of his body obscured by the darkened landscape. From his head grew the shape of horns or antlers. Lord Cernunnos.

Around Chaplin, the stones toppled. Ulla screamed, but Chaplin dared not stop. He knew his fate. He must finish 'Ur Siol' or die. The shape of Cernunnos was reaching out his huge hand as though to claw something back. Just these, Lord, Chaplin's mind screamed. Just these six . . . He was reaching the beginning now, which was the end. The names of the five Thanes . . .

'Not yet, Sandro! It is not time!'

He paused as long as he dared, but she didn't understand; he had to go on, he couldn't stop now. No, he wasn't stopping. The last names of 'Ur Siol' were shouted as his voice cracked and gave up. When no more words would come, he was screaming to fill the void. The figure of Cernunnos faded from the skyline and Chaplin collapsed into blessed unconsciousness.

# CHAPTER EIGHTEEN

When they met at the crossroads in the foothills to the west of the Blue Mountains it was the longest day of the year. The winter sun hung heavy on the horizon and the freezing air, although this place was at least fifty miles inland, still held something of the sea. Chaplin was three days late and Talisker had decided to wait only one more day before setting off on the task Mirranon had suggested. He stared out across the wetlands at the rising sun, sipping morosely at the tea Malky had brought him. 'What if he doesn't come, Malk? What if I killed him in the close? Stirling told me both he and Finn were missing.'

'Ah dunno.' Malky shrugged. 'Ah s'pose he would have disappeared from Sutra. That means Makhpiyaluta would be left on his own. Who knows what he'd do?'

'I know what you mean, Malk. I'm not convinced about the Prince's commitment to Morias's plan either.'

Both men sat down on a tree stump but continued to stare towards the horizon.

'How will ye feel, Duncan, if ye've killed him?' Malky asked.

A look of puzzlement passed Talisker's features as though he was examining the idea closely for the first time. 'I'm not sure.'

'Ye've never liked him.'

'No, you're wrong, Malk. I've known him since I was about seven. Chaplin and me, we were best friends once.'

'What happened? It had to be a woman – right?' Malky chuckled.

'Six women, actually.'

'Huh?'

'The murders. It seemed to make it worse for Sandro that we had been friends at school. It was as though I'd tainted him by association. So he's hated me more than any stranger could have done. He's hated me because I was his friend.'

Both men stared silently at the horizon.

'They'll be here,' Malky said quietly. But he sounded less than convinced. It was difficult to see what could have delayed Chaplin's party by three days – other than wandering Corrannyeid.

A harsh wind was blowing across the wetlands, whipping and snapping the red flags Mirranon had given them to guide Chaplin towards their small encampment. 'At this time of year a flash of red in the bitter wilderness is like a fire in the soul,' she had said. The haunting cry of a curlew was the only other sound to break the solitude of the place.

Suddenly the bird's call changed to a note of alarm.

'Look, Duncan.' Malky pointed to the west. A great eagle flew there, gliding effortlessly where the chill winds met the warmer air currents in the bleached blue of the sky. 'D'you think it's Makhpiyaluta?' Malky asked excitedly. He jumped up and down waving his arms above his head. 'Hey! Hey, Mak! We're ower here!'

'Malky?' Talisker said. 'What are you doing?'

'I'm just—'

'He's an eagle.'

Malky shuffled in embarrassment. Talisker couldn't quite suppress a grin – Malky showed a lot of spark for a dead man.

Makhpiyaluta circled the encampment once then landed on a tree just outside the circle of flags. He and Talisker regarded one another coldly, and Talisker had the uncomfortable feeling that the mighty bird was considering shredding him apart with his silver talons, which glinted ominously, even in the weak winter sunlight.

'Isn't he going to—' Malky began in a hoarse stage whisper.

Talisker ignored his friend. 'I haven't got it, Prince. The gem . . . *Braznnair*, isn't it? We gave it to Mirranon as we discussed. She has it.'

The eagle's eyes had flickered as Talisker used the Sidhe name for the stone, and Talisker held his breath, expecting the bird to strike.

'They're coming – look!' Malky pointed to the west. In the distance, a small band of people moved slowly across the horizon.

Something about their slow progress and their bearing worried Talisker. 'Are they injured, Makhpiyaluta? They are walking so slowly.'

The great bird remained impassive. Talisker knew that Makhpiyaluta was perfectly capable of communicating while in his eagle form but now he did not choose to do so.

'Bank up the fire, Malk,' Talisker snapped. 'I don't like the look of this. I'm going to find out more.'

Malky glanced at Makhpiyaluta. 'It could be a trap, Duncan,' he growled, 'if this one has changed his colours.'

Talisker was already mounting the horse Mirranon had given him. He looked back at the Sidhe Prince, and finally a message came from the mind of the eagle, its form jagged and alien in Talisker's mind.

*No. I am no traitor. At least, not to the Fine.*

Talisker nodded curtly at him and set off at a canter.

Their paths crossed on the dirt road that led north to the fortress city of Soulis Mor, and Talisker saw at once why the band of heroes moved so slowly through the landscape that had been theirs two hundred years ago. In appearance they were similar to Malky – dead men, ghosts – and the impression was heightened by the dirt and dust that clung to their clothes, which were stained too by the blood of the wounds that had killed them. However, they had none of the Highlander's speed or alacrity of mind: they moved as though in a trance, their eyes unfocused and dull.

'This is them?' Talisker said incredulously.

Chaplin's face was grim. He nodded, too tired to speak. He was supporting the weight of the lady Ulla who seemed similarly exhausted.

'Lady Ulla? How did—?'

'Never mind, Duncan,' Chaplin grated. 'Can you take her on the horse? We'll catch up . . . eventually.'

'So, more ghosts walk the land,' Malky mused. They were sitting around the fire and had exchanged news of their separate exploits since returning to Sutra. For the moment, neither Talisker nor Chaplin would discuss the events in Edinburgh. It seemed that the *Fir Chrieg* had been in the same condition since Chaplin had completed the 'Ur Siol', seven nights ago. They ate, slept and functioned, but as though they were moving under water. They spoke seldom, and then in grunts and short slurred words. Chaplin introduced Talisker and Malky to the group but there was little response. Only the biggest warrior's gaze changed as Chaplin said his name.

'This is Kentigern,' he said. 'Kentigern Murdoch.'

Talisker touched his shoulder and the man's eyes locked with Talisker's as though he were drowning. Then, Talisker knew what the heroes knew and how they felt. It was some time since he had felt the empathy that had cursed his existence in Edinburgh but now it reached out for him again and he was as helpless as ever.

*Darkness. Blood and fire. Kentigern looked out on the land and saw the ravages of all time. The souls claimed by any Corrannyeid, unable to leave or rest, bound to the land by the evil manner of their death, moved among the living, their ghostly forms turning into unrecognisable shadow as their anger and spite overwhelmed them. Death was not the end. There was no release, just the beginning of pain. Kentigern had moved among this black company for two centuries, and now his awakening was hard. Pain from his death wounds seared through his corrupted flesh. A scream echoed across the landscape of his perceptions and moved towards Talisker's opened mind like a dark contagion.*

He leaped back as though he had been scalded, his breathing coming fast. 'Christ, Chaplin, what have you done?' he demanded. 'They're in such pain. It's – it's sickening.'

Chaplin was staring at him, his face drained of colour. 'It's true,' he said.

'What's—'

'You felt that.'

Talisker watched the truth of their shared past finally hit home to Chaplin, eating into his self-assured façade like acid. There was no joy in the moment, no sense of vindication, only the emptiness he had felt before.

'It was always true.' Chaplin stared up at Talisker as though seeing him for the first time.

'Game's up the pole, Sandro,' Talisker said softly.

'Oh, my God,' Chaplin whispered. 'Fifteen years.'

Makhpiyaluta's voice cut across their conversation breaking the reverie of both men. 'What did you see, Talisker? What is wrong with them?'

Talisker told them.

'So it means that no one killed by the Corrannyeid can rest?' Ulla said. 'My Dom . . .'

'But you saw her there, didn't you?' Chaplin had taken Ulla's hand.

'Yes, Sandro. I saw her and walked with her until I could go no further.' Ulla swallowed. 'I was so heavy with sorrow that I did not wonder at the lack of any other souls making the journey.'

'So something has gone from there,' Talisker speculated, 'something that leads them home or to heaven – wherever they go.'

'Possibly,' Makhpiyaluta agreed. 'Only a god could do such a thing.'

'Bloody Corvus,' Malky spat. 'It has to be him that's done it.'

There was a long silence as twilight fell and those around the fire mourned those spirits prevented from dying.

Dawn. Talisker had the last watch and he was on edge. He had been unable to sleep: every time he shut his eyes, the black wraiths of the dead appeared to him, screaming their consuming anger and pain. When he opened his eyes the grey outlines of the heroes could be seen. They lay in a straight row like so many corpses, which was what they were. Yet these men and one woman represented hope to the shattered Fine. The rebirth of legends. Now, presenting them at Soulis Mor would bring only despair. What could their message be to the young warriors other than surrender? It was a mockery of what they had planned with Morias. The White Eagle had been right: only the gods – the few who were left – could help them now.

He meditated on his star while fighting his own despair. The company had agreed that no one should know what Talisker had discovered about the fate of those killed in battle with the Corrannyeid, and with that agreement had come a sick sense of complicity. Today, he and Malky would set out to search for the goddess Rhiannon but Talisker felt little hope for the venture. In his experience, people had their own agendas and why should gods be any different? If they lived for eternity, why should they care if Corvus played with the Fine like so many toy soldiers?

'Talisker? May I join you?' It was Chaplin. 'They don't seem much different from when they were stones,' he muttered. 'At least then you could lean on them. Look, I just wanted to say—'

'Forget it,' Talisker grated. He didn't want to hear Chaplin's apology.

'It's important, Tal— Duncan.'

'No. You're not saying it for me. You're saying it for you. That's what apologies are, a kind of absolution. You should know about these things, as a Catholic.'

'You're wrong,' Chaplin said.

'You thought you were doing the right thing, Sandro. I can see that. I can even understand why you might hate me because of what happened to Diane.' Talisker sighed heavily. 'It's my curse to be a reasonable man in a world gone mad.'

'Two worlds,' Chaplin corrected.

They sat in silence as the dawn came, the light washing across the wetlands with a promise of warmth that would remain unfulfilled throughout the coming day.

'I'd like to come with you and Malcolm to look for Rhiannon,' Chaplin said eventually. 'Maybe I could be useful. I've already seen Cernunnos. It seems that *Seanachaidhs* have some powers. And I'd like to help.'

'What about our heroes?'

'Ulla and Makhpiyaluta can take them on to the city. If Rhiannon offers any cure for them we can meet them there – the rate they're travelling at, we'll probably get there first.'

'Can Mak be trusted?' Talisker wondered aloud.

'I think so, although I'm not a hundred per cent sure,' Chaplin admitted. 'I don't think he'd hurt Ulla. He has great respect for her. He doesn't like me much, though.'

'Immaculate taste I'd say.' Talisker chuckled, and was surprised to see disappointment on Chaplin's face. 'Sorry, I was only kidding. Force of habit.' He thrust out his hand, slightly self-consciously. Chaplin made to shake it and Talisker laughed. 'No, like this.' He grasped Chaplin's wrist, and they exchanged fealty as warriors.

Saying goodbye to Ulla was harder than Chaplin had expected. They had a few moments alone as Talisker spoke with Makhpiyaluta, seeking his assurance that he would protect Ulla and the others during the journey.

She stood by one of the red flags and, again, Chaplin realised she had chosen her position carefully so that he would see her best side. He took her hands gently and turned her towards him. 'We are friends, Ulla. That means I would see all of you, remember?' He touched her scarred cheek. 'Will you be all right with Makhpiyaluta to guide you?'

She tilted her chin, expressing that mixture of defiance and vulnerability that made her somehow more regal than a thane. 'Remember who I am, Sandro. The verses you spoke inside the stones, they were my lineage.'

'And I'm your friend,' he said. 'Let me worry if I want to.'

She smiled for the first time in several days, which reassured him more than any words. 'All right,' she agreed. 'I give my permission for you to worry but only once a day.'

He took her hand and kissed it, then felt a tremor run through her. He gathered her into his arms and held her. 'I'll see you in Soulis Mor,' he said. 'I promise.'

At the summit of the hill Talisker reined in his horse and stared out across the wild reaches of the storm-tossed sea. There was the island, its outline softened by the blue haze of distance. The home of the goddess Rhiannon. He dismounted, his gaze fixed on the horizon, his thoughts ahead of the game. The sea wind whipped at the edges of his plaid and the taste of salt was on his lips and in his beard. He imagined he heard voices in the wind but was unable to discern the soft words. Perhaps it was the Sidhe, warning of the dangers of this errand, yet Makhpiyaluta had said that none of their kind lived this far west. He waited patiently for Chaplin and Malky to catch up. Their voices came in snatches carried by the wind as they crested the last of the blind summits that characterised these cliffs. Talisker turned towards them. As he did so, a great wave struck the jagged rocks below and the spray reached high above the height of the cliff.

For fleeting seconds, as the elements surged around him, Duncan Talisker was part of this land. For the first time something made him real here, not transplanted from another world. His hair and beard had grown in the time he had spent in Sutra and the coastal winds had made them wild. His plaid was caked with mud, bracken fronds and sprigs of heather clung to its fraying edge, and his rough linen shirt was sweat-stained. He leaned easily on the long-spear he had chosen as his weapon, which enhanced the impression of his great height. 'Well, it looks like we can't go any further tonight,' he said.

'We may as well camp in the lee of the hill,' Malky suggested.

As they prepared their shelter, a steady grey drizzle began to fall, and by the time the rough lean-to was erected, the ground was soft. They sat huddled beneath the leather ceiling saying nothing; staring out at the landscape, which was now, in the twilight, soft shades of grey shadow. The horses had been tethered loosely in a nearby cluster of rowan and elder trees. The branches were too thin to provide much shelter for men or horses but at least they took the sting out of the wind, which followed the contours of the hillside and was blowing inland from the sea. As darkness fell, Malky lit a small fire; the wood was damp and it smoked badly, but the tiny dance of flames in its centre gave a comfort that was more than physical.

Chaplin stared into the flames for a long time. He let his mind drift away. At length he spoke. 'Long ago, before the Fine and the Sidhe peopled this kingdom, before even the Raven King ruled with cruelty and dark magic, the gods were here in this place. They walked this land, and the land still remembers . . .

'Now, the fairest of them all was Rhiannon, daughter of Soulis. Fair but wilful she was, and she would have no man to her bed. Many suitors she spurned, and she would ride across the moors on her white mare, laughing that gods could be made so weak. Her golden hair would fly behind her in the wind and she wore no clothes so that she could feel the wetness of the rain and spray against her flesh. Rhiannon loved a mortal man . . . There were few then, and mostly they came from the south; they were warriors, for in the time of the elder gods, life was often brutal and short. His name was Ryn mac Tremmor and he had the heart of a poet. She teased him at first, like all the rest, but one day he stood beside the seashore and sang. His voice was like no other she had heard and she was captivated. He caught and held her when she came close and bound her with words of power he had learned. In fact, they were not needed for she fell in love with him then. Time passed and they met often by the shore. Always he would sing for her and they were content with their lot.

'One day Rhiannon's father told her that her wilful ways must end. She was to marry one of the younger gods – Midar, who is now called god of thieves. She contrived to run away with Ryn and sent him a message carried by one of her horses who, according to myth, were half horse and half man. However, Midar intercepted and killed the creature. The message never arrived.'

Chaplin paused. The echoes of the tragedy were all around, in the earth, in the flames and in the water.

'They were to meet near this spot but, of course, Ryn never came. He was sleeping soundly . . . When she discovered he was not there, Rhiannon's heart turned to ashes. In the distance she could see the torches of Midar, who would claim her as his own in that very hour. There, from the bottom of the valley – can you see the oak? – she began her ride. She galloped her horse up the hillside, never stopping to look behind her. Sensing her intention, Midar cried out to her in sorrow, but he was too late. She did not stop. She rode the white mare off the edge of the cliff.'

'But she was a goddess,' Malky objected. 'Couldn't she fly?'

'Some say so. At the moment she left the cliff, some say she cried out a curse on the fickleness of men. She did not curse her lover, although he had broken her heart. He awoke from his sleep and would never sleep thereafter . . . She was never seen again to the eyes of men except at the time of the Great Battle. Some say she flew across the western reaches and awaits Ryn on the island until the end of time.'

The fire sparked and Chaplin came to himself with a wry, almost apologetic smile. 'Course, it's only a story. I still don't know where they come from.'

'Yeah,' Talisker said. 'But you can't dismiss them. We know that now, after the "Ur Siol". This place . . . this land . . . its legends are alive.' He picked up a rough piece of basalt. 'It's in everything. That's what you said. "The land still remembers." You must trust what you feel.'

'I know I should,' Chaplin admitted, 'but I'm not in the habit of trusting what I feel. I wouldn't have thought you were either.'

'Aye, but Duncan's right,' Malky said 'Ye've bin changin' intae a *Seanachaidh* ever since you came here. There must be a reason. Look, you're sitting on a boulder. Mebbe she rode over that stone, mebbe the stone really does remember. Fer Christ's sake, man! What have we seen since we've been here? We've seen things like we couldnae e'en imagine. Magic is real here, what we would call magic onyways.'

'Magic,' Talisker muttered under his breath.

Chaplin stared into the dying flame. 'And Rhiannon? Is she waiting on the island still, d'you think?'

'Dunno,' Malky conceded.

*Rhiannon.* Talisker said nothing to the others but he could see her. As Chaplin told the tale, he had seen her in his mind as clearly as if she had stood before him, laughing – not from malice but from the purest joy of being. He had seen the leap across the darkness and felt her despair. Her laughter was long gone now. If she waited still for her lover, had she turned to bitterness and spite? Talisker was not a sentimental man but the idea of the decay of her great beauty saddened him. 'Her faith is gone,' he said quietly. 'If she is waiting still, she'll be . . . different. Bitterness will have done it to her.'

His companions looked puzzled but said nothing.

'She wouldn't be the first woman in creation to have no faith in men.' Talisker stood up and began to pace around the fire speaking his thoughts aloud. The shadows he cast danced with the flames.

No one said anything until Talisker reached the arc of the circle his pacing had created. He whirled back to face them, grinning. 'What would Rhiannon demand? I'll tell you,' he said, with theatrical flair. 'An act of faith.' With that he loosed the belt that held his plaid, which dropped in a damp heap into the bracken. Then he removed the rest of his clothes, chuckling as he pulled his tunic over his head. Naked in the darkness and the rain, his skin appeared totally white and the muscles of his strong legs and torso were picked out by the light of the moon and the flickering fire. It was disconcertingly as though a marble statue stood before them.

'Duncan?'

'Talisker?'

'We need to see the goddess Rhiannon. We need to get to her island. Follow me.' He stepped out from the shelter of the trees looking towards the top of the hill.

Chaplin and Malky scrambled to their feet and walked over to him. 'Well, Ah' m no' takin' my cleas off,' Malky grumbled.

Talisker turned to him, still grinning. 'Sorry, Malk. I just felt I wanted to be naked for this. Maybe it was Chaplin's story. I feel . . .' But he was unable to put into words the warmth that was spreading within him.

Chaplin muttered something that the others could not hear above the night sounds. By now Talisker's skin was slick with the rain but he showed no sign of feeling the cold. He turned back towards the cliff top, took a deep breath, spread his arms wide and shouted, 'RHI-AANN-NON.'

The sound echoed and rebounded from the rocks of the encircling hillside, but instead of dying away, it seemed to build and swell. The noise of the ocean stopped, or so it seemed, to listen, until they were surrounded by the sound of her name. As it died away, Talisker started to run up the slope of the hill, his long strides moving him quickly.

Suddenly Chaplin and Malky knew his intent and were spurred into action. 'Naw, Duncan, come back!' Malky gasped. 'Come back, man.' But the white form flitted ahead like the ghost of a legend.

Almost at the top. Talisker could hear the sound of

the ocean swelling in his ears. The pounding of his heartbeat and the gasping of his breath seemed far away. His feet were cut to ribbons by the sharp rocks and he was shouting as he ran, the words carried away by the strong ocean wind that tugged at his beard. Talisker was the wind, the surf, the sea. Talisker was faith. And he was coming to Rhiannon.

As they neared the top, Chaplin was almost upon him. He could hear Talisker's ragged disembodied voice blowing back towards him from up ahead. 'Trust me. It's okay. I have a good feeling about this.'

'No.' Chaplin felt responsible for this: the words of a *Seanachaidh* had power, he of all people should have known that after the 'Ur Siol', but still he hadn't learned to respect and control that power. The legends still used him. A red haze was drifting in front of his eyes. He'd not run so fast or so far in years, but nothing could have made him stop. Suddenly he saw the edge of the cliff and he knew it was now or never. He flung himself forward on to his face, arms outstretched before him.

As he crashed to the ground, everything slowed. For a moment, through the redness, Talisker's foot filled his vision. The heel was towards him and the white skin was glistening with rain and blood. He could see the long angular sweep of the foot and the smashed remains of the fourth and fifth toes. Chaplin's own hand appeared in view, claw-like, grabbing, and seized the heel, which slipped from his grasp in a spray of blood and water. At the same time, he heard that name again: Rhiannon. He raised his head and watched his friend leap.

Only at the instant that his feet left the cliff did

Talisker feel any doubt. It coursed through his body like a dull electric shock. His legs were still pumping as though he would run through the air, but then he fell. Defiance took over, the stubbornness of spirit with which he had always been cursed: it held at bay for precious seconds the physical discomfort. Then, cold, pain, despair and the bitterness of a man who knows death is upon him threatened to overwhelm him. And yet, as the wind sucked the breath from his lungs, he cried out her name once more.

It was the last thing the watchers on the cliffside heard from him.

On the black cliff, neither man spoke. Chaplin pressed his face into the earth and Malky watched the point past the breakers where Talisker had disappeared, unable to believe what had happened.

Then, 'Wait . . .' he said. 'There. Beneath the waves.'

Chaplin raised his head and gazed dully out to sea. It seemed to him as barren and grey an expanse of water as he had ever seen.

'I thought I saw . . . a light . . .' Malky's voice trailed off and he sank down on to the grass. 'Dear God,' he said.

The rain became harder. The hissing sound of the drops hitting the water could be heard above the tumult of the breaking waves. The wind grew stronger and colder, pulling at their sodden clothes, chilling them to the bone, yet neither had the will or strength to move. It seemed as if the storm centred around them: they were the eye of the hurricane, and it contained a bleak calm.

'We'll die here,' Malky whispered. 'It's your fault, *Seanachaidh*.' His voice contained no hint of sorrow.

Chaplin lay where he had fallen, his arm outstretched as though still reaching for Talisker. He knew he had broken some ribs. Gradually, both men sank into a state of unconsciousness or sleep, but neither dreamed, and the wrath of the storm continued, abating just before the dawn.

Malky woke up to find his whole body numb. He rolled over on to his side and looked at Chaplin. The *Seanachaidh*'s skin was ashen, and if he was breathing, it was too shallow for Malky to see. The storm had passed and the new day held the promise of renewal, but Malky was too frozen to care. He sensed that if he lay where he was much longer, he would lapse into an unconsciousness from which he would never awaken.

A movement from further down the slope caught his eye. Chaplin's horse was nearby. It had a blanket slung over its back. Malky forced himself to sit up, although a deep internal quaking shook his frame. 'Here, horse.' His encouragement was hardly more than a whisper but the black gelding pricked its ears and looked in his direction. 'Please come here, horse,' Malky begged. 'Please, horse, Ah'm goin' tae die . . .' Cracked laughter escaped his dry throat and he swallowed it, afraid he might frighten the animal, but it had decided to investigate and came to stand between the men. It began to sniff around Chaplin's face, obviously recognising its master. Reaching out a trembling hand, Malky slowly tugged the blanket from its back.

Half an hour later, he still felt appallingly weak, and as the feeling came back into his limbs, they hurt like hell but he knew that if he didn't help Chaplin soon the

*Seanachaidh* would die. It took some time to stand upright, but eventually he took hold of the horse's reins and, leaning against the beast's neck, forced himself to stumble down the hillside. Walking helped and by the time he reached the campsite Malky felt almost human. He was sweating under the blanket but he kept it gripped tightly around him.

Soon he returned to the top of the cliff, riding his own horse and leading Chaplin's, to which he had strapped most of their meagre supplies. He was relieved to see that Chaplin had moved, although he still appeared to be unconscious. Hurriedly he wrapped the prostrate man in three heavy blankets and was shocked by the absolute coldness of his flesh. Then he laid a small fire and brewed an infusion of elder leaves and water. He had no idea if the leaves contained any healing properties but he had drunk the same brew in the past and knew its bitterness might help to revive the *Seanachaidh*.

As he raised Chaplin's head to put the draught to his lips, he glanced out to sea. The tide had gone out a long way: a vast expanse of grey-white sand was glistening in the weak morning sunlight.

'Malky?' Chaplin's voice was weak and incredulous – he was surprised to have woken at all. His normally tanned face was shockingly white, almost blue, against the woven brown check of the blanket.

'Chaplin,' Malky said quietly. 'I thought we'd lost ye an' all.' He'd never liked the man, his loyalty having always been to Talisker, but the *Seanachaidh* had impressed him with his frenzied chase to save Talisker's life and his grief of the night before. 'Drink the rest of this. It'll put a heat in ye.' He looked back out to sea: there was almost no water visible now. You could walk . . . 'Christ,' he muttered.

'What is it?' Chaplin asked. 'You're not trying to give me the last rites, are you?' He didn't have the strength to laugh at his own joke.

'There's a path,' Malky suddenly felt irrationally excited, 'tae Rhiannon's island! Look!' Malky grabbed Chaplin under the arms and hauled him into a sitting position. Chaplin yelled with pain. 'Ah'm sorry,' Malky said, a little chastened. 'Ye'll have tae turn roond onyways.'

Chaplin did so, clenching his teeth. He stared out in amazement at the empty channel, while blinking the feverish sweat from his eyes. It was true. In the distance he could see the outline of the island. Along the edge of its cliffs was a dark line where the water had been the night before; now it had the appearance of a large boat stranded on the tideline. It was about three miles out in the channel and they still had to get off the cliffs, hopefully in a less dramatic fashion than Talisker had.

'It's no' natural,' Malky said warily.

'Let's go.'

'You're in nae fit state tae go anywhere,' Malky protested.

'I'll warm up if I'm moving. It's got to be better than lying here on the cold ground even with blankets.'

The matter was settled.

Two hours later they were only about a third of the way across. It had taken half an hour to find a way down from the cliff using a rough trail made by sheep or cattle. Chaplin lurched around on his horse, leaning towards its neck and shoulders. He didn't say much but clutched his blankets around himself, looking grimly determined despite his intense pain. Malky said nothing, even when Chaplin fell off his horse – fortunately into a clump of heather. He simply helped the *Seanachaidh* back into the saddle and carried on. He had never been much good at giving sympathy and he was still grieving for Talisker. At least the *Seanachaidh* was alive, and although he was sorely injured, he would probably survive.

When they reached the sand, the going was even slower. Although it was quite compacted, the horses didn't like the feeling of it under their hoofs, refusing to go faster than a reluctant walk. Chaplin had lapsed into semi-consciousness, which, given his condition, was probably a blessing. It was almost midday and their shadows were long and black behind them. There was no sound, no mournful crying of birds, no crashing of sea. Ahead, the shimmer of a heat haze had begun to creep across the drying sands. The combination of heat and silence was oppressive.

Some time later they drew level with the ivory bones of a whale. Malky had never seen a living one but he had heard stories of giant fish. He reined in his horse and looked curiously at it. Seawater still gleamed in all the tiny indentations of the bones, giving the shape a clean and somehow lively appearance. Malky marvelled that such a creature could have lived in the first place and wished he could have seen it swimming. As that thought struck him, another followed it: where was Talisker's body? They had come past where he fell an hour since and there had been nothing. Even if he had landed further north or south, his body would have been easy to spot due to the flatness of the seabed. He rode on, pondering. Something else was bothering him: where had all the water gone to? If it was being held behind the island by some magical force, how could they trust the magician to keep it back until they had crossed? Again, he tried to hurry the horses and this time they consented to move faster, as if they sensed his rising panic. He was just soothing his mount, which was side-stepping and threatening to bolt, when he saw movement ahead.

Through the haze he could make out four or five shapes, probably men on horseback. On the edge of his hearing, he could hear the faint drumming of hooves. His hand dropped to the basket hilt of his sword but he did not draw it: he and the *Seanachaidh* would be defenceless if the riders were hostile.

As the party drew closer, he gasped. 'Chaplin! Wake up!'

# CHAPTER NINETEEN

They could only be kelpies, and there were five of them. Their hugely muscled flanks glistened in the sunlight as they galloped, their upper torso, that of a man, naked and bronzed. They all had long wild hair that flew out behind them as they moved and their features were broad and strong. If they were horse-like at all, they had the wild, rugged beauty of the feral ponies that roamed at will in the harsh moors and mountains of this land. They did not acknowledge Malky as they drew nearer – in fact, the leading three did not slow their pace. One let out a shrill cry and they came on at full tilt. Malky drew his sword but they were out of arm's reach until they came behind his and Chaplin's horses. Just as it seemed they would pass by, they reached out on either side and delivered a stinging blow to each of the frightened horses. Malky's reared up, whinnying in terror, then bolted with Malky clinging around its neck. He had no time to see what happened to Chaplin but he could hear more whooping and calling behind him, which drove his mount to further frenzy.

'Basturts!' he screamed.

The fastest kelpie – the piebald, which had slapped his mount – drew alongside him. For a moment Malky thought he would try to stop his panicked horse, but instead he punched Malky hard on the arm. Malky lashed out instinctively in return, but his opponent was already pulling ahead so Malky grabbed at its trailing mane and refused to let go. The creature reared, screaming in anger, and kicked out with its back legs. Malky grinned in satisfaction, but the kelpie was already gone, leaving him with a handful of coarse white hair. He could hear hoots of laughter coming from those still behind.

Suddenly he found himself enjoying the game – he was almost sure that that was what it was – and decided he must reach the beach before them all. His horse was slowing, so he delivered a hard slap to its rump and clung on with new resolve. As he passed the black and white kelpie, he let out a wild call. 'Tae me! Tae me!'

The kelpie seemed surprised, and Malky thought he heard a throaty laugh but he wasn't sure. He reached the beach first and as his horse's thrashing limbs made contact with the shingle, it bucked once more and this time threw him to the ground. He landed hard, jarring his elbow but he was up and brandishing his sword as the first kelpies reached the beachhead. The three who had led the chase stopped a few feet away and stood looking at him curiously, bunched together and skittering about on their hoofs like the colts they were. The two slower, larger kelpies were a little way behind.

'C'mon then!' Malky panted. He still had a handful of the piebald's mane so he lifted his fist and shook it defiantly. 'C'mon.'

The piebald frowned thunderously and the other two laughed – somewhat disloyally, Malky thought – at his discomfort, but none of them moved. They seemed uncertain what to do, and it occurred to Malky for the first time that, perhaps, they were a little frightened of him. He bared his teeth and snarled dramatically: Highlanders had been terrorising their opponents that way for hundreds of years.

'Hold, friend.'

The larger kelpies had caught up with the group. The biggest of them all – a grey – was carrying Chaplin on his back. The *Seanachaidh* was barely conscious and Malky crouched low, ready to spring into action should they harm him.

'Hold, I say,' the eldest kelpie repeated. 'Rhiannon has sent us.' He walked towards Malky as he spoke, and the younger three parted to let him by, bowing their heads to him as a mark of respect. 'You must forgive these young colts, but they will have their fun.' He stopped dead in front of Malky, so close that the Highlander could easily have reached out with his weapon and killed him. 'Please put your sword down,' he said pleasantly. 'Do you not know of our skill as archers? If you were to kill me, you would be cut down where you stand.'

As he spoke the others were quietly taking their long-bows from where they were slung across their backs. Malky sheathed his sword.

'Thank you.' The kelpie inclined his head graciously. 'My name is Niyso. This is Morchell.' He indicated the other larger creature. 'These brothers are Ebas, Peri and Gavia.'

They all nodded somewhat nervously at Malky, apart from Gavia, whose hair he still held in his hand. He scowled petulantly.

'I can see that you and the *Seanachaidh* have spent a hard night. Let us waste no time in taking you to meet the lady Rhiannon. First you must rest and your injuries must be tended.'

As Niyso spoke, a great weariness fell upon Malky. The muscles in his legs cramped and the depredations of the previous night caught up with him.

'Can you still sit your horse or would you have Morchell carry you?' Niyso asked.

Malky was unable to answer; his throat had gone dry. He looked behind the kelpies: the sea had returned to the channel, and the first wave that crashed upon the beach was like an assault on his ears. He staggered backwards and Niyso gestured at Morchell, who came to stand beside the Highlander. Ebas and Peri lifted him on to Morchell's broad back.

'Gently,' Niyso chided. 'He has shown great spirit.'

Just before Malky blacked out he heard Morchell agree: 'Yes, and Talisker will be happy to see them both.'

Evening was drawing in again when Malky woke and remembered that they had done it. They had reached the Island of Rhiannon. Their passage had been bought by Talisker's leap of faith. As his sadness at his friend's death threatened to envelop him once more, he remembered the deep, vibrant tones of the kelpie Morchell. But perhaps he had dreamed the conversation as he drifted into unconsciousness . . .

He sat up and looked around. He was in a large dome-like shelter, which was fashioned from a living thicket, the branches intertwined and woven to a height of around eight feet. The roof was formed from the branches of tall trees, which must have been growing outside the circle of the thicket. The shelter was not watertight but would check the progress of the most stubborn winds. A soft green light suffused it and it smelt of dank forest loam. Malky decided it must be the dwelling of a kelpie: it had a natural, restful feel to it. On the other side of the room, Chaplin lay asleep on a pile of bracken and blankets. His colour had returned almost to normal, and his breathing was steady and deep. Malky stood up to walk over to where the other man lay and became aware of how rested he felt. He wondered briefly if the kelpies had given him some medicine: he would not have expected to feel so much better after so little asleep.

Chaplin opened his eyes. 'Malky, I had the strangest dream . . . Where are we?'

'On the Island of Rhiannon. And ye wiznae dreamin'. How d'ye feel?'

Chaplin touched his ribs gingerly. 'I feel fine,' he said, surprised. 'Do you think they've cured me by magic?'

'Does it matter?'

'No. I guess not.'

'Oh, aye,' Malky added, 'Ah think Duncan might be alive. I heard one o' the kelpies say somethin' aboot it afore I conked out.'

'Kelpies? Is that what they are?'

'Oh, aye.'

Chaplin was staring at him in disbelief when the covering of the doorway was flung back and Gavia put the front half of his body through the entrance. It was the first time that Chaplin had seen one of the creatures, and with the curtain partially hiding his hindquarters Gavia looked more man than horse, although his features were unusually wide-set, and his hair – as Malky had discovered – was wiry and strong. Offset to one side on his abdomen was a tattooed symbol of concentric blue circles, and where his bristly coat gave way to weatherbeaten skin, more blue circles were tattooed in an apparently random pattern. The divide between pelt and skin was not defined: clumps of short soft hair carried on up his torso, and on his back a line of it merged with his mane.

'Greetings, *Seanachaidh*,' Gavia said to Chaplin, and gave Malky a curt nod. 'You are both to come with me. Perhaps you are hungry?'

They followed Gavia outside. The huts formed a large ring around a clearing thronged with the creatures. The females were tall and graceful, their features finer than the males', their breasts exposed to the sunlight. Most wore their hair loose with tiny plaits woven into the length of it; a few had several larger plaits. All were busy preparing a feast for their guests; the soft sound of their laughter and the reedy notes of the wooden flutes that a couple of the younger kelpies were playing drifted into the warm evening air. As the company drew near, an air of hushed expectation fell on the gathering and they drew back to form a pathway, which led to the head of a large trestle table.

Niyso stood there, looking solemn. 'Greetings. May the darkness of your soul take succour in the quiet of this place. May the birds of Rhiannon sing for you, and the silver moon light you a path that leads you ever back.'

Chaplin and Malky bowed, recognising the formal structure of the greeting. There was a short silence and then Chaplin spoke. 'Our thanks and greetings to this company. May the road rise up to meet you and the wind be ever at your back.'

There was a murmur of approval as he said this, and Niyso smiled broadly. 'Well said, *Seanachaidh*. Let's eat.'

As if a switch had been thrown, the laughter and music began once more, although everyone waited until Malky and Chaplin helped themselves to some food. There was an abundance of chicken and hare, and the two men heaped their plates high and gladly accepted the flagons of beer they were offered.

'Aye, well said, *Seanachaidh*.' Malky nodded grudgingly. 'Where'd ye learn that?'

Chaplin bit into a large glistening piece of meat. The juices ran down his chin. 'My auntie had it written on a tea-towel.'

Malky hooted with laughter and slapped him on the back. 'Christ, Ah'm starvin'. Ma stomach thinks ma throat's been cut.'

'Yeah, she had that one as well.' Chaplin chortled, and the kelpies watched in good-humoured amazement while he and Malky laughed themselves silly. The Highlander wiped away tears and Chaplin held his healed but still bruised ribs until eventually they calmed down. Niyso came and sat with them, folding his legs gracefully under his body. 'Rhiannon will come soon,' he said.

'Doesn't she live here?' Malky asked.

'No. We do not know if she has one place where she lives. She is a restless spirit. And she can be fickle as the young bucks over there.' He pointed to where Gavia and his friends sat. 'Be warned. Although her heart is warm, her patience is thin. She grows easily bored so her magic is unpredictable.' He smiled. 'We love her.' He touched his heart as he spoke, and both men found this simple gesture endearing in such a noble creature.

When the food had been eaten the music began in earnest. Gavia's friend, Ebas, played a long, haunting tune on a set of rough bagpipes. Malky grunted his approval although the tone was higher than the pipes of his day, more akin to the Irish sound. Chaplin said nothing: he'd always hated the bagpipes, but now he realised that he'd never really listened to them, that the soldiers playing on the corners of the High Street had always fought a losing battle. Had there been this silence, this contentment, with only the small sparking sounds of the fire, he might have heard what he was hearing now. The trick was to ignore the drone of the bag, accept it, go beyond it, focus on the melody, the lament.

One of the young females came forward, her friends urging her on from the sidelines. She carried a small harp, which she rested against her side as she played and sang. Her voice was high but strong, and she sang in a tongue unknown to the two men. Chaplin thought she was the most beautiful thing he'd ever seen: she was a sleek silver-white and her hair cascaded down her back to join the rougher hair of her tail. Her upper body was almost as pale, and as the wind stirred about her, the tiny pink points of her nipples were exposed as the breeze lifted away their covering. Her cheeks were slightly flushed with excitement, and she sang with a shy smile hovering about her lips. The mixing of her quiet beauty and her music was erotic somehow and

Chaplin realised with a shock that he desired her even though she was not human.

'What is her name?' he whispered to Niyso.

'Eymer,' the kelpie replied. 'She is my daughter.'

Malky, who was sitting to the left of Chaplin, nudged him. 'Never mind that, ask him aboot Duncan,' he whispered.

As Chaplin turned back to Niyso, Eymer's music ended but, instead of applause, there was a burst of birdsong. Tiny bright red and yellow birds skimmed low into the clearing, their colours almost illuminating the gathering dusk. The kelpies laughed with delight at this entrancing departure from the evening's agenda and held out their hands for the birds to land on. One perched on Eymer's and she tilted her chin and spoke to it in an equally musical tone; Chaplin could not have looked away from her had his life depended on it. Laughter followed the flight of the birds, such clear high laughter that it seemed to encompass the whole assembly in a warm crystal rain.

Niyso smiled. 'Rhiannon comes.'

She stood where the shelters of the kelpies gave way to the wild forest, tall and slender, just as the *Seanachaidh* had imagined her when her story had formed in his mind. Her hair was unbound, green, red and gold leaves scattered randomly through it – even a few small twigs and creepers. She wore a loose green shift of a thin translucent fabric, through which her naked form was easily visible, and she was still laughing. For a moment it seemed to Chaplin that he could detect an edge of cold spite in the sound but he dismissed the thought as a smile crept across his features. She held up her hands and all of the birds flew towards her still calling and singing. When they were an arm's length from her body, they flew into a spiral. More and more joined the joyful music, until they appeared as a whirling maypole of colour obscuring the form of their conductor. Then, with a clap of her hands, they disappeared, and Rhiannon could be seen again, her green eyes shining with delight.

She is like a child, Chaplin thought, but he was still smiling.

The kelpies applauded, and Rhiannon walked over to where Malky and Chaplin sat, her bare white feet making no indentation on the grass. When she reached them she smiled warmly and beckoned to Niyso. He stood up and she climbed on to his broad back and sat comfortably, her shapely legs dangling over one side for all the world as though he were an easy chair. Malky and Chaplin made to rise but she motioned to them to remain seated. The gathering was hushed, and many crept closer, sat down as Niyso had done with their legs folded beneath them. By chance, Eymer sat near to Chaplin.

When Rhiannon spoke, her voice – unlike her laughter – was surprisingly low, her tone vaguely mocking. 'Ah,' she said, touching her heart as Niyso had done earlier. 'The *Seanachaidh*, Alessandro James Chaplin, and the warrior, Malcolm Talisker McLeod. You are welcome in this place. I trust you have rested and eaten well.'

Chaplin and Malky bowed their heads in response. 'Our thanks to this company, Lady Rhiannon, but our hearts are sore with worry for our comrade, Duncan Talisker,' Chaplin said.

She smiled. 'He is alive, Seanachaidh.' She paused. 'I understand you are the chosen successor of Morias. It is a greater honour than you know. Morias is an ancient being, not godly but quite separate. He is, was, an adviser to us all aeons ago. I suspect he seeks to shake us from our inaction.'

Chaplin was astounded. 'Morias?'

Rhiannon nodded. 'Do not be fooled, Alessandro. Although Morias has some power, like us, he grows weaker through the ages and now he needs help to achieve his aims.'

'Which are?'

'Oh, worry not. They are honourable if a trifle naïve. Morias has always loved the Fine and will conspire to save them at any cost.' She looked a little irritated. 'We always called him a meddler . . .'

'But don't you also want to save the Fine, lady?'

She arched her delicate brows and looked amused by this. 'The Fine are not really my concern any more, *Seanachaidh*. My domain is here . . .'

'But—'

Her patience with the exchange had ended and she held up her hand imperiously. 'Come, now, I will take you to your friend. He was badly injured so the kelpies took him to the spring to be healed. They were moved by his gesture of faith and consider him a great man. Walk with me in the forest awhile and we shall find him.'

Without further ado she dismounted lightly from Niyso's back and moved into the tree-line, a tantalising vision. Chaplin and Malky stumbled to their feet, the rich beer they had drunk making them unsteady.

Rhiannon turned and quirked an eyebrow at their condition, but said nothing. Instead she gestured to Niyso and Morchell. Before they knew what was happening, both men were hoisted unceremoniously on to the broad backs of the kelpies. It was especially difficult for Malky to come to terms with riding such a creature: the stories he knew of kelpies concerned them luring people into a watery grave, and their capricious nature had been already proven to him. Still, the motion was similar to the movement of a large horse, and the journey through the hushed forest acquired a not unpleasant dreamlike quality in the gathering darkness. The figure of Rhiannon moved ahead of the great beasts and it seemed that her outline glowed against the black patterns of the trees and branches. She began to sing, and with each chorus Niyso and Morchell joined in, their strong baritone mingling with the sounds of the forest and a fast-flowing river. After a while the singing stopped and only the music of the river remained. Finally, Rhiannon pointed ahead. 'There,' she said.

Talisker sat on a lichen-covered boulder beside a small waterfall. He was naked and it occurred to Chaplin that he should have been cold. A silver-white mist was rising and the scene was lit only by the chill brilliance of a full moon. Talisker waved, showing no sign of discomfort. He had shaved off his beard and appeared once more as Chaplin knew him.

'You must bathe also,' Rhiannon said. 'It will ease your pains.'

'You must be jokin',' Malky said ungraciously, 'It's freezin'.'

'The water's warm, fool,' Niyso snapped, irritated by Malky's lapse in manners. 'Now, get off my back because I'm going in so you'll be in the spring if you want to or not.'

Once Niyso had pointed it out, they saw that what they had initially mistaken for mist was in fact steam so the water was, indeed, warm.

The group moved to the edge of the pool, Malky hurrying to Talisker. Once he reached his friend he felt awkward and punched his arm. 'So, ye're still alive, ye wee scunner. Gave us a bit o' a fright, though, Ah must admit.'

Chaplin came up behind Malky, smiling self-consciously. He shook Talisker's hand as though they hadn't met for years and suddenly seemed quite emotional. 'I never thought I'd say this, Duncan, but I'm glad to see you. It was my fault – the stories, they . . .'

'It's okay, Sandro,' Talisker said. 'It was a bloody stupid thing to do. I don't know what came over me.' He smiled, then looked serious. 'Doubly stupid, because it achieved nothing. I've spoken to Rhiannon and she thinks that Corvus is none of her business. She and the Fine parted years ago.'

'Chaplin was aghast. 'But surely . . .'

'She thinks she did her bit the last time.'

'But that was two hundred years—'

A shrill scream split the night air followed by an inhuman sound. Horse and man. A soul divided, screaming, whinnying in fear.

Makhpiyaluta shifted impatiently from foot to foot. He

was worried. Knowing that his journey with Ulla would pass through the valley where the council would meet, he had sent messages out to call this meeting then left Ulla and the *Fir Chrieg* with a guard of eagles while they slept. He was uneasy, regretting his decision, remembering too late how long these ritualised proceedings could go on. In the warm darkness the large cave smelt of woodsmoke, and he looked up to the hole in the roof where the fumes leached out into the night sky: the stars were brilliant tonight.

'So, the question must be, do we succeed at the expense of the Fine?' The voice echoed around the chamber. There was a pause but each participant knew that this was merely for dramatic effect. Nabbuta, a shaman of the bear clan, was a great orator; each word he spoke was chosen with care and polished like a fine jewel. He cast his gaze around the cavern. Before him sat representatives of each of the Sidhe tribes: bears, lynx, eagles and, subject to a harder gaze, wolves.

'I say no,' he continued. 'Without *Braznnair*, the Fine are finished. We are condemning men to death. They are not merely our friends, they have been our partners, our mentors, since we came to this world. In our arrogance we think of ourselves as their superiors because they have little magic or arts of their own. Yet although we sow and harvest nothing, they feed us willingly, which is no little consideration. Would we return to Lysmair with the stain of guilt on our consciences? Is our gratitude such a worthless thing?'

*Sit down, you pompous old fool.* The largest silver wolf had stood up, his fur bristling indignantly. Although in his wolf form, the Sidhe projected his voice into the minds of all those assembled. *You overstate their case and you know it.*

Voices were raised in objection to this interruption.

'Eskarius,' Makhpiyaluta's voice cut through the babble, 'Nabbuta has the floor.'

'Yes.' Nabbuta banged the end of the council staff on the floor. 'You must wait your turn.'

*There is precious little time for such formalities,* the wolf snapped. *As we speak, Braznnair is travelling north.*

'How do you know this, Eskarius?' Makhpiyaluta's eyes narrowed and the atmosphere in the chamber stilled.

As if in response, the silver wolf transformed into his human guise. Like Makhpiyaluta, his features retained something of the creature; his sharp hooked nose and dark skin almost unnatural against the steely silver mane of fine hair. His smile, directed at Makhpiyaluta, was defensive and nervy. 'We are a free people, Makhpiyaluta. We wander, as is the nature of wolves, throughout eternity.'

Makhpiyaluta said nothing. Eskarius walked towards Nabbuta and snatched the staff from his hands. He whirled round to face the rest of the assembly, the tattered cloak and feathers he wore catching the updraught of the fire. He held the stick before him and shook it dramatically. 'Hear me, tribes of Sidhe. Could it be that only *my* people remember the leaving of Lysmair? That only the hearts of wolves cry out for our ancestors when we bay at Rumari, the moon? The Fine are not helpless. They are not even sure of the role *Braznnair* must play in their war against Corvus.'

'As we are not sure, Eskarius,' Makhpiyaluta remarked.

'But we know that we must have *Braznnair* to return home. We know the prophecy.'

'But the Fine have a prophecy of their own, do they not? We all need *Braznnair*.'

Surprisingly, Eskarius smiled in agreement, although his smile was not pleasant. 'At last, the bird speaks some sense. Need I remind this assembly that it was one of your kind, Makhpiyaluta, who succeeded in bringing *Braznnair* here only to give it knowingly to the Fine?'

'Beware, Eskarius, lest I consider you insult the honour of my people,' Makhpiyaluta said coldly. 'Many men have died for such insolence.'

'Not just men, though, bird,' Eskarius spat. 'Don't speak to me of honour.'

It seemed then as if all in the chamber held their breath. Eskarius had gone too far, and Makhpiyaluta would surely strike him down. In fact, he said nothing for some time, but when he next spoke his voice was closely controlled in his effort to curb his anger. 'If you speak of Mirranon, the White Eagle, you know that she was outcast from my people for many years. However, I would say before this assembly that I feel she has acted with honour and I will seek her out when I can to offer fealty once more.'

Nabbuta stepped forward, glad of Makhpiyaluta's hard-fought calm. 'This does not address the issue, Eskarius. What do you propose?'

'It is simple. We take what is ours – *Braznnair*. And we kill this Talisker if we must in order to obtain it.'

There was a gasp from some members of the assembly, although those of Eskarius's clan did not react. He held out his hands in a placatory gesture. 'It is only fair,' he reasoned. 'Our forefathers were propelled here as the spell was laid that binds the Raven King. Without that event the Fine would have been wiped out two hundred years ago and we would have remained in Lysmair. All that we have done is help to buy them generations of extra time. I say we owe them nothing.'

A murmur began in the further reaches of the chamber.

Makhpiyaluta raised his voice, feeling his command of the situation threatened. 'But it did happen, Eskarius. We can only deal with the facts as they stand. We do not know how our prophecy may be fulfilled either, only that we must bring *Braznnair* here. Then what? What will you do on the morning of the day you have murdered Talisker and the Fine, only to discover there is no magic here big enough to take us home?'

'Enough!' Eskarius was furious at the suggestion. 'I say we take *Braznnair*. Who is with me?'

If he had expected a cheer of response from all the assembly he was disappointed, for only his own clan answered, those in their wolf form baying, setting up such a din that it echoed around the walls of the cavern to reach an almost deafening pitch. He held up his hands for quiet. 'I see you have all become misguided. But you will gather here, will you not, on that morning Makhpiyaluta speaks of, to see the clan of the wolf leave this accursed world? Know this. Those who are not for me I consider my enemies. None shall go but us, if we get to *Braznnair* first. Long have we walked alone in the wilderness. If we must walk the last mile alone also, so be it.' With that Eskarius gathered his grey robes about him and strode from the assembly, his wolves at his heels. He paused only to spit in the dust at Makhpiyaluta's feet.

An uncomfortable silence fell in the gloom of the chamber. Makhpiyaluta stared out after the departed wolves. Their pawprints in the loose dirt of the floor left an erratic trail, which caught the light of the full moon making a silver pathway away from the assembly fire. A sudden nausea gripped him, a prescience of tragedy. He longed to fly from this place and feel the coolness of the winter winds cut beneath his feathers.

'Makhpiyaluta? What say you now?' Nabbuta spoke quietly.

Makhpiyaluta looked around at the creatures within the chamber, the bears, lynxes and eagles that remained, their shadows looming darkly on the red sandstone walls. They stared back silently, their mood sombre, almost frightened.

A lynx walked forward and sat by Makhpiyaluta's huge talons, which could crush her with ease. She stared up with placid yellow eyes. 'We understand your pain, Makhpiyaluta, as we understand Eskarius's. Our tribe will be guided by your judgement.'

'As will ours.' A black bear moved forward from its fellows. 'What say you?'

Makhpiyaluta paused. 'I say the Sidhe should have *Braznnair* as is their right . . .' There were stifled exclamations of surprise and he raised his voice: 'Hear me! We will not condemn the Fine to get it. We wait. It is possible that the day of their need will come sooner than ours. Please wait. Do not interfere with the passage of *Braznnair* to Soulis Mor.'

'Makhpiyaluta, I must speak with you before you leave.' Nabbuta's face was grave as the assembly took their leave. Makhpiyaluta turned to say something to Artasia and the elders of his tribe. 'Alone!' Nabbuta hissed. So startled was Makhpiyaluta by his tone that he nodded and told the others he would catch up with them, probably at Soulis Mor.

'What is it, Nabbuta?' he asked, when they had gone. He had transformed into his human form as he felt it only fair when he and the elder shaman were to be alone. They sat by the remains of the fire, but although the night was freezing Nabbuta had not kept the blaze alight and Makhpiyaluta took this to mean that their secret meeting would be short.

'You were wrong, Makhpiyaluta, so wrong. I didn't want to tell you in the assembly because I thought . . . well, I thought it best not to. The day of need you spoke of, the Fine and the Sidhe day of need, it will be the same day. Only one may have *Braznnair*.'

'How do you know this?' Makhpiyaluta asked.

'I have spoken with the wise man of the Fine . . . the Oakshadow.'

'Morias?'

Nabbuta nodded slowly and, with a charred stick picked from the edges of the fire, began to trace an image on to the rock face of the wall. It was a simplified picture of the many-faceted gem, *Braznnair*.

'*Braznnair* is the key to worlds,' he said quietly. He drew lines radiating outwards. 'Such is its power that it may be used to open or close portals to other places. Most of what we know of *Braznnair* concerns its use two hundred years ago when we of the Sidhe were propelled here through a huge vortex.' He wrote 'Lysmair' beside one of the lines. 'However, the Fine must be concerned with using *Braznnair* to keep another gateway closed.' He drew a cross beside another line and a deep V to indicate a bird. 'Through this gate Corvus is held.'

'He is not here on this world?'

'No. These other places . . . Oakshadow tells me this is where Tal-ees-ker comes from, but this way is now closed. This other is unknown.'

Makhpiyaluta studied the diagram. 'But why must the time of the Fine and the Sidhe be together? Why can we not use *Braznnair* in turn?'

Nabbuta sighed. 'Because its power is dying. It was created here and there is little power or belief left. Perhaps it is a natural death, perhaps it is more like the dying of a sun. If the Sidhe use *Braznnair* its power will be spent.'

'And if the Fine use it first . . .' Makhpiyaluta mused. 'Nabbuta, what have I done? The Sidhe have listened to my counsel and it is false.'

'No. I did not tell you before for just this reason. I did not want to provoke wholesale slaughter of the Fine. They are not our enemies. But you must pursue *Braznnair* alone . . .'

An icy breeze entered the chamber, whipping the ashes of the fire and the dust from the floor. Makhpiyaluta stared at the rough outline, cold fingers of anxiety gripping him. 'And I must win,' he said, 'or the hopes of the Sidhe are doomed.'

*

The water's edge was a seething, roiling mass of foam. Rhiannon stood transfixed by the happenings in the pool. Morchell, who had only been in the water up to his fetlocks, made to gallop into the water, yelling to Niyso, but Chaplin grabbed his arm to pull him back. It was clear to Talisker, Chaplin and Malky that there would be no helping the stricken creature. Already, the dark shadow shape of a centaur mirrored Niyso's image.

'Corrannyeid!' yelled Malky. 'Gimme a sword!' But they had no weapons: Chaplin and Malky's had been left at the encampment with their packs. Talisker raced round the pool to where his clothes lay.

Niyso had collapsed in the shallows, his legs thrashing the water. In his agony his contorted features appeared more horse-like than ever: his eyes were wide, rolling in panic, his dark mane plastered against his face, mercifully obscuring most of it.

'Help him!' Morchell bellowed. 'By the gods!' He was helpless too, unable to enter the water lest the Corrannyeid strike him down. But even as he shouted, Niyso's struggles ended and he lay still, blinking as though stupefied by pain.

Rhiannon rushed forward.

'No!' Talisker yelled, from the other side of the pool. 'Lady, you must kill him now. You must!'

'What?' she breathed. 'But he's—'

Everything happened at once and yet, when remembering it afterwards, Talisker could visualise every detail of the scene: Niyso's first racking convulsion as the black tendrils of his attacker erupted from his flank, Rhiannon's stricken expression, Chaplin and Malky holding back Morchell as the mighty centaur shouted his grief into the darkness. All these things were imprinted on his mind, with the bright flash of silver, which was his sword – his oath – as he ran into the water oblivious to the danger. His own berserker roar was heard again in Sutra, echoing the pain and grief of the kelpies and their goddess. Raising his sword high above his head and gripping the hilt double-handed, he brought down the blade as hard as he could in a huge sweeping blow. The waters turned red beneath the silver moon and it was seconds before he realised he had failed.

'Duncan! He's still—'

Another blow. Finally, the creature that had been Niyso lay still and a stunned silence settled over the scene.

'Talisker, get out of the water.' Chaplin's voice was quiet but urgent. 'Get out now.'

Talisker waded through a tide of blood and hair to the edge of the pool. 'Did I do it in time?' he rasped. Already the red mist that accompanied his battle fevers was fading. 'Did I kill him before the Corrannyeid?'

'I don't know, Duncan.'

Rhiannon had come to say something but now she looked imploringly at Chaplin. 'There is no rest, lady,' he volunteered. 'Those slain by the Corrannyeid are bound to this realm for ever.'

Her delicate white features were a mask of fury in the cold light. 'Oh, no,' she said firmly. 'Not one of mine. Corvus will pay for this.' She walked towards the pool, her head bowed as though in sorrow, her gaze fixed on Niyso's corpse.

A flash of amber lit the night sky, making everyone start. Without a sound, the pool had exploded into fire and the shape of Niyso's body was still visible among the flames. It was an uncannily silent pyre, burning without sound or heat. Rhiannon stood before it calmly, the expression on her face unreadable. The watchers shrank back as, assuming the aspect of goddess, she grew in stature until she was as tall as the trees and the height of the flames. She no longer appeared delicate and willowy and strength flowed from her. She walked forward into the flames as an unnatural rumble of thunder echoed across the winter landscape. The clouds above the burning pool parted to reveal the deepest clearest blue. It seemed as if the sky now held the reflection of the sullied water. For a moment there was silence, and then an image formed against the blue background. It was Niyso. He stood as though uncertain, shifting from hoof to hoof, his brows creased as though in concentration.

'Niyso.' Rhiannon's voice was sad and gentle, but in her present godly form, it seemed to reverberate and fill the world.

'Where am I, lady?' the kelpie asked.

'Do not be afraid, Niyso. I will send your soul to its rest even if my cousin's creatures have claimed you. You do trust me, don't you?'

Niyso touched his heart as he had earlier in deference to Rhiannon. 'With my soul, lady,' he said. 'Look after Eymer for me.'

Rhiannon smiled and nodded to reassure him. Then she reached out her hand palm upwards and slowly closed her fingers. As she did so, the image of the great creature faded to be replaced by a tiny dancing mote of light.

'To me, Niyso,' she commanded quietly. The light moved down towards her, its path wavering and uncertain but eventually it rested in her palm. Rhiannon looked down on it and its radiance lit bright tears in her eyes. 'Goodbye,' she said simply. Closing her hand she extinguished the light that had been Niyso.

There was a long silence in the glade, unlike any Talisker had heard before, the rushing of the waterfall seemed a backdrop for the grieving of Rhiannon and Morchell, and some prescience told him that all the kelpies on the island already knew of the death of their kindred. As he thought this he looked at Morchell who nodded sadly, reading Talisker's mind.

Rhiannon had returned to her more human aspect and sat near the edge of the water, her head bowed, the breeze catching her silver hair. Talisker thought she was weeping but then she turned her face towards him and he recognised the anger that burned through her like the flames of Niyso's pyre. Her eyes glowed and there was a force behind her anger that was as frightening and elemental as the Corrannyeid. From her fingertips and behind her eyes, a blue fire flashed chaotically, small particles earthing themselves in the rocks around the shore. Talisker, Chaplin and Malky exchanged a worried glance. In her anger, Rhiannon was reduced almost to revealing the chaos from which she was made and it seemed that gods were not simply good or evil: they wore the masks they chose. Sensing their discomfort, she sighed and stood up, visibly fighting for control. 'Go back to your battle, Talisker,' she said. 'I will meet you in Soulis Mor before the day of Corvus's game. I am going to fetch my brother, the Lord Cernunnos.' She narrowed her eyes and attempted a small smile, which was less than reassuring by virtue of the eldritch light that played around it. 'Just remember, you asked for our help.' With that the lady Rhiannon vanished.

# CHAPTER TWENTY

Una stood at the casement window and stared out across the snow-covered moors. At this time of morning the fortress of Soulis Mor was still quiet. Occasionally muffled noises rose from the kitchens far below but apart from that the soft breathing of her companions was the only other sound to break the hushed stillness of the landscape. Una had lived all her life in what some would consider the north of Sutra but she had never before travelled to the most northerly reaches and the starkness and cold of the landscape here both thrilled and horrified her. It was hard to understand why the men and women of Isbister's clan chose to live in this harsh unforgiving place.

Less than a hundred of Thane Ferghus's people had stayed behind to rebuild the interior of the shattered city of Ruannoch Were. All the warriors who had survived the battle had been sent to Soulis Mor, the fortress city. It was steeped in ancient mystery but, more importantly, acted as a barrier between the poisoned lands where Corvus's minions were gathering and the rest of Sutra. Soon there would be a battle at this place to eclipse any other.

Una shuddered, pulling her shawl tighter around her shoulders. She wished now that she had said more to Talisker before he left. More to show what she felt for him. She had been so concerned then to appear strong that she feared now her farewell had seemed more of a dismissal. Still, he would be here soon with the *Fir Chrieg*. She could imagine the sight of the legendary warriors riding through the huge oak gates, their horses ploughing up the snow as they galloped, cheering the battle-weary soldiers' hearts. It was not too fanciful to imagine Talisker leading them . . . She checked herself sternly. There was much to think about between now and then – at least ten days hence. She suspected that one of her charges would deliver.

She sighed and turned back into the room. Four women, in various stages of pregnancy, and she slept in the stuffy little attic: Gwen, Brigid, Katlyn and Misty – well, Misty was really Bronwynn, but the others had teased her because she cried at little provocation, as some women did in her state. Only Brigid still had a husband; the others would bear fatherless children and it would be hard for them, even if the battle was won. Misty was only sixteen and her young husband had been eighteen; he had been killed in a Corrannyeid raid during her seventh month of pregnancy. All of the women wanted boy children. Gods protect them, Una thought.

There was a quiet knock at the door and the Thane entered. Una curtsied but Isbister smiled wearily and made a dismissive gesture at such formality. 'I've come to see Brigid,' she whispered. 'How is she?'

'She is doing well, lady. I expect she will be delivered soon.' Brigid was the Thane's younger sister and, as Kyra and Ulla had been, the two were as different as night and day. Una had been surprised to find that Soulis Mor had a woman thane, but on meeting Isbister it seemed perfectly natural. Isbister was handsome, short and stocky with long red plaits and as much muscle as any of her warriors. It seemed that Brigid had inherited the femininity of the clan, and Isbister the duty of care and rough edges her position required. She cared about her little sister as fondly as she did any woman or child of her clan. Men, it seemed, were another matter.

'You do well to look to the south, Una,' she said gravely, gesturing towards the window. 'The view to the north is less encouraging.'

Una smiled, unsure of what to say. Her charges had been forbidden to go beyond certain points in the city from where they could look towards the poisoned lands. Una had heard rumours in the kitchens that the sight of massing Corrannyeid would be enough to make any of the women miscarry, or worse . . . Not superstitious, Una kept her own counsel on the subject, although she had to concede to herself that it might be true. Anxiety did cause the women to miscarry but she hoped her skill might keep them alive in such an eventuality. Only Gwen's child would be too early to survive . . .

Brigid stirred in her sleep and Isbister smiled indulgently at her, apparently satisfied, and turned to go.

'Lady?' Una said. 'I wonder if you might have a word with Brigid if it's not too much trouble.'

'Something ails her?' Isbister frowned.

'Oh, no. Not really. It's just . . . well, she keeps saying she wants a boy. She is preparing for a son.'

'And?'

'My experience tells me, at least from the way it is

lying in the womb, that it will be a girl. A daughter.'

A grin of sheer delight lit Isbister's face. She chuckled. 'Well, well . . .' Then she noted Una's concerned expression.

'I don't want her to be upset, lady.'

Isbister was grave again. 'I understand your worry, Una. I will speak to her. Myself, I think to bring another woman into Sutra can only be wonderful.' She stared down at the sleeping women, a faint hint of sadness crossing her face. 'Wonderful,' she repeated quietly. 'Strange, is it not? On one side Corrannyeid, creatures from the darkest pit, and here the beginnings of new life. Here is the future of the land, Una. Guard them well.'

Una curtsied low, and when she looked back to the doorway, Isbister had gone.

In order to reach Soulis Mor by the year end, which was only a week away, they would have to ride hard for about eight hours each day. For the first two days Talisker, Chaplin and Malky said nothing about their unlikely target, simply gritted their teeth and rode with the grim determination that seemed to bind them together. On the third morning, heavy rain had begun to fall from leaden grey skies, chilling them to the bone. Their clothes were not waterproof – Chaplin cursed himself for leaving his trench-coat behind – and the moorland they were crossing fast became a bog, frightening the horses as their hoofs sank deeper into the mud with each passing step. Around noon, Talisker called a halt, pointing towards a clump of trees that would give a little shelter.

'We're no goin' tae make it, Duncan,' Malky grated, as he dismounted. He was the first to voice what they were all thinking and the Highlander, usually optimistic, was looking at Talisker as though for an answer to their predicament. His wiry red hair was plastered to his face and his plaid was stuck to his body. The blue-white skin of his chest was slick with rain and glowed white against the brick red of his shirt. He grimaced. 'It's jist no' possible in these conditions. Ah'm sure Corvus'll no' mind startin' without us for a' the difference we'd make now.'

Talisker frowned, not understanding.

'Well, we've no' got *Braznnair* now. It's up to Deme tae get it there. Just as well, probably, since we widnae know what to do wi the damn thing onyways . . .' He laughed unexpectedly. 'Aye, we look like three drookit rats and no mistake.'

The others said nothing, their mood as grey as the weather. They both knew that Malky was right: now that they had passed on the responsibility of the gem and completed the task of petitioning the gods, they were more or less redundant. There was no reason to imagine that the battle would wait for them: all they amounted to was three extra sword arms against the Corrannyeid. Talisker had thought often about Una since his decision to stay in Sutra but, really, they had made no commitment to each other. Their short affair, which had happened in the shadow of a battle, had burned like a bright flame in the time since, but despite Una's promise to meet him in Soulis Mor, her farewell had seemed cool as though she had counted him gone the moment the echo of his horse's hoofbeats had died away.

*

Midnight of the same day: a mere ghost of a shadow flits across the moorland towards the small copse where the camp has remained for the rest of the afternoon and evening in the hope of better weather. Moving silently, the shape shifts in and out of focus as though it is moving between worlds, which indeed it is. Gradually, the outline becomes more definite and the shape recognisable as a huge black horse on which the delicate figure of a woman is perched, her legs splayed wide across its back. It is Phyrr. Oblivious to the biting wind, she rides, as ever with purpose and style, her good eye fixed on the copse of trees but her mind at one with her mount. Stopping at some distance from the camp, she dismounts while her steed is still moving and, as before, she binds him with magic so that he will return at her beckoning. A blue flame flares briefly between them and the horse is gone.

A light is burning in Talisker's tent. Phyrr sniffs the air: the tents have been given by Mirranon – she can smell the cursed taint of the eagle. For a moment she stands still by the entrance, checking, spreading the net of her consciousness wide to find Talisker's companions and deepen their sleep. Entering the tent, she looks towards the figure on the bed. Her promise to Corvus that she would bring him Talisker's head echoes through her mind. She has not forgiven her brother, but she needs to make this last gesture, to show him that he needs her. She gazes thoughtfully towards her prize, her eyes becoming accustomed to the glow of the rush-light.

Talisker is lying on a rough pallet of clothes and blankets. He sleeps on his stomach, his knees bent for support, one hand reaching out, as ever, for his sword. Phyrr wonders idly where on his own world he may have learned such caution as she nudges away the blade with her foot. Crouching beside the sleeping form, drawing her dagger in the same movement, she studies his face dispassionately. This is the man whose very existence has thwarted her brother, has sent him into paroxysms of mindless rage. He has a handsome face, although even in sleep it is marred by bitterness. A strand of red hair has fallen across his eyes and something about it seems intensely bright, somehow defining the contradictions Phyrr can see in those features. A brief memory of their duel at Ruannoch Were flashes through her mind, the moment when both she and he knew it was finished. Phyrr had seen foolhardy bravery many times, had killed without pause while men posed or blustered, but that look, that second, had been unique. Within that instant a cessation of the fires that drove them both – her anger, his bitterness – had simply happened. A shared tiny fragment of peace, which for them both was no less than a tiny miracle. Her thought is dismissed by the pragmatic side of her nature – which, could she but know it, was something else they shared – but she reaches out to brush aside the lock of hair.

He awakes, his hand grabbing her wrist as his eyes snap open. She pulls away, hoping he is not fully aware, but his grip holds.

'Phyrr?' He seems puzzled. He hasn't seen the dagger in her right hand and her grip tightens on the hilt, but she doesn't use the weapon. She remains motionless for the space of three heartbeats, her breath loud in the confines of the tent, her subconscious berating her for her uncharacteristic indecisiveness.

'Talisker.' She gazes at him a moment longer, waiting for him to relax his grip, fingering the blade at her side.

Her blue gaze is as piercing, as elemental, as he remembers, her jet mane obscuring most of her face. Could it be – he asks himself after – that something of her mood affects his judgement? He reaches forward with his right hand, pulling her closer, and gently pushes back her hair to reveal her left eye. The marble-white retina glows like an opal in the halo of the rush-light amid its network of scars and bruising. 'What happen—'

She snarls like an animal, fury contorting her features, fury that he should pity her, fury at her own moment of weakness. With a curse he does not recognise, she raises the blade high and, too late, he sees the glint of steel. But then, suddenly, she vanishes, and the blade drops to the ground before him. In the space of a second she has spared his life; no flash of light, no warning, she is gone. Neither he nor she knows why.

For hours afterwards Talisker sits on the bed, playing with the blade, listening to the cold soft sound of the rain.

*. . . and all the beasts are one beast*
*one beast of Lysmair. Rivers of silver*
*dreams move and flow*
*through veins of fire. The message*
*moving across a land so like,*
*and so unlike. Towards which, we fly*
*and run.*

*Driven by the bright music of the sons of Lys*
*destined, doomed, to travel for ever*
*towards home.*

Makhpiyaluta moved through the midnight sky, an echo of the impending storm he rode, shifting and dipping his mighty wings. He knew there was more of the verse, which his mother had taught him, and yet, like her, it had gone, and it seemed that each generation took a little of the dreamtime with them until it faded into the dark. Already some of the Sidhe believed Lysmair to be a fable. He wished he could remember . . .

Down there, somewhere among the rough shadows of the heather and rocks of the moorland, such a Sidhe was travelling. A silent grey cat, carrying the birthright of the Sidhe – *Braznnair* – to Soulis Mor at the bidding of Mirranon. It had been earlier that day as he travelled with Ulla and the so-called heroes that the decision to make this night excursion had formed in the mind of the Prince. Since the meeting at the crossroads he had known that the Sidhe Deme was now carrying the gem – reading Malky's uncluttered prosaic mind had been an easy task. He hoped Eskarius did not have the same information, although it seemed unlikely that he did not: the silent grey wolves were everywhere. Now, at last, Makhpiyaluta had reached a decision for the Sidhe and it felt right. 'I am no traitor – not to the Fine . . .' As he had spoken the words, the seeds of his choice had been planted. Had Duncan Talisker the wit to look into the mind of a Sidhe – of which he was easily capable – he would have seen Makhpiyaluta's surprise at the strength of his own feelings: *Braznnair* belonged to the

Sidhe and if Talisker succeeded in enlisting the aid of the younger gods, the Fine would surely have no need of it. The needs of Makhpiyaluta's people, ignored or forgotten for generations, were greater by far.

He shifted, slowing his flight as a movement in the heather caught his attention. There she was. Deme of the lynx clan. He steeled himself. If she would not relinquish *Braznnair* to him it would be regrettable. He called to her, 'Deme. Greetings,' and she froze in mid-stride.

The eagle alighted on a rock a few paces ahead of Deme. She sat down as though awaiting an explanation and sent no thought message in return as was polite custom. In the yellow light of the waning moon it could be seen that the cat carried a soft kid pouch around her neck, which held Makhpiyaluta's prize. There was a long moment of silence on the moors and the wind, the wind of souls, danced and wailed around the two creatures, which faced one another.

'Makhpiyaluta, I presume,' Deme remarked finally. 'Mirranon, White Eagle, warned me you would come.'

'If you knew I would come, then you must know why. You must also know that Mirranon is considered a traitor by some and you are allying yourself with her.'

'Perhaps those who would consider it fair to desert the Sidhe might say such things – those who believe in old stories of Lysmair, which is gone.'

Makhpiyaluta ruffled his feathers. 'Deme, I will forgive your impertinence should you give *Braznnair* to me, but beware. Men and Sidhe have died for such blasphemy. You cannot know . . .'

'Yes, I can. Mirranon has told me. Such a glorious tale. The Sidhe return to Lysmair by some magic of the stone. Shame, you neglect to mention that only those of certain lineage can go. In fact, that means less than a hundred Sidhe – Mirranon reckons around forty-eight, including yourself, of course.' She stood up, her tail twitching in agitation and distress.' Please excuse me, Your Highness, I have a delivery to make to those in great need.'

'No! It's a lie!' Makhpiyaluta protested. He was confused and distressed by the little cat's version of the prophecy. 'Mirranon lies. What does she care for the Sidhe, we who have shunned her?'

'It may interest you to know that the White Eagle is of the necessary lineage – on her mother's side, at least. She could go if she wanted.' Deme began to walk away and Makhpiyaluta hopped after her, clumsy on the rough ground.

'It cannot be true,' he shouted after her. 'All the Sidhe may go!' The wind howled around him and his instincts told him to fly; from the sky he could strike the defiant cat with ease. Spreading his wings he took to the air, riding the storm once more. 'Deme,' he called. 'Hear me, Deme! Surrender *Braznnair* to me now.'

Like a silver ghost, the tiny cat became one with the rocks and landscape and disappeared from sight.

For hours, Makhpiyaluta watched and followed Deme as she travelled fleet-footed across the moorlands. His mind was in turmoil. If the lynx was correct and Mirranon spoke the truth, the Sidhe had been lied to for generations by their elders. Why would they do such a thing? It was almost unthinkable and yet it made sense. The legends of Lysmair kept the traditions and foundations of Sidhe society alive . . .

A movement below attracted his eye. It was not Deme: the lynx moved with a rhythmic pattern of which she was probably unaware and which was evident only from the skies to a bird such as himself: she moved unconsciously with the grey strata of the underlying rock, exploiting the grain of the land so that even when she was obscured by trees or heather, Makhpiyaluta could predict where she would reappear. All earthbound creatures moved in such patterns and the pattern of the animal that now followed the lynx was instantly recognisable: it moved in deceptively lazy curves, hugging itself to wood rather than stone like Deme. It was a wolf. Even from this distance Makhpiyaluta could identify the black and white feathers it wore in its earring. Eskarius.

Makhpiyaluta folded his wings and dived towards the moors, not clear of his own intentions but grimly certain of Eskarius's.

Talisker had lain awake for hours. It was the night following Phyrr's appearance but the tension was unabated, like the rain outside although its soft spattering against the roof and sides of the tent was calming. He had said nothing to Malky and Chaplin about his encounter of the night before and he was unsure why. The sense memories of their meeting burned in him as though Phyrr had bewitched him, and he was sure she would come back, but whether to kill him or not he wasn't sure. In a perverse way, he almost hoped she would attempt to: at least he could deal with that. Talisker's jaw ticked as he clenched his teeth. Despite the chill of the night, a light sheen of sweat covered his body and his limbs felt heavy and warm.

Thinking about Una, trying to visualise her face, served as a talisman to keep away . . . what? He didn't know. Mirranon's warning that Phyrr could kill him at any moment echoed through his mind. It was true. The image of chaos revealed by the goddess Rhiannon when her guard had been lowered was enough to convince him: *They wore the masks they chose.* Phyrr did not have to waste her time coming to his tent like the proverbial thief in the night, she could dispose of him by magical means or have the Corrannyeid deal with him. Instinctively, he knew the answer – he had seen such a quality before while in prison but never in a woman: Phyrr enjoyed the kill. The feeling of power and triumph each time she ended a life must be euphoric, he thought. And this was her weakness, the reason she had hesitated the night before, because she desired him: as the warriors of Ruannoch Were had related around their campfires, it was not essential for Talisker to be alive for her to take her pleasure. The men of the western clans called her Morrigan, or Battle Crow, he remembered, so often had her dark shadow been seen around the fields of border skirmishes.

'Very astute.' The voice came from nowhere, low and mocking. Outside the tent, the shape of a dark bird fluttered briefly in silhouette, its shadow encircling the flimsy canvas. Talisker knew the voice to be Phyrr's but the shape that formed in the corner of his tent bore no relation to her. It was an old woman, toothless and wrinkled, a hag. Only Phyrr's eyes remained, one a brilliant blue, the other pearl white, and her voice.

'I've come to pay you in kind for your pity, Talisker.' She grinned hideously. 'Do you pity me now?' Without waiting for a reply she dropped her tattered grey rags to the ground and moved towards him. Talisker shuddered at the sight: her yellowing flesh hung loosely from her bones in a way that suggested she was melting; the fleshy remains of her breasts hung obscenely like wasted fruit almost to her waist. As he tried to back away, Talisker realised he was powerless to move. Phyrr chuckled at his anguished expression and reached out to grab his foot.

'You fool,' she said. 'Never pity me. You were right. We wear the masks we choose.'

There was a faint greenish glow and the image of the hag moved and buckled. There was clicking and cracking as Phyrr's bones moulded themselves into a new shape. Still unable to resist, Talisker yelped as the clammy fingers that gripped his foot became talons. A huge she-wolf stood over him growling and slavering, its hot breath washing over him in a tainted rush. His mind was searching desperately for a faint glimmer of hope that his life might be extended for more than the next few minutes. That Phyrr intended to possess his body – to rape him – was irrelevant: whether she killed him first was more pressing. The she-wolf moved forward, her legs at either side of his shoulders and knees, and brought her muzzle to just before his nose. Her growl deepened almost to a quiet purr, and her saliva trailed across his cheek.

'Phyrr,' he gasped. 'Phyrr, listen to me. Please. I have something to tell you.'

The wolf stopped growling and seemed to study his face – that was good, he told himself, she didn't see him merely as prey. Phyrr changed again, the sound of her bones a sickening parody of the clean drumming of the rain. This time, the transformation was more alarming.

'Una? Oh, no, Phyrr . . .'

'Does this shape please you more?' She laughed.

Although his rational mind knew that the woman before him was not Una, that she contained a core of feminine evil, Talisker drank in the warmth and scent of his lover and his body responded. Triumph crossed Phyrr/Una's features and she moved against his thighs, drew him inside her with ease. Shame washed over him that his body could betray him. 'Una. No . . .' Still, he looked through his half-closed eyes and the mist of his lashes aided the deception further. She sat quite still and touched his face, not with tenderness, rather with curiosity. The instant her fingertips made contact with his cheek, Talisker felt as though a circuit had been created by the joining of their bodies; her spirit engulfed him.

The chaos being that was the goddess Phyrr, so bright, so powerful, was all around him and what was happening to his body – a warm wet rush, above which the sensation of the rain was still audible – was only an accompaniment to the music of her soul. Talisker's mind was frail, embittered by comparison and he knew she would crush him if she discovered he could approach her godhead in this way. Never before when touching other souls had Talisker been so powerless to withdraw from the shared sensation. He knew, in these short seconds, everything that comprised the soul of Phyrr: around the image of the woman his eyes could see, there moved a galaxy of dark images disassociated from any landscape, swirling and moving, flashing teeth and claws on the edges of existence, spirits, demons, djinns of chaos, all the poisons of existence that had no physical form. Talisker cried out in stark fear for his soul, and Phyrr, mistaking his cry for passion, scratched his chest with sharp fingernails, drawing blood.

'No . . .' He closed his eyes but knew that he could close out only the physical image. The darkness remained, rushing in towards him like a black and purple tide in which he sensed the timeless soul that chose to manifest itself through Phyrr. It was moving closer as Phyrr relaxed, preoccupied by her act of power, unsuspecting of Talisker's ability. Something was happening as the soul approached: it grew brighter, until Talisker was encompassed by light. He opened his eyes again, to focus on the red hair of his lover and she appeared in the centre of the light, naked, moving above him, his blood on her lips. He was drowning in a cold brightness, which was not simply Phyrr – he could see that now. Within the sphere pulsed a rarer more fragile heart that had once been the soul of a child born and taken by godhood. Reaching out instinctively towards the light he anchored his hands in the warmth of her hair as the physical rush claimed him, pulling her towards him, clinging to her physically and emotionally, suffocating, gasping, watching the duller pulse that had something in it of humanity, shaped by the fears and beliefs of the Fine.

Suddenly, she sensed his seeing. She screamed in fury and disbelief, and Talisker's world exploded into white flame.

Malky heard the scream from Talisker's tent. It sounded as if it had been uttered by a huge cat but his instincts knew better and the hair on the back of his neck stood up. 'Duncan!' he roared.

The tent was burning with a sulphurous fire, hissing as the raindrops splashed on it. Most of the hide fabric had melted away to reveal the naked, prostrate form of Talisker on the earth floor.

'Duncan! Duncan, wake up, man!' Malky screamed. Chaplin appeared beside him and began to beat at the flames with a blanket. It seemed to do no good. Something about the fire was unnatural: it burned with tenacity, fuelled by the spite of a goddess. Both men were driven back, choking. 'It's nae use,' Malky coughed. 'Duncan . . . C'mon, Sandro, we've got to go in or he's gonny die.'

Chaplin wrapped his cloak over his nose and mouth, and both men ran into the flames. The smoke engulfed them and they knew they had made a fatal mistake. Chaplin's cloak flared into incandescent light and he screamed as the heat seared his skin. He fell to the floor, and rolled around on the damp earth. Malky raced towards Talisker then hesitated, realising that Chaplin was in mortal danger. Suddenly the framework of the tent collapsed and Malky was thrown to the floor where willow canes uncoiled across his back in a burning brand that pinned him down. He could hear Chaplin screaming, but there was nothing from Talisker. Perhaps he was already dead. Malky reached into his pouch and drew out Deme's gem. It was pulsing, a weak, delicate light. It was losing its power.

'Please,' Malky whispered. 'Please . . .' He blacked out as the smoke and pain overcame him.

## CHAPTER TWENTY-ONE

*It's not like before. He can still smell the flames. He can still hear her screams of rage as she curses his soul. But she can't reach him here. Not in the void. He lies still in the darkness, coughing out the smoke that has travelled to this plane with his body; caught in the cage of his chest and lungs. He's thinking of her; or maybe not really of her but of Una. He tells himself that Phyrr has forced him into this dishonouring of Una but, really, if he's honest – and the void is no place for lies – it was his own weakness she exploited. If he had been stronger . . .*

*'Duncan?' The voice chokes into a spasm of coughing. 'Where the hell are we?'*

*It's Chaplin. He's lying on the ground and his clothes hang on him in blackened tatters. From where he lies, Talisker smells the sickeningly meaty smell of charred flesh. He gets on to his hands and knees, and crawls over to him. 'We're in the void, Sandro. It's an in-between place where I think my soul waits for some kind of opportunity to jump back into my body in Edinburgh.'*

*Chaplin tightens his limbs against the pain. 'But it doesn't usually happen to me. I just wake up back there,' he says, through gritted teeth.*

*'This time . . .' Talisker hesitates. 'I'm sorry, Sandro, this time your life must be in danger.'*

*Chaplin says nothing: his burns are so painful he is*

*almost unconscious. Talisker takes his hand. 'Don't worry, it'll be soon,' he says. 'The darkness never lasts long.' The realisation that Chaplin's life is ebbing away makes him feel desperately alone, and he casts around anxiously for Malky.*

*'I never thought you'd risk your neck for me, Sandro, that was a brave thing you did.' He looks down at Chaplin again and sees that he is smiling slightly. 'Your dad would have been proud.' He doesn't know why he is babbling. 'I don't want to go back to Edinburgh,' he says. 'I'm afraid. Shula's gone. They all hate me. You hate me there . . .' He feels so weak, he knows he can't do this journey any more.*

*'I don't hate you there, Duncan,' Chaplin whispers. 'I never hated you. Not really. I was just angry and alone. I—'*

*'Sandro! Sandro!' Talisker grabs Chaplin by the shoulders and shakes him. There is no response; at best, Chaplin is deeply unconscious.*

*'Duncan. C'mon, let's go.' Malky appears beside Talisker and puts his hand on his shoulder. Talisker stares up at him, wild-eyed. 'Where have you been?' he demands.*

*'What kinna question is that? Ah don't know where Ah've been, do Ah? I mean, you just appear in this place. Ah know we've got tae go, though. Mirranon's wee gem, it's nearly spent – look.' He waves the dimly glowing stone in front of Talisker's face. 'Ah think if we dinny get out o' here soonish like, we might be trapped. C'mon, Ah've seen thon hare that led you out afore.'*

*'But I can't leave Sandro,' Talisker frets.*

*'We've got tae hurry. Look, chances are, if you get out,*

*he'll be out an' all. That's how it's worked before.'*

*'But we don't know that. He's never been here before.'*

*'Hurry up, Duncan.'*

*Talisker stand up and lifts Chaplin on to his shoulder in a fireman's lift. Just as they set out at as fast a pace as they can manage, he catches Malky giving him a wry puzzled look. 'After everything . . .' the Highlander says.*

*'He's my friend, Malky.'*

At first he thought he'd really died this time, but eventually he realised the darkness was a natural, grainy darkness, not the black of the void. Talisker sat up and waited for his eyes to adjust to the shadowy space in which he lay. It was strange, he thought, that he could still smell and taste the ashes of the fire in Sutra. He noticed, with grim satisfaction, that his left hand and arm were heavily bandaged.

There was a groan from just behind him. 'Duncan? Is that you? What's going on? Why's my shoulder all bandaged up? '

'Erm, I think it's probably where I shot you. We're back,' Talisker said flatly. 'But unless the police force has resorted to some pretty strange methods of interrogation, I'd say we're in some kind of trouble. Malky?'

'I'm ower here, Duncan.' The Highlander's voice came from a few feet to his right where, as Talisker's eyes became accustomed to the darkness, he could make out the shape of a doorway. 'Ah'm sorry Ah had tae bring you back again. Ah know you widnae choose tae be here. It was the only thing Ah could do.'

''S alright, Malk.' Talisker closed his eyes again

wearily. 'I'm so tired, I don't think I care.' Outside he could hear heavy rainfall and the choking, gurgling noises of a drain or guttering. The sound of the rain transported him, and as though he was reading his thoughts Chaplin spoke through the darkness.

'What happened, Duncan? In the tent?'

'It was Phyrr. She . . . well, she and I . . . never mind. Let's just say she doesn't take rejection very well.'

'At least you're still alive,' Chaplin remarked evenly. 'You almost didn't make it.'

'You too, Sandro. But I wish I could wash my mind out. I feel—'

'Em, lads,' Malky interrupted, 'Ah think there's someone else here an' all.'

'What? Where?'

'Ower there, behind ye, Sandro. It looks like a person tae me.'

'Hello? Is anyone there?' Talisker called.

Both men stared into the corner, which couldn't have been more than a few feet away as the room was small. As the shape became more distinct, it appeared to be a person. Talisker wondered briefly if it was a tailor's dummy, but something about the way it was standing, slumped forward as though pulling against the wall, made it appear too articulated. Chaplin reached into the pocket of his coat and found his lighter. He held it aloft and the light flared, bathing the corner in yellow. Both men gasped.

'What is it?' Malk called, as he came across the room. 'Oh.'

It was a skeleton. It had been chained to the wall, which was why it was still standing. The warm dry air of the basement had mummified it and, in places, dried flesh still adhered to the bones. The head had flesh down one side of the jaw, which hung slackly open; the eye-sockets were empty and the dome of the skull bare.

Talisker reached forward to touch the face.

'What are you doing?' Chaplin asked.

'I wondered if I might see something.' Talisker shrugged. 'I'm more empathic here. It might give us a clue as to why we're stuck in the basement with this guy.' He touched the skull gently at the temples. 'No,' he whispered after a moment. 'There's nothing there.'

'Looks like he died in a lot of pain.' Chaplin held the light lower to the floor, which was stained a rusty sepia where the victim's blood had flowed. 'I'd guess, from the amount of bloodstains, it was a gut wound, and he died slowly . . . unless someone took pity and shot him.'

'Poor wretch, eh?' said Malky.

'Talisker, I think you'd better see this.' There was an edge to Chaplin's tone, and Talisker's stomach lurched as it had when he heard about Shula. More light flared in the corner: Chaplin had found a candle stub to light. He was sitting on the floor staring down at the thing he'd found.

It was a rusty tin that had once contained Walker's shortbread. Talisker crouched beside him and looked down at the contents. 'Oh, my God,' he whispered.

Malky came over and frowned, not understanding the significance of what he saw. 'It's just jewellery, keepsakes an' the like, isn't it?'

Talisker and Chaplin did not reply.

Finally, Chaplin picked up a silver bracelet and

turned it over in his hands. 'It's hers, isn't it?' he breathed.

'Sally Willis.' Talisker nodded. 'And here, look,' he picked up a silver belt buckle with a rather kitsch-looking daisy. 'Rosalind Baxter's.' He was about to put it down again when he gave a frightened cry. 'No! I can see – I can see—'

'Duncan!' Chaplin grabbed the buckle and threw it back into the tin, 'Snap out of it, man.' He placed his hand on Talisker's shoulder and shook him lightly. 'Don't you think you've suffered enough for those girls?'

'Would someone mind tellin' me what's goin' on?' Malky asked somewhat peevishly.

Chaplin showed him the tin. 'We never told anyone about this stuff, Malk. The killer took a souvenir from each body. It was one of the things that helped convict Duncan – he knew about Sally's bracelet and we'd made no mention of it to the press.'

Malky jerked his thumb at the suspended corpse. 'D'you think he was another victim, then?'

'I'm not—'

The door opened suddenly and a figure was silhouetted in the doorway. 'Ah, I see you've met my father. If you look closely, you can just see where I had to stick his head back on,' a voice said, almost pleasantly. There was a click and a dull electric light flooded the cellar. Finn stood in the doorway.

'What the hell's going on, Finn?' Chaplin demanded.

'You tell me, Inspector Chaplin. That's why you're both here.' Finn blinked rapidly as he spoke. His dyed blond hair was matted and unkempt, as though he hadn't combed it for days, and his face and eyes were red. More importantly, he held a pistol in his shaking hand, which he had aimed at Talisker and Chaplin.

'People will be looking for us, you know.'

'No, they won't. Not yet. You signed out your prisoner to take him to the secure psychiatric unit at the Royal Ed.'

Talisker and Chaplin exchanged glances.

'It might be true,' Talisker mumbled unwillingly. 'I did attempt suicide at Ladyfield. You know, after Shula . . .'

'Put the gun down and we can talk,' Chaplin said soothingly.

'Stay back!' Finn jabbed the weapon towards them.

'Finn, look at me.' Talisker moved towards Finn as imperceptibly as possible. 'You said we could talk once, remember? At the beach?'

'See? That's it,' Finn snapped. 'You're doing it now. I'm not stupid. You make it sound as though it was ages ago but it was only two days! You'll start talking to someone next – I know, the Highlander.' He waved the gun at Chaplin. 'Even he believes you.'

'But you did say we could talk?' Talisker insisted.

Finn licked his lips nervously. 'Yeah,' he agreed.

'Did you kill them, Finn? All those young women?'

'No!' Finn looked surprised and indignant. His gaze flicked between Chaplin and Talisker. 'Is that what you think? I—'

Talisker saw his chance and took it. As Finn looked, almost beseechingly, at Chaplin, he rushed forward, head and shoulders down as though in a rugby scrum. There was a shout from Chaplin as Talisker knocked aside the gun and pushed Finn to the floor. But Finn was possessed of the wiry strength of insanity, and before Talisker could achieve anything he knew more about the depths of his aggressor's soul than he wanted to.

*There's a sound. White noise. A television is hissing in the corner of a room and there's only a dull light from a standard lamp. A young boy of perhaps sixteen is curled up in a foetal position in the armchair. He's been crying and possibly drinking, but he wouldn't want anyone to know. He scrubs his face as he does when demons torment him. It's Finn. The door of the small room opens and a tall man is standing there: he's covered in blood and breathing heavily. Finn looks up at him and begins to cry. His face contorts into a mask of anguish, and tears are the least of his sorrow. 'You promised,' he wails. 'You promised.'*

*Without warning the man walks over and picks up the boy by the lapels of his dressing-gown. He flings him effortlessly to the floor and, as the boy scrambles to get up, pulls a thick leather belt from around his waist. 'You saw nothing,' he commands. His voice is deep and heavy. It washes across Talisker's labouring mind in a cold wave. It is the only time he will ever hear the voice but he knows what it is: the voice of a serial killer, the murderer of six women. The man lashes out with the leather strap, once, twice . . . but on the third stroke, Finn grabs the belt. He is crying hysterically, his face reddened in stripes where the edge of the belt has caught him. 'It's got to stop!' he screams.*

Talisker let go – he had no choice: the vision overwhelmed him. Before he could recover Finn's face was in front of him, staring down the barrel of the pistol and grinning maniacally. 'One more move and I blow his head off,' he said, looking directly at Talisker but addressing Chaplin.

'Calm down, Finn.'

'Listen to him,' Talisker advised. 'Finn, you've only killed one person in self-defence. Don't make it any worse.'

Finn blinked rapidly. 'How do you know that?' he whispered.

'You just told us, Finn. It was your father, right?' Finn loosened his grip but the gun remained pointed at Talisker's face. 'That's him, isn't it? Over there?' Finn nodded, but Talisker's gambit failed: Finn didn't glance back at the corpse. 'I bet he beat you too,' Talisker continued.

Finn let go of him and his hand strayed up to rub his cheek. 'He was a monster,' he whispered. 'He deserved to die. But once I started hurting him, I couldn't stop. That's what was so horrible about it.' He moved away from Talisker. 'You see, I must be like him, deep down. I enjoyed it.' A nasty little sneer crossed his features and his demeanour changed. 'You wouldn't understand about killing people. It's power.'

'No, it's not,' Chaplin intervened, moving between Talisker and the gun, intending to placate Finn. Talisker pushed him aside. 'What are you doing?' Chaplin hissed, grabbing the back of his shirt.

Talisker ignored him. 'And what about me, Finn?' he demanded. 'You must have seen the trial on TV. They took my life away and you just let them. Yeah, you *are* like your father. He was a coward, and so are you.'

'Duncan, leave it,' Chaplin snapped.

'C'mon, Duncan.' Malky moved, as though to pull him back from a bar-room brawl. 'Let it go.'

'Stay back,' Finn warned, 'or I'll shoot.'

'Go on, then, shoot, why don't you?' Talisker taunted. Chaplin had him around the shoulders now as he tried to pull forward to get at Finn. 'You haven't got the guts . . .'

Everything happened at once. Talisker broke free of Chaplin's grip and lurched forward into Finn. All he knew was that he was angry. And that anger, directionless for so long, had found its focus in Finn and his dead father. Finn fired as Talisker came at him but the bullet went awry, ricocheting off the wall in a trail of sparks and hitting the light, plunging the room back into darkness. As the light went out, the door crashed open.

All was darkness and confusion. The smell of cordite filled the small space and they were unable to hear anything until their ears recovered from the explosion. Talisker didn't stop to consider where the gun was pointing. He was on top of Finn now, having knocked him to the ground. Chaplin was trying to pull him away, vainly hoping to recover the situation. 'Duncan, get off him!' he was yelling.

'Get the gun! Get the gun!'

'Jeez . . . heads up, boys!'

There was a further yell and a muffled banging, and Talisker knew what had burst through the door. The demon. At that moment Finn looked up. Both men froze in their struggles.

'Oh, my God,' Finn whispered, 'that's it, isn't it? What you call the Highlander?'

'What?' Talisker was momentarily confused then saw that Finn had put two and two together and arrived at seventy-five. 'Yeah,' he agreed hastily. 'It's the Highlander.'

Since their last meeting the demon had suffered. It had allowed its form to slip and was unable to repair it. The mask that had served as its face had melted and was now situated bizarrely in the middle of its chest. The dark eyes still stared out vacantly and the slack mouth moved and drooled.

Talisker glanced to the other side of the room. The demon had thrown aside Chaplin who was now lying awkwardly by the skeleton on the wall. The creature moved, surprisingly fast for its bulk, towards Talisker and Finn.

'Malk? Is Sandro—'

Malky, unable to influence the outcome of Talisker's encounter, was already with Chaplin.

'Aye, but—'

There was no time to finish: the creature was upon them. Finn screamed and fired the gun twice. The second shot made a direct hit, shattering the obscene face into a pulp of blood and bone. The demon reeled back but recovered immediately and grabbed Finn by the arms with its skeletal claws. It hoisted him into the air as he kicked and screamed and in a moment of sickening certainty, Talisker knew that Finn would not survive. He backed away, unable to take his eyes off Finn's struggles as the demon's claws pierced the flesh of his arms and the tops of his thighs. Talisker knew that, weak and confused as he had been, Finn did not deserve the terror of such a death. He was screaming again, a raw sound that filled the basement room with almost tangible fear.

'Duncan! Ower here! There's a weapon,' Malky yelled.

Talisker backed towards the far wall, and bent down without taking his eyes off the demon. He felt around on the floor and found a piece of piping, a heavy, cold length of steel. 'I'm coming, Finn! Hold on!'

Even as he spoke the demon was twisting and wrenching at Finn. Its claws held its victim firm and blood spurted from Finn's forearm where an artery had burst. He didn't stop screaming even as his spine cracked and fractured. Talisker hefted the pipe into a double-handed grip and held it before him like a sword.

'Duncan?'

'Yeah?'

Malky's voice was strained above the screams. 'You've got tae finish it this time,' he roared. 'The beast. You canny leave it here in the city. I dinny think Corvus tidies up after himsel' . . .'

There was a thud and the screaming stopped abruptly. The demon had tossed aside Finn's body. Mercifully, the impact had broken his neck, but as his lifeless corpse fell, an arm caught the candle, which fell behind the packing case on which it was placed. Flames and smoke immediately sprang up behind the dry wooden crate. Talisker had no time to worry about this for the creature, sensing that Finn had been a distraction from his main target, rushed towards him. As it came nearer, time seemed to still for Talisker; the light from the doorway lit the smoke from beneath and the growing heat and glow from the flames behind him made the scene move in a surreal fashion. The smoke drifted towards him in swathes of white and Talisker's eyes streamed as he inhaled it, but in this *slowtime* he dared not blink: even the blink of an eye would be enough to seal his fate. Hefting the pipe, he stepped forward to meet the force of the beast and hit out as hard as he could. To his delight, the beast roared with pain and moved back, its legs buckling.

'C'mon, you bastard,' Talisker yelled. 'That's for Shula.' He knew better than to believe his opponent could be maimed so easily and moved in to press his advantage, hitting out again, ducking low and striking for the beast's legs. Although the force of the blow must have been immense, this time the demon did not give ground. Talisker felt a wave of desperation: the heat from the fire was becoming stronger and if he retreated he had nowhere to go. It was fight or be killed. He struck out again, aiming for the bloody area of the chest where the face had been.

'Duncan,' the voice, from a long way away, was panic-stricken, 'the fire . . . Ah canny . . .'

Talisker watched his next blow land with horrified fascination. Blood, or some demonic equivalent, flew out from the already pulpy mess and, although it was now faceless, a loud keening noise came from the beast. The flames were all around and there were just two souls within the ring of fire . . .

'Duncan! Duncan!' Malky was still calling, still desperate, but Talisker could feel the heat of different flames: the red mist, his berserker rage, overwhelmed him, but this time, for the first time ever, he welcomed it like an old friend. He knew hatred now. He knew that this creature, blameless in its way, had lifted Shula, had twisted and broken her just like it had Finn. And, God knew, he wished the thought would stop coming, but she must have screamed just like Finn. His precious girl. She who had forgiven him.

'Die!' he screamed. 'Die!' He struck again. This time, the demon fell to the ground and Talisker didn't pause but ran forward to stand astride its bloodied body.

It was still *slowtime*. Talisker stared down at the beast, aware that his own face, covered in its blood, wore an expression every bit as monstrous, and that perhaps he had, in the end, lost something to Corvus. He didn't care. At this moment he wanted to kill. Raising the weapon high above his head, he struck again and again, screaming aloud. It seemed to take hours to die but the moment it stopped thrashing, its hold on Talisker's perceptions was broken. Time returned to its normal flow and, as the last blow landed, the sound and the fluids that had flowed from the carcass of the beast became nauseating.

Talisker dropped the weapon, self-disgust washing through him like a shockwave. 'Tell Corvus he's next,' he mumbled.

Smoke, flames and grief claimed him as he stumbled away from the lifeless shape, and he sank to his knees, choking and sobbing.

'Duncan? Can you hear me? This way. Look, I think there's just enough—'

He crawled towards where he thought Malky's voice was coming from. Vaguely outlined in the gloom he could see Chaplin's body but beyond it the basement wall was gone: there was just a familiar blackness. Numbly he reached out for Chaplin, but he wasn't moving.

'He's waking up!'

Talisker opened his eyes and knew that he was back in Sutra. Malky was peering down at him and the coolness of the morning air against his cheek could only mean that he was outside. He sat up, dimly surprised at how normal he felt. Malky and Chaplin were sitting beside a fire, drinking something hot from steaming mugs.

'Ah, so you finally decided to join us, Mr Talisker.' Chaplin grinned. 'We'd just about given up on you.'

'Sandro, you're all right?'

'Don't look so pleased.'

'No, I mean . . . I remember you being pretty scorched. And in both worlds too.' He looked around. They were still at the same campsite and behind where they sat the tattered remains of his tent lay in a sorry-looking heap. 'That was Phyrr,' he muttered.

'I reckon she did us a favour,' Malky said. 'We had to go back, Duncan.'

'I feel bruised all over and I've got some funny marks where I think I was burned the worst. But I'm okay,' Chaplin added.

'What d'you mean we had to go back?'

'We had to kill it.'

'We?'

'All right, then, you had tae kill it. And if we hadnae gone back, we would never have known about Finn and his dad, eh?'

Chaplin handed Talisker a mug of Malky's best elder tea. 'He should have gone to the law years ago. Duncan did time for him.'

Talisker sipped the bitter liquid, enjoying its warmth. 'Don't be too hard on him, Sandro,' he said quietly. 'I know I was really angry back there and I can't deny I was ready to beat the living daylights out of him, but I saw his childhood when I touched him.' He remembered the dark, sonorous voice of Finn's father. *You saw nothing* – 'I wouldn't wish that on anyone. It obviously drove him over the edge. I can't help thinking I didn't try hard enough to save him.'

'Come on, Duncan,' Chaplin insisted. 'There's such a thing as justice, you know.'

'No, I don't. I don't think Finn knew either.'

Malky came and sat companionably between them. 'Right, don't start again, you two,' He put a hand on each man's shoulder. 'I'll tell you what, boys. Ower there, that way, is Soulis Mor, and beyond that is Corvus. Now, tae my mind, justice doesnae just come tae the victims.'

Talisker and Chaplin exchanged faintly surprised glances. 'We hear you, Malk,' Talisker said. 'Just gimme a minute to drink my tea and I'll be right on it.' He watched, bemused, as his friends cracked up with laughter. 'What did I say?'

Once the relief of returning alive had passed, Talisker sank into a deep depression. The journey into the valley floor was slow and arduous, giving him time to brood. Malky was right, of course: it was good that he had gone back to Edinburgh because he had finally severed Corvus's influence in his world. Implicit in Malky's statement, however, was that they wouldn't be going back again. To a large extent Talisker didn't care about this, but being here would never be right either. Not as long as Phyrr was in Sutra. Corvus was different, but his sister had somehow violated Talisker. Not by the physical act of seduction but by their moments of shared consciousness. Of all the things he had experienced in Sutra, proximity to the soul of an evil-tainted goddess was the hardest thing to bear.

Over the next two days he became increasingly withdrawn and Chaplin and Malky exchanged worried glances. He had to be emotionally tired, they told themselves. He'd snap out of it.

# CHAPTER TWENTY-TWO

Brigid's screams were terrible to hear. Una had delivered many babies over the past few years and her instincts told her there was something badly wrong with this birth. Brigid had been in labour for ten hours already and, although this was not uncommon, her pains had been ferocious from early on. She was weakening steadily, and Una feared that she would not see the dawn of the next day. In the tiny casement room, Katlyn and Gwen stood together by the door, their expressions taut with fear. Misty sat on the bed where her friend was resting, holding her hand and wiping her down with warm water. Although a fire was burning in the grate, Una was struggling to keep the room warm. A chill blast was blowing through the cracks in the ancient shutters and Brigid's hands and feet were cold, especially her feet.

'Una?' Brigid whispered. 'Can I walk around again? Please?'

'You need to conserve your strength, Brigid, to push.'

'Will it be soon, Una?' Brigid's eyelids fluttered, and Una feared she would lapse into unconsciousness: her face was shockingly white, her lips tinged blue, yet the girl did not seem to sense that she might be dying.

'Soon, Brigid, soon.' Una fought tears. She had never lost a mother yet, although when she was training she had attended one such tragic birth.

'It's coming. Another pain,' Brigid whispered. 'Oh, gods . . .'

Una signalled to Misty and the two women pushed Brigid into a sitting position to assist her bearing down. Brigid screamed shrilly as the contraction hit, and this heartened Una: if she had strength to scream, perhaps there was reason to hope. However, the contraction was short – too short for this stage of labour. Una did her best to smile encouragingly and settled Brigid back on her pillows.

'Una, may I speak with you?' Isbister had appeared in the doorway in full battle armour carrying her helmet. Her expression radiated concern for her sister but she appeared uncomfortable, as out of context in the chamber as any male warrior. She did not approach the bed so Una went over to her, wiping her face with her apron.

'How is she?' Isbister asked, in a low voice. Una glanced at the other women and walked out into the stairwell with the Thane.

Una steeled herself. 'She is not good, lady. I fear she may not survive the labour unless the babe is born soon.'

Isbister paled. 'Is there nothing you can do to remove the infant?'

'I have given her a draught that will make the pains come more strongly – that will help her body push harder – but she is very weak. I am afraid we must prepare for—'

Suddenly there was singing from the foot of the stairs, and the voice of a drunken warrior carried to them. 'Is the bairn no born yet? Brigid! Brigid, will ye no. . .'

Rounding the last bend of the stairs the inebriated man found himself confronted by Isbister, who slapped him with surprising ferocity.

'Damn you, Alistaire! My sister is fighting for her life in there,' she snarled.

'I – I am sorry, lady,' the warrior garbled, striving for sobriety. 'I was just worried—'

'About yourself and an heir only,' she snapped. 'You have never treated her well. Get out of my sight. I trust you will conduct yourself with more dignity in the face of Corannyeid.'

The man stumbled back down the stairs, and Isbister watched him go with a bitter expression. 'She has always deserved better,' she said softly.

'Is that Brigid's husband?' Una marvelled. 'He has never been to see her all this time.'

'He thinks this child will secure him some power in the Fine, that is all.'

There was a low moan from inside the chamber and Una turned automatically to attend to her patient.

'Una?'

She turned back, expecting a rebuke from the Thane.

'The warriors – they are drinking before the battle. For some it will be their last night and I have not the heart to stop them. It may be wise to lock the door to ensure the women's privacy. When there is . . . any news . . .' Isbister cleared her throat . . . 'send word to me. I will be on the north wall with the commanders.'

A winter storm began at midnight, the shrieking of the blizzard replacing Brigid's moans of pain as she had no voice left for it. The room was freezing as there was no fuel left for the fire, and Una would not allow the women to unlock the room – twice already a small group of warriors had rattled the door and shouted lewdly to the women inside. Una's unease increased each time it happened and she cursed the men loudly. Brigid lapsed into a state of semi-consciousness between her pains. She was weak now because she had lost so much blood. Una's heart was sore but she knew she could have done nothing to prevent this tragedy – before the labour Brigid had appeared perfectly well.

'She will freeze to death before this babe is born,' Misty commented, 'I cannot stand this much longer.' She dropped her voice. 'She is dying, Una, isn't she?'

Una gave a tiny nod, and someone stifled a sob. 'Let's make her comfortable, shall we?' Misty took off her cloak and shawl and wrapped them around Brigid's shoulders. Gwen and Katlyn followed her lead. For a moment there was silence then more banging at the door.

'Let me in, you witch whore! What are you doing to my wife in there? I will be admitted, damn you to hell!'

'Una!' Brigid screamed suddenly. 'Una! It's coming!'

'Let me in!'

Brigid screamed loud and long, and the storm gave answer, the window shutters crashing open, the blizzard throwing the room into chaos.

'The babe . . . Oh, sweet gods!' Misty shrieked, and the other women raced to Brigid's bedside.

Una battled with the shutters and turned back to her charge. Something was clearly wrong. The women were shocked and dazed. Gwen stood with her hand clapped over her mouth. The baby must be dead. Una steeled herself and went to see if anything could be done for the mother. 'Out of my way, Gwen,' she muttered, shock and tiredness engulfing her. She fought to sound calm. 'There is still a mother to cons— oh.'

Without further comment she gathered up the child, wrapping it quickly in the nearest cloak.

'Misty, make Brigid comfortable,' she snapped. Moving away from the bed, she stared down at the bundle in her arms.

Brigid had given birth to a sadly misshapen baby. It was a boy child, but its limbs were withered and tiny in proportion to its body, its back was hunched and distorted, making the neck jut aside so that the head was held at an impossible angle. There was breath and warmth in the tiny shape, and Una cursed the gods who had seen fit to give life to such a poor being at the expense of its mother. Its eyes were closed as though it – he – slept, unaware of the chaos of his coming.

'Una.' It was Misty. She seemed calmer than the others, who sat motionless by Brigid's side. 'The end is near for her, I think. She wants to hold her baby . . .' Her eyes rested on the shape in Una's hands and she suppressed a shudder.

'Get me two more cloaks, Misty. Quickly.'

They wrapped the child in as much fabric as they could, disguising its shape, leaving only the face showing. Then, forcing bright smiles, they took it to Brigid as she lay dying. She smiled a soft, heartbreaking smile, and touched the tiny face.

'It's a boy, Brigid,' Una faltered. She could hardly speak for the constriction of her throat.

'He's not dead, is he?' Brigid frowned. 'His little eyes are closed.'

'No, he's just asleep.'

'Asleep.' Brigid was fading.

'Oh, Brigid . . .' Misty whispered.

'It's all right, Misty. It doesn't hurt any more. I'm warm now . . . Una? Where are you? I can't see . . .'

'I'm here, Brigid . . .' Una took her hand.

'Will you look after my baby?'

'I – of course I will.' Una stroked her hair. 'Brigid?'

She had gone. Una took the child from its mother's arms and stared down at it. Encased in the cloaks, the tiny infant appeared like any other newborn. Suddenly the eyes snapped open and Una was surprised to be looking into deep pools of brown merriment. She knew that all babes were born with blue eyes, whatever colour they might become later. Unexpectedly, she smiled down at the child, warmth washing through her.

'Here.' Gwen touched her shoulder and proffered a pillow.

Una stared at it blankly, refusing to acknowledge what she knew the other woman meant. 'What?' she whispered.

'It's the only way.'

'Open up! Open up, you bitch! Where's my wife? Brigid!' The women froze. The hammering on the door increased until it seemed the door would burst open, then stopped. They heard a low cursing, then footsteps going down the stairs.

Una looked at the pillow in Gwen's hands. 'Don't you think one death is enough for tonight?' she said coldly.

'Gwen's right, Una,' Katlyn said. 'The warriors will

surely kill it if they get their hands on it. It is the worst possible omen.'

'*It* is a he,' Una said fiercely. 'Didn't you hear me promise his mother that I would care for him? Misty, go and find the Thane. Speak to no one else. Tell her . . .' she swallowed. 'Tell her both mother and child passed away during the birth.'

The women stared at her in horror. 'Una, do you know what you are doing?' Misty breathed.

Una looked down at the tiny wrinkled face, and the wise brown eyes smiled up at her. 'You've been here before, little one,' she whispered. She didn't know what had made her say it.

'Una?' Misty said urgently.

'Go,' she hissed.

Without another word, Misty unlocked the door and raced from the room. Gwen followed behind her to lock it again but was not quick enough. Alistaire was wedged in the space before she could close it.

'My wife. I want to see my wife!'

Una ducked behind the door, her eyes widening in horror.

Gwen saved the day. Keeping herself firmly between Alistaire and access into the chamber she spoke calmly. 'Sir, I am sorry but your wife has passed away during her confinement. Please give us a few minutes to prepare her and you may pay your respects.'

'Very well,' Alistaire said roughly – his tone implied that he was less than grief-stricken. 'What of my child?'

'It – it died also, sir. Please. I will open the chamber in a moment so that you may see Brigid.'

Alistaire drew back from the door, allowing Gwen to

close it. The women panicked, and Una stood in the middle of the room crippled by indecision. Gwen picked up the pillow again. Una misread her intention and almost cried out as she clasped the baby to her.

'No,' Gwen mouthed, putting her finger to her lips. She lifted the lid of the wooden bench seat below the window, placed the pillow inside and Una laid the baby on it. Then, when they had tidied Brigid's hair and bedclothes and composed themselves, they admitted the widower to the chamber. He stumbled in, his breath smelling of beer, and stood swaying by the bedside. Una almost felt sorry for him but reminded herself that he would kill the child if he saw it. There was a long moment of silence and the strains of the night caught up with Gwen and Katlyn, who cried in earnest for their friend as the storm abated and the first tinges of dawn lit the chamber. Finally, Alistaire spoke. 'Where is my child? I would see my son.'

'It was a girl, sir,' Gwen lied, hoping to deter him. He could not hide the disappointment that crossed his face. 'Still,' he said, 'I would see it – her.'

Una stepped forward and curtsied. 'Sir, your wife requested that we cremate the child so that their souls may be together.'

Alistaire stared suspiciously at the fireplace, his eyes narrowing. 'It's very clean – the grate,' he muttered.

'I have . . . chemicals, sir, for my midwifery.'

He nodded curtly and started back towards the door but just as his hand touched the latch, there was a faint cry from the window-seat.

'What witchery is this?' Alistaire stormed. Striding over to the window he flung open the lid. Dazzled by the light, the baby began to cry, reaching out with his stumpy little arms. The blanket fell aside to reveal his body.

'Sweet gods!' Alistaire cried, his face screwing up in disgust, and drew his sword.

'No!' Una shrieked. Before she had time to think, she had flung herself in front of the weapon, lashing out blindly. The unexpected ferocity of her attack caught Alistaire off guard and he staggered back, catching her arm with the blade. He reeled, his eyes darting between Una and the window seat. Una seized on his moment of doubt. 'Yes,' she panted, holding her wrist, 'you'll have to kill me first. Brigid asked me to care for him and I will.'

'You can have it, lady,' Alistaire growled. 'It is nothing of mine. Nothing!' The baby cried out again and, as if struck, Alistaire dropped his sword, clapped his hand over his mouth, and fled from the chamber.

Gothic. That was what Talisker thought when he sighted Soulis Mor for the first time. In the pre-dawn light a freezing mist was drifting just above the snow, and the dark shape of the fortress city, which spanned the width of the valley, loomed before him. Hewn from the black basalt that lay beneath most of the land this far north, it seemed a natural extension to the mountains that girded it at either side, its black walls slick with ice. From this distance the steady line of people leaving the city appeared as a colourless streak moving steadily towards the foothills, where Talisker and Chaplin now stood watching.

Talisker sensed that they were both thinking about

the inhabitants of Ruannoch Were, killed as they fled the Corannyeid, and he hoped the Thane of this city had taken precautions to protect the people who were now leaving their homes. As the wind shifted towards them, the disembodied sound of a child crying was carried on the wind. The only thing of warmth about the scene was a fire burning in the tallest of the numerous towers randomly scattered along the width of the wall. Even from this distance, it was clear that the tower would be burned out: it seemed that the battle had begun with the first touches of the dawn. Fainter noises carried towards them, and it was difficult to tell whether the eerie sound was the screaming of warriors or the cries of the large crows that flew out of the turret. Talisker's thoughts turned to Phyrr – the Morrigan – a black, evil bird like her brother. His memory of the night when she had seduced then attempted to murder him plagued him like a festering wound. But down there in Soulis Mor was Una, the real Una, flesh and blood and warmth. He recognised his need for her, which frightened him almost as much as any battle.

Malky had crested the hill behind him. 'Shall we go, then?'

As they grew closer, the sound of dying warriors issued from the cavernous city gates as though from the maw of some distressed creature. They entered unchallenged, passing those refugees who, out of fear, love or loyalty, had deferred their flight until the last moment. Two young sentries stood by the gates, surprised that anyone should be entering Soulis Mor against the tide of departing Fine. Talisker slowed his horse to a walk and stared at the youths, his mood sombre. He had wrapped the upper end of his plaid around his face and only his blue eyes could be seen against the glare of the snow. The youths shrank back instinctively, confirming what Talisker already knew: his encounter with Phyrr and his journeys between worlds had branded him with a cold fire.

'You there.' Chaplin stopped his mount beside Talisker, glancing sideways at his friend. 'We would see Lady Ulla mac Ferghus of Ruannoch Were. Do you know her whereabouts?'

'Sh-she is in the west wing, sir,' the youth stammered. Then he caught sight of Malky, who gave him his best grin. 'She – she arrived three days ago. I'll take you to her.'

Ulla sat in darkness, listening to the cries of the dying. Isbister had politely requested that she and the *Fir Chrieg* remained within their chambers and, as the daughter of a thane, Ulla understood and respected her reasons. Rumours of the return of the heroes had arrived with the remnants of Ferghus's people from her city. The last thing the warriors needed before doing battle with the Corrannyeid was the knowledge that those heroes were the ghost-like figures who had walked beside her like so much animated rock. They were resting now in the lower cellar rooms, which had acquired the silence of a tomb. The sight of them lying still and pale as death on their pallets was chilling. They demanded nothing, and only the white wisps of their breath in the cold air gave any sign that they lived. Ulla feared that they would soon return to the rock that had been their existence for the past two hundred years. The grey calm of the situation sapped her resolve, and the tide of grief she had dammed to help Chaplin and the walk to Soulis Mor had claimed her. Dom, Kyra, her mother Erin who had died years earlier, even her father – alive, but lost to her – those who were dead achieved more life in her mind than the *Fir Chrieg*. In her mind's eye they moved before her, their smiles and laughter bright and so poignant that she wept for long, miserable hours.

'Lady Ulla?' At last the silence was broken by an almost timid knocking at the door. 'There are people here who wish to see you . . .'

Sandro? Even Makhpiyaluta who had deserted her party would cheer her now. She pulled distractedly at her hair, automatically obscuring the scarred side of her face, painfully aware that she had used no salve for days, and that her skin was raw and inflamed from the salt of her tears.

'I'm coming.' She limped to the door chiding herself for her pleasure at the idea of seeing Chaplin, aware that the weakness in her legs was not entirely due to pain. But the memory of his rejection still stung. She should appear calm, perhaps a bit distant . . .

She unlocked the chamber door. 'Yes?'

'Ulla?' Chaplin was framed in the doorway and bright morning light shone around him. Ulla smiled uncertainly but as he opened his arms to her she rushed into his embrace.

'Ahem.' Behind Chaplin stood Malky and Talisker, looking tired and cold but faintly surprised by the warmth of Chaplin and Ulla's mutual greeting.

Now she felt reassured of Chaplin's friendship, Ulla stepped back and smiled at the travellers. 'Forgive me

Duncan, Malcolm, I trust all went well with your search?'

'That remains to be seen, Lady Ulla,' Talisker said quietly, his eyes grave. 'We found Rhiannon, but who knows what she will do?'

There was such bleakness in his statement that Ulla was reminded of the *Fir Chrieg*, lying in darkness in the cellar below. 'Come,' she said, as brightly as she could against the backdrop of the dead and the dying. 'Sandro, perhaps you can get the fire going and we can warm some mead.'

For a while they sat around discussing how they had fared since parting weeks earlier. Chaplin seemed surprised by Makhpiyaluta's desertion but Talisker said, 'He's gone after *Braznnair*. I never trusted the damned bird anyway.'

'D'ye think he would kill Deme to get it, though?' Malky frowned.

'Who knows? Anyone who kills women is capable, I would say.'

'That's jist a story, Duncan. Remember Tayna? She widnae think sae much of him if it wiz true.'

'What was true? Who's Tayna?' Ulla asked.

'It doesn't matter,' Talisker replied. 'Malky's right. All we know is hearsay, Sidhe stories.'

'How goes the battle, Ulla?' Chaplin asked. 'Has anyone told you anything?'

'No. It started at dawn this morning but judging by the noise it's not going very well. You get to recognise the sound . . .' her voice faltered, 'of that last . . .'

'So much fer the great heroes, sleeping it off in the cellar,' Malky grimaced.

'It's not over yet, Malk,' Chaplin said quietly.

'Well, Duncan, what do we do now?' Malky asked.

'Do what you like.' Talisker frowned. 'I'm your friend, that's all. I'm not about to order you into some battle that is not your fight.'

'But it *is* my fight, Duncan.' Malky glowered. 'Ah'm here, aren't Ah? So're you. Don't ye care what happens tae the folks here? You canny just run aroond sayin' it's got nothin' tae dae wi' you. Not now. What about Tayna? What about all the folks that have died . . . all the mothers 'n' the children taken at Ruannoch Were?' Malky was angered by Talisker's apparent disinterest. 'So you've done yer bit gettin' *Braznnair* tae the White Eagle an' talkin' tae Rhiannon, but ye canny jist stop now. You canny jist sit back an' say ye're finished while this world is fallin' apart around ye. You may jist as well have stayed in the jail an' me in . . . wherever I wiz . . .'

Talisker drained the last of his mead. His haunted blue eyes had sparked almost dangerously as the Highlander spoke to him, and for a split second Chaplin thought he would reach out and strike him. Malky seemed unaware of this. Ulla reached forward and touched Talisker before she spoke. 'Talisker,' she said, 'when I arrived I sent word to Una, as you requested. I don't know if she received my message. I was told she was caring for some Soulis Mor women who were pregnant, and they were quartered in the west tower. Anyway, the lad who brings my food told me this morning that there is some kind of trouble in the tower, I'm not sure what.'

Images whirled unbidden through Talisker's mind.

Una, astride him, smiling lecherously, his blood on her lips. No. It wasn't her. A small white feather drifted across his thoughts. It danced and moved on waves of torment yet still it was sublimely simple and bright. The sound of Una's laughter washed across him. Soft and warm and . . .

'Una? In trouble?' It seemed as though he had awoken from a dream. 'Where is she?'

But he had to see it first. The dying place. The screams, the sickening thuds, the howls of pain were the same as the day of Ruannoch Were, but this time there was no red mist, no pounding rush of adrenaline.

Talisker stood at the top of the stairwell of the central tower and stared aghast at the carnage around him, all thoughts of reaching Una gone. There could be no victory here. The black shadow of the Corrannyeid covered the bleak landscape of the poisoned lands as far as the eye could see, moving like a huge swarm of insects towards the battlements, ripples running through their ranks as though they were a field of slick black corn. Above them flitted the ghostly shapes of the *Bultari*, the creatures which had so wounded Mirranon – the sky was thick with them. The walls had not been breached but it made little difference: the flying creatures descended with the accuracy of the Sidhe eagles, enveloping their hapless victims within their leather wings, only opening them when a warrior of the Fine lay dead at their feet. The kill was soundless but, as they flew, they emitted a banshee wail, which suggested to Talisker that these things – whatever they were – were in pain. The light of this world pained them or offended their dark soul. Whatever corner of the void Corvus had pulled them from, they had come unwillingly and would kill any living creature they were directed towards. The Corrannyeid, moving as indistinct, vaguely human shadows, were scaling the walls using tall trees they had felled and ropes to take them the rest of the distance. They did nothing to secure a route for their fellows and once again it seemed to Talisker that they were not an army in any normal sense but, rather, a multitude of seething soulless minds intent on murder and destruction.

Despite their lack of a tactical plan, it was evident that the Corrannyeid were slaughtering the Fine, their massacre only constrained by the speed at which they were able to gain a foothold on the battlements. Never, even at Ruannoch Were, had Talisker witnessed such mass despair and desperation. Men were weeping openly as they fought, curses and sobs punctuating the screams of the dying. The corpses of those already dispatched by the Corrannyeid crowded the battlements so that those still alive trampled them in their desperate fight, tripping over their kinsmen and kinswomen, even using the dead as a shield or barrier to hide behind. Those whose death had erupted from within their form lay shrouded in the twisted black tendrils. Only Talisker could see their ghost forms, shrieking still at the terror of their demise, jumping from the battlements into the black sea beneath or sitting hunched beside their corpse, unable to leave, their eyes blank. There was no glory here, no heart, as there had been at Ruannoch Were, only the charnel stench of blood, bile and death. Talisker thought fleetingly of Phyrr and the hellish nightmare of her soul: here the nightmare was made flesh.

'You there! Yes, you!'

Talisker turned to see a small muscular woman with long red braids waving a sword in his direction. She was spattered in blood and breathing heavily, and her eyes were blazing with near berserker fury, which Talisker recognised. Isbister spat and wiped her cheek on her leather glove smearing the blood further so that her face appeared as a crimson mask.

'This is no day for craven sons of bitches,' she cursed. 'If you won't fight, make yourself useful and help the dying.' She hefted a sword towards him and turned to slash into a Corrannyeid, which had lumbered behind her and was shadowing her form even as she spoke to Talisker.

Talisker could see how he must appear to the woman, and he still stood rooted to the spot, overwhelmed by the sheer scale of the killing. Worse, he held on to the rail of the stairs as though anchoring himself to the tower. Then a *Bultari* descended behind the already beleaguered Thane. Ibister screamed, not in fear but in fury. Despite her reckless bravery the sound was still eminently female and Talisker, his trance broken, rushed forward to slash at the grey being with the sword Ibister had thrown to him. The *Bultari* turned towards him as he descended the last few steps and his downward thrust caught the black leathern surface of its left wing, slicing deep into the joint between the wing and the spine. The creature bled a bright sulphurous yellow, which matched the baleful glow of its eyes, but it did not recoil or cry out.

Isbister had despatched the Corrannyeid she was fighting, lopping the head from its body with a powerful blow and spun round to Talisker's aid just as the *Bultari* snapped open its shattered wings, catching Talisker's arm at the end of his stroke and knocking the blade from his hands. He yelled as a sharp hook at the apex of the wing sliced into his forearm. The glint of a curved silver dagger could be seen in the *Bultari*'s talons as it moved forward and Talisker was defenceless against its dark embrace. Isbister cursed – the opponents were too close to allow any hacking stroke and she was fending off another Corrannyeid while trying to move to the back of the *Bultari*. Just as the creature reached out a spindly arm and grabbed Talisker's shirt, pulling him towards the blade, Isbister struck. The hideous face shattered, yellow blood gouting forth, spraying Talisker as Isbister's axe split its skull apart. The body fell forward and Talisker threw it away from him, his stomach knotting with nausea.

Isbister grinned through the blood and filth. 'So, you *do* know how to use that thing,' she taunted.

'Wha—' But there was no time to speak before the next Corrannyeid and the next . . .

In this manner Talisker was drawn into the battle as the red mist came down and the day of blood began.

# CHAPTER TWENTY-THREE

The wings of the eagle trembled as he lost the height of the thermal he rode and failed to hold his flight. Makhpiyaluta screamed his fear and frustration into the encroaching wall of dark cloud and flexed his aching wings. He was lucky: the northern wind, Salkit, forgave his lack of respect and bore him upwards. He flew so high that his flight was soundless as though the silver-blue of the airless realm was the space between worlds and Makhpiyaluta, Grey Ghost Stalker, Prince of the Sidhe, moved between them, a tiny speck against a cold, darkening twilight. His golden-brown feathers were limed with white frost, brittle as beaten copper. Within his talons he carried *Braznnair*, and as he passed through the high bank of cloud the dying rays of sunlight arced through the stone, colouring the lower clouds with vibrant green flashes, turning the sunset into the realm of Ashutu, the great ocean.

He knew that he was failing. Soon he would whirl and fall, out of control, his strength gone. For Makhpiyaluta's people it would be a shameful way to die but at least none would see his shame except those awaiting his demise. Still, he flew onwards, his poignant cry filling the cold white reaches with the sound of the unforgiven.

As an early winter dusk came to Soulis Mor the stench

of blood and burning filled the air. The Corrannyeid had withdrawn as the light grew ever weaker but not before the Fine – what was left of the original force of four thousand – had been forced to pull back to the secondary tier of the city's defences, abandoning supplies and many horses stabled in the outer rim. This furthest level had been sealed successfully leaving a distance of less than half a mile between Isbister's demoralised army and their attackers. Battle-numbed men and women who sank gratefully against the cool stones of the secondary wall wept as the terrified whinnies and squeals of the mass slaughter of three hundred horses reached them. One woman warrior, whom Talisker had aided earlier in the afternoon, sprinted across the distance screaming and cursing as a final rush of fury and adrenaline coursed through her. She had a gash to her left calf but seemed oblivious to the pain, screaming over and over again the name of her horse, Cruach. Those nearest her tried to restrain her but she pushed them aside, punching one of her fellows in the stomach almost without pause. Beyond a certain point none would follow her, knowing they were too exhausted to fight on. They could only watch, fascinated, as she disappeared among the rubble used to seal the main gates. There was a long quiet as those who would have imagined themselves past caring gazed at the place where she had vanished from view, unconsciously holding their breath.

Almost miraculously, the woman reappeared, moving more slowly, her energy reserves obviously gone. She was leading a ragged-looking black pony by its mane, encouraging it to run faster. However, behind her, three Corrannyeid were closing fast. In an unthinking response to her bravery, a small group of warriors rushed to her aid as others raced to secure the breach. The Corrannyeid, stranded in the space, were cut down, the Fine warriors venting their final fury on them. As the band moved to within the safety of the wall, people smiled wearily and clapped one another on the shoulders. No one saw fit to reprimand the woman for her recklessness: the Fine fought always with passion, which often led to such incidents, often with an unhappier outcome.

Talisker and Chaplin watched this happen without comment as they sat like the others with their backs against the stones. Both men recognised the foolhardiness of rescuing one small black horse and putting at risk the lives of men and women who had survived such a day, but Chaplin smiled as people gathered around the bewildered pony to pat it, as though it might bring them luck.

Talisker's eyes were grim. 'They're slaughtering us just like the horses. It's just a matter of time . . .'

'What?' Chaplin asked. Talisker had spoken so quietly that he was unsure if his friend had said something.

'Time,' Talisker repeated. 'It's just a matter of time.'

'Have you seen—' Chaplin stopped, unsure why the question had occurred to him and what Talisker's response would be.

'Phyrr? No. I think she's done her worst to me. Corvus is responsible for this. She doesn't care . . . doesn't think like this. Sandro?'

'Yes?'

'I can still see them, you know. The dead. Just like I see people's past lives when I touch them. They are still here, all around, still screaming . . .'

To Chaplin it was unimaginable . . . 'Maybe when Rhiannon comes with Cernunnos he can do something.'

'What are they waiting for? The eleventh hour? Perhaps they won't come. You've seen Rhiannon. She's like a child – she's probably forgotten us already.'

'Why don't you go and see Una, Duncan? Maybe it will help to be with someone you feel close to.'

Talisker turned to him and, in the gathering darkness, he appeared to be fighting for control of himself. 'I can't, Sandro. I . . .'

'Duncan! Sandro!' Malky had run over to them. Talisker wondered how the Highlander had enough retained energy to show such excitement. 'Ah heard one o' the sentries tellin' his officer that he'd seen a green flash in the sky jist ower there.' He pointed south. 'You don't suppose it could be onything tae dae with *Braznnair*?'

Talisker stood up. 'Let's go and see, Malk, shall we?'

They found him less than a mile from the southern gates of Soulis Mor. Makhpiyaluta had fallen from the skies. Unable to hold to his eagle form as his lifeblood leached from his wounds, he had returned to the shape of a Sidhe warrior. He lay caught between the rocks of a narrow crevasse, his limbs crushed and broken, his torso twisted in such a way that it was plain his back was broken. Even through his intense pain Makhpiyaluta had an air of calm expectancy, and he managed a thin smile as the three men clambered across the rocks to him.

'White Eagle told me you would come, that I must not fear failure, that the rest is down to you, Tal-ees-ker.' He pronounced Talisker's name in the way of his clan.

'But White Eagle is dead,' Malky frowned, 'isn't she?'

'She is flying, Malcolm, towards Lysmair.'

'Where's Deme?'

'Killed. By Eskarius, for *Braznnair.*' Makhpiyaluta closed his eyes, his strength ebbing.

Talisker crouched down beside him and touched his bloodied face. 'Makhpiyaluta, where is *Braznnair*?' he said gently.

'It's over there.' Chaplin pointed.

Just behind where Makhpiyaluta lay the snow was bathed in a warm green glow. As Talisker turned towards it Makhpiyaluta's hand shot out and pulled him with unexpected strength back to face him. 'Come closer,' he whispered, 'I want you to know the tale of the Sidhe, so all will know what we have done. Without us, the Fine would perish . . .'

'They may still—' Malky began, but Talisker held up his hand for the Highlander to be silent. Makhpiyaluta reached out and touched Talisker's chest just over his heart. 'Do you feel it? Do you feel the heartbeat of the Sidhe?'

Instinctively Talisker closed his eyes.

*He saw. He felt. In the green warmth of* Braznnair *and beyond to a place he knew to be Lysmair. All the beasts were one great nation there, the eagles flew and the creatures of the land lived in harmony. Only when they gathered in one place did the Sidhe transform to their other state of being, and Talisker sensed that all the joy of their existence remained within their totem beasts:*

*all the knowing, all the seeing of the life and colours of the land. Being human to a Sidhe was like being a shadow. And yet the Sidhe had held this form for most of their time in Sutra because they needed to live in harmony with the clans of the Fine, who instinctively distrusted the bear and the wolf, and only tolerated the lynx and the eagle. Lysmair was the home of their soul.*

*And now he heard the voice of Makhpiyaluta speaking the prophecy. 'And, with Tal-ees-ker, each shall go forward, eagle, bear, lynx, wolf and eagle. The circle of spirit will be complete and the way of Lysmair will be opened. The Sidhe will find redemption.* Braznnair *will . . .'*

Makhpiyaluta died, seeing the truth, finding his own redemption. Talisker turned to Malky and Chaplin, his eyes bright with tears. '. . . take them home,' he ended. '*Braznnair* will take them home.'

'What is it, Duncan?' Malky asked. 'What did ye see?'

'Their prophecy, Malk. It wasn't what they thought, it was about letting go of the past, making Sutra their home. "Each shall go forward, eagle, bear, lynx, wolf and eagle . . ." It was their deaths in that order. They believe their spirits return to Lysmair. Mirranon, Tayna, Deme, Eskarius – Makhpiyaluta killed him – and now Makhpiyaluta.'

'Deme?'

'Yes. They all died for this, so that we could bring it here and save the Fine, even if we haven't a clue how we're going to do that. Even if the gods have deserted us.' He held up the gem, which Chaplin had passed to him. It was coated in blood and snow. 'Can you see the blood on it?' he grated. 'It's cursed . . .'

His gaze travelled to the deeper line of the crevasse.

Within the basement where the *Fir Chrieg* lay sleeping, a conversation was taking place that was just outside the bounds of human hearing. It grew progressively louder, each word more distinct, and as the sound grew, so did the pools of shadow that clung to the edges of the room until the shadows took shape and form. Two tall figures stepped through the wall. They were arguing.

'And I am telling you I cannot awaken them, Rhiannon, without the stone. How could you be so stupid as to offer my assistance without speaking with me first?' The voice was a dry rich sound, with a discomforting sibilant edge.

Rhiannon pulled a mock-petulant face. 'Cernunnos, you are a god. The power of life and death is yours. The souls of the dead are yours to command. What are you saying?'

Cernunnos stood beside the stone slab on which Uisdean lay. In the cold darkness of the chamber, the shape of the god could be seen only as a huge looming shadow, but his green eyes gleamed with annoyance. 'Have you seen what is happening out there? Corvus defies me. The souls of the Fine are being stolen by the Corrannyeid. Each death makes them stronger and us weaker. You never did understand the complexities of godhood, did you?'

'Don't patronise me, brother,' Rhiannon fumed. 'You have spent your existence in darkness for millennia, taking the souls of men only when they are spent. You are as guilty as I of ignoring the plight of the Fine. And now it has come to this. You cannot restore a mere five?'

'I have already restored them, Rhiannon.' Cernunnos's tone was one of careful patience, as though he were explaining to a child. 'The *Seanachaidh* Alessandro Chaplin came and asked me by way of the "Ur Siol" so I could not refuse him.'

At this, even Rhiannon looked impressed. 'Really, these outworlders are an interesting breed, are they not? Is there nothing we can do, then? What if we have the gem?' There was a silence. 'Well?' she said, impatiently.

'It would be a mixed blessing, Rhiannon. True, I could restore these five and send the trapped souls of the Fine to their rest . . .'

'But?' It was Chaplin who had spoken. He and Talisker stood in the doorway to the chamber. In such close proximity to the gods who had fashioned it, *Braznnair* gleamed brightly even from the depths of Talisker's pouch.

Cernunnos looked towards the two mortals and bowed his head in acknowledgement to Chaplin. 'Corvus would be freed,' he said. 'The magic of *Braznnair* is limited, as others who have sought it already know. Were any of its power to be diverted, Corvus's bonds would fail. He would be here physically.'

They heard a sudden shrill scream as a luckless female warrior succumbed to the Corrannyeid. Talisker stared into the shadowy outline of the god, his eyes trying to make out detail where there seemed just darkness. Only the green eyes were real. 'Do it,' he said. 'If he's here, we can kill him.' He nodded towards the sleeping figures of the *Fir Chrieg*. 'Maybe they'll be useful after all.'

He took *Braznnair* from his pocket and threw it across the chamber to Cernunnos, whose eyes gleamed approval as if in reply to the stone. Green on green.

Talisker adjusted his reins and stared fixedly at the great oaken gates of Soulis Mor, waiting for them to open. At last he felt right about this. At last he would see the face of the Raven King. His stomach churned, his legs felt weak, but he was no longer afraid. After three days of watching the men and women of the Fine die needless, horrible deaths, his anger burned brightly. His growing sense that Corvus was not merely an evil god but amoral outraged him. The faceless waves of Corrannyeid that broke relentlessly on the walls of the citadel spoke to him only of an almost disinterested cowardice and that Corvus had endless boxes of soldiers. At least Phyrr's dark passions suggested some perverse feeling for mankind where Corvus played a cold, malicious game – the spite of a young boy – edged with insanity. Now it would be personal, Talisker would make sure of it.

'Remember,' Rhiannon's voice cut through his thoughts, 'I may not be able to maintain the force that protects you. You must reach the site as quickly as you can, lest I fail.'

'Aye, lady. We have waited for this day.' It was Uisdean who spoke. The revived *Fir Chrieg* were ready to ride out as a vanguard for the three outworlders, as Rhiannon insisted on calling them. Cernunnos had used *Braznnair* to wake them and, at the same instant, a massive shaft of blue light had rent the skies to the north of Soulis Mor, earthing itself among the furthest ranks of Corrannyeid. By first light there was nothing to indicate that anything had fallen to earth yet it was plain that Corvus had arrived. The Corrannyeid did not begin their morning attack as expected, but seemed to be awaiting instruction. The few remaining Fine were glad of the respite yet the silence was uncanny. Unease pervaded the citadel, and was only partially lifted by the appearance of the *Fir Chrieg* when half-hearted cheers carried into the stillness.

Talisker had seen Una. It had been a brief, unsatisfying encounter; both of them emotionally numbed and physically exhausted. They had simply clung together when their paths crossed in the kitchens. People passed them by unheeding: displays of emotion were common at such times, heightened by impending oblivion. There was so much to say, so much to tell, yet neither said anything. Gathering her hair in his fist Talisker buried his face in her neck. A small sound escaped him, part laugh, part sob. Someone called him and he let her go reluctantly. He left without saying goodbye – neither of them could bear to hear the word again.

'Duncan, are ye all right?' Malky sat his horse to Talisker's left, Chaplin to his right. The two men had insisted on coming, and Talisker felt a rush of affection for his friends, tinged with an uneasy shame that their loyalty to him might take them to their deaths.

'I'm fine. Look, you don't have to do this, either of you, especially you, Sandro. You're a *Seanachaidh* now.'

'Do you remember what you said about apologies?' Chaplin said. 'And you were right, Duncan. "Sorry" is just a word.' He gripped Talisker's shoulder. 'We're friends, aren't we?'

Talisker returned his embrace, then looked at Malky, trying to shake off the wave of emotion, knowing he couldn't afford it now.

There was a heavy sound, like hollow thunder, and the gates began to open. As one man the three spurred their horses forward, each secretly afraid his courage would desert him.

Corvus paced across the room of the dwelling he had created for himself. It was constructed from the only materials available in the immediate vicinity: mud and turf. It had escaped his notice that he had laid out the room in exactly the same way as his prison. Sluagh sat on the back of his throne and watched his master.

'He's coming here. Talisker is coming. She could have killed him but, no, now he's coming here.' He stopped. 'What am I saying? He's only mortal. Who cares? Let him come . . . But why him, Sluagh? Something is happening.' Suddenly he flung open his arms expansively. 'But look, Sluagh, I'm free!' He walked to the door of the chamber and pushed it open but stopped on the threshold.

A Corrannyeid lumbered towards him. It was large, but vaguely human in appearance. Corvus squinted at it thoughtfully. 'You've stopped the attack. Why? Get on with it.' He slammed the door shut again.

'Corvus.' In the corner of the chamber, a shadowy outline appeared.

'Phyrr, you whore, why aren't you here?' Corvus was irritated.

'You could say I'm moving on, brother.' There was no reproach in her tone but something in her demeanour was frightening, something intangible.

'I'm free, Phyrr,' he boasted. 'Look.'

She did look, for long moments, at her brother sitting in his chair, and her smile held a mocking edge. 'I'm free too,' she said. 'I've only come to warn you. Get out of here. Dissolve the Corrannyeid. Something's coming . . .'

'He's only mortal.'

'Just get out, Corvus,' she repeated. 'Goodbye, brother.'

'Phyrr, wait!' But she was gone.

# CHAPTER TWENTY-FOUR

The riders were half-way across the plains when the Corrannyeid moved forward. At first the creatures ignored them: Rhiannon's shield seemed to make them, if not invisible, a less attractive target. Maura and Conniech of the *Fir Chrieg* took the long-awaited opportunity to kill some of the beasts as they passed. They whooped, cheered and screamed as the Corrannyeid fell like cattle. Uisdean and Raghnald laughed and swore roundly but Kentigern said nothing, his dark eyes darting back and forth trusting neither their luck nor their shield to hold.

Talisker was thinking the same, and the recklessness of the two younger warriors irritated him. He turned on his horse. 'Save your energy, for Chrissakes,' he yelled. 'Look around you. How many do you want to kill?' The dark ranks stretched as far as the eye could see. Chastened, Maura and Conniech sheathed their blades but not before Conniech spat in Talisker's direction. Talisker said nothing but turned away scowling. They rode on in stony silence.

'Talisker, look.' Chaplin pointed to the sky. At first it seemed remarkable only in that none of the flying creatures were there but then he looked into the winter sun. A shadow lay across it, as though someone had taken a bite from it. Behind it, there was another, less distinct shape. A couple of the *Fir Chrieg* drew their swords again and, without thought, Chaplin crossed himself.

'It's an eclipse,' Talisker told them. He turned to those behind him. 'Look, there's nothing to fear, the path of the sun and the moon have just come into alignment. In a few minutes, everything will go dar—' He stopped and glanced at Chaplin, who was still staring at the sun. Then he looked back at the sun. Behind the weak yellow glow was the vast black shadow of a bigger star or planet. 'Sandro, it's just an eclipse. They must be different here.'

'Yeah.' Chaplin tore away his gaze. 'You must be right, Duncan, it's just . . . awesome.' He turned to Kentigern. 'You must not look at it. It will hurt your eyes.' The old warrior nodded, then spoke with the others, passing on Chaplin's instructions.

'Let's go,' Talisker said, 'or we'll be fighting in the dark.' He spurred on his horse, fighting the impulse to look up once more. He wasn't even sure he had convinced himself.

Rhiannon also watched the sky and cursed. The last time such a thing had happened . . . She knew that within moments her shield would fail and the riders would be defenceless.

It was growing darker. Still they rode, looking forward, but now their silence was a pall of fear. Only the horses' hooves could be heard, a flat, muffled noise, as though it was being absorbed into the earth. In the gloom, Corrannyeid moved past them soundlessly, the monstrous shadows they cast in the sickly yellow light heavy black upon the corrupted plain. Suddenly a scream split the stillness, throwing the horses and riders into confusion. It was Maura. Black tendrils were erupting from her and her mount.

'Maura!' Conniech screamed. He galloped back to where her horse had collapsed and dealt the killing blow.

'Conniech, come back!' Malky yelled. 'We've got tae stay together.' It was useless. In his fury, Conniech struck out again and again at the passing Corrannyeid, but once more it seemed the riders were invisible to the creatures, who made no attempt to defend themselves.

Chaplin reached the only conclusion. 'Rhiannon's defences are failing. Come on! We must go!'

The remaining riders spurred their mounts into a gallop – there seemed no choice but to leave the unfortunate Conniech if he would not come. Kentigern drew his horse level with Talisker.

'We are here to protect you, Talisker,' he panted. 'Stay between us.' He and Owein rode at either side of Chaplin and Malky while Uisdean and Raghnald brought up the rear. They rode like the proverbial wind into the gathering darkness. Talisker stared fixedly ahead, his whole world compressed into the space between his horse's ears. The yellow light was suffocating, the nightmare landscape seemed far away, all sound coming as if from a great distance. His fear was a growing mass of tightness in his chest. He released it in the only way his instincts told him. '*Corvuuuus!*' he yelled. 'I'm coming for you, you bastard! Aaaaagh!'

'Stop! Duncan, stop!' There was a sudden lurch as

someone pulled on the bridle of his horse and Talisker was swung around sharply.

His horse stood on a precipice. He was at the edge of a huge crater about a mile wide. The smell of burning lingered from its creation and, in places, the earth was still smouldering. In the centre, half a mile down, a rough building of sorts had been erected. Something about its appearance suggested chaos in its purest form. The mud and turf used for its construction had coalesced into a structure that had organic life. It was almost dark now. Talisker risked a look at the sky: only a segment of the sun remained. There was no light within the building but he sensed that Corvus was in there.

'Where's Owein?'

Malky shrugged sadly. 'He didnae make it, Duncan.'

Talisker had a fleeting memory of the young warrior that morning: he had had a refined, haughty look, tempered by the suggestion of a laddish sense of humour. Although he knew that the *Fir Chrieg* were here only to settle an old score and 'find a better death', as Kentigern had put it, Talisker wished he had known him. That was what Corvus did. It was more than just the opposite of creating life. It was theft.

'Let's go down,' he said. 'There are fewer Corrannyeid down there.'

They had to walk. The horses would come only so far down the slope and they left them in a sad little group tied to the remains of a tree.

'It's too quiet,' Kentigern muttered. 'It might be a trap.'

'Aye,' Malky whispered, 'but we've nae choice.'

A raven flew overhead, and mocking laughter floated from the building.

Along the walls of Soulis Mor there was a brief cessation of battle. All that remained of the Fine, two hundred and thirty men and women, stood along the battlements watching the dying of their sun. There was no panic although a few wept silently. Isbister was among those who wept. It was surely the end of the world and she had lost everything – her sister, her army, her citadel, which was in ruins. Someone put a comforting arm on her shoulder and before she thought to shrug it away – as would have been her normal response – she looked into the scarred face of Ulla ap Ferghus, who smiled kindly. 'Cousin, if it be the end, we of the Fine will face it bravely and together.'

They entered the building together as the land was thrown into darkness. Uisdean, Kentigern and Raghnald remained by the doors, swords in hand, in case of any trap. The remaining *Fir Chrieg* were stoic and appeared unafraid. Talisker, Malky and Chaplin crept in, each hoping they appeared as calm.

'Stay together,' Talisker whispered.

Suddenly, there was a blaze of light, not yellow like the dying sun but pure white, and the chamber lit up. It was a vast space: walls, floor and ceiling had the rough appearance of a cave but their surface was a reflective white. In the middle of the chamber stood a tree whose branches reached up to the apex of the ceiling and outwards over the space. The large raven perched in the branches and, at the foot of the tree, sat a man. He wore a plaid, white like the surroundings but held in place by a green gem as large and brilliant as *Braznnair*. He had long black hair and blue eyes, just like his sister's.

'Corvus,' Talisker breathed. As the word left his lips, the chamber was plunged once more into darkness. It became warmer, and a faint, worryingly familiar smell reached them.

'Sandro? Malk? Are you still there?'

'Yeah.'

'Aye.'

'Keep talking to me so I know where you are.'

Silence

'Did you hear me?'

Silence.

There was a rustling noise and Talisker took a step forward. Something made a cracking noise beneath his foot. 'C'mon, Corvus, show yourself,' he muttered. He held his sword aloft ready to swing downwards – Talisker's Oath, he reminded himself. Sweat had formed above his top lip because the chamber was now so hot.

'Sandro? Malk?' Still no answer. Only faint mocking echoes of his voice, which held the first faint edge of panic.

Light. Horror. All around lay carrion, corpses – men and women of the Fine – and feeding on them, huge fly-like insects, maggots breaking forth from the corrupted flesh. Talisker retched bile but recovered in time to hack out blindly as one of the creatures turned its attention towards him.

'Ohgod ohgod ohgod.' He heard his horrified whisper echo around the chamber. 'Malky!' he yelled. 'Where the hell are you?' Still no response, and it occurred to Talisker that he was in hell already. He moved towards where he thought Corvus had been sitting, and his feet made crunching noises as they made contact with something that released a putrid smell. He gagged. It was an illusion, he told himself. He didn't believe it. To his left a large black and yellow wasp deposited its eggs on the corpse of a Sidhe eagle; gel clung and dripped from the feathers of the eagle's breast and an obscene wet noise accompanied the act. Something played tantalisingly at the fringes of Talisker's subconscious. Then he made the mistake of looking down at his feet. His mind reeled away from what he saw: Chaplin's body. The policeman's head was twisted round as though his neck had been snapped: his eyes were open, devoid of life but filled with terror; beneath his flesh, something was moving, was about to hatch. Talisker couldn't bear to watch it. 'No!' he screamed. 'Sandro, no!'

Low laughter echoed around the chamber, and Talisker tore his gaze away from his friend. 'No,' he shouted. 'If Sandro was dead, I'd know.' He vaguely realised that he'd said something important. 'Sandro, Sandro.' He wasn't sure if he was weeping.

'Duncan?' The voice was weak, but recognisable. 'Ah'm ower here – tae yer left. Ah dinny think Sandro kin hear ye thinking, though. He wiz tae yer right last time Ah saw him . . .'

Talisker opened his eyes and looked to the left, it was where the wasp-like insect had laid its clutch. Cautiously, he sidled towards it, sidestepping. The wasp looked up and rasped her wings. Talisker stood still. 'Malk, I think they can hurt me.'

'Aye, Ah think they kin kill ye too.'

'Cheers, Malk.' Talisker brandished his sword and the huge creature took off unexpectedly, lowering her abdomen to present a massive sting the size of Talisker's blade. As she came towards him, he threw himself aside, slipping on the ichor beneath his feet. He heard her fly overhead, like some engine. Slipping and groaning he pushed his way towards the body of the eagle, every instinct in his body screaming that he should run the other way. The wasp creature had turned round in flight and was returning to protect her brood. Talisker whirled around and struck out blindly, slicing the wasp's thorax from her abdomen. As she fell to the ground, the front half of her body was still moving, her spindly legs walking her towards the eagle although her abdomen and sting lay a few feet away. Talisker's gut twisted and he struck out again, severing her in half. Still, her legs twitched and moved. In mounting horror, Talisker hacked again and again.

'Duncan, she canny hurt ye now.' Talisker turned towards the eagle, which was now a heaving mass of larvae. Suddenly, from its breast, a hand appeared. He stared at it in horror. 'Take it, ye fool. It's me.'

He reached out to grab the hand and then stopped. 'Malk?'

'Yeah?'

'How do I—'

'—know it's not a trap? Ye don't. But right now, we're runnin' oot o' options, are we no?'

'Shit.' Bracing himself and fighting back his mounting nausea he reached forward and took the hand.

The chamber went black.

'Malk?'

'Yeah?'

'Tell me that's your hand I'm still holding.'

'Aye, ye big jessie.'

Despite himself, despite everything, Talisker grinned into the darkness. He could tell that Malky was grinning too, dead cheerful.

'This doesnae mean we're engaged, like.'

'No. Just keep hold and we won't get separated again.'

Then the floor gave way.

Outside the doors, Kentigern gave his companions a baleful look. From inside, the sounds of Talisker's struggle rebounded in a cavernous echo. 'Well, I don't know about you lads, but if Corvus is in there I'm not for standing out here. I say we owe him some pain.'

'You're right.'

The three men walked into the cavern.

For the first time Una looked out to the north. During her confinement with her charges she had been forbidden to go outside but now she stood on the battlements with the rest of her clan, the survivors of Ruannoch Were, and watched the skies. Because of the darkness, she had brought the baby, well wrapped up to disguise his misshapen form. If it was true that they would all die when the sun disappeared for ever, he should be with her for comfort. If they were to survive, he and all the Fine should know that he had witnessed this event. She thought it was snowing now – a thin chill was enveloping her – but still she stood in silence like the others.

'Lady Una?' She turned to see Alistaire standing beside her. He seemed sober and quiet like all the others and glanced at the baby in her arms. 'I owe you an apology,' he grated. She was about to speak when he continued, 'I know now that there was some mistake, that the babe I saw was not mine, and it died, as you said, during delivery. I am sorry if I hurt you. It was a mistake. You understand.'

She was amazed. He had obviously convinced himself that this was the truth, and although she was outraged by his hypocrisy and longed to thrust his son towards him and say, 'Look! Look into the eyes of this child and deny him,' she did not. She curtsied.

'Yes, sir. Just so.'

As he turned to go he nodded towards his son. 'Better for this baby, really, if it hadn't survived.' He inclined his head towards the edge of the battlements.

She smiled brightly. 'But he did survive, sir, unlike his poor mother. His name is . . . Tristan.'

'It means sorrow,' he said, and walked away.

Then Una saw something in the darkening skies. It flew overhead, its form indistinct, ghostly, its flight somehow inspiring. It was a white eagle. She smiled, perhaps there was hope in the land.

They didn't fall far before they hit the rock floor in the chamber below. Malky cursed and groaned. 'Duncan, Ah think I've broke me leg. Eiyah, ahh, it hurts. Duncan, are ye still there? 'Are ye all right?'

'Yeah, Malk. Just a few bruises.' He reached out and

took the Highlander's cold hand again. 'C'mon. He wants to separate us, but we can't let him do it. Can you walk?'

'Aye. Mebbes it's no' broken. Bloody hurts, though. Wee basturt that he is. Why's he no' jist kill us, Duncan? He could, fer sure, jist kill us wi' a lightnin' bolt or that.'

'I don't know. Maybe the eclipse is affecting him, like it has Rhiannon, or maybe he's just curious. Huh – maybe we're a challenge.'

'Well, I reckon he could be jist keepin' us busy till he gets his powers back, so we'd better find Sandro pretty quick. What wiz that? Did ye hear?'

There was a rattling sound and the chamber lit up once more.

Two creatures were stationed towards the right wall. Half snake, half woman, they writhed towards Talisker and Malky, who instinctively took a step back.

'Jeez, Duncan, what kin we dae now?'

'I say we up the pace a bit, Malk. Look, they came from over there so I bet that's where Sandro is.' Talisker drew his sword again and stepped forward.

'But they're wimmin,' the Highlander objected lamely. He drew his sword anyway.

Talisker struck out and the nearest snake-woman parried unexpectedly with a long-spear she had been concealing behind her back. At the same instant she whipped her tail round, just missing Talisker's ankles. He yelped and leaped back. 'Don't let her knock you down, Malk,' he shouted, 'or you're finished.'

Malky was similarly embroiled with his opponent. The snake-women made no sound, except with their tails, which rattled ominously.

Talisker made some progress towards the wall but the snake-woman fought furiously. Curiously, her expression was mild and occasionally she smiled at him as she tried her best to kill him. Talisker could not deny the first faint stirrings of arousal. He had learned that this was common among warriors before and after battle but not simultaneously with it. She smiled again and for a fraction of a second he lowered his guard.

'Duncan!' He was pushed aside and fell heavily to the ground. When he looked up Malky was embroiled in the creature's deadly embrace. She had captured him in her coils. Now moving her face towards him she parted her lips, revealing a forked scarlet tongue that quivered in the air before the Highlander's horrified face. Her intention was plain.

Frantically, Talisker tried to get up but slipped in the pool of blood gathering beside the corpse of the other snake-woman, whom Malky had killed. His hand closed around her spear and he threw it with all the strength he could muster from his position. Propelled by desperation the missile struck true, entering at the hip and impaling the creature. For a few moments her coils thrashed around as her muscles went into spasm. Malky rolled free, grabbed his sword and hacked the reptilian half from her body. He stared down at it in horror, then vomited.

'Malk,' Talisker panted, 'we must be running out of time before the eclipse is over. C'mon, before he thinks of something else to throw at us.'

They ran towards the far side of the chamber and stopped when they reached the wall.

'Now what?' Talisker muttered. 'Sandro, can you

hear me? If you can hear me, reach out to your left.'

There was no response. 'Oh, no.' Malky groaned. 'Look, Duncan.'

Talisker glanced back towards the corpses of the snake-women. Slowly but relentlessly, each severed half was growing new flesh, the torsos new tails and the severed tails new torsos. There would soon be five, as Malky had split the tail of the second. It was a sickening process to watch.

Suddenly Talisker remembered what had bothered him earlier. 'Surely Corvus can't create anything? I know from my last . . . encounter with Phyrr. They can't heal or create. He must be using our fears.'

'Fascinating,' Malky muttered. 'Sandro, ye wee brammer! Look!'

Sticking out of the rough stones were the tips of the middle three fingers of Sandro's hand. One of the snake-women stood up, flexing her arms, and looking for her spear.

'Sandro!' Malky yelped. 'Take a side step. Hurry!'

The fingers disappeared. Two of the snake-women were now moving towards them.

'No!' both men roared. 'To your left!'

'Shit,' Talisker cursed. He turned round to face the assault. At that moment Uisdean, Kentigern and Raghnald entered from the far side of the chamber and rushed to engage the snake-women.

'Duncan, c'mon.' Malky grabbed his sword arm at the wrist, and Talisker both saw and reached for the hand at the same instant.

The result was not quite what he expected.

It felt like fire, growing, expanding. For an instant

Talisker saw his two friends beside him. They were smiling as though this was right. Malky reached out with his left hand and Sandro with his right. They closed the circle of three.

Behind them, the three *Fir Chrieg* reached forward, each man touching the shoulder of the one in front so that they made a double circle. A circle charged with past and present time. Each man was shining with an electric blue flare. Then they were no longer visible to Talisker because they were in him, part of him. Still growing, still expanding, a vast being. Talisker was Malcolm and Alessandro and Talisker. And Kentigern and Raghnald and Uisdean. Their wisdom, their strength, their belief. The being was all this and he was more: he was the hope of the Fine, their past victories and their retribution. Within it, Talisker held sway as the empathic and physical link.

Darkness gathered around the blue light and Talisker stood within the void where Corvus had fled, knowing that only its reaches could contain him. 'Corvus, I have come.' His voice boomed and echoed across the empty space. He drew his sword.

There was silence before Corvus appeared, just out of reach of his weapon. He was smiling as beneficently as ever but both he and Talisker knew his fear. 'Talisker. At last we truly meet. I know it's you. It can't last, you know. The conjunction will be over in a few moments and then you will return to six rather pathetic mortals.' He sniggered.

'Then I will kill you now.' Talisker took a step forward.

'No! I am an innocent man . . . god.'

The Talisker-being looked confused, as though something had struck it.

Inside, the babble of voices:

*'No, Talisker, he's lying.'*

'But what if it's true?'

*'Strike, Talisker!'*

'Injustice. Fifteen years. Two hundred years. Injustice burns.'

*'He killed them all.'*

'But what if it's true?'

Corvus seized his moment. 'That's right,' he continued smoothly. 'It was her. My sister Phyrr. She used me, imprisoned me in her place. She could do that, you know, because we're twins. You know her – quite well, in fact . . .'

Talisker took another step forward. The voices would not stop:

*'Kill him! He's killed thousands.'*

'Phyrr? Yes, I remember . . .'

Phyrr. She could have done it. She's just as capable. I can't. I can't take the chance . . .'

Corvus purred on. 'Of course, what's happened since . . . well, you, you of all . . . things, should understand the need for retribution, an innocent such as yourself. You understand the anger, the burning. I'll dissolve the Corrannyeid. Look, I'll do it now . . .' He waved his hand.

The being lowered the tip of its sword. Its form, a blue opaque shadow, wavered. Dissolution was close.

*'No! No! Do it!'* They were screaming now.

*'We're running out of time.'*

*'Remember Tayna.'*

*'Remember Makhpiyaluta.'*

*'Remember Kyra.'*

*'Remember . . .'*

*'Remember . . .'*

*'Strike!'*

Corvus sensed that victory was close. Only seconds remained. He smiled.

Suddenly, another being entered the void: it was the spirit of the White Eagle. She flew behind Corvus, her vast wings making silver-white trails, her great hooked maw open as though a scream would issue forth, although none came. She stretched her silver talons towards Corvus's back as though she would rake them through him. But she was only a ghost.

'Mirranon!'

*'Strike, Tal-ees-ker!'*

He raised his blade and struck the head from Corvus's body in one stroke.

Quiet sobbing. As he opened his eyes, blue sparks danced before them. Blue sparks and white feathers. He grinned and tears rolled unbidden down his cheeks.

'Malk?'

'Duncan, you'd better come over here.' It was Chaplin's voice.

Still dazed, he tried to get up but he was too weak. He crawled across the floor, noting that they were back in the chamber where they had started. He could see Chaplin's back and Malky's . . .

'Malky? Malk? Oh, God, no.'

Sitting on the floor, the three warriors were clustered

around Chaplin, who held the Highlander cradled in his arms. Malky was near death.

'What– what happened?' Talisker stuttered. He looked down at his friend and stroked a lank piece of red hair back from his brow.

Malky spoke quietly, straining for words. 'Ah dinny think Ah wiz strong enough, Duncan, tae be part o' that thing we became. Jings, yer no greetin, are ye? Dinny greet, man. Every day wiz somethin' o' a bonus. We got the wee basturt, though, eh?'

'Aye. We got him. Not just for us, though. Can you feel it, Malk? They're gone. The Corrannyeid have disappeared, just like he said. Sutra will be clean again. Tayna would be—' He broke off. 'Malk?'

'Hmm?'

'We loved ya.'

'Aye . . .'

He was gone. They sat in the darkness of the chamber for a while, mourning. With the shadow of destruction gone, weak winter sunlight shone in through the doorway.

# CHAPTER TWENTY-FIVE

*Edinburgh*

It has been snowing again, and the city nestles beneath its white cocoon like a gloomy butterfly. The sense of waiting has gone. That time when the mist between worlds was breached, has passed unnoticed by almost every soul. But still, as the morning dawns and the seagulls scream their cold welcome to the day, there is sadness here, and bewilderment. Around a derelict tenement building, police and fire crews cluster, performing their duties quietly. The fire was extinguished during the evening of the day before, and the soot and ashes that remain are like a grim scar against the whiteness of the landscape. It will heal eventually, until people will never know it was there.

'Do you think they were here?'

Beatrice's arms were crossed, protecting her from the biting cold. 'It's impossible to tell, sir. The fire brigade boys reckon that with the airflow through the building the basement became like a little furnace. They say the temperatures in there could have melted just about anything.'

Stirling frowned and tapped his teeth with his pen. 'But it didn't melt everything, Bea, did it? We've got two corpses: Finn, who appears to have been mangled, and some unknown bugger chained to a wall. Surely there'd be some evidence of Sandro and Talisker? Are you all right, Bea?'

She was crying silently. Tears trailed through the soot and grime on her cheeks, but she tilted her chin defiantly and pretended to smile. 'I knew them all, sir, Shula Morgan, Duncan Talisker – and Sandro, of course. We were all at school together, although it was Duncan and Sandro who were best friends. Shula and I were in the same year . . . You know I'm Effie's godmother, don't you?'

'Of course, poor kid, I'd forgotten,' Stirling said distractedly.

'Sandro came to the opera with me the other night,' Beatrice continued. She sniffed and dabbed her eyes with a tissue Stirling handed her, wiping a clean spot amid the grime. 'He was such a sweetie. He hated opera, especially Bizet, but he came to keep me company and meet Miles.'

'C'mon, Bea,' Stirling said, patting her shoulder. 'Let's get you a coffee or something.'

'No, sir, I'd better finish up here so the team can take the bodies away.'

Stirling looked tired and drawn. 'If Sandro was in there,' he said, 'you realise there's no one to mourn him.'

She patted his arm. 'We'll miss him, sir.'

An hour later, Beatrice was still sifting through the soot. The fire crews had finished damping down and seemed confident that there was no chance of the blaze rekindling. The first indications were that it had been accidental. Beyond that, the scenario in the basement was almost impossible to imagine. Only Beatrice and her assistant, Tom, were still working silently in the basement.

'Bea, what do you think of this?' Tom came over, looking excited. He held out a charred black object. She took it carefully and examined it.

It was a biscuit tin. Around the edges where the lid had been, she could still make out the faded colours of red and green tartan. 'Let's have a look, shall we?'

'But we're not supposed to . . .'

Beatrice silenced him with a look, then gingerly prised off the lid. She stared down at the contents with a dawning realisation of exactly what she was looking at.

'Do you think it's significant, Bea?'

She ignored his question but stared back across the room to where the unidentified corpse was still manacled to the wall, awaiting further photographs. 'Tom,' she said quietly, 'stay with that body. When we get it back to the morgue, I want a full report as fast as you possibly can. I want everything – age, height, shoe size, blood group . . . and, Tom, I need to know if he was a redhead.' She stood up slightly shakily.

'Are you all right, Bea?' Tom asked anxiously. 'You look like you've seen a ghost.'

'There are no ghosts in this business, Tom, you should know that by now. There's only evidence.' She looked down at the tin. 'I'll take this to Stirling. It might just make his day.'

When their shift was over Beatrice and Stirling walked by the Water of Leith together, stopping by the iron bridge to feed the ducks. They didn't talk much, but each were glad of the companionship of the other.

'We might never know what happened to them,' Stirling mused. 'I can't understand how every trace could be gone and yet the other two corpses . . .'

'Hotspots, sir. The fire crew were explaining.'

'Yeah, yeah.' Stirling threw the last of his bread to the ducks then pulled his coat tighter around himself. 'Whatever. Like you said, Bea, we'll miss him – Sandro, I mean. It's just a shame he didn't let more of his men get to know him better.'

'That's how he was, sir. Private.'

'But Talisker . . . guilty or not at the end of the day, I could see him fair enough. He was a cold fish.'

She linked her arm through his and they continued walking. 'He wasn't always like that, sir. I remember when we were at school . . . One morning . . . '

Her voice echoed beneath the iron girders of the bridge then faded into the distance swallowed by the sound of the river.

*Sutra*

'So this is really goodbye, then?' Talisker shook Chaplin's hand warmly and slapped his friend's shoulder.

'Well, until late summer. I'll want to see the baby.'

'Bring a good story for her, *Seanachaidh*, won't you?' Una smiled.

'The best,' Chaplin assured her. 'You seem sure it will be a girl.'

Talisker grinned. 'Una is something of an expert in that department.'

They stood outside the house that Isbister had

granted Talisker and Una in the foothills of the Blue Mountains, in the southernmost reaches of her domain. The first warm touch of spring was in the air and the surrounding woodlands were as vibrant with the promise of life as Una was herself.

Talisker began to walk Chaplin towards his waiting horse, reluctant to take his leave of his friend. 'So, have you spoken to Ulla?' he asked.

'Yeah. She's gone back to Ruannoch Were. Ferghus died just after the year and she will be Thane. I tell you, Talisker, whichever world we're in, we're ruled by women.' They laughed together, then Chaplin became serious. 'I'm going to visit her before I arrive back here, so I'll keep you posted. For now, I've got something of a mission.' He glanced back towards the house but Una had already gone inside. Reaching inside his jerkin he pulled out a small bundle and unwrapped it.

Talisker gave a low whistle. '*Braznnair.* I never thought I'd see that again.'

'Rhiannon gave it back to Isbister, who gave it to me. She thinks we owe the Sidhe, so I'm taking it to them. I've no idea what they'll do with it.'

Una watched the two men from the window. The wooden frame made all the spring colours seem so bright somehow. She touched her stomach and frowned. It was only dreams, she told herself. She was a midwife, and she knew that no such thing could touch a babe within its mother's womb. Life was a blessing. Tristan began to cry and she went to pick him up. His little limbs pained him sometimes. 'There, little man, did you have a bad dream?' As she said the words, she shuddered. Perhaps she should tell Duncan . . . but tell him what? That she had dreamed of a great dark bird who came and spoke to her baby? A shadow, a nightmare? He would surely laugh at her.

'Ssh, Tristan,' she smiled, 'go back to sleep.'

It was late summer. Even the so-called poisoned lands were recovering from the scourge of Corvus. Here and there, among the blackened earth and rocks, small bushes and scrubby plants were sprouting, clinging to darker seams where water trickled and collected in small pools. Beside such a pool the Morrigan was crouching, her black cloak spread beneath her.

It would be an easy thing, Phyrr told herself. Mortals did it all the time. Cattle did it. Still, she screamed loud and long and the sound echoed for miles across the empty reaches where none could hear of her plight.

By midnight, it was over. It was a boy. Unsure of what she was doing, Phyrr wrapped the pink fleshy bundle in her cloak and smiled down at it. 'Well, little one, what now? I could leave you here to be eaten by the wolves, I suppose . . .' She looked around her at the bleak moorland then back at the baby. 'Or we can see how it works out. Mother has much to teach you about mortals. As you are part god there are some things you should know.' The baby gurgled in response and the cloak fell back from its head to reveal a shock of bright red hair. Phyrr laughed. 'Now, what should I call you?'